TAKE HER FROM YOU

McRae Bodyguards - #3

Jolie Vines

Cover design - Natasha Snow https://natashasnow.com/

Formatting - Cleo Moran / Devoted Pages Designs

Cover photography - Wander Aguiar

https://www.wanderbookclub.com/

Cover model - Christian M.

For all of you who've ever wanted to take down a hot guy's man bun and drag your nails over his scalp

BLURB

A single mom in hiding and the bodyguard roommate she can't resist

Mia

Hiding out in the Scottish Highlands, I've fled my old life. I need a home for my little daughter, a job, and the eyeful of my roommate naked in the shower has me thinking I might need a hot Scottish boyfriend, too.

But the gorgeous bodyguard only offers fun nights between the sheets. While he's preoccupied worshipping my thick thighs and claiming he doesn't want commitment, I'm meant to be busy on the dating scene.

For longterm, he's telling me to look elsewhere, but what if it's him I fall for?

Valentine

My new roomie is a wet dream come true. With her kind personality and curves for days, I can't keep my mind off her. A welcome distraction from the broken relationship with my brother and the ex-fiancée who won't leave me alone.

Except Mia's looking for more than I can offer. I had my fingers burned by love and won't ever go there again.

Only when people come looking for her do I realise just how easily she could be taken from me.

--

Take Her from You features a plus-sized single mom, her Scottish roommate with golden retriever energy, and an intimate toy she creates using *him* as a template.

This swoony, friends-to-everything, steamy read is a standalone in the *McRae Bodyguards* series and set in the gorgeous Scottish Highlands.

Join Mia and Valentine's adventure in love today!

READER NOTE

Dear reader,

Thank you for picking up Take Her from You, the third in my series about the McRae Bodyguards team.

The audiobook https://adbl.co/46ChLvv featuring Aaron Shedlock and Addison Barnes is delicious.

These books are focused on the romance and lighter on anything potentially triggering, but please note a warning for custody threat, rape (historic, minor reference), and injury.

Like with the previous two books in this series, there's a hidden code in this story. Join my Jolie Vines Reader Group https://www.Facebook.Com/groups/joliesfallhardfans on Facebook or go to the acknowledgements at the end for more information.

Love hot Scottish heroes? I have five series of them. Once you're done reading this smutty and delicious story, check out the full works and reading order at the end of the book.

There's also a map of the McRae lands you can download for free here: https://www.jolievines.com/mcrae-estate-map

Love, Jolie x

1

Mia

In the past, when picturing a life of freedom, I'd never imagined it coming with a side of big, swinging dick.

Well, maybe I'd hoped so, but my goals had been a new place to live, a little job, *safety,* and peace of mind.

The huge, naked man in the shower of my temporary home was a bonus to my wish list of essentials. Long hair, steamy water sluicing over a muscular, golden frame, and a very hard dick in his hand—the guy was a vision.

I was here earlier than planned, and Daisy, my new boss, had jumped to show me around. Even now, she chattered from the bedroom, unaware of what I could see on my peek in the bathroom. The man I was spying on.

Abruptly, he locked his gaze on mine.

And held it. He made no effort to cover himself.

I froze.

A thrill spiked my heart rate. I needed to leave, but instead, I let my gaze take its fill. Blame shock or still being on high alert, but I was out of my comfort zone and thriving.

After everything I'd been through, this was a weird kind of gift. Spank bank material I didn't know I needed. I'd been unloved for so long that I'd forgotten the insistent pull of lust and how it drove away everything bad.

It set aside my fear at bagging up clothes and toys and concealing them in my car. Stealing them away so we could move out piece by piece. It dislodged my worries over how my daughter would handle staying away from me while I got us set up someplace new.

Instead, I just let myself feel.

The god in the shower trailed his gaze down my body, lingering on my breasts. I was a bigger woman, and in the past, that had been used to make me feel bad about myself.

The man with his dick in his hand didn't seem to have a problem with it. He smirked, gripped himself again, then pumped harder.

Goddamn it, hot guy.

Need pulsed. If he could use me for inspiration, then I was going to use this image of him in exchange.

"Mia? Did you hear me? I was saying the noise of the hangar stops by mid-evening." Daisy said, closer now.

I jumped and slammed closed the shower room door.

Then I turned to face her where she stood in the doorway to the women's dorm.

"The occasional helicopter goes in and out overnight," she continued, "but the mechanics shut up shop, so you don't get the clanking of tool noises unless there's some emergency maintenance."

I couldn't summon a response, temporarily stunned by the memory of the red-hot male.

The pretty brunette cocked her head at me. "Everything okay?"

"A man's showering in there," I confessed in a rush. If she opened the door herself, things were going to get awkward fast.

Her eyes rounded. "No! God. What did he look like?"

A god sent to walk the earth.

"Really tall. Long, black hair."

She pulled an amused face. "That's Valentine, one of the bodyguards and your new roommate. Oops, should've locked the door there, Val. But it's also my bad. I told him you'd be here this evening. Did he see you?"

No way was I sharing the tiny, heated exchange I'd had with the man. "I think I got away with it."

She fake-mopped her brow. "Phew. That could've been a situation, considering you'll be living together. When he's done, I'll introduce you. It's just the two of you staying here this week, unless someone else needs a roof over their head, but I checked with the flight school, and they aren't expecting any students. The other team that uses the bunkhouse is the mountain rescue crew, but that's unpredictable, of course, and most live locally, so unless there's a major incident, it should be quiet. I know it isn't much, but I hope it's okay for a little while."

I intertwined my fingers and crossed the living room to join her. The bunkhouse, a structure made out of shipping containers and stowed under the cover of the huge aircraft hangar, was a blessing compared to where I'd been.

It had a wood-burning stove which crackled with a merry flame, teal-coloured couches, and even a bookcase. There were two dorms with six bunkbeds in each, one of which was all mine, and I'd never felt so relieved to be somewhere as right now.

"It's perfect," I breathed. "I can't thank you enough for all you've done."

My new boss cupped my elbow, giving me a soft look. "It's nothing. I'm pumped to have you come work for me, but I'm also thankful because at the interview, I was worried for you. But you made it. You're here."

I'd told her I needed to get away from our living situation. I'd also asked her to put me on the books under a fake name so I couldn't be traced. When cleaning clients' homes, I was Megan, but I was still the real me, Mia Walsh, on my payslip where I couldn't avoid it.

Daisy watched me for a moment, presumably wanting me to say more.

I used to pride myself on being a good judge of character. When Daisy interviewed me, I instantly liked her. She was an American, like me, settled in the UK, and about the same age. Her Californian tones had me missing my mother so badly it hurt.

But I'd learned that first impressions weren't all they were cracked up to be.

"I'm more grateful than I can say," I mumbled.

She exhaled, letting me keep my secrets, then finished the tour, showing me out of the bunkhouse and across the hangar.

Engines roared and tools clanged, sparks flying from where someone in a mask welded metal. Behind what appeared to be an office unit, a fair-haired woman approached a guy, whispering something in his ear with an expression that was decidedly sexual. She backed up, and he followed with a predator's stalk, and my jaw dropped. I was so out of touch with the adult world that even two people flirting had the power to shock me.

It also drove home another truth. This was no place for a little girl to live. As horribly as I already missed her, Tobi was better off with my friend.

"This is the rec room," Daisy told me.

We entered a bright and slightly warmer space. There was a shiny coffee machine and basic breakfast facilities. No real cooking would be possible, but that was fine. My stay here would be short-lived—it had to be as I couldn't be away from my girl for more than a few days. My next priority was getting an apartment or even a small house and bringing Tobi home.

We were exiting the rec room when a deep voice hailed us.

"Daisy, wait up."

We both turned. Shower God crossed the space, hands up to dodge a group of men and women in jumpsuits, some of whom hailed him with smiles.

He'd dressed, which was a shame but probably sensible, as out here, a frosty blast swept through the hangar from the wide-open frontage, and he'd tied that gorgeous black hair up in a man bun with a leather strip.

Fresh lust descended over me.

What the heck was up with my nervous system? It had gone haywire.

His gaze danced my way, something teasing in his expression. "Hey, I'm Valentine. Ye must be my new roommate."

"This is Mia," Daisy introduced. "I'm sorry we were early. I hope you didn't get a shock when I showed her around."

His curious gaze slid to me.

I jumped in fast. "I briefly opened the door on you in the bathroom. You had your back to me. I apologise."

Valentine exhaled, his amusement returning fast. "Right. The lock's broken. I'll fix it this afternoon."

His eyes twinkled. Warmth swarmed in me.

Daisy asked him something, but my brain blipped out. Being so close to such a fine specimen of man was doing something to my head.

I'd never seen a dick as big as his.

My mental image retained all the details—a throbbing vein, a thick base that disappeared into dark hair, his firm grip with his big hand, the way he'd stared at me...

The guy was my new roommate, and we'd already crossed a boundary we really shouldn't have. Maybe I didn't care.

New-Mia made decisions that suited her. For over four years, I'd suffered other people's choices, and it had nearly broken me. Never again. I'd made the break and now had the chance to change everything. Who said I couldn't be a woman who had one-night stands?

Sexy escapades she actually wanted.

In an aircraft hangar filled with active and attractive men and women, I'd bet a lot of sex happened in that bunkhouse, or wherever the couple I'd seen were running off to. My roommate had the sort of swagger that made me picture him easily taking women or men into his bed.

I could be one of those lucky people.

New determination grabbed me. If I made it through the night with no one coming after me, no disaster, and no drama, I was grasping every opportunity that came my way.

My list—to find a home and bring my daughter back—expanded to add a third item.

To get laid.

Life looked sweet for the first time in forever.

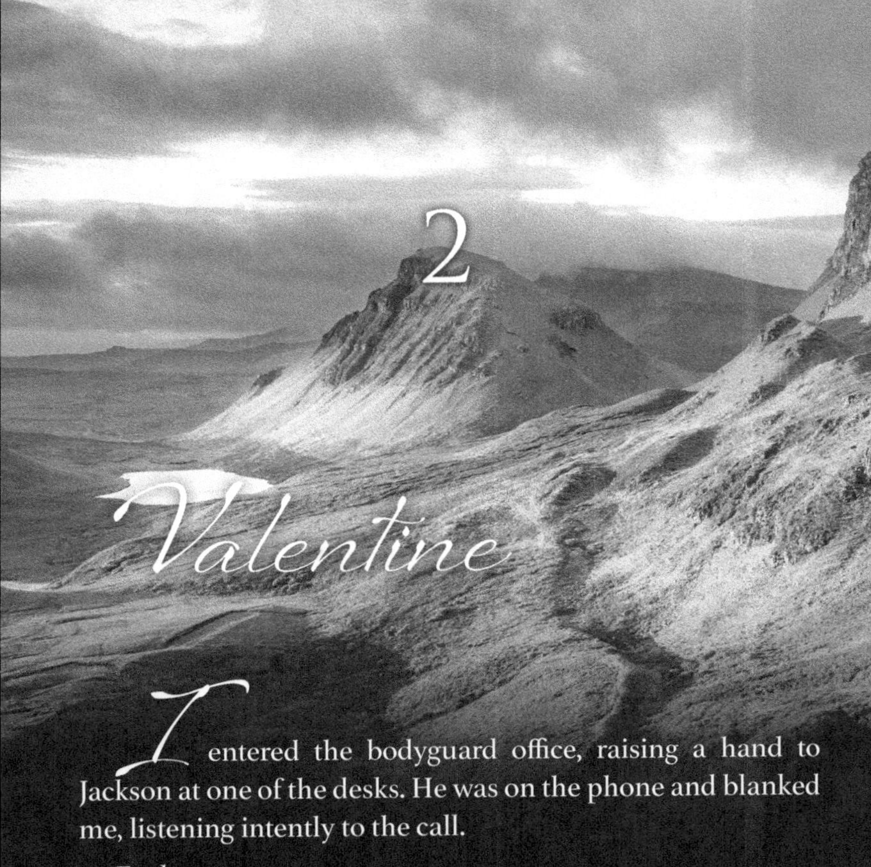

2

Valentine

I entered the bodyguard office, raising a hand to Jackson at one of the desks. He was on the phone and blanked me, listening intently to the call.

Fucker.

From the boss's desk, I peeled a Post-it note from a pack. Balled it up. With a casual flick of my wrist, I fired it his way, landing a direct hit to his forehead.

Jackson jerked then eyed me, lowering his gaze. "Aye, the twenty-fifth," he said to his caller and drifted his hand to the floor.

The ball of paper sliced through the air, whip-fast. It hit my chest and bounced away. I'd barely seen his hand move.

Game on.

Peeling another five from the stack, I rolled them between my palms and lined them up along the front edge of Ben's desk in a neat row, a few inches between each. Across the room, Jackson picked up a book.

I crouched behind my ammo, lined up my shot, and flicked the first ball.

It arced towards him.

Jackson lurched, parrying it with the book, a satisfying low *thwack* resounding.

I flicked the next, but it went wide.

He tutted. Then winced, shooting me a glare. "No, sorry, carry on," he spoke down the phone.

I cracked up silently, readying the next missile.

Life was good. A happy mood had taken over me, made out of getting comfortable in my new bodyguard job in snowy, gorgeous Scotland, but also from the attention of my spy earlier. The woman I'd be sharing the bunkhouse with could've called me out for my unintended exhibitionism, except she didn't. She'd watched, God love her, and given me the visual of a bountiful pair of tits and a pretty face that I'd needed to tip me over the edge.

Even now, I could picture her. Those flushed cheeks. The way she stared. That stunning, curvy body.

Holy fuck, little spy.

I darted another paper ball at my colleague, right at the second someone else entered the room. A large someone in the shape of my boss.

The ball pinged off Ben's arm. His blond eyebrows dove together, and he switched his confused gaze to me.

Fun time was over. I brushed the final two into the bin.

He made no comment, crossing the office to his desk. He'd called us in for an afternoon update meeting, so I found a seat, right as Jackson finished his conversation and Raphael strode in.

Ben gave us all the once-over, waiting for us to settle.

"Thanks, everyone, for coming in. I wanted to officially recognise our newest recruit to the team. Welcome aboard, Raphael."

Jackson repeated the welcome.

I reached to fist bump our latest member. "Thanks for taking the new-guy position from me. Appreciate it."

"If this is the start of hazing, I'm not playing," Raphael replied, his expression cautiously pleased.

He was a deal younger than the rest of us, with me at thirty, Ben three years older, and Jackson in his late twenties. Raphael was barely twenty-one, but he'd recently qualified as a helicopter pilot. A big asset to our team when our job was to keep our rock-star client and his family safe.

"Making no promises there," I replied.

From a bag on the floor, he brought out a tub. "I made cookies to keep everyone sweet."

I opened my mouth. "Ye baked bribe cookies for us? Deal. No hazing. Gimme."

Raphael held out the tub, and I claimed one of the biscuits, demolishing the sugary treat in a single bite while he passed them around.

Butter melted in my mouth.

Ben accepted a cookie then got on with the show. "With Raphael joining, that makes a core team of four, and perfect timing to have a full complement. Leo has been lying low after the birth of his and Viola's second baby, but his typical year is a lot busier. Such is the life of a world-famous musician—he needs to be out there in the world. Next month, we'll be in active service guarding him on tour, and his family are going, too. For the next several weeks, I'll be dividing up our tasks between training and escorting Leo on UK-based appearances and meetings."

He went into details of the tour—all the dates in stadiums across Europe—then walked us through a training programme.

"We start tomorrow with weapons instruction," Ben continued. "Focusing on disarming anyone who comes at us with a bladed item, or worse."

I snorted and slapped the back of my hand to Jackson's chest. "Our boy here doesn't need the help. He's way ahead of the rest of us. Maybe ye should ask him to teach?"

Jackson shoved me, his lips pressed together.

A couple of weeks ago, some maniac had rushed the stage when Leo was being interviewed. Jackson swan-dived onto the guy, neatly neutralising the threat and earning himself a reputation as a jump-first-ask-questions-later guy.

Ben's lip curled like he wanted to smile but couldn't because I'd made the joke.

I didn't blame him.

The moment passed, an awkward silence descending.

"Before that," Ben continued, "I have an extracurricular task that I need volunteers for this evening. No problem if you're busy, but Daisy and I could use the help. It's a mix of manual and skilled labour."

Jackson raised a hand. I did, too, no excuse not to, though I'd rather stick my dick in a blender than hang out with Ben.

Raphael threw a glance at the door, where even the office soundproofing couldn't keep out the whirr of rotor blades. "I've got airtime booked this evening. If there's work left to be done, I'm your man tomorrow."

Ben gave us our orders and let us go.

Out in the hangar, I couldn't help my gaze sliding across the floor in search of the woman from earlier.

A couple of weeks ago, I'd self-sabotaged a sure thing with

a lass at a bar in the nearby village. She'd been giving green lights all over the place, and I opened my damn mouth and told her I was engaged.

Ex-fucking-cuse me?

Five years ago, that had been true, but my marriage plans had imploded in one fuck-awful evening. I'd gone from being a military man, who travelled to the US as often as possible to see my bride-to-be, to the one everyone pitied.

Thinking about it made me want to break things, so why the ever-loving hell had my mouth summoned those words?

I'd cock-blocked myself and had no clue why.

Perhaps I should've been relieved when the little spy on my shower session hadn't got the same response from me.

In any case, she wasn't in sight now, and Jackson and I loaded into our cars and followed Ben out into the snowy roads for the evening work we'd signed up for.

A short drive later, we were pulling up outside a long, white, single-storey building with spindly wooden columns holding up a front porch which stretched the length of the frontage. Despite the shelter, some of the panes of glass in the windows were broken.

It was probably old accommodation of some kind, run-down, but in the prettiest spot. Below us, a half-iced-over river meandered around a Scottish Highlands hillside. Beyond, the glen gave way to a thick stand of lightly frosted fir trees, their dark green the only pop of colour in the winter landscape.

I could watch that view all day.

It was even possible to see Castle Braithar where Leo, our rock-star client, and his family lived, plus a few other houses dotted here and there.

"Whose place is this?" I asked, my boots crunching into the snow.

"No one's yet," Ben replied. "Gordain had it on a list of properties to be renovated as potential housing but hasn't got round to finishing the task."

Gordain was father-in-law to Leo, and Ben's boss. The older man usually came out with our crew and was fitter than most of us, despite being over sixty.

"The roof's new," Ben went on. "One of the back walls was rebuilt and underfloor heating put in. The front door's been stuck tight since, though. There's windows to install, a pile of rubble that needs shifting, and a whole load of other shite to get these liveable."

"These?" I asked.

"It's been divided into two homes, both two-bed. A good starter for small families."

I eyed the task then kicked one of the porch struts, rotten wood flying in a chunk. "It's a few days' work."

"Hard work never bothered ye," Ben replied.

I shrugged, dismissing the familiarity I didn't want to share. "Never said it did. Got tools? Materials?"

"Ready and waiting." He indicated to his car.

I glanced at Jackson who shrugged, already tugging on gloves.

The only thing I couldn't stand was having nothing to do. Ever. It left me restless. A typical evening saw me working out, or heading to the pub with Jackson, or even fighting with a couple of the airmen who liked a rumble.

"Let's get it done," I decided.

Ben opened his car, and we started extracting a plethora of tools and shite.

Another vehicle pulled up. Daisy climbed out, another lass following, both bundled up in winter coats.

My roommate. My pretty, blonde spy.

I stood taller, shoulders back.

"This is it," Daisy said. "I know it doesn't look like much, but it will."

She added something too low for me to hear, but my mind was working overtime. So this project was to give my brand-new fantasy woman somewhere to live. Which meant she'd be hanging around.

Adrenaline filled me, and I turned away to carry a circular saw into the house, keeping my head down so she wouldn't see my dumbass grin. I could sniff out a new friend at fifty paces, and she had fun written all over her.

From my pocket, my phone buzzed with a text. I grabbed it and peered at the screen.

Kelly: I know it's been a long time, but I need to talk to you. Can you call me?

Fucking hell.

My stomach seized up.

My ex hadn't messaged me in years. We didn't speak, despite the fact she worked for my parents at their inn thousands of miles away in the States. Whenever I went there, I avoided her. I'd spent months in Washington State after leaving the military and managed not to have that confrontation once, living for most of the time in a cabin in the woods.

I felt nothing for the woman except judgement on how she'd handled breaking up with me. Fun fact: It had hurt. Something inside me had sheared off and broken, and I was done with all thoughts on relationships and any of that level of bullshit.

After her damning words that killed off my love, I wasn't interested.

Whatever she had to say could be to herself.

Stowing my phone, I set down the heavy saw and shoulder barged the stuck door. It popped open on my first hit, opening to a spacious room with a flagstone floor.

Then I twisted back to locate Daisy's friend, ready to talk shop with her about the new home we were setting up.

But the lasses were hugging, and my new insta-crush got into her car and drove out of sight without me even being able to ask why.

3

Mia

Six AM rolled around by the time I crept back to the aircraft hangar. The darkness suited me, concealing my car in the country lanes. It hadn't been my intention to stay away all night, but my daughter had needed me, so I'd driven the two hours to reach her and slept around her tiny frame on the borrowed mattress. Then I'd woken early and driven back.

All my things were in the bunkhouse, even my toothbrush, so I had to pop back in to ready myself for the first day in my new job.

I started in thirty minutes, and excitement infused me.

My thrill was undoubtedly a little pathetic—it was just a cleaning job, nothing elaborate, but it was mine. I'd applied and got it. For me, it was a big deal.

The hangar was mostly empty, the big overhead lights chasing shadows across the wide space, helicopters here and there, work stations with tool racks, offices in a block, and big display boards around the section I guessed was the flight school area. A mechanic stomped by, hefting a toolbox. She spared me a wave, and I waved back then continued to the bunkhouse.

Holding my breath, I twisted the door handle.

It creaked.

I grimaced, not wanting to wake my roommate, and pushed it wider to slip inside. Warmth and the scent of smouldering logs replaced the chill and the oil scent of the hangar.

Truth be told, I hadn't minded spending the night with Tobi. It hadn't been comfortable, but I'd had a mild panic over the man I'd met here and how I'd reacted to him. He was so far out of my league I was dreaming.

Was I really going to make a move? Offer him...me?

Disgust soured my tongue. I'd spared myself humiliation at his certain rejection and I'd start over when I saw him next.

Hopefully that wouldn't be too soon.

"Hello, little spy."

I jumped, whipping around. A light sprang on, and from the doorway of the second dorm, a fully dressed Valentine emerged, one hand holding the frame so he didn't hit it with his head.

Good God. I'd forgotten how big he was. Easily a foot taller than me at maybe six-five, but not only that, his t-shirt sleeves stretched over biceps that bulged. I'd never in my life seen a man so well made.

"You're up early," I squeaked.

"Better than the way I was up yesterday or worse?" He grinned at me.

He was flirting? I stared some more, unable to start a sentence.

"I should probably apologise for that," he continued, "and tell ye how I cleaned the bathroom thoroughly last night, but the way ye watched makes me not want to bother."

"I, um…" I stumbled. "It's early."

God, what nonsense was I saying?

Valentine squinted at me, choosing to take pity. He went to the wood burner, drawing across a black metal lever beneath the glass window. "Never could sleep in. I left this on high so it would be warm when ye returned."

"I appreciate that," I finally managed.

"Nae bother. Get lucky last night?"

His words were casual, but I winced all the same.

"No. I have a daughter. She's staying with friends while I get established here. She's had sleepovers with them in the past, so I'd hoped she'd be okay being away from me, but she needed me last night."

Valentine tilted his head, his gaze taking me in. "Makes sense why Daisy had us busting a nut to fix up that house yesterday. How old's your bairn?"

"She's four."

"And she's having to stay away from ye?" Something ticked over in his vision. "Christ. And ye didn't bring her because you're sleeping in a shared space? That isnae right." He took up his phone and tapped out a text with sharp jabs of his finger.

An icy chill slid through me.

I'd done the best I could for my little family. I hated being away from Tobi, but we'd left with almost nothing. I needed to earn money, and that meant being here, with the job I'd found. To bring her to the hangar with all its dangers felt risky, particularly when I'd had the generous offer of a warm pullout bed and a home with toys.

But Valentine's horror at my actions panicked me.

"I know it isn't right." I crept a few steps deeper into the room. "But she's only two hours away. I can get to her when she needs me. I wouldn't do it if I had another option. Please, who are you contacting?"

"Ben. My boss, I mean. I'm asking if we can start early on the home repairs. We've got training this morning, but other than that, I'm going to crack on with your wee home. It's nae good ye getting up at four AM to drive to work."

His phone dinged. He squinted at the screen.

"Jackson's down. Raphael, too. Ben has a meeting, but he'll show up later. I'll see who else I can round up."

He sent a reply while all I could do was try to breathe.

Daisy had shown me the house yesterday, but it hadn't really sunk in that it could be my new home. People didn't just offer up houses, nor was it habitable. I'd figured that once I was done with work for the day, after going to the preschool to register Tobi, I'd be house-hunting.

A knock came at the bunkhouse's door.

Daisy poked her head in and smiled when she sighted me. "Good morning. Oh hey, Val. Mia, are you good to go?"

Shit. I hadn't even changed yet or brushed my teeth.

"Can I have two minutes? So sorry. I just got back."

"No problem. I'm early because I was going to get us a coffee for the road. The first job involves a drive up into the mountains. Go get ready. I'll wait."

"I'll be as quick as I can."

I darted into the dorm room and snatched up clothes and my toiletries bag, then ran for the bathroom. My strip-wash and teeth-brushing took a minute, then I combed my hair out, tying it into a high ponytail to keep it out of my way.

Even in the midst of first-day nerves, I couldn't help stealing a glance at the shower.

The image of Valentine in there was permanently embedded in my brain, and I wasn't mad about it. It also solidified how I couldn't bring Tobi into such an adult environment. The hangar was dangerous for a little one, and the bunkhouse had its own hazards.

Done, I dashed back to the dorm room and grabbed my cleaning caddy, then returned to Daisy.

She and my roommate were having some kind of in-depth conversation which ended with my arrival, Valentine's lips pursed and his dark eyebrows drawn together.

One guess what their topic had been.

I swallowed. Had to make a good impression, and I was already slacking. "I'm ready. I apologise for the delay."

Daisy waved off my concern and ushered me outside. I gave a hurried goodbye to Valentine, not meeting his eye.

"We'll take my car, if that's okay." Daisy directed me to the side of the hangar. "This job is a double-handler, so we'll spend the morning just blasting through it. After, we'll return here for lunch and I'll give you the address for your afternoon booking. That one will be a weekly slot, if you want it. Sound good?"

"Very good. I really need a full schedule and regular work."

"I've got booking requests coming out of my ears, so that won't be a problem. Good cleaners who are willing to drive out around the Cairngorms are apparently hard to come by."

She unlocked a red car with a vacuum cleaner and cleaning goods in the trunk. I added my caddy to the collection and climbed in the passenger side.

Daisy drove us onto a mountain road. We passed a sign for a snowboarding centre then headed out into white-covered hills, dark trees here and there, their boughs laden with snow.

The sky was brightening with the approaching dawn, the

world muted and soft.

"It's so pretty here," I mused.

"Right? The beauty is unreal. It's one of the reasons I never intend to leave, other than the fact my bestie lives here."

"Ariel who interviewed with you? I really liked her."

"That's her. It might be isolated here, but there's a tight circle of ladies, and we all support each other."

A trickle of warmth replaced some of my uptight nerves. I'd always been a girls' girl, though that had been to my detriment with regard to one woman in particular.

"I love that. It must be lovely to have people you're so close to nearby."

Daisy gave a laugh. "Also my boyfriend. I should've started with him maybe, but he was my third reason to stay in order of time. He's Ben, the head of the bodyguard service."

I made the connection to the blond man I'd seen yesterday with Daisy. "Valentine's boss?"

"And his brother. Though you wouldn't know it."

I squinted at her. Valentine and Ben, from the brief sighting I'd had of the latter, didn't look all that alike. Maybe it was just the hair colour throwing me, with Valentine's warm black nothing like Ben's honey yellow. They hadn't seemed close either.

But my employer moved on, changing the subject back to work, and I got my head in the game.

I didn't want to get personal. Not yet.

This was day one of living here, and there were questions I didn't want to answer.

At the house in question, Daisy took a deep breath. "The owner wants it done in four hours but said the people who'd rented it had left it in a state. It's going to be a miracle if we finish."

It was a sizable home, but what kind of mess took over eight combined hours of work? I braced myself, determined to shift my butt to prove my worth.

My new life depended on it.

By eleven-thirty, we'd finally finished. The five-bed home was a holiday property that had been rented by a group who'd partied hard. A bottle of wine had been left in the middle of the lounge carpet like someone had played spin the bottle, just without emptying it first so it had puddled in a vinegary stench. From there outwards, devastation ran wild.

Food on the walls.

Mud tramped through the kitchen, into the hall, and up the carpeted stairs.

Trash *everywhere*.

Daisy had divided up the work, popped in headphones, and got stuck in. I'd leapt to follow. Hard work never scared me, but this was so disrespectful to the homeowners that it made me mad.

True to my word, I'd scrubbed, scraped, swept, and polished, and it had all come up good.

We carried bags of rubbish out to the bins and returned the keys to the lockbox.

"The owner said it was bad," she said. "But that was far worse than I expected. I'm sorry. Talk about a baptism of fire for your very first job."

"Did I do okay?"

She raised her eyebrows, checking the junction to pull onto the road. "God, yes. Your work is amazing. I was worried that you'd turn tail and run."

Relief trembled inside me. "I never would. Least because I can't afford to run. You can throw anything at me and I'm your girl. I probably shouldn't say any of that, but it's true."

Daisy exhaled. "I'm trying to be respectful and mind my own business, but I have to admit I was concerned after your interview that you were in danger."

"I just need to find my feet," I said fast.

"While avoiding some people?"

"Exactly that."

Tension played out between us. Again, I held in all the words I wanted to blurt.

Daisy reached for the sound system, turning it on. "Pick a song."

"I'm sorry?"

"I want us to be friends, and you can tell me as much or as little as you like, whenever you're ready. In the meantime, we'll bop all the way home."

So we did.

My new boss and I alternated our song choices, more Taylor Swift than any other artist, and the return journey zipped by. I was still on edge, watching the roads, expecting to see familiar cars on the hunt for me. But so far so good.

Daisy slowed as we entered the hangar's parking lot, stopping with her focus on something across the expanse of flat moor. I followed her gaze.

Valentine and a group of men were out in the open,

working through some sort of action sequence. One of the men advanced on Valentine, holding out an object. The huge man—taller than the others by a few inches—blocked the attack and had the first guy on his back in the blink of an eye.

"That is so attractive it should be illegal," I breathed.

Daisy giggled. "Valentine? He's single, if you're interested in knowing."

I goggled at her, my cheeks heating. "Oh no. He wouldn't look twice at me."

Unless he was stroking his dick in the shower, but then probably any woman would do as a visual aid.

"What do you mean?"

"He's gorgeous. Have you seen me?"

Daisy's expression turned fierce. "Honey, no, we don't let women put themselves down here. Didn't your mama ever tell you you're beautiful?"

God. My lip trembled.

In all I'd done to walk away from my and Tobi's old life, I'd had to put a pin in thoughts about Mom. I'd *lost* her. I missed her so much it killed me. But I had to keep going or I'd lose more than her alone.

Daisy's face fell. "I just said something stupid, didn't I? I'm sorry."

I managed a shaky laugh. "Please don't apologise."

"I did, though. I was aiming for supportive tough love. It wasn't meant to be flippant in any way."

I took a long breath, returning my gaze to Valentine. He spotted the car. Raised a hand then nudged one of the other men.

"My mother died six months ago," I forced out.

Daisy exhaled, starting a sentence but slow with her words.

But I couldn't wait. I had goals to meet, and succeeding at work was the main one right now.

My boss stumbled over another apology. I pressed her hand.

"Thanks, but it's all good. Can you give me the address of my afternoon job? We overran this morning, so I don't want to be late."

"Of course." Her shoulders sank, and she texted me the details and gave me pointers on what I needed to know.

I left her there with red cheeks and chagrin written all over her.

It would be nice to have a friend, to be part of the close-knit group she'd spoken about, but life rarely gave good things easily.

At least it never had to me.

4

Valentine

Dust rose from the rubble on the poured concrete floor, stinging my eyes where I swept it into a wide bucket, ready to go into the back of Ben's car. Since starting the work at lunchtime, the crew I'd formed had divided up the long list of tasks required to get this place ready for its new occupants, the knowledge that Daisy's employee was here without her child spurring us all on.

I hefted the full bucket to my shoulder and carried it outside, setting it down in the truck alongside tools and a stack of two-by-fours.

"Making progress." Ben approached from the other direction, a drill in his hand from where he'd finished a window.

He regarded the house, and I did the same, activity concentrated on the left-hand side of the structure. The other half of the building had been ignored for now. If someone needed it for a home, that could be managed separately, but there was a thick wall dividing it from what would be Mia's home, and the roof overhead had been renewed. It wasn't our priority.

"What's your take on the electrics?" my brother asked.

I gave an easy shrug, the supplies needed for the minor electrical work already on my radar. "I can do it."

He slanted a look at me. "Safely?"

Oh, fuck him. "I wouldn't offer if I couldn't. Military training, remember?"

"Shite. I wasnae doubting ye."

That's exactly what he had done. I didn't dignify him with an answer, and an uncomfortable pause played out. I wanted to know more about the new resident—my temporary housemate seemed nervous, and that didn't sit right with me. But on any given day, Ben was the last person I'd chitchat with.

I turned to walk away, but he said my name, halting me.

"Regarding the second property."

"What about it?"

"Daisy thought that perhaps you'd want to move in."

"Daisy thought?"

"I think it's a good idea, too. Once we're done with the first place, we'll move straight on to the second. Get ye set up with a real home after weeks in the bunkhouse."

Snarky replies formed in my mind.

It wasn't fair to blame Ben for what my fiancée had done, but he'd been involved, and the concept of a comfortable home had gone when she had. Ever since, I'd avoided putting down roots. I'd moved around with the military, visiting friends in my downtime, and when back in the States, I'd holed up in the cabin, the facilities basic at best. I'd grown out my hair, and for a year, did my best impression of a wild man of the woods.

Still, my gaze darted over to the adjoining property. The

porch ran across the front of both, and I pictured it in the spring with a couple of chairs outside, warmer days and a sun trap to enjoy them.

"Save it for someone who'll appreciate it," I said, then walked away, leaving him in my dust.

*D*arkness fell, and I returned to the bunkhouse, exhausted but with a decent chunk taken out of the renovations list.

Curled up on a sofa and lit by a lamp and the flickering fire, Mia talked on a video call, her face shiny like she'd just taken a hot shower.

Awesome. Exactly the person I wanted to see.

"You did? Can I see it?" she uttered, replying to a sweet voice that had to be her baby girl.

Mia's gaze lifted to me, and I gave a small wave and pointed to the bathroom. I meant to indicate I was going to wash up, and only that, but pink spots appeared on her cheeks.

A hit of lust slammed into me.

Maybe I could blame the adrenaline from the hard work, or the fact that my muscles were well used, but her tell drove hunger through me.

She was a pretty lass. One hundred percent my type, down to a T.

Purposefully, I drifted my gaze over her body, testing her out. Though her focus was on her screen, the pink darkened to a full-on blush, and I gave myself a mental slap for messing with her while she was talking to a child.

I grabbed some clothes and took my shower, sporting a semi with her name on it. This time, though, I left myself alone.

When I emerged, she was off the call and paging through something on her phone, her composure regained.

"Everything okay with your bairn?" I asked. "No long drive down the country to see her tonight?"

Her gaze leapt to me. "How do you know she's down country?"

"A guess."

Her shoulders went down. "Sorry, I'm a little jumpy. Tobi's good. She had a happier day, and Molly, my friend who she's staying with, thinks she'll be okay without me this evening, which is a relief because I'm starting early again tomorrow."

I dropped onto the second sofa, spreading out my arms. "Sweet. Listen, since you're hanging around, want to get dinner? There's a pub in the village that does decent food, and I can catch ye up on the renovation work."

"Dinner?" Anxiety widened her eyes again.

I backtracked, considering what I said. "Just as roommates. I didn't mean as a date. There are fuck all choices around here unless ye want toast or cereal from the rec room."

Mia's gaze slid to the door then back to me, her expression shifting to something more curious. "Not a date," she stated.

"Not even a hint. I'm not the dating kind," I promised.

"That sounds nice, but I can't afford to eat out."

Her saying *eat out* did something strange to my brain. Desperation surged in me. I wanted to feed her up. Get her smiling. "My treat as a welcome to the estate. And maybe as an apology for what ye had to witness yesterday. Let's start over, aye?"

Her lips curved in amusement. "If you're sure? I'll reciprocate once I get paid."

I clapped my hands to my knees and stood, stretching a hand out to help her to her feet as well. Her warm fingers met mine, and a swift pulse of electricity followed.

Mia flushed red again. "Don't you need to dry your hair?"

"Eh. It'll dry itself in the cold air. Let's go."

Muttering about how that never worked for her hair, Mia collected her coat, and we left the hangar together.

At the car park, I gestured to my ride. "Want to follow or hop in with me? Ye can even drive, if you'd prefer."

Huddled in her thick coat, my roommate considered her choices. "You'd really let me drive?"

"If it makes ye feel safe, why not?"

"Most men wouldn't think like that." She blew out a frosty breath. "I'll follow you in my car, if that's okay."

No problem for me. I waited for her to be ready, then gunned my engine and drove away from the hangar, tracking the river past Braithar, then Castle McRae, and over the bridge to the exit for the estate. From there, we rounded the loch and took the faster road east for a couple of minutes until we came to the village. I parked up outside the pub, watching Mia back neatly into a space one over. I opened her door for her with a sweeping hand gesture and a bow.

She giggled.

My blood heated. Why did everything about this woman turn me on so much? I had to remember my vow that this wasn't a date, despite my dick having other ideas.

In the bar, I found us a table and pulled Mia's chair out, pointing at the blackboard for the meal choices. "The steak's good. I had their beer-battered cod a couple of times as well and I'd go back. Can't attest to the rest of it, but pick whatever takes your fancy."

Mia draped her jacket onto the back of her seat, giving me full chance to stare at her. In the cosy room, with the old boys by the fire, the heavy wooden furniture, and the scent of ale in the air, she stood out, her blonde hair glossy and her figure driving me wild with every dip and curve.

Mia settled, and her gaze moved to something I couldn't see.

She leaned in, pitching her voice low. "There's a woman glaring daggers at you. She just walked in the door."

I lifted my eyebrows, my curiosity on high alert. "Is it safe for me to look?"

She gave a subtle headshake. "Not yet. Nope. Wait...now."

I snuck a quick peek over my shoulder, finding the lady in question instantly. Facing Mia again, I winced. "Oh dear."

"Oh dear there's your ex?"

I gave a dramatic shudder. "Nothing quite so horrendous. No, that lass is someone I turned down recently."

It wasn't the nicest memory, recalling how my anticipated night of fun had turned into sabotage.

Mia glared back at the woman. "Rude of her. You don't owe her anything just because you weren't interested."

I wrinkled my nose. "No, it's fair. I led her on, then at the last minute, I don't know, panicked, maybe. I told her I was engaged, and she leapt from me like a scalded cat."

Mia snorted laughter then quickly schooled her features. "Oh shit. She's coming over."

For fuck's sake. I summoned strength and turned to face the incomer.

The woman arrived at our table and planted her hands on her hips. "Hello again. I'm surprised to see you out with another woman."

Before I could answer, Mia stuck out her hand. "Hey there. I'm Mia, Valentine's fiancée."

The woman dragged her shocked gaze to my roommate. "Then I'm sorry for you. Your boy is an outrageous flirt. I wasn't going to say anything, but I saw him whisper something to you that made you laugh, and it pissed me off. From one woman to another, you need to have a word with him about his behaviour."

Mia tilted her head. "I appreciate the concern, but the only person responsible for Valentine's behaviour is Valentine."

The woman shook her head. "You don't understand. He was ready to take me home. He was going to cheat on you."

Fuck that. "Mia's right. I owe an apology for giving ye the come-on, but I've never cheated, and I never would. That's unfair."

The woman, whose name I wasn't sure I'd known, appeared slightly mollified by my words, her hostility simmering. "Then you weren't chatting me up?"

How the hell did I answer that without condemning myself? "Pretty sure flirting is my default mode. When it came to the crunch, I told ye my facts."

"That's...true. Maybe I'd had a drink too many and read into it. Apology accepted." She slid her gaze back to Mia. "Good luck with that one."

She left us and returned to her friends, their backs to us at the bar, though all of them threw us baleful glances.

Mia pulled an awkward expression. "I'm not sure I helped

any there."

"I don't know. It's kind of fun to be engaged again without warning."

"My bad. I've no idea why I said that."

Embarrassment had her scrunching up her nose. I'd never seen anything so cute.

"Believe me, this experience beats the last by a landslide."

"Oof. Sounds like there's a story there."

I gestured to the blackboard, standing. "Choose your meal, and I'll go order it, then I'll give up one of my secrets. But, on the condition that this is a reciprocal thing."

She blinked at me, and I elaborated with a wolfish grin.

"My stories for yours, roomie. I want to know who I'm living with, and ye have mysteries written all over your pretty face. Do we have a deal, or should I just bore on about home improvements all evening?"

I was reaching, without much expectation for her to give up anything, but to my surprise, she gave a slow nod.

"For the sake of getting to know each other, okay. I want that, too. Oh, and Valentine?"

My heart thumped, anticipation filling a void inside me I hadn't known was there. "Anything, little spy."

"I'll have whatever you're having."

God did that give me a raft of ideas, only some of which related to food.

5

Mia

Valentine returned from placing our order, setting down two bottles of beer, condensation beading on them and running down to the coasters. Then he dropped into his seat, propped his chin up on his hand, and raised an expectant eyebrow.

"Oh no, you first," I insisted.

I wanted an excuse to look at him. Already, this evening was mixing me up. First, picturing myself in the position of the woman he'd flirted with. Having that intensity focused on me would probably burst me into flames.

And second, he'd called me pretty.

Besides Daisy, and my mom, I wasn't sure anyone had done that before.

Well, Tobi's father, but I wasn't touching that thought with a ten-foot pole. I didn't trust any memories when it came to him.

Valentine relented, taking a long drink of his beer. He

wiped his mouth with the back of his hand and settled into his story. "Many years ago, back at the dawn of time, I had a long-distance girlfriend. I was in the military, and she lived in a little town in Olympic National Park where my parents also made a home."

"They live in the States, not here?"

He inclined his head. "I was born in Scotland, to a Scottish da and an English mother. My family emigrated, and I didn't return until I was nine or ten. I was in boarding school from thirteen with Ben, and then the army, but I returned to the US often because our family had gone back. The girl in question sought me out on every visit, and I very quickly fell in love. She tolerated the long months of us not seeing each other and didn't ask for much. When I popped the question, she accepted happily. Every minute of our relationship felt so straightforward, right until the end."

I leaned in, the picture he was painting enthralling. I needed all the details. How could something so perfect have gone wrong? "Go on."

Valentine took another swig of beer. "Nope. Your turn."

I recoiled. "What do you want to know?"

His mouth fell open in an expression of amusement tinged with outrage. "Uh, anything? I know nothing about ye except that you're a walking wet dream, and obviously running away from one life while trying to set up another fast. Believe me, I'm fascinated. Spill it."

Fascinated? Oh my.

I hesitated, and he heaved a dramatic sigh. "Tell me why ye left wherever your previous home was, and I'll serve the identity of the guy who was instrumental in the implosion of my engagement. You've met him."

"It's someone I know?" I barely knew anyone here, plus

he'd been engaged in the US.

He gave a purposeful nod.

It could only be... My jaw dropped. "Ben?"

Valentine sighed.

"Fine," I grumbled. He'd been betrayed by his own brother. I could share. "The people I was living with wanted to control every part of my life, and I had to break away."

"Your baby daddy one of those people?"

"No, he's dead."

Valentine widened his eyes. "Damn. Are we sorry about that?"

Despite myself, I broke out with a laugh, and crammed my hand to my mouth to stifle it. "No one has ever asked me that before. Honestly? I feel bad that my daughter will never get to ask him questions, but no, I'm not sorry."

"And the people weren't your people, which makes them his?"

God, he was perceptive. I shook my head, gesturing to him. "It's your turn. Why, no, how did Ben screw up your engagement?"

"That, my new friend, is a story too far."

I knew those well.

A man appeared at our table, two plates in his hands. He settled them in front of us, and my stomach growled. Valentine had chosen the beer-battered cod, and it came with a heap of fries, peas, and a wedge of slightly charred lemon.

"Oh my God, I'm suddenly ravenous," I uttered. "Thank you so much. I mean it. I can't remember the last time I had a decent meal."

He gave me a wink, so effortlessly sexy that my heart skipped a beat.

In our short exchange of information, I'd come to realise a couple of things about Valentine: his heart had been broken badly, and he used flirting as a defence mechanism. He'd called me a wet dream. He'd had another woman ready to go home with him.

The barman reappeared with two side dishes, one chicken wings in a sticky sauce and the other with a rainbow selection of veggies.

"Don't be shy. Share with me," my roommate said with a grin.

Wasn't that the most tempting offer I'd had all year?

We ate, conversation ceasing for a while. I'd worked so hard today that replenishing my strength took over my thoughts.

Valentine consumed his dinner like a man on a mission, and to fuel a body as big as his, that probably wasn't far from true. After he'd offered me the final chicken wing, he sat back, hands to his belly, and smiled.

"I needed that. My stomach thought my throat had been cut."

I laughed. "Didn't you have lunch?"

"Too busy working on your new place." He winked at me. "Another drink?"

I stared then managed a headshake. "Were you really there all afternoon? I saw you on the field doing martial arts training."

"Went there after and worked straight through until dark. I told a lie about eating—Daisy brought us coffee and some little cakes. That was it."

An unfamiliar sensation swirled in me. My mother aside, I wasn't used to anyone voluntarily doing anything for me. Definitely not something so huge as working his backside off for no reason.

"Why?" I sputtered.

"Why what?"

"I mean, thank you. I just don't understand."

He regarded me with curiosity. "Guess I can see why ye left home if that's the treatment you'd expect." He gestured to himself. "You're in need of a place to live. I'm willing and have the time. What possible reason would I have not to help out?"

"You don't know me. I'm a complete stranger."

"Is that true? Feels like we've been in a compromising situation that broke through that barrier. My dick's already your friend."

Another laugh sprang from me unbidden. "Are you always this candid?"

"Naw, only with people I like."

He grinned and took his leather tie to his dark hair, binding it up in a practiced move. Ready, easy lust slid through me, heating my belly in a coil. His relaxed flirting made me like him in far shorter a time than I should've. Nobody was this straightforward—I didn't kid myself that I knew him—but I had the feeling his depths were more of the same.

Decency and kindness. Carefree and determined.

"What are ye thinking over there?" Valentine asked with that same devilish smirk in place.

"That you played with your hair so I could imagine running my hands through it."

Where the heck had that flirting come from?

He poked his tongue into his cheek, the smile growing. "Guilty. And there was me promising this wasn't a date."

I raised a shoulder. "I've seen you naked, and we got engaged within five minutes of arriving at the bar. I think that ship sailed."

His gaze held mine. His eyes twinkled. "Touché, little spy. How about we get out of here?"

The food was done. Our stories had been left unfinished. In an instant, I couldn't care about anything other than getting back to the bunkhouse and seeing where the draw to him led.

Tension pulled me tight, the sense of feeling alive blooming inside me and dancing over my skin.

On the table, my phone lit.

Molly: She's fast asleep, no trouble tonight. I'll message in the morning.

"All okay?" Valentine asked.

"Just my friend telling me Tobi's gone down well."

"Thought you'd have to leave."

I shook my head slowly, tapping out a reply saying I'd see them tomorrow. Then I put away my phone.

My daughter didn't need me right now.

Other things were possible.

Valentine rose and offered me a hand. I took it solely for the excuse of touching him, a delicious play of electricity tingling over our connection. He kept me with him through the tables of other customers and to the door. I had to break the link to shrug on my coat.

Outside, a frosty wind swept over the car park. Valentine didn't make for the cars, instead, turning to face me in the entranceway.

The noise of the bar fell away with the door snicking closed.

My pulse beat loud in my ears.

"In case I forget to say, I'm glad ye came to dinner with me. You're good company," he said.

I watched him, a quip on my tongue about why he'd forget left unsaid.

His dark eyebrows merged, and he set a hand on the wall by my head, leaning in. "Also, in case it needs stating, I am blessedly single, and I think ye are, too."

"Very," I managed in a breathy rush.

His gaze dropped to my lips. But he didn't move.

I waited a beat, the suspense killing me. This was my life now, brand-new-me able to go out with guys and be fit to burst with feelings. The realisation staggered me. I could do anything, with anyone. I was free.

"Valentine?" I said.

"Aye?"

"Are you just going to stand there, or do I have to ask you to kiss me?"

Amusement crossed his features. Then the big Scot closed the distance and brought his mouth to mine.

Our lips touched. My knees weakened, but that was fine because his arm curved around me and bolstered me up. He gave a low groan that went straight down the centre of me, sending fireworks off in all directions.

Valentine angled to connect better, and then I was entirely lost in a decadent slide. He nudged me to open for him, and his tongue touched mine in a burst of fresh heat.

I gave up some kind of whimper.

The kiss got harder.

Sex, let alone good sex, was far from my radar. I was no virgin but I wasn't experienced either. Something about the way he touched me told me he'd be an amazing lover.

He gave up his hold on the wall to cup my face, his other hand skating down my spine to align our bodies. Need built in me, a shockingly fast wave that had me clutching on to his arms, desperation for something, anything, building.

We sped up, moving in unity.

The door opened behind me, and I tore my mouth away.

"Ugh, get a room." A woman breezed past us.

I peeked around Valentine to see the lady he'd turned down. Embarrassment chased my man-fever, and I took a breath.

Valentine didn't falter, though. He gave a laugh that sounded like satisfaction and pressed his lips to my forehead. "Follow me home, aye?"

Across the car park, I threw myself into my car, turning off the heat to let the cold fix my face.

Who the heck had I just become?

And was I really going to do more once we got back?

6

Valentine

A group of people stood together outside the hangar, backpacks on and waterproof maps in hand.

The mountain rescue team.

Shite. I'd signed up for training with them and been told I'd shadow Lochinvar, the leader, on a callout. If they'd messaged me to tell me to attend tonight, right when I was fucking aching for my new friend, I'd die.

I slid my phone out, holding myself taut to peer at the screen.

No messages.

Fuck yeah. I punched the air under the line of my window. In the next car over, Mia switched off her engine. I hopped out to open her door.

"Such a gentleman," she said to the ground.

"Won't be saying that in thirty minutes when you're screaming my name," I quipped back.

Mia's startled blue eyes shot to mine.

I choked on a laugh. "That was presumptuous of me."

She shook her head, one hand to her chest. "No, I'm just not used to this. I've lived in a very non-adult world of raising a baby for the past few years."

"You're out of practice?"

Mia pulled a face. "I don't think I was ever in practice."

She slammed her car door and locked it. I did the same, and we set off to the hangar. I waved to friendly calls of my name, but my attention was locked on the woman I'd either freaked out, or turned on.

I couldn't call it.

Which meant I had to back the fuck off and let her decide.

At the bunkhouse, Mia opened the door and entered, holding it for me. I followed her in but kept a respectful distance, stripping my jacket and tossing it into my dorm room.

"It's not that deep," she muttered, as if convincing herself this was no biggie, her back to me as she hung her coat on a hook.

Too. Much. Innuendo.

I pressed my lips together and rested a shoulder on the wall, not answering.

Mia slowly looked at me. At whatever she saw in my expression, some of the tension left her.

"How do you do that?"

I tilted my head. "Do what?"

"Just be so effortlessly sexy? You're not even freaking out."

I held my ground, though my body yelled for me to do the opposite. "Ye said yourself, it's not that deep. Which, by the way, ye can't say to a guy without him picturing all the ways he wants to go very, very deep."

Her pink lips parted, and a boost of attraction heated my blood.

I forced myself to continue. "Sex should be fun. There's no better way to relax, but I get that it's different for men and women. So here's my deal. I have never once shamed a woman for who she chooses to sleep with. I've never once kissed and told. And I've never, ever left a lass dissatisfied. Use me if ye want, but my balls are entirely in your court."

Short, sharp, and factual. A hint of desperation might have edged my tone, but I couldn't help that. I was dying for her. Perhaps because it had been a long while since I'd got off to anything other than my own hand, but I hadn't felt like this a week ago. Or ever.

I wasn't kidding how she was my wet dream come true. Everything about her turned me on. The furious blush on her curved cheek. Her soft voice. Her fine-as-fuck body.

In the amber light from the single lamp in the bunkhouse living room, Mia watched me.

"I'd give anything to know the thoughts in your pretty head right now," I confessed.

"Why me?" she managed.

I prowled a step closer, drawing my gaze up and down her in a slow, provocative manner. "If I list all the ways, we'll be here all night. Top three. You're fucking gorgeous. Sweet as hell. And if I don't get my hands on those tits, I'm going to explode."

She shivered, her fingers going to her throat, then drawing down to just above her cleavage. "I haven't had sex in a long time."

"But ye want it now?"

Her single, fast nod drove all my blood south.

"Then you're in need of an orgasm or three. Sit down."

Flushing even redder, Mia perched on the sofa. I strode to the bunkhouse's door and locked it.

Without pause, I returned to her and dropped to my knees. Put both my hands on hers.

"Kiss me, little spy, while I play with these." I grazed the side of her breast. "Then I'm going to push ye back into the cushions and lick your pussy until ye scream. Sound good?"

"Very good," she breathed.

"Then get to it."

I held my ground. Mia regarded me then reached for my collar. Drew me in and brought my lips to hers.

The second the connection was made, I was lost. A groan of relief ripped from me, and I palmed her knees and spread them, inserting myself into the gap so I could get closer. She gasped but kept up the kiss, taking ownership.

My damn heart thudded, my pulse skipping beats.

Mia's careful kiss turned needy, fast.

Brushing my touch up her legs and over her body, I finally got my hands on the objects of my not-so-minor obsession for the past couple of days. That spectacular rack of hers. With both hands filled, I cupped her, flexing my fingers against her flesh.

God, they were heavy. I tested the weight, my mouth watering and my dick pulsing in sheer, happy lust.

Her breath hitched. One of her hands landed on mine.

Then it went to the button of her shirt.

I smiled against her lips. "That's my job."

Her fingers stilled and moved away, but I nudged her, inching back to command her attention.

"Know what's cool? This is a two-way street. I get to touch ye, and ye can have at any part of me you're interested in."

"Anything?"

"If ye don't, I'll assume I don't interest ye that much."

Her eyes opened, and she stared in outrage.

But curiosity got the better of her. Mia reached for my hair, gliding her fingers back to find the leather strip. "Is it okay if I take this out?"

"Ye can ask me to stand on my fucking head and sing the national anthem while slapping my dick and I'll do it."

She giggled and tugged on the tie. My hair fell loose. She played with it, grazing her nails over my scalp then teasing out the lengths.

I closed my eyes, lost for a second in the sensation.

Her tits in my hands, her playing with my hair. I couldn't remember anyone touching it since I'd grown it out, and it was instantly my new turn-on.

I ducked to press a kiss to her chest. "While ye do that, I'm burying myself in here. Don't worry if I don't come up for air."

Mia arched into me, pushing those gorgeous tits into my face.

Fuck. My dick pulsed again, hard enough to hammer nails into wood. I made short work of the remaining buttons on the shirt. It only opened halfway, the line of buttons ending at a point that was not nearly enough to expose her completely, but stripping her naked felt like a step too far for this first time.

I reached into her shirt, bypassing her bra to touch her bare skin. Her hard nipple grazed my palm, so I yanked the material aside to see it.

"Ye have gorgeous tits," I said. "Can I take my mouth to them?"

"Y-yes."

Diving in, I enclosed her nipple in my mouth, plumping

her up for my attention. Mia dropped back on the cushion with a moan of pleasure that hit me right in the balls.

She liked nipple play. Thank fuck for that.

Following her down, I drew my tongue around her, elongating her taut bud further. At the same time, I got a palm around her other tit, the space narrow but not defeating me.

This was my heaven. Right here, right now. I could spend all night doing this. Leaning over her, I sucked until I got another moan, then I brought my finger and thumb to my mouth.

Retreating, I waited until her gaze was back on me, then I licked my digits, returning the wet fingers to the nipple I hadn't got to know yet.

Mia watched me, her chest rising and falling with shaky breaths.

"Do ye like this?" I asked.

"God."

"Answer me or I'll stop."

"No! I mean yes. Please."

I gave a wicked laugh, returning to focus on the delicious feast laid out before me. A perfect pair, big and bouncy, and all mine.

My phone buzzed.

I yanked it from my pocket and tossed it across the room, not giving a fuck where it landed.

Another buzz came.

"Shit. That's mine," Mia breathed. "So sorry."

A little delirious, I released her. She had a kid. Could be something to do with that. My dick ached in the torment of stopping.

From her bag on the floor, she found her phone. Blinked at the screen.

"It's Daisy. She said she'll be here in ten minutes to talk about the rota with me. Ben's coming, too."

"Probably him messaging me," I managed to reply, but my tone was gravel.

Goddamned worst timing.

"I can't believe we have to stop." Her wide eyes beseeched mine.

Aw, hell no.

"Who says? We've got ten minutes. That's more than enough time for me to get ye off."

I palmed her thighs, driving my fingers up to the waistband of her leggings.

"Give me permission and I'll deliver a good, hard orgasm, like I promised."

She took a breath. "Please."

"Set a timer for nine minutes on your phone. You'll need the last to remember how to breathe."

She did it. In utter relief, I yanked down her black leggings, shifting back to pull them and her underwear off her. I tossed the clothing in the direction of the bathroom then grabbed her thighs again.

Without further warning, because this boy was on the clock, I kissed her pussy, right over her clit. Then I opened my mouth and licked her, gliding my tongue inside her for a brief second to drive myself insane with her taste.

She was so wet for me, this was going to be torture, but of the very best kind.

Mia tipped her head back and gave up a sound of pleasure.

It was everything I needed to get to work.

I spread her with my fingers, teasing her lower lips then pressing one long digit inside her. Her inner walls gripped me.

"Fucking hell," I groaned. "You're so tight. If this was my dick, I'd come in a shamefully short time."

Mia mumbled words I couldn't make out. I added another finger to the first, drawing them in and out of her. At the same moment, I returned to sucking her clit, getting straight into the fastest form of relief the lass needed.

My dick would've been better. It fucking wept for not being involved.

Each time she spasmed around my hand, I pictured driving into her. When she moaned, I memorised the sound to replay and use at my leisure.

Those noises she made got faster. More desperate with everything I did.

Repeated actions, a good pace, delivering over and over into her flesh.

Mia keened and gripped my hair, tugging on the roots.

I didn't need to check the clock to know I'd been at this for no time. She'd been so badly in need that she was hanging over the cliff.

If we'd had longer, I would've drawn it out. If I'd had any other options, I would've pretended we weren't home. But the choice wasn't mine so I kept on going.

Fucking her with my hand.

Working her now-swollen clit.

On her back on the couch, naked from the waist down and with her blonde head tipped back, the lass was a goddess.

"You're so fucking gorgeous," I said.

One more suck, and she broke.

A long moan came from her, but she slapped her hand over her mouth, stifling the sound while she pulsed around my fingers.

I leapt up, dragging her fingers aside to kiss her mouth, kneeling on the sofa between her legs, still seeing her through her climax with gentling strokes.

Mia slumped, finally through it.

I gazed down at her, a little dazed by how good that had been for me even without getting my dick near her delectable body.

A knock rattled the door.

"Shit, they're early," Mia gasped.

She shoved me aside and leapt up, scanning for her clothes.

I turned her, pointing them out in the bathroom doorway. "Go in and compose yourself. I'll keep them talking."

She disappeared, her shirt hiding the sight of her bare arse from me.

Pity. I really wanted that picture.

More slowly, I grabbed a bottle of water from a side table and scrubbed over my mouth, wiping my face in my sleeve— no need to give the game away to anyone else. Then I righted my clothes, twisted my hair back into a bun, and shook out my limbs, trying to get rid of my erection.

"Val?" my impatient brother shouted.

"Coming," I yelled back.

I ducked first into the dorm room and grabbed a dumbbell from under my bed. Carried it with me to the door to give a visual for why I was probably rumpled.

At last, I unlocked the door, revealing Daisy and Ben on the other side.

My brother scowled. "What took ye so long?"

"I was mid-rep. Where's the fire?"

The room smelled of sex. Hard to avoid that, but damn.

I stepped outside.

"Daisy needs to see Mia," Ben said, "but I have a new assignment for ye starting in the morning. Can we talk?"

I gestured to the office block. He pursed his lips but turned and marched away.

"Mia was in the bathroom, I think," I told Daisy.

"Uh-huh." My brother's girlfriend peered at me with a quizzical frown but went into the bunkhouse and shut me out.

I trod after Ben, leaving the dumbbell behind.

In the bodyguard office, he waited behind his desk. "Jackson, Raphael, and I are escorting Leo down to London for a couple of days starting tomorrow. Viola and the kids are staying here, but she could use some help with Finn."

Finn was our client's six-year-old.

I wrinkled my nose. "What kind of help? And why am I not going on this trip?"

"It's only meetings with his record company so doesn't need a full crew. Raphael isn't strictly necessary, but the training for him to fly us into the city space and land at a busy heliport is well needed. Plus ye have two reasons to stay here—the work you're doing on the cottages is one—you have the expertise to work on the electrics which is the next big job."

"What's the second reason?" I grouched.

"Getting to know Finn. Soon enough, when we're out in the field, we'll be in charge of the lad, and he needs to trust and know each of us. Viola has her hands full with baby Torran, and that'll be the way on tour. One of us will be assigned to Finn at all times."

It made sense, but I didn't like the feeling of being left behind while my team went off on a trip.

"What do I do with a kid?"

"Take him to and from school. Hang out with him for a couple of hours after. Jackson and Raphael will get this assignment, too. You're just the first. Is this going to be a problem?"

Ben was reading my body language—my crossed arms and the scowl that sank my forehead into lines—but it was the interrupted time with Mia that pissed me off.

I stood, tense as hell and needing air. "It's all good. I've got no problem with the job."

"Then what's with the sour face?"

In the doorframe, I paused. "Sexual frustration."

Then I left my boss to chew on that while I took myself off for a much-needed run.

7

Mia

"Are there boys at the school?" Tobi eyed me across the café table, her half-eaten dinner abandoned and going cold.

I'd finished work and drove like the devil to pick her up. Thankfully, the gods of traffic and road closures had been on my side, as Molly, my friend, was having an early dinner at her in-laws this afternoon so I couldn't have been late.

My daughter had leapt into my arms, holding me tight and not releasing my hand all the way here. She had a sweet and easy-going personality, but I couldn't rely on that to keep her content without me for long.

"Of course there will be. It's a small village school with a preschool class in the same building. It's so pretty there. We can go for walks every day when I pick you up."

"Do I have to?"

"Walk?"

"No, Mama, change school. I won't see my friends."

My heart panged. "Sorry, but we don't live near there

anymore. You'll love the new school, and I just know you'll have friends straight away."

She picked up her library book and held it in front of her face, not sobbing, but in a mini sulk that I totally understood.

Tobi was on Easter Holidays from her old preschool and attending a daily holiday club with Molly's daughter. It was the perfect time to move her, and the new setting in the village where Valentine and I had gone to dinner had spaces.

The school was so remote there, they were more than happy to take a new child in, and guaranteed to me that the privacy of their students was taken seriously. On my visit there, I'd asked if they could promise no letters would be sent to my old address, revealing my new one, and they assured me of it.

Not that I had a new address yet, though Valentine had left me a note this morning saying he'd be working on the cottage for most of the day.

I was such a coward. After Daisy left last night, I'd hidden in my bedroom. What he'd done to me had me blushing every time I thought about it. The first man to ever go *there*, and the speed in which he'd—

"Are we all finished?" a voice asked.

I snapped my attention to the café worker, a familiar face as we'd been in here often. "Hi, Bette, I think so. Tobi, are you going to eat anything else?"

My daughter lowered her book to wrinkle her nose at the cold chips and congealed ketchup. "Did I eat enough to have pudding?"

A healthy eating ethic didn't fly when she was having to live away from me. "I'd say so."

"Yay! What can I have?"

"Anything you like."

"What a kind mother ye have," Bette said. "Come see what

we've got behind the counter."

Tobi jumped up and trotted after the woman. I went to follow, but my phone beeped with a message.

Daisy: Valentine wants your number so he can ask a question about the renovations. Is it okay to pass it on?

Mia: That's fine, thank you for checking.

It still didn't feel real that I'd get that cottage. I didn't want to believe it, mainly because who knew what the rent might be. I'd searched locally, looking at ads and asking estate agents, but flats were few and far between, and houses out of our price range. The only places I'd found were a long drive away and not in the catchment area for Tobi's new school.

Besides, I didn't want to be travelling in and out of a town— it was the reason I'd picked the mountains.

Being out in public risked too much.

Here, in the library in Molly's hometown, there was next to no chance we'd be found. None of the people I used to live with would set foot into a community centre, and they definitely wouldn't stoop to eat in its café.

More so, the McRae estate felt perfectly secure.

I wanted to stay there. I wanted us both there, and yesterday.

My phone beeped again, and I peered around for Tobi first. At the counter, she chattered away to Bette who was all smiles for my little blonde cherub.

I checked the message with my heart hammering.

Unknown number: Hey, Mia, it's Valentine. I'm wiring up the electrics for your cottage this evening. Free to chat quickly?

I saved him as a new contact, then before I could chicken out, dialled him.

New-Mia wasn't quaking at the sight of a previous conquest. We lived together, for now. I needed to be able to look him in the eye.

He answered immediately. "Well, hello. Guess where I'm standing right now."

"Where?" I said, twisting in my seat to watch Tobi ponder the cake choices.

"In the middle of your bedroom."

"At the cottage, I hope."

He answered with a low chuckle. "I guess that did sound kind of creepy. I'm not in the bunkhouse, rooting through your underwear."

I wanted to flirt back, but there were families nearby. "Good to know."

"My question is, ye have overhead spotlights already, but only monsters use the big light, right? So, I'm putting in plug sockets for lamps either side of where the bed will go. Another can go by the door. Is that enough?"

"I think so," I breathed.

"Nice. They're all double sockets, in case ye need to plug anything else in when you're in bed."

I pressed my lips together. "How did you make that sound so...?"

"Dirty? It's a gift."

"You're very talented."

A pause played out.

Tobi pointed to her choice—a purple fairy cake with sprinkles—and Bette put it onto a plate. I half stood, my purse at the ready, but she waved me away.

When Valentine spoke again, his tone changed to more curious. "Where are ye anyways? With your daughter?"

"I am."

"In a secret location somewhere in the country that I won't ask or even guess at."

I smiled. "Appreciated."

"Not even a hint?"

"You're a terrible gossip, so no."

He took a shocked breath. "Damn, sweetheart. Arrow to the heart."

I winced, my words unfair. I didn't know where they'd come from. "Sorry. I didn't mean you were untrustworthy."

"I like a good story as much as the next man but I'll take your secrets to the grave." He hummed. "Will ye be staying in that mystery locale?"

"Yep. I'm sleeping here tonight."

"Then I'm on my lonesome."

"I'm sure you'll find something to do."

He made a low rumbling sound. "With the images I have of last night in my head? I think I'll cope. The shower might get abused, though."

I gave a breathy, startled, definitely turned-on laugh.

"Will I see ye tomorrow?" Valentine added.

"You will. I'll probably drive straight to my first job but I'll be back at the bunkhouse in the evening."

Oddly, I didn't want the call to end, but my daughter was on her way back, her tongue out in concentration and both hands gripping her plate.

"It's a date. By which I mean a non-romantic page on the calendar. Unless ye say otherwise. Until then, I'll send a few pictures," he said in a purr.

"Pictures? Of what?"

"The cottage. Now who has a dirty mind?"

He hung up, and I stared at the phone, my body warm from the brief chat alone.

Tobi set her plate down on the table, her thumb in the cake. "Bette let me have it for nothing."

"That is so kind of her. People can be lovely." Here, two hours north, just not where we'd come from. I brushed a curl back from her face so she didn't eat it. "Listen, for your first day in your new school, I have an idea. We'll bake something nice and take it in for all the other children."

"So everyone will like me?"

"Just to be kind, like Bette."

Tobi grinned big, dropping fairy cake crumbs. "I really want to do that."

My phone dinged, and she angled to see the screen.

"What's that?"

A photo of the cottage's exterior displayed. Gone were the broken windows and piles of rubble. I stared at the sweet home, flicking through the three other pictures Valentine sent.

I imagined painting it. Finding furniture. It was a dream I wasn't sure I could afford.

"Is that our new house?" Tobi tried again.

"I'm not sure yet. I'm still searching."

"But can it be? Then I don't have to sleep away from you."

I hugged her to me, kissing her soft hair. If only it could be, everything could all work out so well.

*H*alf an hour later, the library café was closing and we needed to move on. We'd killed time but couldn't go back to Molly's yet. She wasn't back for an hour, and I didn't have a key.

Outside the library, a chilly April gale swept over us, so we ran to the car, Tobi clutching her sparkly backpack. Rain splattered on us, soaking my hair and sliding down my neck, so I dived into the back of the car with my daughter to get her into her car seat without standing in the downpour.

Closing us in, I stripped her coat then mine. The windows fogged.

While I got to grips with the buckles, Tobi drew on the glass with her finger. She took a rush of breath.

"Mama, look."

"What, baby?"

"It's Greg."

Horror slammed into me. I froze then slowly lifted my head.

On the main road, beyond the library car park's railing, a metallic-orange four-by-four crawled past, the driver just visible from our angle.

Tobi was right. Tall, fair, and smug-faced Greg was one of the people who absolutely could not find us. If he did, my entire plan would fall apart.

In a panic, I dropped flat to the seat, my heart rebooting and skittering like a scared rabbit.

"Duck down so we can play a game," I whispered, sinking my fingers into Tobi's hair to gently guide her low.

Our windows weren't completely obscured. Her bright-blonde hair, and mine, would stand out like beacons in the dull afternoon.

"But don't we want to stop him and say hi? Greg!" Tobi called.

He wouldn't be able to hear her cry, nor recognise the car, but if he'd seen us, this was all over. I'd used my very last child maintenance payment to trade in my old car for this one. He couldn't see us in it.

My pleading with my daughter finally got her to hide with me, and we played a word game, though my brain raced over the sighting. They lived in Dundee. We were in Stirling. The distance wasn't far, a shade over fifty miles, but I knew the family. There was no reason for him to be in this town. None at all.

Maybe he was just passing through, but why leave the main road and cruise around the suburbs? Was he hunting us?

It felt unlikely, but I wasn't sure I believed in coincidences.

The family had known I had a friend called Molly, but I'd never told them where she'd moved to.

A minute passed with only the drumming of the rain on the car roof. No engine moved closer. Nothing to say he'd seen us, though he might now know my car model and numberplate.

Carefully, I peeked up then around. The metallic-orange truck had gone.

What could I do? I couldn't take Tobi back to the aircraft hangar, but if Greg had somehow discovered Molly's details, we couldn't stay here either.

Greg's car might've vanished, but my illusion of safety had evaporated with it.

I had no clue what to do next.

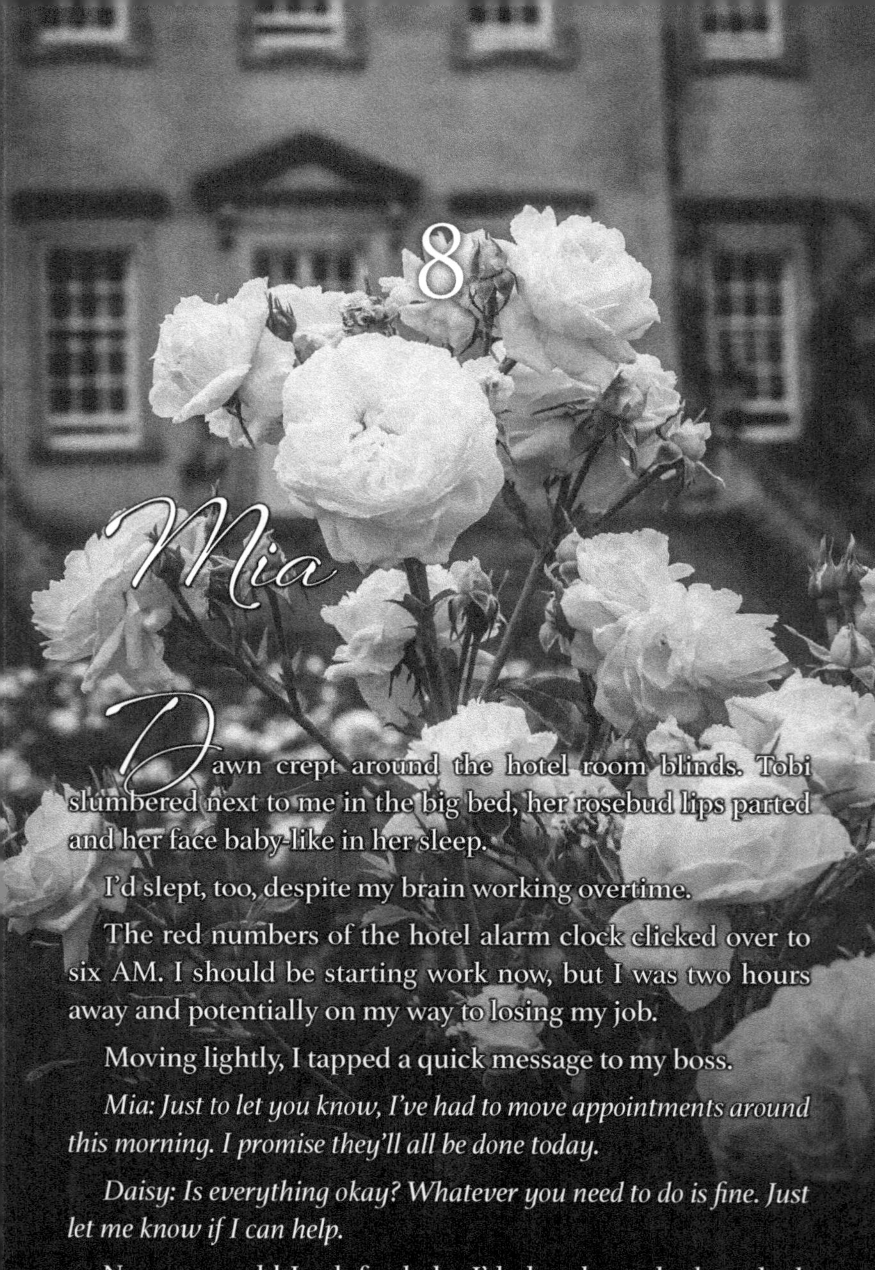

8

Mia

Dawn crept around the hotel room blinds. Tobi slumbered next to me in the big bed, her rosebud lips parted and her face baby-like in her sleep.

I'd slept, too, despite my brain working overtime.

The red numbers of the hotel alarm clock clicked over to six AM. I should be starting work now, but I was two hours away and potentially on my way to losing my job.

Moving lightly, I tapped a quick message to my boss.

Mia: Just to let you know, I've had to move appointments around this morning. I promise they'll all be done today.

Daisy: Is everything okay? Whatever you need to do is fine. Just let me know if I can help.

No way would I ask for help. I'd already pushed my luck far too much. There had been no choice over what I'd done, though.

After seeing Greg's car, returning to Molly's had felt too dangerous, as had setting out on the road, so I'd searched for local hotels with private parking, then brought us straight here. I had a change of clothes, and luckily Tobi did, too, in her backpack. We'd hidden away all evening.

The time alone together had been a gift, as much as a necessity. We'd snuck out to get vending machine snacks for supper, played games and read books, then finally watched Bluey until it was time to sleep.

My phone lit with a call.

I squinted at it, spying Molly's name, then rolled from bed to answer in the tiny bathroom.

"Hello?"

"Hey, is everything okay? How did you both sleep?" Molly asked.

"Pretty good. Did anything happen?"

My friend took a breath. "No. Nothing. There was no knock at the door or anyone lurking in the street. I made a point of taking the kids next door for a quick chat on the step, just in case your ex-family was watching. I'll do the same again this morning. Linger about a bit to prove you aren't here."

I exhaled relief. "You're such a good friend."

"I'm just repaying favours. Think of all the times you took Jessica for me when I was working. This is the least I can do." She clucked her tongue. "I was thinking about getting Tobi to the holiday club."

"I was as well. If I drop her off, they might see me and try to take her at pick-up. She'd go willingly with them, too. The same applies if they're watching you."

"I'd never let them grab her," Molly spat.

"I know. But they're powerful." Threat of legal action had been one of the reasons I'd fled.

Molly was a single mom like me. Neither of us stood a

chance when up against the machine that was the Winchester family.

"I had an idea. My aunt can come get Tobi from the hotel and take her to the club later than us. That way, if they're following me, I'll have led them away, and you'll be able to go to work. She'll pick Tobi up, and we'll work out a way to smuggle her back here."

Molly's aunt was a formidable lady who drove a bus. Tobi and I both knew her. If she was able to do this, I'd be able to get to work and not miss any more clients.

"Are you sure she can do it?" I asked.

"She never liked the Winchesters when I lived near them so she'll be glad to help. Leave it with me. But after this…"

I knew.

We said our goodbyes, and I texted an update to Daisy, cringing with each word. This plan might work today, but I needed a better one for tomorrow.

An hour later, Molly's aunt parked up in the hotel's covered foyer, and I strapped Tobi into her car. She'd flipped the plan to take her in early, which suited me better even if the very last thing I wanted was to let her go.

"George and Simon Winchester can suck it," she muttered, climbing from her seat. "And their mother."

I thanked the woman, not having the heart to tell her she'd got Greg's name wrong, and hugged my baby goodbye, holding in a wave of emotion.

Back in the hotel room, I sobbed.

Parting from her never got any easier. The wrench of seeing her go tore me up. Aside from my mother, she'd been all I had for years. I gave myself a minute to have a mini-breakdown then packed up our few belongings and checked out, driving north once more with a head full of problems with few solutions.

The rest of the day passed in a blur. I'd missed two clients but promised both I'd fit them in, so worked straight through without a break until eight in the evening. Tobi had been successfully smuggled back to Molly's, which was a relief, but every ding of my phone in the hours after spiked my panic.

Finally, I returned to the hangar and into the bunkhouse.

I needed food. A shower.

Strangely, I buzzed with energy.

The place was empty on my arrival, so I took myself straight into the bathroom and washed away the grime of the day. When I came back out, I had company.

On one of the teal sofas, Valentine stretched out, a beer in one hand and a slice of pizza in the other. He peered up and grinned. "There she is. Hungry? I have food."

I switched my gaze to the pizza boxes on the table which had been dragged closer to the fire. "Where the heck did you get takeaway pizza from?"

"It's Friday."

"That...makes no sense."

"There's a guy who parks his wood-fired pizza truck at the side of the A9 every Friday evening to catch the passing trade heading home for the weekend. I discovered him a couple of weeks ago and am obsessed. I even took a food bag to keep it warm, but it's cooled down now."

It smelled so good my mouth watered.

"One's for ye," he added. "The lower box. Daisy said you'd had a mare of a day, so I wanted to make ye smile. Take off any toppings ye don't like."

In a kind of daze, I sank to the rug and drew out the second box. Opening the lid brought a rush of amazing scent. The pizza was still warm, and he'd loaded it with a selection of toppings. Meatballs. Sweetcorn. Onion.

I lifted my gaze back to him. "Did anyone ever tell you you're a beautiful man?"

Valentine mimed flicking back his hair. "Not in the past hour."

"Well, you are."

"Just eat," he ordered.

So I did. The first slice barely registered, my hunger overtaking everything but the consumption of much needed calories. Pizza had never tasted so good.

When I was done, I pointed at Valentine. "I like you."

"I like ye, too. I wish I'd bought more."

"Oh my God, was that for sharing?"

"No. I meant watching ye eat was somehow so hot that I want it repeated."

I laughed, settling back against the second couch. My phone dinged, and I grabbed it, but it was only Molly saying the kids were asleep and nothing had happened.

When I lifted my gaze, Valentine was still watching me. "Want to share whatever had ye panicked today? All I heard from Daisy was that ye had an emergency."

I owed my boss a better explanation than the hasty, panicked ones I'd given throughout the day, but in a rush, I was sick of keeping secrets. It wasn't comfortable, and if I planned to bring my daughter here, a child who loved to chat, our story would be partially out anyway.

Hugging my knees, I pieced through what was safe to share. "The drama relates to the baby daddy I told you about."

"Mr dead guy, uh-huh, I remember."

"Tobi and I were living with his family."

"His parents?"

"No. His wife and sons."

Valentine gawked, his shock comical. "He was married? How old are his kids?"

"Grown up. The oldest is twenty-four, so a year younger than me, and the other twenty."

"Fuck, so he cheated."

"Yup. I worked for his company in one of their offices, and he would come by once a month or so, always with nice compliments for all the women. He had a reputation as a silver fox and a charmer, but mostly everyone liked him. Then there was a party to celebrate a major contract being won."

"He plied ye with drink and one thing led to another?"

My breath caught. Valentine was so close to the truth, but that information was a step too far.

"Something like that. I got pregnant unexpectedly, and when I told him, he was strangely happy about it. He set me up with child maintenance payments, even visiting Tobi a couple of times while I was on maternity leave."

"But ye weren't a couple."

I shuddered. "Not at all."

"Did he tell ye about his other family?"

"Nope. That was a big shock. I only found out after he died."

Valentine's jaw dropped again. My story wasn't a fun one— at least living it hadn't been—but getting the big reactions from my roommate was becoming enjoyable.

Valentine's expressions were making me want to share.

"Who told ye?" he asked.

"Human Resources, inadvertently. While on maternity leave, I had regular contact with my old office, though they knew nothing about who'd fathered my child, and it was a mass email that informed me of the manager's funeral arrangements. I was so shocked, and sad for Tobi."

"Did ye go? Is that how ye met the evil stepmother? Please tell me ye dressed in black lace and made a scene."

Another laugh bubbled up. "I wish I had just so I could tell you, but no. I took Tobi in a carry sling and went solely for the purpose of meeting whoever was managing his finances. I had no income, and my mother was sick…"

I trailed off, not meaning to have said anything about Mom.

Valentine waited, his grin falling. "Sorry to hear about your ma. I'm guessing ye lost her, too?"

"Yeah, but can we not go there? It's been such a day, I'll probably burst into tears." My voice wobbled. I patted my cheeks with the backs of my hands, cooling them.

Valentine reached into a bag and collected a beer bottle. Popped the cap with practised ease and handed it to me. "Right. Back to the dramatic funeral scene with the evil stepmother. Go."

I took a swig, pressed the cool glass to my face, then got myself under control. "I strode out into the middle of the funeral and held up my daughter Lion King-style, hollering to the mourners that she was their new ruler."

"Ye did not."

"No," I said with a grin. "I slipped in at the back of the church pews then waited until the end of the service. It was obvious who the lead mourners were, but I assumed the woman in black was his sister. She went deathly pale when I walked up and introduced us."

"Did she get nasty?"

I held the scene in my head, no small detail missing even after nearly four years. "She's a calculating woman. I didn't know that at first. After her very visible surprise, she welcomed me and Tobi in with open arms. We even moved into an annexe on their house for practical reasons, and she insisted on calling us family."

Valentine held his steady gaze on me, clearly ticking over my story. "Not many women would be so accepting of the lass their man had cheated with."

"I know."

"Or the new bairn whose existence meant their children had an inheritance to split three ways instead of two."

That was less of an issue, so I shrugged, taking another swallow of the drink. "The house was hers, and the company wasn't doing all that well. I don't think there's much to inherit."

His intent stare continued, and I cocked my head at him.

"Most people who've heard this story, which is few, judge me for it."

"Why?"

"Because I got pregnant by a married man."

"Ye didn't know. He's the bad guy."

Valentine unfurled his limbs and sat rigid on the couch edge, his gaze laser-focused on me. His attitude had changed entirely. Gone was the jokey, sexy roommate, and in his place was a different kind of man. The bodyguard. Sharp intelligence in his eyes and his attention honed.

I leaned in, fascinated with the switch.

He steepled his fingers. "So the evil stepmother convinced ye she was a kindly witch while being shady. Ye told me the people you're trying to avoid were controlling. The sons, too?"

I shivered, still riding adrenaline from that car park glimpse. "That's who we nearly ran into last night. The older one."

"Did he see ye?"

"No."

"Sure of that?"

"About ninety-five percent certain." But that five percent still haunted me.

"Where's Tobi now? Back with the same friend she's been staying with, I'm guessing."

At my slow nod, he pressed further.

"And is she safe there tonight?"

"I believe so. But tomorrow, I'm going to move her on, just in case I'm wrong."

"Where?"

"I...don't know."

Valentine waited for a moment, that intensity in him building. "Ask for my help."

"What?"

"I'm right here. I've heard your story and I have ideas."

I recoiled, embarrassed that I had no answer. The sense of failing when I'd barely got started strengthened, and it wasn't a nice feeling. "I didn't tell you any of that to get your pity."

"Do I look like I'm pitying ye? For fuck's sake. I'm a bodyguard. Ex-military. I have the capacity to help, so open those lips and say the words."

In a hot second, him telling me to *open my lips* for him switched my turmoil into something darker.

A coil of lust twirled low in my belly.

Valentine dropped his gaze to my mouth. "Save that needy expression for a minute and tell me I can get involved."

I'd be a fool to refuse, and I couldn't afford the pride being rapidly buried by lust. "What were you thinking?" I managed.

"Bring her here. To the bunkhouse. It has a bed for her and a lock on the door. I'll find somewhere else for the night so ye have the place to yourselves, then I'll work like a fucking maniac to get the cottage finished."

I cast my gaze around. The bunkhouse was an option, but I had back-to-back clients tomorrow, and Daisy had been so kind about today.

"You're amazing for even offering it, but I'd need to find something for her to do during the day while I'm cleaning. I haven't found weekend daycare yet."

"When does she start school?"

"The new term begins on Monday. I enrolled her in the village but haven't confirmed her first day."

Another problem I hadn't worked out how to tackle.

He took out his phone, his forehead lined in concentration. "So ye need cover for tomorrow and Sunday only. Let me get some minds on it. Plenty of families with weans her age around the estate."

He typed a message, responses coming in fast that earned more frowns and tapping out of replies.

My mind was a mess. I'd prepared as best I could under the worst of circumstances. Mom's death had left me reeling, while also propelling me to take action and change our lives. But I couldn't do it alone. The most important thing in the world was getting Tobi back with me.

By the way Valentine's mouth curved, he'd found a final piece to the puzzle.

"Sorted. After work tomorrow, I'll take ye to fetch her so you're nae risking being in the same car from yesterday, then we'll come back here for dinner with Cameron and his family. His wee girl, Avery, has just turned four so she will be in the same year group as Tobi. Cameron worked on this team a few years back, and he's happy to have your lass over for a playdate while ye work."

My control snapped.

So easily, he'd fixed my problems. Not just in getting Tobi

here but in gifting her a friend for her first day—something that had been taking up brain space and for which I had no solution.

A rush of need overtook me. I rolled up on my knees, got into his space, and kissed him.

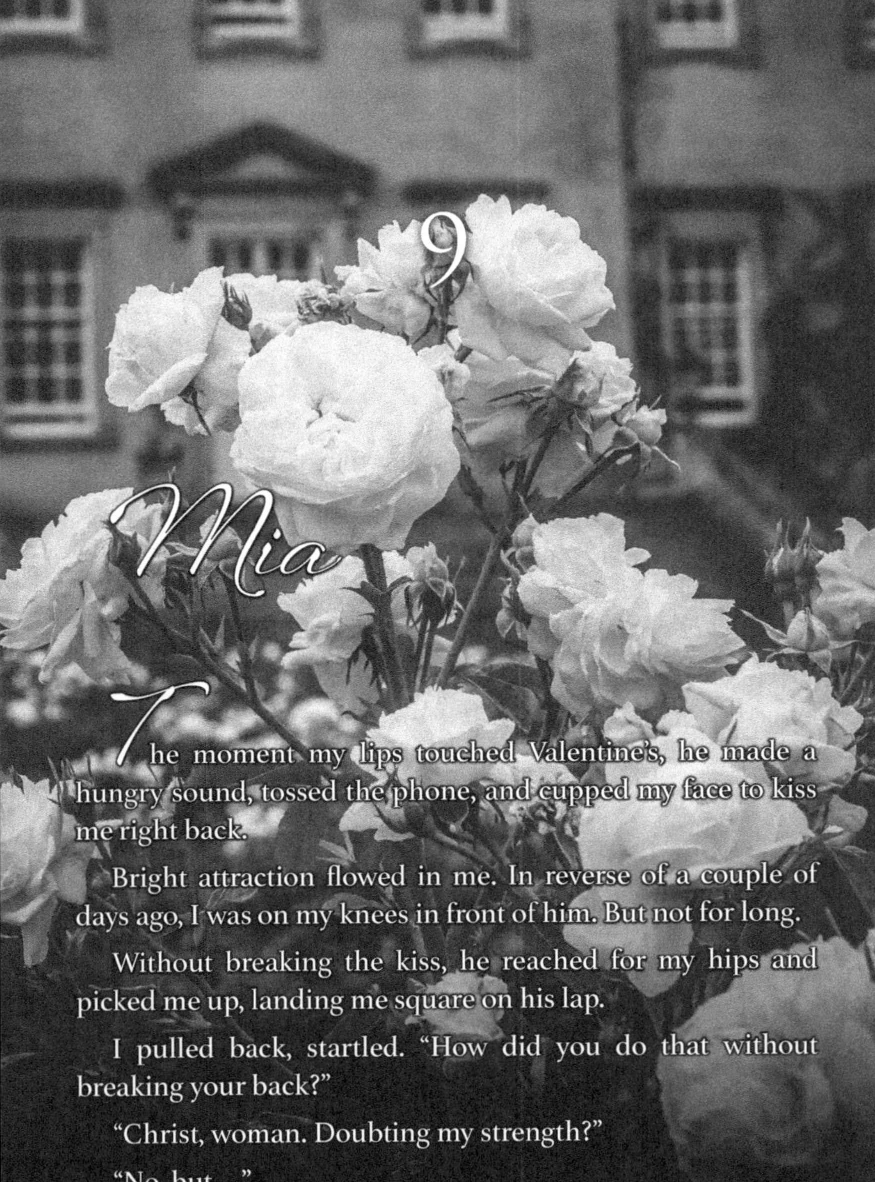

9

Mia

The moment my lips touched Valentine's, he made a hungry sound, tossed the phone, and cupped my face to kiss me right back.

Bright attraction flowed in me. In reverse of a couple of days ago, I was on my knees in front of him. But not for long.

Without breaking the kiss, he reached for my hips and picked me up, landing me square on his lap.

I pulled back, startled. "How did you do that without breaking your back?"

"Christ, woman. Doubting my strength?"

"No, but—"

"Then get your mouth back here."

Obeying him was no trouble. I kissed him again, harder, parting my lips. Pure heat zapped me at the first touch of his tongue to mine. God, this man could kiss. Even letting me take control, he gave the exact right pressure, coaxing, teasing, and driving me crazy.

His fine bristles scratched my skin, and I grazed his cheek with my fingertips.

"Do that thing with my hair," he asked, his voice deliciously gruff.

"What thing? Playing with it?"

"Aye, and your nails on my scalp."

I tugged the leather strip so his hair fell loose then brushed my fingers through the strands. On a second pass, I used my nails, drawing light lines.

Valentine made a sound of pleasure, bringing his focus down to my breasts, right under his face.

I took my hands to the hem of my shirt, ready to peel it off.

He squeezed my hips. "Hold up a second. There's something I need to say first. All that shite tomorrow is going to happen regardless of this."

I squinted, confused.

"I mean, I don't want ye to feel ye owe me anything."

I choked on a laugh. "Did you really think I'm paying you in sex?"

Under me, his dick pulsed.

"Sex," I said again, testing him.

He throbbed once more, hard enough to poke into me through our clothes.

Valentine appeared dazed, his eyes hazy. "Fuck, little spy. How is it you've taken control of my dick like that?"

"Just by saying sex?"

A third pulse came with another groan from him.

I let him off the hook. "I want to do *that* with you because you've done nothing but turn me on since we met. I'm not paying you with my body, but if it's a problem…"

"Fuck, no. Don't move."

"Not even to do this?"

The shirt came up over my head. I discarded it behind me.

Valentine's gaze shot to my breasts, just as I wanted. I didn't even care that I'd only put on a plain black t-shirt bra after my shower, as under his avid, instant need, I was the sexiest woman alive.

I pushed my ladies forward until they were right in his face.

Valentine cupped them both, sliding his fingers around the curves then drawing his palms under, taking the weight. His expression morphed into desperate need.

"Fucking hell. Aren't ye the most gorgeous pair? I want to bury myself in ye and never come up for air. I'll die a happy man."

I gave a breathy laugh. "Are you having a conversation with my boobs?"

Without looking up, Valentine hushed me, drawing his thumbs over my nipples. "Do ye mind? We're having a moment here."

Amusement battled how turned on I was becoming, but I shut my mouth and arched my back, giving him the green light to play. The huge Scotsman didn't hesitate. He ducked his head to kiss the swell of one breast, plumping up my flesh to create a deep valley of cleavage. Then he buried his face in the gap, giving up a groan that went straight down the middle of me. He kissed one side then the other, then licked my skin, all the while flexing his fingers, toying with me.

Heat streaked out from every place he touched me, my cheeks flaming, and my core pulsing with need. I only had to be close to the man to get turned on, but him losing himself in my body was something else entirely.

His touch drew fire along my skin. His wet mouth moved

from my cleavage over the top of my breast, pausing while he slid his hand inside my bra cup.

"This okay?"

I gave up a kind of moan that was answer enough, because he freed my boob and instantly enclosed my nipple in his mouth.

Another cry spilled from my lips, and I tipped my head back, the sensation of him on my sensitive flesh almost too much. Valentine took it slow, flicking the taut bud with the tip of his tongue, sliding one side of it then the other, coaxing it to pebble for him. He pulled back and blew on my wet skin, giving a sound of satisfaction at what he could see.

My eyes had closed by themselves.

But I could feel. Knew what was happening when he curved a thick arm under my breasts to present them to him. The pulse of his dick under me told me he liked what he saw.

He enclosed me once again, and this time, sucked.

Hard.

I moaned, barely remembering what he'd asked me to do. With a light touch, I drove my nails up the nape of his neck and into his hair.

Valentine stalled his actions and panted around my nipple. "Question for ye."

"Anything."

"If I told ye I'd never wanted anything more than to have ye sit on my dick so we can fuck while I suck your nipples, are ye going running?"

I opened my eyes to find him watching me.

The man was too good-looking, with that dark hair and beautiful, expressive eyes. There was nothing I wanted more than sex with him. The hangar could burn down around us, and I wouldn't care.

As if he could read my mind, Valentine gave my breast another possessive squeeze. "I swear I'll make it so good."

"Yes, please," I said in a rush.

"Thank fuck for that." He kissed me fast, at the same time shifting me to the sofa. Then he climbed up and strode to the bunkhouse door, locking it.

From his jacket on a hook, Valentine produced his wallet. A condom from inside.

I shivered, watching him prowl back over, his jeans tented and nothing in his eyes but sheer need.

He stripped his shirt. Tossed the condom packet to me.

"Clothes off," he said.

I caught the little packet and held it to my chest. God, the man was stunning. Wide, rounded shoulders that led to thick biceps. A broad chest that tapered to a narrow waist. In a rush, I felt my entire lack of experience and every inadequacy I'd ever imagined about my body.

"Can you turn off the lamps?" I asked, my voice a squeak.

Valentine popped the button of his jeans. "If I have to, I will, but I want to see ye. Every curvy inch."

"I don't look like you."

"If I wanted dick, I'd be sleeping with dudes."

A laugh flew from me. "That isn't what I mean."

Valentine stood in front of me and placed his hands on the back of the sofa, either side of my head. With his face inches from mine, he pressed a decadent, languorous kiss to my lips. "You're gorgeous. Your full, curvy body is making me crazy. Now finish the job of opening my jeans because if I'm not inside ye in the next five minutes, I'm going to go insane."

Without breaking the kiss, he nudged me to get to work.

This, I could do. I flew my fingers to his waist and carefully undid the next few buttons of his jeans, drawing them over his butt and taking his boxer shorts with them.

Valentine rumbled approval and broke his grip on the sofa to rid himself of the clothes. He returned to his pose over me, this time with one huge dick pointing at my face.

"Suit me up."

My jaw dropped. Not just because of his body but his confidence, too. Mostly, the size of the dick.

"You're so big."

"Thanks for noticing."

I fluttered my fingers at the condom packet. "I don't know what I'm doing. I've never done this before."

"Open the packet. We'll do it together."

I would, but I had another idea first. Gingerly, I reached for his hip, then drew forward until I enclosed his dick in my mouth. Masculine flavour burst over my tongue. Valentine gave up a sound of deep pleasure. It sent a rush of sensation to my core, the fright leaving me and being replaced by much better feelings. I drew my lips over my teeth and inched forward. There was no way I was fitting the whole of him in my throat, but I could try.

I sucked him, pulling back.

Again, I rolled up and down his dick, spreading my tongue this time to tease his ridges.

Valentine's fingers drove into my hair, and he cupped the back of my head. Standing over me, he held me still then worked himself in and out of my mouth for a couple of strokes, fucking my mouth. His breathing quickened.

"Ye should see how pretty ye are sucking my dick. Do this naked and I'll lose control in an instant. Fucking hell, woman. I want to come over your tits, but I need to be inside ye more."

God, I needed this. The relief and release that sex would bring. I was certain that he had all the skills I lacked, and desire crested in me.

With urgency, I came off him and held up the packet. "Can you do it? I'm scared I'll get it wrong."

Valentine took it, tearing open the foil and donning the condom in seconds.

Nerves shook me, but I scrambled to take off my leggings and panties, leaving me in just my bra top. It didn't provide much cover, but getting completely naked was beyond me in that moment.

I could be bold and courageous to a point. The walls of my new life shook with too many challenges to my sanity.

Somehow, Valentine seemed to understand because he didn't push me any further. Instead, he gestured me aside, sitting back on the sofa. Then he held a hand out for me to climb back on.

I wanted to babble excuses, speed-talk my nerves, but he reached to kiss me, swallowing my words.

The kiss, I could follow. That made sense when everything else didn't. Valentine guided me back to his lap, his dick under me.

My heart thumped, a drum pounding.

Valentine squeezed my hips then eased his hands back to feel up my ass. I kept my eyes closed, still panicked but focusing on the kiss. On the hard length of him under me. I wanted to be the woman who could have casual sex with a hot man who was offering. It was fine. Like playing sport with a new partner.

Then his fingers rounded me to cup my pussy.

My hitched breath turned into a moan when he slid a finger inside me. It said a lot how wet and ready I was. Even seeing him turned me on, so being naked on his lap? Game over.

Valentine glided that finger in and out, using the heel of his hand on my clit, his tongue stroking mine. His other hand grazed my breast, once more diving inside my bra to take the handful he so liked.

I whimpered, arching into him more. Needing this so badly.

Valentine read every sign like a book. Not once did he pause. Not once did his rhythm falter. He toyed with my nipple, sucked my tongue, worked my clit. It was all I could do to let him. We were so close, so hot together.

Another thick finger speared me, and I moaned, the insistent coil of an orgasm approaching.

In exacting moves, Valentine built it up, stoking a fire in me until I was surging against him, riding his hand, mindless, driven on. Then I broke, shuddering with the release I'd so badly needed. It danced through me, drawing a wave of sparkling lights and bliss.

Holy cow. How...?

I couldn't finish a thought.

He broke our connection, breathing hard, and drifted his knuckles down my cheek. "Fucking hell, little spy. You're so gorgeous, hear me? Watching ye fall apart on my lap is branded in my brain, and all I want now is to slide my dick into ye so I can feel another orgasm tightening around me. But I have to say we don't have to take this further. Ye might've initiated it, but I let my attraction to ye drive me on. If this doesn't feel right—"

"It does."

I was adamant. I wanted this.

He switched his gaze between my eyes. "Thank fuck. Then there's something else I need to be sure about. This is going to sound messed up, but I still need to say it. Tell me you're naw in love with anyone else."

I tilted my head, dizzy but confused.

His history returned to me. The story he told me in the bar. The woman he'd planned to marry had been in love with another man.

"There's no one else," I promised.

"Good. And the other thing is I can't promise more than sex. I can't offer anything beyond making ye feel good. Just need to put that out there, too."

"No problem for me. I don't want more."

He took a breath, his chest inflating. "Anything ye need to confirm?"

I'd never considered my own terms, but one was instantly there, cramming forward to be heard. "You actually want to do this with me," I said.

Valentine grinned. Under me, his dick pulsed. "There's your answer, but for the record, I've never wanted anything more. We good?"

I was halfway to inclining my head when he grasped my hips, got into position, then filled me with one deep plunge.

A groan ripped from me, echoed by him. He let me settle, just holding me while I adjusted to the size of him. To that huge dick inside me. He stretched me, parts of me lighting up in a series of mini explosions.

My eyes closed, and my arms banded around his neck without even being aware, every sense trained on what he'd done.

My pulse skipped along like a scared little bird.

Nothing had ever felt like this. Both strange and incredible. I was a twenty-five-year-old woman, a mom, and in stark realisation, I knew I'd never had good sex before.

"Hold on to me," Valentine muttered, his tone gruff.

With his arms supporting me, he lifted me from his lap so he could drive in and out of me. I gaped against him, struggling to breathe through my desire.

"Tell me how that feels," he asked.

I untangled myself from him, seeking his mouth to kiss him. "Incredible."

His hands eased from my hips to my chest. He stroked my breasts, returning to the action that had started all this. "Ride me while I play with these again."

Emotion shook me. I was in danger of embarrassing myself by not being cool about this. Giving away my inexperience.

We were just two people using each other's bodies. It should be fun. I had no idea why I suddenly felt emotional about it, but I needed to act better.

Settling my knees into the cushions, I eased up Valentine's dick a few inches, tensing my thighs to drop down him.

"Fuck, yeah." He yanked down my bra cups again, exposing both my tits to him.

Palming me, squeezing me, and finally sucking on a nipple, Valentine teased me while I rode him.

I took it slow, working out the position and the pressure. If I dropped down hard, somewhere high up inside me panged with absolute pleasure. If I circled my hips, something lower gave up brilliant sparks.

This was beyond what I could have imagined.

It was also compelling me towards the finish line. I panted, moving faster. I couldn't allow anything to get in the way. No interruption would end this. Not my own insecurities suddenly realising that I was mostly naked with the most beautifully made man.

All I knew was I had to get him to finish like I'd already done.

I focused on one place, one rhythmic hit, over and over.

Valentine came off my nipple and brought the other breast to his mouth, sucking hard on the skin of the upper curve. He repeated the hard suck an inch or two to the left, using the edge of his teeth.

An ocean of desire built where he touched me, and I pushed into his mouth more, rising and falling with increasing pace.

He groaned. Pulled away.

"I'm leaving marks," he suddenly said, his tone confused, like his act surprised him.

I glanced down at the red bruises. Love bites. "Keep going."

He sucked again, closer to the centre now. Both my breasts cupped, and his thumbs sweeping over my nipples while he worked.

Everything about this experience was startling and new, but the marks on my skin sent fresh need coursing through me. I fucked him harder.

My hands had kept a tight grip on his shoulders, and I used the leverage in my efforts until I was bouncing on his dick.

Valentine finished his line of love bites that went from one breast across to the other, and sucked a nipple back into his mouth, holding my boob in place while his other hand drifted between my legs. He'd already devoted a lot of time there, but I instantly keened in pleasure.

My skilful lover swept over my wet core, his fingers splaying over the place we were joined. They came back to my clit and wasted no time in making steady circles into my flesh.

It was all I needed. The help of his fingers working me. The rhythmically timed flick of his tongue as he sucked my nipple.

I'd started off in control but lost all ownership now. I moaned, my climax nearing, my pussy tightening around him. His dick thickened, and Valentine took over, hammering into me.

The action at my clit, the suction, the onslaught of good feeling...

My second orgasm smacked into me like a wrecking ball.

I cried out, dimly aware of the loudness but not giving a damn. All I knew was the rush of brain-cell-destroying pleasure. Around his rigid length, I clamped down and fluttered.

Then rush after rush of happiness lit every inch of my body, distinctly different to my first orgasm and all the better for gripping around him.

My strength gave out. I sagged onto Valentine.

But he wasn't done.

In a burst of energy, he rolled me to my back on the couch, fucked into me a few more times with repeated, hard thrusts, his mouth open and his focus going from my face to my breasts then lower.

My trembling arm weighed so much, but I raised it to scratch my nails over his scalp.

Valentine gave a broken cry and pulled out.

He reared over me, ripped the condom off, and came over my chest.

I gasped, lips parted at the dark desire in his expression. The groan of pleasure he gave.

Strings of cum decorated me, and Valentine sank to press his mouth to mine. He kissed me. Then he dropped onto me and breathed, his shoulders rising and falling and his heart pounding fast.

I hugged him, not caring about the mess. Not caring about anything but how free and alive I felt.

"Thank you," I whispered.

Valentine squeezed me. "You're thanking me? Christ, sweetheart, it should be the other way around. That was insane. I lost all control with ye."

But I didn't just mean the sex.

My life had been a small one, and I knew I'd needed more. This only went to prove what I'd been missing all those years.

*H*ours later, the cheerful beeping of my phone's ring tone woke me from a heavy sleep. After my eventful evening with Valentine, I'd taken another shower then hidden myself away when he had his turn.

I didn't know how to do the return-to-normal thing. The acting like sex was no big deal. So I'd climbed into my bunk, killed the lights, and slept hard.

I reached for my phone, the bright screen lighting up my narrow room.

Molly, read the caller ID.

My heart skipped a beat. It was after three AM. A phone call in the middle of the night from the woman looking after my child couldn't be anything good.

I fumbled to answer. "Hello?"

"Mia? I'm so sorry to wake you, but something happened."

I was already throwing back the covers and climbing up. "What is it? Is she okay?"

"Tobi's fine. She and Jess are sleeping top to toe, and I haven't heard a peep from them all night. No, this is something else. I woke with the baby crying, and I got spooked, so I was watching the doorbell camera on my phone while I fed him. I scrolled back through to yesterday, and I saw something."

On the edge of my bed, I perched, gripping the frame. "What was it?"

"A man posted a big envelope into my parcel box by the gate," she whispered back. "I haven't checked it in days because we weren't expecting anything. He didn't ring the doorbell, so I didn't get an alert, but the camera still picked him up."

"Did you recognise him?"

Her pause sent a chill down my spine.

"It was Greg. According to the time stamp, he was here right after you saw him at the library."

Shit. I closed my eyes, panic chilling me to the bone. He knew where Tobi was. He'd been there. Seeing his car hadn't been a coincidence after all.

I forced my lips to move. "What's in the envelope?"

"I don't know. I'm too scared to go outside."

Clothes. I needed to get dressed. To get my daughter away. "Stay there," I told Molly. "I'm on my way. Whatever you do, don't answer the door."

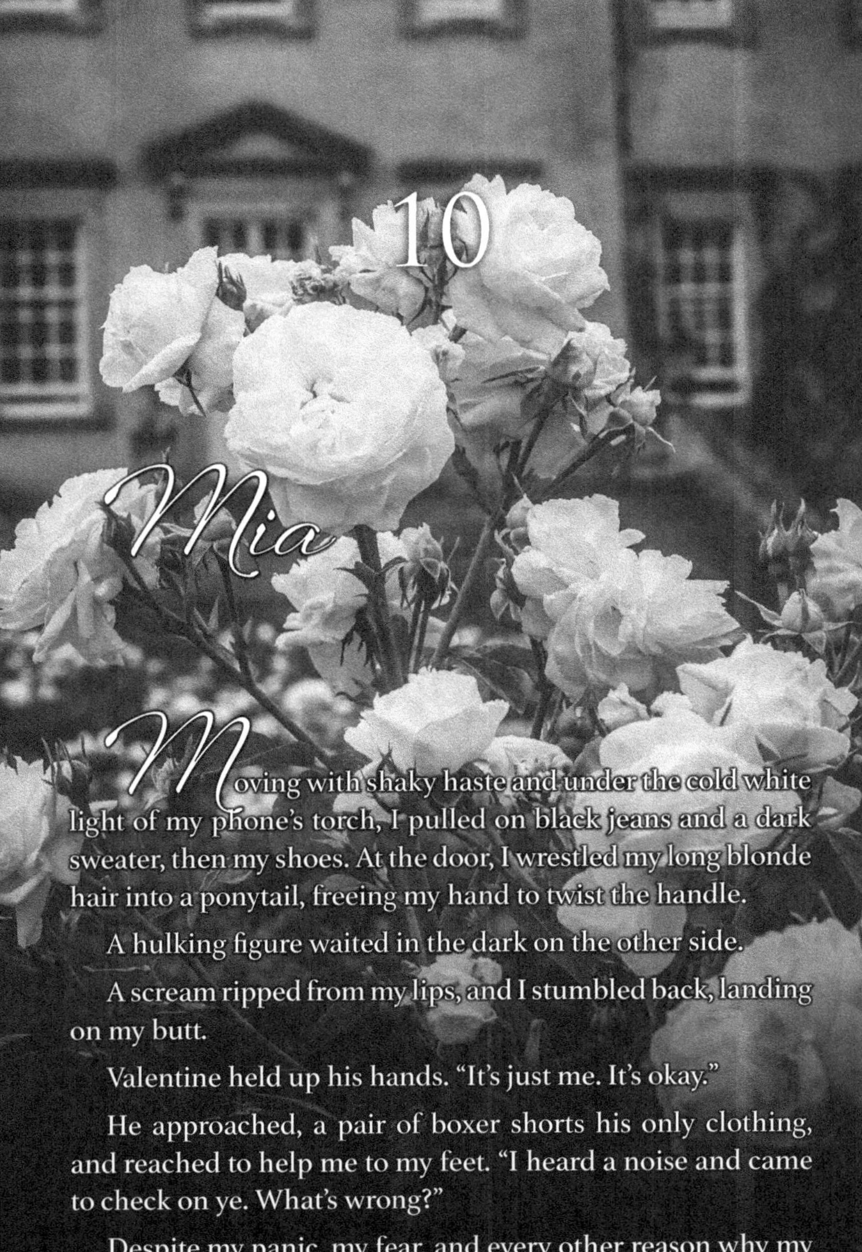

Mia

Moving with shaky haste and under the cold white light of my phone's torch, I pulled on black jeans and a dark sweater, then my shoes. At the door, I wrestled my long blonde hair into a ponytail, freeing my hand to twist the handle.

A hulking figure waited in the dark on the other side.

A scream ripped from my lips, and I stumbled back, landing on my butt.

Valentine held up his hands. "It's just me. It's okay."

He approached, a pair of boxer shorts his only clothing, and reached to help me to my feet. "I heard a noise and came to check on ye. What's wrong?"

Despite my panic, my fear, and every other reason why my mind shouldn't go there, warmth trickled through my veins at his touch. But as incredible as last night had been, it was in the past and done, we'd both agreed.

I'd washed him from my skin.

"Sorry," I breathed, my voice choked. "I had a call. I need to go."

"To fetch your daughter?"

I nodded. "Greg knows where she is. I have to get her out."

He scrubbed a hand over his hair, backing up to the main room. Any vestige of sleep fled him, pure action in his moves. "Give me thirty seconds."

"You don't have to," I called after him, relief adding to my mix of emotions. He'd offered to help, but that didn't mean he needed to get up in the middle of the night for me.

The light sprang on in the living room, then the one in his dorm room. Trailing behind, I peered through the open door, an unashamed spy now, watching as he shrugged on jeans and a close-fitting shirt, a zip-up jacket following. Then he grabbed a backpack from the floor.

I couldn't help noticing the two packed sports bags on the bunk next to his.

He followed my gaze. "I've emptied the bunkhouse of my things and given the place a scrub down. Would've stripped the sheet, but I was still using it."

I blinked. "When did you do all that?"

"After ye decided against cuddles and took yourself to bed."

My cheeks heated.

He grinned, tugging on two huge black boots. "I didn't want to be lurking when we brought your girl back."

Our plan had been to leave in the afternoon. Not the middle of the night.

"Where will you stay?" I muttered.

"Aw, ye worried about me?"

"A little. I'm throwing you out of home."

"Someone's giving me a bed elsewhere. I'm good."

Did that mean another woman? Why the heck had my mind gone there? It was none of my business, except I was the reason he was having to go.

Maybe it was better if I didn't ask.

Either way, now dressed, Valentine was all action. He passed me, taking my coat from the hook and his car keys from inside his backpack. We exited into the darkened hangar, and I zipped up against a cold breeze from the open front.

Valentine directed me to the black truck I'd followed in and out of the village, and I moved Tobi's car seat into it, nerves shaking my fingers so badly it took multiple attempts to clip it in.

While I worked, Valentine jogged back to the hangar and returned with something in his hands. He knelt at the front of his car. "Trade plates so no one can track my registration. Just in case."

Inside the comfortable car, with the heating on, I huddled in the passenger seat, my knee jumping and my mind flitting over what I needed to do and what could go wrong.

"Give me my destination then tell me what happened," Valentine requested.

"Stirling," I said with a breath. Then I related what Molly had seen on her camera.

"Sounds like he was scoping the area hoping to find ye, then delivered whatever's in that envelope. I just wish we knew this yesterday. Talk to me about Molly's place."

"It's a small, three-bed terraced house on a cul-de-sac. She has three kids and is a single mother. She used to live closer to my old home, and our daughters went to the same toddler groups and preschool. She moved away, but we kept in touch."

I stopped talking, realising he needed tactical details, not commentary on our friendship.

Valentine hummed acknowledgement, his gaze on the road where his headlights pierced the dark. We were far off dawn, which could only be a good thing.

"It's a quiet road," I continued. "Everyone knows each other."

"Any footpaths going onto it?"

"There's a few that run behind the houses. They exit onto other streets."

"When we're closer, show me on a map. Now, I realise ye might not want to talk about this, but I'm going to ask anyway. What happens if these people find ye?"

Valentine knew barely anything about my situation, yet he'd been willing to jump into action. I couldn't be more grateful, but I could definitely be more forthcoming.

Taking a deep breath, I demolished the wall I'd put up around my trust. "I told you they were controlling. The Winchesters. That's their family name. Vanissa is Tobi's father's wife, and her sons are Greg and Simon. In the lead-up to me leaving, there was some kind of legal stuff they wanted me to sign. There was even a threat."

"What kind of threat?"

"That they'd take Tobi from me."

"On what grounds? You're her ma."

Shame pierced me, and I stared out the window so I didn't have to look at him. "Of me being unstable. When my mother died, I was a mess."

"Holy fuck. Of course ye were. That would break anyone."

"I think I was worse than most. My grief came and went unpredictably. Some days I'd be coping fine, the next I'd be devastated. One night, after Tobi was asleep, I missed my mother so much that I just sat and sobbed. Vanissa came to see me. She had something to talk about, but I was inconsolable.

She ended up calling a doctor to sedate me so I didn't upset Tobi if she woke."

"What the fuck? That's the threat she's using against ye?"

I raised my hands in a shrug. They shook. "That incident is on paper. Vanissa threatened me with it, but in a kindly-help sort of way. She said if I was unable to cope, they'd take Tobi off my hands for both of our sakes. It was the final straw and the reason we left. I hate myself for how long it took me to break away."

"Fuck that bitch. She's evil. Like land-a-house-on-her level." He worked his jaw. "What was the legal shite she wanted from ye?"

"Something to do with winding up her husband's business. Probate had taken years because he didn't have a will, and I wasn't in the right place to care about it so I didn't listen."

There was a pause. A comfortable silence. I'd shared so little of my story with anyone else, and nothing of the threat Vanissa held over me, not even to Molly. The act had me breathing easier. I'd needed this.

"Can I ask what happened to your ma?" Valentine said quietly.

"Cancer. It's the reason we came back to Scotland. She's from here originally but relocated with her gran, her only relative, to California years ago. She loved the life and went full American. She got pregnant, stayed with my dad while I was small, but they broke up, then she got sick. I was fourteen the first time it hit her. The second time, we came back to the UK for her treatment, and Mom beat it. When I was pregnant with Tobi, it hit again. She died last year."

I kept my gaze away, lost for a moment in the abject sadness that had come with slowly losing Mom. Then one hand landed on my knee. Squeezed.

"We'll get your girl back. I promise ye that."

He didn't offer platitudes about my mother, just gifting a simple truth of how the morning was going to go. I believed him.

I barely knew him, but I was certain Valentine delivered on every promise he made.

With my quietly whispered thanks, into the dark night we continued.

Valentine asked a few more questions about the Winchester family, their descriptions and what cars they drove, then asked me to hold up his phone. I unlocked it for him and navigated to the message screen he directed. He left a voice message to what I guessed was his team, stating that he was taking me to retrieve my daughter, and asking Raphael to check in with availability. I had no idea what that meant, but he was done and the message sent.

Valentine filled me in. "The basic plan, if ye agree, will be this: We approach with caution, keeping a lookout for the cars belonging to the people we're going to avoid. We'll park up on a nearby road with lane access, and I'll scout the area and retrieve that envelope. Assuming all is well, we'll take the car to Molly's, I'll get out and run inside to get her bags. Molly will bring Tobi to ye in the back seat. No lengthy goodbyes or chat. No hanging around. Once we've got her safe, we drive for a while so I can ascertain if we've been followed. If we have, we go to plan B. If not, we'll return home."

I stared at him. "When you said you were in the military, you weren't messing around."

He gave a head waggle that was decidedly hot.

"What's plan B if we're followed?" I asked, shivering for multiple reasons.

"Did Raphael reply yet?"

I picked up his phone, noting the answer from his teammate.

"He gave a thumbs-up."

"That means he's available if we need him to pick ye and Tobi up by helicopter."

My jaw dropped open. "You're joking."

"About safety? Never. If we have to enact that plan, it's only a short flight. I'll hang back and lead the family elsewhere."

I'd fallen into an alternative universe with ultra helpful people and resources to burn. I was either lucky or dreaming. I couldn't work out which. But the whole point was getting Tobi back, and if it meant taking what others had to offer, I'd do it.

11

Valentine

A blue-black sky blanketed the streets of Stirling, the snow melted here—a benefit to those out on the prowl like myself. I slunk along the hedgerow, silent, and with my senses alert for any sound.

We'd made good time on the road, and it was gone five in the morning, few cars around and even fewer people, only a milk delivery van cruising by on its electric engine, the driver not spotting me.

My heart beat at a steady pace, and I breathed slowly, telling my body to remain calm, even though my adrenaline was up.

Back in the car, concealed two streets away, Mia had shown me on a map the house that was my target, then called her friend to tell her to be ready.

I was dead opposite the property, my focus on the lockbox in the front garden.

What reason would the arsehole family have to serve papers to Mia? They'd been trying to get her to sign something and issued threats against her daughter. They obviously wanted something, and I'd bet any money it would be at Mia and Tobi's expense.

The front door of the house opened, and the homeowner peeked through the gap. She peered up and down the street, not spotting me, laid something on the step, then shut the door after herself.

I waited for a minute, nothing stirring. Sneaking across the road, I dove over her low fence, then darted to the shadows of the front door.

A thick white envelope waited, Mia's name in bold type with her friend's address beneath.

My stomach tightened.

This wasn't what we'd agreed. Mia's friend was supposed to have left me the lockbox key so I could retrieve the packet. But she'd already moved it.

With a muttered curse, I opened my backpack and took out my bug hunter. Passed it over the envelope. The indicator light turned red, my device silenced but the impact just the same.

There was a tracker hidden inside.

"Fuck," I grumbled under my breath, another hit of adrenaline priming my limbs.

Decision time.

Movement of the paperwork would already have been picked up by whoever was monitoring that tracker. They'd almost certainly be on their way now.

Our time to take this slow was at an end.

At the top of the road, the milk delivery vehicle turned, and an idea sprang into my mind. I tore open the envelope, extracting the clipped-together pieces of paper. Probably fifty sheets, stapled in groups.

A quick shake released the tiny tracking disc—one anyone could buy online—and I scrunched it back into the empty envelope, checking that there wasn't a second in the paperwork.

The milk van cruised past my hiding place. Taking aim, I tossed the balled-up envelope onto the back of the vehicle. It landed neatly between crates.

As solutions went, it wasn't perfect. If the delivery driver had other houses in the local area to go to, that didn't give us much breathing space to get away. But it would distract the people following us and was better than nothing.

Adapting a plan on the go was my sweet spot.

At a guess, we had minutes to get clear of the area. If I were the one staking out Molly's property, I wouldn't ignore the tracker moving away, but I'd have eyes on the moving target as well as the original one. Mia had mentioned two brothers.

Finding my phone, I called her.

"Drive my car around to Molly's," I ordered.

This wasn't what we'd discussed, but the lass shifted, her car door clunking open. "What happened?"

"The envelope hid a tracker. I got rid of it, but we need to move."

She took a rushed inhale. "On my way."

We'd lost the element of surprise, so I paced down the path and secured Molly's gate open. My tap at her door was opened quickly, a wide-eyed lady on the other side taking me in.

"What's your name?" she challenged.

"Valentine."

She gave a single nod then tipped her head at the room behind her. "All the bags on the rug are theirs."

"Thank ye. Mia will be here with the car in a moment.

Please go fetch the bairn." I moved past her to the darkened living room.

In the tidy space, a pile of belongings sat on a circular rug, and I stooped to collect them in two big handfuls of carrier bag handles. A completely out-of-place pang hit my heart. This was their worldly belongings. Everything else had been left behind when they'd fled their home. All their furniture, any bigger items.

Where the hell had that sentimentality come from?

I had no space for emotional shite. It wasn't going to help us any now. I adjusted my grip to put the paperwork into a bag, then carried it back into the hall.

On the road, my car drew to a halt, Mia reversing and parking neatly. I jogged out, and she was there, opening the boot and helping me shove everything inside.

"They're trying to track me?" she said, her voice tight. "I can't believe it. I mean, I can, but that's horrible."

"Grab your girl and we'll get out of here," I replied, just as gruff.

A second later, a little voice sounded in the dark. "Mama!"

Mia gripped my arm then sprinted away. In the doorway, her friend handed over the girl, a soft blanket bundled around her. Somewhere in the background, a baby wailed while the women hugged it out.

Mia's daughter sobbed.

Another wave of emotion hit me, something poignant and fucking cloying in my chest. So strong I rubbed my knuckles against the ache. Once, I'd wanted kids, but that had been a long time ago. I couldn't imagine it now. The heartache of trying to be everything for someone who relied on me and my partner. The panic and fear that went with the responsibility. Of how it all could implode and fuck up a child's life.

That's all it was.

A warning that my life had changed. It was better this way. I was free to help people like Mia and Tobi. Free, and single, and definitely not in any way fucked up from seeing a lass and her bairn reunited.

I closed the boot with a low clunk and opened the back door. Mia whispered goodbyes to her friend then fled back to me, hurrying to get seated. I climbed in the front, and with a backward glance to be sure they were clipped in, drove us away.

For several minutes, Mia and Tobi kept their heads down, Mia whispering reassurance to her daughter. Though there were few other people around, we were far from out of the woods. I kept my attention on the road, scanning for the milk van I'd sent off with the tracker, as well as every dark street that we passed.

Headlights shone in my rearview mirror. Laser-focused, I took a turning. A second.

They kept on our tail.

Right, fucker. I caught a glimpse of the vehicle type as it passed under a streetlight. A metallic-orange truck. Exactly what Mia had told me one of the family drove.

"Mia, do ye remember the license plate of the older brother's vehicle?" I asked.

"No, I've no idea," she said in a rush.

"Did he buy it new?"

"Yes. A year ago."

Shite. I couldn't make out the plate without him getting nearer, but that was definitely a newer model. Nor could I speed away, not in a residential area, but I was good at evasive manoeuvres.

Ahead, a three-way junction appeared, the lights on green.

I assessed the choices in a fast reckoning. Taking the left meant more suburbs and quiet streets. Dead ahead was the town centre. The right-hand turning joined a faster road and our route north.

"We're going to need to take action sooner than I thought. Keep low and out of sight."

With calm agreement, hiding nerves I sensed coming off her, she whispered something to her daughter.

"Why have we got to hide?" Tobi said. "Can't we go back to bed at Molly's house?"

"Not now, baby. You're coming home with me."

"But it's dark, and I'm cold."

"I know. Cuddle against me, and I'll tuck the blanket around you like this. If you close your eyes, we'll be there soon."

"Who's that man?"

"Valentine. He's a friend. He's going to get us home."

I wanted to reassure the little lass myself, but I was a stranger to her, so it was better left to her ma. Besides, all my attention had to go to crossing the junction. My green traffic light turned to amber, warning me to stop. If I did that, I'd give the truck a chance to get right behind us.

Instead, I floored it.

We burst across the junction, speeding through ahead of the lights switching to red. I didn't slow, my focus ahead and on getting away. I'd picked the option with the faster road. There were fewer opportunities for concealing us but greater risk in lingering now that he knew what our vehicle looked like. Hitting the accelerator, I punched through the gears. The speed limit was fifty, and there were big gaps between the cars so I could under and overtake easily.

I could get us away. I had no doubt. But the priority was the safety of the woman and the girl in the back.

My car ate up the city streets. I'd picked it for speed and agility, and that was paying off.

But a glance back put the orange truck in my rearview again.

I gritted my teeth.

For a minute, I watched him. If I sped up, he did, too. If I held my pace, he retained his position, several cars back but not budging.

There was no doubt in my mind now that we were being pursued.

I'd planned for this. For Mia and Tobi's extraction. But the decision wasn't mine.

From my shirt pocket, I pulled out my earpiece and fitted it. Then I glanced back at Mia, finding her gaze on me. I didn't want to scare her daughter, so picked my words carefully. "That second option we talked about earlier, the plan B, it's a possibility."

Already pale, she gave a shaky nod and huddled closer to her bairn. "I understand."

"We'll need to choose now to give Raphael time."

If he wasn't already at the hangar, my colleague would need to get there, set a flight plan, and agree a touchdown location with me. I'd take a diversion, leading Mr Orange Truck in a different direction so he didn't know the ultimate destination had been north.

I'd get Mia and Tobi there, see them away safely, then it would be just me and the pursuer, one-on-one. Exactly the way I liked to handle bullies.

"Can we stay with you?" Mia asked.

I peered back at her, furrowing my brow.

She continued, her gaze beseeching mine. "Would that be

okay? The idea of leaving you is..." She slid a glance at her daughter. "What I mean is I feel safe here. With you. I don't think I would if we had to get out of the car."

That same feeling hit my chest, an arrow to a bull's-eye, burrowing deep. It wasn't a comfortable sensation, but somehow, I couldn't say no. I couldn't refuse the woman anything.

I tore my gaze away and adjusted my plan once more. "If ye want. That means losing the jerk ourselves, and possibly taking longer to get home."

"I'm good with that. You'd have to do it anyway, right?"

"What's a jerk?" Tobi asked.

A choked laugh flew from Mia's lips. "Someone we don't like, baby."

I could've apologised, but fighting with the strange emotions threatened my focus. Bolstering myself against it, I put everything into finding an escape route. My car had a panel with a mapping system, so I turned it on and, with one eye on the road, paged through the map.

What I needed was an exit into a town with the right kind of streets to lead the orange truck on a dance. I'd done this before, and it was a thrill playing a cat-and-mouse game.

Luckily for us, the city of Perth wasn't far ahead. I put my foot down until we reached it, easing off the roundabout into the outskirts, our speed coming down but my heartrate still flying.

A business park was my destination.

I killed the lights and ignored the first two car parks, spinning the car into the third—a much bigger one with trees and hedges and a good amount of vehicles already parked. A space between a van and a chunky Range Rover made our hiding place.

With the engine off, silence reigned.

I watched the road beyond the hedge, waiting for my quarry.

Lights cruised down the road.

I squinted into the dark. The sky was brightening to purple at the edges, the coming dawn making it harder to see, but it didn't obscure the spectre of the orange truck. The driver paused at the entrance to our car park, stalling to have a good look. We'd got into our bay in time to not draw the eye—the strategy of not picking the first turning paying off—but if he entered and drove around, he'd spot us.

And the fucker wasn't moving on.

We needed a distraction.

Tobi started to say something, but her ma hushed her with a quiet word. Abruptly, I snatched up my keys. Passed them back to Mia.

"Lock the doors after me. I'll be right back," I uttered.

"What are you doing?"

"Keeping ye safe," I promised then closed them in.

Icy air curled around me. I'd boosted the heat for Tobi and Mia's sake, so the wintery blast sharpened my senses.

I paced towards the entrance road, keeping concealed behind the rows of cars as I scanned my surroundings for something to use. An opportunity.

A second car passed the orange truck. White with a siren on the roof. The markings snagged my focus for a beat. No, not a police car. This was even better—a security patrol.

It cruised into my car park and towards me. I flagged it down, keeping on the offside to the road.

The driver drew up alongside and lowered his window. "Can I help you?"

"Security?" I asked.

"That's right."

"It's about time. I'm Paul from Human Resources. We've left multiple messages about unauthorised vehicles taking up spaces here. I've come in on my day off to deal with this because no one is getting back to us." I was pushing my luck. In jeans and a black jacket, I appeared anything but corporate. At least my hair was tied back.

The security guard blinked. "It's the first I've heard of it."

The orange truck entered the car park.

Fuck.

"That's not good enough," I argued. "We've had the director and multiple important visitors unable to park outside our own office. They've had to walk in the rain to get into our building because their spaces have been taken up. I've asked that all cars be checked for a permit."

He eyed me. "What did you say your name was again?"

"Paul. I'm from HR. Are we going to have a problem?"

The man started. "No, I didn't say that. Leave it with me. I'll make sure the team know."

Mia's follower inched down the central row.

We were on the third to the left. If he got there and turned, the game was over.

"Still not good enough." I pointed to the truck, keeping low to the security car so the driver couldn't see me. "Who's this guy? I don't recognise that car, and he's about to take up one of our spaces. We have meetings today. Go do your job."

The officer jumped his gaze to where I pointed.

I held my breath.

He glowered, nodded at me, and drove on.

Thank fuck for that. I didn't wait around. We had to leave one way or another. Slinking between rows, I jumped a low barrier, appearing at the back of my car. Down the way, the security guard pulled up alongside the orange truck. The guard called something to the driver.

This was our chance. I tapped on my door. It clicked, Mia leaning over the central console to let me in.

"I didn't want to use the keys in case it turned on the lights," she whispered.

"Smart of ye," I commended.

"Valentine, is the jerk gone?" Tobi asked.

In my seat, I twisted to face her, surprised at her talking to me. She was a mini-me of her ma, with the same sweet face down to the quizzical expression. I caught myself grinning.

"Aye, sweetheart. I think so."

The movement of the car headlights showed me the driver peeling away back to the exit.

"Can we go home now?" she added.

I watched the road for a moment longer, inwardly cheering when the lights went left and deeper into the business park.

It left our route back to the fast road clear. My tactic had paid off.

Relief, satisfaction, and an array of other shite mixed up in my chest. My answer was for her, but my focus lingered on her ma.

"We can. Settle in for a wee nap, and I'll get ye home safe."

12

Mia

$\mathcal{O}$ur return to the McRae estate wrapped me in a sense of safety that I'd rapidly begun to associate with Valentine. After neatly evading Greg, he'd got us back on the road, speeding us north again. Though he'd thrown glances regularly backwards, I felt only certainty that he'd done what he'd promised. Brought us home.

Maybe it was tiredness, but that did dangerous things to this woman's heart.

Valentine slowed the car, cruising past the gateposts to the estate. His gaze found mine in the rearview. "What time do ye need to start work?"

I checked my phone. "Half an hour. I only have bookings until lunchtime, though."

He indicated with his head to my sleeping daughter. "I'll call Cameron now and see if he can take Tobi for breakfast."

I wanted to protest, but I'd learned by now to hold my tongue and take the help.

Valentine made the call, idling his car on the far side of the bridge that spanned the river leading to the loch. The water spread out to our right, icy at the edges and calm in the centre, the shape of the towering mountain reflected back. Picture-perfect places I hadn't explored yet, but that were becoming so familiar.

"Grand. We'll be there in a few." He hung up the phone and twisted to speak to me. "Cameron said bring her on by. Avery's excited to meet her new friend. They'll take her until you're done with work."

"Thank you," I said, a wave of emotion threatening me again. "For everything. Without you, Greg would have found me, either at Molly's house or he would've been able to follow me here. Because of you, we're safe."

His gaze held mine, a new expression in it. I knew amused, wry Valentine, sweated over him when he turned on the charm, and sat back and admired his all-action state. This was different. Tender, maybe. He opened his mouth to speak, but no words came out. Instead, the big man reached back to take my hand. His warm fingers enclosed mine for a brief but meaningful second before he turned back to the wheel, shaking his head like he had to dislodge a thought.

On the cool, misty morning, I was reading far too much into that gesture. A dangerous amount I knew was absolute fantasy on my part.

Yet it clamped on to my other emotions and held tight.

Driving on, he took us on a road to the right and up a hill, the opposite direction to the aircraft hangar. I carefully woke my daughter, her smile of happiness when she realised it was me and not Molly, warming my heart.

"This morning, you're going to meet a new friend who you'll be going to school with on Monday, and I've got work for a few hours. Then this afternoon, I'll show you where we're sleeping tonight."

Tobi yawned, her cheeks flushed. "Together?"

"Just you and me."

I yawned, too, and she grinned even bigger. I was the luckiest mama around for my sweet-tempered child. She had every right to be grouchy with me for staying away, having her sleep in a new bed, and now leaving her with strangers, but her bright eyes took in the surroundings with interest.

"Valentine's still driving us," she noted.

"That I am, little lass."

"Did you drive all night? Aren't you sleepy?"

He gave her a quick smile. "I don't need much sleep."

"I can make you tired." Tobi's eyes turned devilish.

"Oh no," I told her. "No tricks."

Valentine peered back at the same moment Tobi thrust forward her hand and formed her fingers into a beak, opening it in staggered stages like a bird yawning. She'd learned it from another child in preschool and did it to me regularly to make me yawn.

On cue, Valentine's mouth opened.

"See, you are tired," she chirped. "Maybe you can nap with my mom later."

He burst out with a laugh that he disguised as a cough, and I distracted her with a promise she could pick something from the pub's menu for dinner tonight.

We arrived at a long, brick building Valentine named as the crofthouse, and which had clearly been renovated to a high spec. Valentine hopped out and opened my door, and I unfastened Tobi from her car seat. A woman with a girl stood in the house's entrance.

At our approach, the woman smiled, and her daughter

hopped up and down on the spot.

Tobi squeezed my hand. "Look, Mom. Hello Kitty."

The girl ahead of us held up her soft toy cat.

In a heartbeat, I knew Tobi would be okay.

"Morning," Valentine said from behind us. "Mia, Tobi, meet Elise and Avery."

A man rounded the building with an older boy, and Valentine introduced Cameron and Zander, his and Elise's almost-six-year-old.

I sought out my daughter, but she'd already disappeared inside.

I smiled at Elise, recognising her, though I couldn't think from where. "I can't tell you how grateful I am for this. It's been…difficult getting settled."

"Are you kidding? Avery is over the moon at having a new friend to start school with. She's got the jump on the other kids because she'll know the new girl first. Let me show you around the house quickly so you know what she'll be up to this morning."

Elise was Californian, too, I noted. My heart warmed even more, though I hadn't been concerned ever for a minute about the people Valentine had picked to care for Tobi.

A fresh warning sound played out in my mind.

My head was filled with Valentine and all the things he'd done. He was everywhere I looked. Helping me, protecting me, hiding in every thought.

A few minutes on, and I had to go. I hugged my daughter, retrieved a couple of toys from the car for her, and promised to return at lunchtime.

Then Valentine drove me away.

This time, I sat up front with him, though I kept my gaze

on the landscape. At the aircraft hangar, I checked the time, cursing myself for not paying more attention. I had ten minutes to get to my first appointment but whole armfuls of bags to transport inside.

Valentine paused me at the car. "I've got this. Go ahead and get to work. I'll put your bags in the hangar bunkroom and lock everything in. I'll be working on your cottage today, so I'll leave the key with someone here."

I had my cleaning caddy in my car and my keys in my bag. I had no reason to linger following his kind offer. Yet all I wanted to do was bury myself in the huge man's body. Steal his warmth. Hug the heck out of him.

Mash my lips to his and kiss his gorgeous mouth.

Deliberately, I took a step backwards. "I'll find it," I forced out. "Thank you again."

Valentine gave me a wolfish grin. "Anytime."

Turning, I fled before I said something stupid, confusing that overwhelming gratitude for something much, much more.

*T*he best thing about cleaning as a job was how quickly the time went. At each place I arrived, I discussed the tasks that needed doing, organised them in my head, then popped in headphones and got to work.

For the first hour, I listened to music, then remembered what Daisy told me she did. She played audiobooks. She'd even offered me some recommendations, though I hadn't taken them.

I'd been keeping her at bay, purposefully.

We lived here now, and I'd already opened up to Valentine. Probably more than I should have. I needed friends. Ones I didn't keep fantasising about.

In my car outside of the second house I'd been booked to clean, I texted my boss.

Mia: Just to let you know all is good today. Tobi is here, so no more running off for me. Also if you've got any audiobook recommendations, I'd love to hear them.

Daisy: I heard from Valentine that you'd driven out overnight. Are you both okay?

Daisy: I have so many book recommendations. If you can handle smutty ones, those are the best.

Mia: Thank you, we're fine. I have my daughter back, so all is good with the world, and I promise I'll be less flaky from now on. Bring on the smutty books!

Daisy: I just knew you were my kind of people. List incoming. Also, if you have time free this afternoon, I'd love to meet your girlie. Come to my place for coffee?

Daisy: PS you were never flaky. Life was happening to you. I got that.

At any other point in the past week, I'd have given an outright no to her coffee invite. Pushed her away and made excuses. That was in the past.

Mia: We'd love to.

The rest of the morning flew by. I picked up an excited Tobi at midday, driving her to the hangar where, Valentine informed me, the bunkhouse key was being kept by a man named Gabe who ran overall hangar operations. I retrieved it and showed my daughter around the huge building. Tobi was all big eyes for the helicopters, pogoing on the spot, zero concerns that this was our home for a while. We had lunch from the breakfast foods in the rec room, then went into the bunkhouse.

"Ohmigod," Tobi squeaked at the women's dorm. "Bunkbeds! Can I have the top one?"

"If you like." I helped her climb up, then grabbed her bag of teddy bears and stuffies, handing them to her one at a time to line up against the back of the bunk.

Each one got nestled into place, Tobi chattering away. "This is our bed now. Don't be scared of anything because we're all together. Mama, is my blue blanket there?"

From another bag, I pulled the blanket my mother had knitted when Tobi was born. It was well-loved and frayed in one corner, and I'd used it to bring my baby home, and to every place we'd lived since.

She tucked it around her toys then reached out so I could jump her down from the high-up bed.

She'd sleep in with me anyway. The stuffies could have that top bunk all to themselves.

Locked in together, I unpacked clothes and got us both washed and changed, putting our toothbrushes side by side on the sink and grinning at Tobi's antics as she played.

Happiness drove away a week's worth of worry and anxiety. Living without my daughter had been a constant pain in my chest. I'd coped. We both had. Having her back was a balm over every jagged edge.

At long last, we'd left our old life behind completely. Sure, we were still in a transition, but this was a huge step on from where we'd been.

In the living room, I added another log to the wood burner.

Try as I might, I couldn't stop thinking of the times I'd

clashed with Valentine here. Watching him in the shower. The two times we'd fooled around on the sofa. He'd cleaned the place down and taken every one of his possessions, removing every trace, but God, the man was in my head and wouldn't quit.

At three, we drove out to Daisy's place, a pretty cottage where I'd applied for my job. A second person waited inside, Ariel, her friend who'd interviewed with her.

I grinned. "Hey."

"Hey yourself." She hugged me in greeting. "I hope you don't mind that I'm here. Daisy said you were coming over, and I wondered how you were doing. You haven't had a proper welcome to the estate yet."

Because I'd been hiding.

I needed friends. I liked these ladies. Both were so pretty, and really kind, too. While Daisy served coffee and cookies, Ariel told us how she'd been teaching snowboarding to kids all morning, and my daughter nearly fell off her seat in excitement.

"Does Avery go out on the snow?" she asked.

I explained. "She spent the morning with Cameron and Elise and their kids."

Ariel grinned. "I teach Zander, but Avery hasn't started lessons yet. Most of the snow will melt soon, so it'll be next November when we start up again."

Tobi blinked at the window. "It's all going to melt?"

"Yup. Happens every year," Ariel said. At my daughter's crestfallen expression, she hastened on. "Tell you what, I've got a board and some kit in my car. There's a slope outside we can practice on. Want to try it out so you know if you like it?"

Tobi sat up tall. "Can I, Mama?"

"If you're sure," I said to Ariel.

Tobi leapt up and bolted for the door, making the decision for us. While Ariel took her outside for an impromptu snowboarding lesson, I sucked in a breath, centred myself on my boss, and in an information flood, began to share.

About why I was running. About the scare last night.

"Thank you for telling me this," Daisy said. "I was so worried, but also unsure about how to support you."

"I was trying to do it all by myself. And failing."

"I can see why you didn't want to trust anyone. When you told me about your mom, I felt awful for you."

All I'd told her was that Mom had died.

The words fell over each other to fill her in on the details. The illness, the relocation from one country to another, how Mom battled it but lost the fight.

To my horror, my tears spilled, but Daisy only hugged me, her eyes watery, too.

"God, we need alcohol for this kind of conversation."

I dried my eyes with my sleeve. "Right? A tequila shot for every time I cry."

She laughed, releasing my hand to collect her phone. "I'm going to do the next best thing and introduce you to the girls. We have a virtual girl group. Warning, it can get spicy. Want in?"

She'd mentioned this earlier, and it had piqued my interest. "Absolutely."

"Good. You live here now so you need a support network."

My phone chimed with messages.

Daisy: Everyone, meet Mia. She's moved here with her daughter and is in need of some love.

Isobel: Welcome to the chat, Mia!

Elise: We met this morning. Avery hasn't stopped talking about your girl.

Casey: Hey, Mia! Daisy, did you warn her about this chat?

Daisy: I did. She's still here.

Viola: Good, because I've got something super fun to share. Welcome, Mia!

I tapped out my own reply.

Mia: Thanks, everyone. You have no idea how much it means to meet you all.

Wasn't that a fact?

I'd found a place to live and people to get to know. I could focus now on settling Tobi into school and doing better at work. Maybe we'd even get lucky and move into the place Valentine was working on. Put down roots.

For the first time, my thoughts slid in a new direction.

What if I had a boyfriend? All my crazy thoughts about Valentine had been leading me that way. I'd been making plans to create a new home while my body had been developing something else.

It hadn't ever been a concern for me in the past, but suddenly it was right up there with my list of goals. With one man square in the frame. The problem was, I was almost certain that if I asked Valentine if he wanted the job, he'd turn and run the other way as fast as I'd arrived.

13

Valentine

Digging into my strength, I wrenched at the plumbing fittings under the cottage sink, finally getting the fucker to sit in place.

"Try it now," I ordered Jackson.

The tap opened, and I watched the drain, glowering at it as if that could stop leaks.

Nothing dripped.

I wriggled out of the tight cupboard space and stood, flipping the flow on full.

Beside me, Jackson squinted at the repair job. "Reckon you've done it."

I huffed a breath, content, but still wired as hell from lack of sleep and a burning need to keep going.

Tomorrow was Mia's day off, according to Daisy. I wanted the place as ready for her as possible so she and Tobi could envisage moving in and be excited about it.

Behind the scenes, there was a small army hustling to find

furniture and home goods. I'd made calls and set people into action, Daisy doing the same.

With the help of my crew and others from the estate, we'd fitted a kitchen and finished up the half-installed bathroom. The double-glazed windows were in, the electrics done, and the heating checked. The place needed a good clean down, but the trade work was mostly complete. I'd even walked the place to carry out a risk assessment, looking out for anything that could injure an active four-year-old.

"Damn, this place is incredible," Daisy said from the door.

I spun around, panicked that Mia was with her. I wasn't ready. But it was just her and my brother, both of them checking out the progress from the bright-white spotlights overhead in the kitchen, to the neatly sealed countertops. Originally, this had been Daisy's project, but I'd taken over almost entirely.

"What's left to do?" Ben asked.

"Not much for anyone else." I twisted to Jackson and Raphael, plus the couple of others who'd helped out this afternoon. "Ye did great. Go on home for the evening."

"Thank you, everyone," Daisy added. "I'm sure Mia is going to love it. We'll give her the tour tomorrow."

There were smiles and backslapping, but I couldn't share their sense of completion. Urgency still filled me. Despite what I'd said to Ben, too many priorities competed for me to think about next.

The cottage quietened with most others leaving. In the bathroom, I screwed on the showerhead, trying not to imagine the curvy, gorgeous woman who'd be using it. When I came back out, Ben regarded me from across the living room.

"Aren't ye quitting for the day?"

I shook my head. "Naw yet."

Daisy joined him. "You've been up since three this morning.

Mia told me all that happened with the drive to get Tobi and all the drama that went with it. You should rest."

Spreading my arms, I gestured to the open space. "What's the first thing Mia is going to see when she comes here?"

My brother furrowed his brow. "The transformation from her previous visit? It couldn't be more different."

I switched my gaze to Daisy.

She tangled her fingers together. "If it was me, I'd notice the layers of dust. That's what you're getting at, isn't it?"

I snapped out my hand, my action bigger than I intended, but adrenaline was still riding me. "Exactly. She cleans for a living. She can't come here and not see the mess, no matter how good the rest of it. Believe me, I know her expectations are low. People have taught her that she isn't deserving of more. But fuck that. We're going to welcome her here, not burden her with more work." I marched back into the kitchen and returned with a broom. "I'm going to spend the rest of the evening cleaning, then in the morning, hopefully we'll have sourced some furniture. When Mia and Tobi set foot in the door, this is going to feel like a home."

For a long moment, my brother's girlfriend just stared at me. I didn't know what she saw. As far as I was concerned, I was doing what anyone else would do who'd taken the lead on a project. Fixing up a place to live for people who needed it. Nothing more, nothing less. If I was stressed, it was probably tiredness.

I'd rest when it was over.

Daisy clucked her tongue then switched her gaze to Ben. "Can you drive home and fetch my cleaning kit? Valentine's right, and we're going to work alongside him."

My brother took up his keys and kissed Daisy's cheek, muttering something to her with an interesting look coming my way.

I didn't understand their scrutiny, but the help was welcome. Mia deserved it.

For the next several hours, we swept, scrubbed, cleared out all the remaining rubbish, mostly packaging from fittings, and polished the fuck out of that cottage until it was sparkling.

By the time I dropped onto the mattress on the floor of Raphael's room at Castle Braithar, barely awake enough to hold a conversation or joke about how neither of us was willing to sleep in the spare bedroom of the apartment Ariel shared with Jackson, I was finally ready to accept sleep.

Damn if I didn't dream of Mia's expression at the first glance of her new home.

The next morning, the people of the McRae estate came up gold.

I had a double bed first on my pick-up list, followed by a single for Tobi. Callum and Mathilda at Castle McRae provided two thick rugs, a chest of drawers and lamps, also retrieving a sturdy, iron-studded coffee table from their cellar. Gordain and Ella offered up a wardrobe from Castle Braithar that nearly broke my back carrying it to Ben's flatbed truck, but it was quicker than breaking it down into pieces. Their daughter, Viola, organised a toy and clothing run for Tobi. I sourced curtains so no one could spy.

Piece by piece, throughout the morning, the cottage took shape.

Mia and Tobi, according to Daisy, had spent the time exploring, walking to the school and having lunch in the pub with Cameron and Elise and their kids. It had given us the space needed to get the place ready. By two in the afternoon, I was down to the final task of giving it another clean to rid it of the dust from moving in the furniture.

In the centre of the living room, I dug my fingers into my hair, strands coming loose from the leather tie, and turned on the spot, hunting for anything that dared be out of place.

"It's done," my brother offered from his lean on the kitchen doorway.

I shrugged. "I can see a dozen more things I want to do." Nothing had been painted. All the walls were uniformly white. But I couldn't pick out colours on their behalf. They needed to see the place and make their own decisions. What else?

"It's done enough," my brother tried again.

Taking a deep breath, I relented. "Aye. Maybe."

He hollered to Daisy.

She returned inside, a tub of sprays and cleaning things in hand, and looked at me. "Text her and tell her to come."

"She's your employee," I challenged back.

"And your friend," she retorted. "You've done all the work. Tell her to come."

I dropped my gaze and found my phone, hesitation slowing me. I hadn't talked to Mia since yesterday morning when I'd texted her the whereabouts of the bunkhouse keys. We'd spent days in each other's company in that place, followed by the late-night flit down to collect her daughter. It made no sense now for me to feel strange about messaging her. No sense at all. I pulled myself together and sent the text.

Then it was a waiting game.

Daisy and Ben talked in low voices by the door. I took myself to the kitchen, fussing with the back door which was still stiff though I'd greased it.

Tension built in me. The more minutes passed, the more my stomach tightened.

She didn't text back, but a dozen checks showed me she'd

seen and read the request.

Then tyres crunched the gravel outside.

Voices followed.

Mia's hesitant tones, Tobi's happier ones, then exclamations as Daisy brought them inside. My boots were glued to the floor. Not physically, but somehow I couldn't budge. The same sensation as not being able to message her had returned tenfold, holding me in a death grip. There was something messed up in my head, and I frowned at myself, pissed off that I was missing that very expression I'd wanted to see.

But witnessing it...that felt dangerous, too.

The voices moved through the house, going from room to room until they came my way. Standing by myself in the kitchen, I resembled a statue, or a stalker, so I snatched up a screwdriver, the last tool left in the place after I'd done the rounds of tightening screws.

Mia entered the bright space, her fingertips pressed together over her mouth and her eyes bright with unshed tears. Her gaze shot to mine. Locked on.

Emotion fucking rocked me.

Peeking around her, Tobi grinned at me. "Valentine's here."

At her back, Daisy gave up my role. "Valentine has worked tirelessly on this place. At a guess, I'd say he's done ninety percent of the work."

Tobi's mouth formed an 'O'. "Even the toy hammock in my bedroom?"

"I think so," Daisy said when I made zero reply.

All I could see was her ma.

To my horror, Mia choked out a cry, instantly stifling it.

My damn heart lurched.

"Uh, Tobi? Why don't we check out that hammock again

and guess how many toys can fit in it," Daisy said.

She led the little girl away, Ben going with them, though I hadn't spared my brother a glance.

Mia and I were left alone.

I forced my mouth to open and my lips to move. "Do ye like the place?"

She took a shuddering inhale. "I love it. You really did all of this for us?"

I jerked my head in a nod, confused by the expanding bolt of something in my chest. I'd expected to feel happiness. This was not that.

Then Mia uttered another sob and flew across the kitchen. In a heartbeat, she was in my arms and burying her face in my chest. I hugged her. Closed my eyes and tucked my head against hers.

Shock. Relief. All manner of things battled within me, but all I knew was this private moment. I didn't want to share it with anyone, and it seemed she hadn't either.

"I knew you were working here, but I had no idea it would be like this," she said, her voice strained and broken. "It's perfect. I've never lived anywhere I loved so much, and I've barely been here a minute. Do you know what you've done? Do you know how much this means to us?"

I didn't know anything, not even my own name, but I was certain about what I needed to do next.

"You gave us a home, Valentine," she finished.

I dropped a kiss to her hair, nudging her face to meet mine. Then when she did, I kissed the ever-loving fuck out of her sweet mouth.

Cupping her cheeks, I forgot all my worry and stress, and lost myself in her lips. Mia fisted my shirt, bringing me as close as I needed her. She matched my energy, her cheeks wet from her tears, and her kiss just as fierce as mine.

We were playing with fire.

Her daughter could walk in. Or my brother and Daisy.

I turned us so my back was to the door. Mia tore her mouth from mine, breathing hard. My chest rose and fell, and I brushed my thumb down her damp cheek.

"I shouldn't have kissed you," she uttered, almost to herself.

I gave a short laugh. "I kissed ye."

Her blue-eyed gaze rose to meet mine. "Then I shouldn't have kissed you back. I need to ask you something."

She stepped back from my hold on her, her expression getting all the more troubled.

"Anything," I murmured.

"Why did you do all this?"

I raised a shoulder. "I had the time and the energy. It's no big deal."

Mia shook her head. "It's a huge deal. Think about it. Think about the list of all you've done."

Something less comfortable replaced my good feelings. I took my own step backward, shoving my hands in my pockets. "Is this to do with me kissing you? Like I said back at the bunkhouse, the two things aren't connected."

"They are connected for me. After everything you've done for us, I can't separate out the two."

"What does that mean?"

Mia's careful gaze studied mine. "It means that I'm getting confused over what you are to me. A friend, a one-night stand, or a boyfriend in the making."

Horror sank the rest of my lust like a stone.

A boyfriend.

God, no.

At my expression, Mia choked on an unfunny laugh. "Don't freak out. I'm not saying that suddenly we're dating."

"Good, because that's never been on the cards," I retorted.

She forced a smile, but it was tinged in pain. "Exactly. And that's why I stopped that kiss. I don't think I can separate out sex and emotions, and in the space of a week, I'm in danger of getting attached to you. You've done nothing wrong, you told me exactly what you wanted, so I know this is all on me. If you wanted a relationship—"

"I don't," I said fast.

"Right. Which is what I thought. Then we can't kiss."

I breathed in through my nose, a clusterfuck of emotion hitting me. This was going wrong. Badly. I didn't know how to stop it. "We laid this all out. Ye told me ye didn't want a boyfriend."

"That was the case, but my mind has changed. Probably because I met such a great guy who gave me a model for exactly what I wanted."

"I…didn't know I was doing that." Fuck. Fuck everything.

"I'm sure you didn't. Which leaves you and me as friends. It can't be more unless it's leading to more. Do you understand?" She held her ground, not meeting my gaze now, but pouring meaning into her words. "I can't tell you how grateful I am, and how much your friendship means to me, but please understand why I'm putting this boundary in place. I've known too much pain in my life, and if we do anything else, I'll give you the power to hurt me. I know you don't want that."

"I don't—" My flare of emotion crackled and burned to a crisp. "The last thing I'd ever want to do is hurt ye."

She waited me out. I took a breath, digging my fingers into my hair with the realisation of what she was saying. Not everyone was like me. Not everyone could handle casual sex.

I cared about Mia, and Tobi, too. I wanted them to be happy here, so what the hell was I doing, readying an argument to prove her wrong?

I swallowed rocks and faked a smile. "You're right. I shouldn't have gone there. It's my bad. I'll keep my hands to myself."

Mia blew out a breath and straightened her shoulders, finally meeting my eye. Under the brights, she was golden. So fucking pretty.

"Great. Then we're friends." She stuck out her hand for me to shake.

A fucking handshake. But I still took it, giving her what she needed, an out-of-body experience guiding me now.

Tobi ran into the kitchen, thrilled with some new discovery that she dragged her mother off to see.

Leaving me in their wake.

"Ye okay?" Ben asked. "If ye need to talk, I'm here."

He sounded like he used to when we were kids. In boarding school when he could've ignored his three-years-younger brother, he hadn't. He'd looked out for me. Helped me fight my battles. I hadn't heard that voice in years.

"Never better," I said.

And I meant it. Everything had worked out for Mia, and that was all that mattered anyway.

14

Mia

Children's laughter mixed with shouts of joy, the school playground full with the new term starting. Tobi clung to my hand, her other arm looped through Avery's. At the far end of our little chain, Avery's mother threw me a reassuring smile.

Once I'd been told who she was, I felt like such an idiot. Of course I recognised her. Elise was a freaking movie star. But more, a new friend in the making, like the half dozen other ladies I'd been talking to and getting to know.

My girl chat group was an absolute hoot. Also an eye-opener. The women hadn't been kidding when they said they openly discussed all manner of topics. Motherhood, work, and sex were all up for grabs. I was learning fast.

"Inside the entrance is the going home book," Elise told me with a gesture to the open classroom door. "If you write my and Cameron's names in there, we'll be able to pick up Tobi for play dates."

I nodded, my mind tripping over our new schedule and everything that came with it. "I'll do the same for you so Avery can come to us. Now we have somewhere to live, we'll be able to entertain."

Elise grinned. "Speaking of entertaining, Daisy said she's planning welcome drinks for you this weekend, now you're settled. Viola said she'd host at Braithar. If her boy, Finn, comes to ours to hang out with Zander, maybe Tobi would like to do the same?"

My boss had messaged me to tell me her plan. I loved the idea. So did Tobi and Avery from the happy sounds they gave up.

"I can't remember the last time I had a girls' night," I admitted.

"Then it's perfect timing. How was your first night in the new cottage?"

"We loved it. Tobi even slept in her own bed, the whole night. Probably thanks to the Hello Kitty sheets and duvet cover you gave us."

Avery yanked on her mother's arm, and Elise stooped to hear her question. Behind her, a familiar figure entered the playground, a small boy at his side.

Valentine.

My breathing hitched. For a long second, I let myself soak up the sight of him. The man in black. Long legs in dark jeans, that close-fitting jacket, and his gorgeous hair tied up in his man bun. He'd left his scruff unshaven this morning, and it only made him more appealing, reminding me of how it had scratched my thighs.

I knew every word of what I'd told him by heart. It was imprinted on my brain. Despite that, my body betrayed need I could hardly contain.

From the way he drew glances from other mothers, I wasn't his only admirer.

A group of children ran up to claim the boy he was escorting, and Valentine stuck his hands in his jeans pockets, pausing for a moment to watch them go inside.

Then his gaze leapt directly to mine like he knew I'd been staring.

I jumped but didn't look away. Instead, I raised my free hand in a greeting.

I didn't get one back. Valentine regarded me for a beat longer then turned on his heel and strode off, exiting the playground to his car. My heart lurched. There had been no malice in his expression. Nothing angry or resentful. I couldn't help but feel that I'd hurt him all the same.

Maybe he thought me ungrateful, though the gift he'd given us of the work done to our cottage deserved gratitude without measure. I'd give him space, but if it killed me, I'd find a way to thank him and get back to being friends again.

The next morning, I had an early cleaning job lined up so had organised for Tobi to join the school's breakfast club. This time when I dropped her off, it was without any risk of seeing Valentine. The same didn't apply at pick-up time, because he was there, waiting for his charge.

I waved again and got a sideways glance and a half-smile.

Progress.

Tobi spilled out of the classroom, falling into my waiting arms with a handful of paintings clutched in her fingers. We hugged out our greeting.

"Did you remember your promise, Mama?"

This morning, she'd reminded me of our idea to bake cookies for her classmates. Managing it on our first morning when we'd barely gotten unpacked at the cottage hadn't been possible, but I was done for the day with work, and we were desperately in need of a run to the shops.

Holding her hand, I led her out of the playground. "Sure thing. We'll go to the shops and fetch everything we need. Think about how you want to decorate them so we can pick up sprinkles or icing."

"Can we do both?" She skipped along.

"If the supermarket has them."

Footsteps sounded behind us, and a deep voice hailed me. I turned to see Valentine close by.

His brows furrowed in. "You're heading to a supermarket? Is that wise?"

I guessed he meant *safe* but was trying not to alarm my daughter with his word choice. I raised a shoulder. "We need food. We've been living off cereal bars and meals at the pub. The cupboards are bare."

His careful gaze was guarded, his usual buoyancy missing. "Which one?"

Which...? Oh, he meant the store. I gave the name of the small supermarket a couple of towns away. It was the nearest, according to the map, and I didn't want to drive to Inverness and risk being too far out in the wide world.

Our hideaway was a refuge, and I wanted to keep it that way.

Valentine squinted down at the boy with him. "Just so happens that Finn and I are going there for a few things. Hop in my car, and I'll drive. Tobi, have ye met Finn? Finn's friends with Zander, Avery's brother. You'll probably see each other on play dates at their house."

While the two children gave shy waves, Finn asking if Tobi had seen Zander's car collection, my attention remained on Valentine. Still, he was trying to protect us.

"You don't have to do this," I said softly.

The huge bodyguard looked away, scanning the other

parents passing by. "It's just a rideshare. One fewer car on the road."

It was more than that, but I relented, moving Tobi's car seat from my old junker to Valentine's much nicer vehicle. With the two kids in the back, he put music on, giving them the alternating choice of song. Then we set out.

I wanted to make conversation, but it was tricky with little ears listening. That was fine. Settled in the familiar passenger seat, I formulated a plan to use the trip as a way of sussing out something nice I could do to show Valentine my thanks.

My scheming went awry, though.

At the store, he marched off, not lingering near us and not reappearing until we were done and through the checkout. He and Finn waited by the exit, both standing sentinel like security guards.

Valentine took control of our heavy trolley without comment.

It didn't escape my notice that neither he nor Finn carried a shopping bag.

The return trip went the same way, the kids choosing songs and singing along, and Valentine studiously not talking.

At the school car park, he transferred our numerous bags into my car, then left without another glance.

Job done, I guessed.

I grumbled under my breath but got us home, parking outside and taking all of our goodies in. Tobi danced inside, switching lights on as she went. The heating timer had the place warming up nicely, and we put away the fridge goods, tins, and packets of food, leaving out the items we needed for the cookies.

Double amounts, because my solitary idea for Valentine was to bake for him.

He liked food, and I was pretty sure a dinner invite would've been refused outright. This was the next best thing.

For the following hour, Tobi and I measured ingredients, mixed them up using our brand-new bowl and wooden spoon, then baked two lots of treats in our new oven. Then we made dinner, eating our first hot meal in our kitchen since we'd moved in.

We perched on tall stools at the counter, a picture of Mom on the wall to watch over us, the window beyond us, with exposed stone and white-painted plaster walls, giving way to a gorgeous view down the hill to a river. There was no garden boundary, but it wasn't needed. Outside the window was our porch—just a roof over a concrete floor, but a place to put seats come summer. Somewhere to sit and look out over the purple heather-strewn Scottish Highlands' landscape.

My imagination drifted to that happy place.

Every little thing here felt like a gift. A kindness from someone we hadn't met yet. After Valentine, Daisy, and Ben had revealed the place to us, the owner of the cottage had visited. Gordain and his brother owned all of the land for miles around, and from what I understood, he was Ben's boss, too. His wife had been by his side with a box of crockery which we were now using, and he'd confirmed the rent and offered us a lease for the cottage which I'd readily accepted. If I worked enough hours, we could afford the place, just about.

We were home.

For the first time in forever, I could take a deep breath, everything in order.

Well, except for my issue with Valentine.

After dinner, while I washed the dishes, Tobi plated up the biscuits with a splodge of icing and rainbow sprinkles on each.

"Do you think everyone will like them?" she asked.

I dried my hands and kissed her forehead, gazing at her handiwork. "Of course they will. You've made them so pretty. Shall we take Valentine his?"

"At the bunkhouse?"

I'd told her he'd no doubt move back in after we left. Tobi had loved the place the single night we slept in the bunks, but I was glad I didn't need to worry about her wandering out and getting stuck into a mechanic's station.

"I think that's where he'll be. We'll surprise him."

Her eyes lit, and she ran off to put on her shoes.

Nerves swarmed inside me, but I was determined. It wasn't late. With any luck, he'd be there to receive our tiny gift. If not, we could leave them for him. Seeing him was a bonus, but all that mattered was he knew we cared.

We trundled over, dusk gathering and the bright lights of the hangar a welcome sight. I held Tobi's hand, clutching the wrapped plate of cookies in the other, and we made our way through the hangar.

There were still people working, the place as noisy and busy as in the day. One of the bodyguard crew perched in the open door of a helicopter. He shot us a curious look, but we continued on, winding our way through to the bunkhouse.

At the door, I swallowed, shaking. "Want to knock?" I said.

Dutifully, Tobi tapped on the metal.

Laughter came from inside. A pretty, feminine giggle with an interesting tone. A male voice followed it. Valentine's?

Then a moan that was decidedly sexual.

My mouth fell open, my stomach compressing tight. I stared, replaying the sound for my brain to confirm what I'd heard.

Valentine was in there with someone else. Someone female

and very happy.

I took a step backwards, horror and disappointment rushing through me. It gutted me.

He didn't owe me anything, and he'd done so much for us. There was no reason for the stabbing jealousy that cut through me at the image of him with another woman. He had every right to take someone to his bed. Every right under the sun to find a beautiful, pliant fuck buddy who could handle one-night stands without things getting messy in her head.

Good for her.

Good for both of them.

I was sure they'd build up a steam together on that same teal-coloured sofa.

My unwanted emotions welled up, and abruptly, I turned, marching Tobi away. If they answered the knock and saw us standing there, that would be far, far worse than the crushing turmoil I felt now.

In the rec room, I deposited the plate of cookies on the countertop, peeling back the foil to show they were fair game to anyone who came in.

"Aren't we leaving them for Valentine?" Tobi asked on our return to the car.

"He'll get his cookies." I forced a smile back.

No pun had been intended, but this time, the joke was on me.

***

*A*lone in my bed, despondent and more than a little

miserable, I paged through a conversation underway in my girl chat group. Daisy had confirmed drinks on Saturday night, and every single woman had responded with a resounding yes.

It eased some small part of my moping.

Then the conversation took an interesting turn.

Viola: The kit turned up today, and I got Leo to do the honours this afternoon.

My mind boggled. A couple of days ago, Viola had shared a link to a product she'd found. A kit to make your own dildo modelled on your partner's...package.

Isobel: Don't be coy there, Vi. We need details.

Viola: A blow-by-blow play? Buckle up. The guy has to get hard, then hold that erection while the mould sets around him. You have to mix up the setting gel first, so timing is important.

Isobel: How big is the mould? Does he have to lie over it?

Casey: Like stick his dick in a bucket? My mind is working overtime.

Viola: You're both hilarious. It's a tube. He just sat on the bed and held it there.

Isobel: What's the result like?

Viola: Have to wait twenty-four hours for it to harden before we can find that out. I'll report back with test results this time tomorrow.

A mass of comments flooded in, the women all delighting in the image Viola had painted of her man sitting there with a tube of gloop around his dick. They were Finn's parents, and Viola's husband, Leo, was the musician Valentine and his crew were paid to protect.

Making a vibrator replica of your dick was such a rock-star thing to do.

It tickled me that they were getting up to this while their son was out shopping with his bodyguard.

I rolled over in bed, scrolling through the messages with my mind pulling in another direction. I'd never owned a sex toy. That was a mistake. Maybe sexual frustration was part of my problem, and why I'd reacted so badly to knowing that Valentine had screwed someone else.

Ultimately, I wanted a boyfriend, but I didn't want to be a jealous, stifling girlfriend to whoever that guy turned out to be. Which meant handling some of my issues.

I needed a toy of my own, but when I thought about it, I could only picture Valentine's incredible dick.

It's a shame they didn't design vibrators based on him.

The pieces slotted together in my mind. The obvious answer right there.

I sat up, dropping my phone to the sheets. What if I asked him to model a vibrator for me? It would be the ultimate way of getting over him and not being a moping weirdo if I saw him with anyone else. Plus I knew him. He'd find the idea hilarious. It would get us back on easier ground.

All I had to do was pluck up the courage and ask.

15

Valentine

The reverb from an electric guitar buzzed through the recording studio, Leo and his band fitting in a practice session. Most of his team had left already to head over to the continent, readying for his European tour. The rest of us would follow in a week, and I was gunning to get out there.

My team had trained hard for this. We'd rehearsed scenarios, planned who we were marking and when, and worked out contingencies until my brain ached. The planning was important, but I was an active guy and I did my best work out in the field.

Across the studio, a glum six-year-old stared at his hands, and a pair of blue headphones nestled into his mop of hair.

I'd come to find Finn to deliver him to his friend's house for dinner. It had taken a while to hunt him down in the castle. At my gesture, he hopped off the sofa and tossed the headphones, trudging after me to the car.

It wasn't like the lad to be so quiet. For a week, I'd been taking him to school every morning and then home in the afternoon, under Ben's orders to get to know him as I'd be protecting him most days.

I was doing a shite job of that right now.

"What's up, little bro? Ye upset over something?" I asked.

Finn peeked over at me then shrugged.

I tried again, slowing my drive across the estate. "If something happened at school, ye can tell me." I knew fuck all about kids and school life, but everyone had good and bad days, regardless of age. "I'm your bodyguard," I added. "If someone's mean to ye, they answer to me."

He mulled over that, fingers twisting in his lap. Then he turned in his seat. "Why do we need bodyguards?"

Damn, I hadn't thought this through. "Ye don't, round here. But when your da is on tour, that's when the crazies... I mean, that's when we have to be around the public. And not everyone is chill."

"Will people try to hurt Da?" His serious wee expression intensified. "Davies in school said a guitar player was killed dead. My da plays guitar."

That's why he'd been watching his da's rehearsal. He'd been guarding him himself.

Davies was going to get a lecture from his teacher, courtesy of me. I gritted my teeth. It wasn't right to lie to kids, but there was no way I was letting him carry that fear. "Your da isn't going to be hurt, but just think what it's like in a big crowd. It's easy to get lost or swept away, and he's so loved by his fans that they all come to see him. What happens with an even bigger crowd? More chance of getting lost. Ben, Jackson, Raphael, and I are there to keep ye all safe."

Finn scrunched up his nose. "So he won't get dead?"

"Naw."

"Or lost?"

"I swear on my bodyguard's honour that nothing will happen to any of your family. Ye trust me, aye? I'm good to my word."

He sat back somewhat easier, though I wasn't convinced he'd bought it. The topic changed to his plans for the evening, and I hid a sigh. It wasn't surprising that Finn was picking up on tension. He would miss school while we travelled through cities in Europe. Anticipation to get going held everyone in its grip.

One thing for certain was the strange feelings that had haunted me had gone. All week, I'd seen Mia here and there and felt fine. If I missed having her around, that was just because she was good company. The few days we'd shared the bunkhouse had been fun. Our antics around that even more.

Leaving the estate for a while would blow away any remaining cobwebs, and I'd be back to my normal self.

We drove on to the crofthouse, where Finn was to spend the evening hanging out with Cameron and his boy. I thumped on the door, and it was pulled open by a wee lass instead. Tobi, Mia's girl, another child with her.

Tobi's eyes brightened. "Valentine! Why are you here?"

I tipped my head at Finn who ran on inside. "Just delivering that one. Your ma here?"

Despite myself, I leaned to peer inside the home, hopeful for a glance of Mia.

"Nope. She's on a night out," Tobi informed me. "Did you like the cookies?"

Did she mean a date? Was Mia out with a man? I didn't like it.

"I love cookies," I mumbled back.

"No, I mean the ones we made for you. We brought them to the hangar."

I squinted at the girl. "Ye did?"

Her shoulders slumped. "Didn't you get any? I decorated them for you."

"Fuck," I swore, then clapped my hand over my mouth. "I mean fudge."

The two girls cracked up, their expressions a mixture of amusement and prudishness at my curse word.

Cameron appeared at the door, wiping his hands on a tea towel. The calm and stoic man had previously been a bodyguard for Leo and had joined our planning sessions for the tour, so I'd got to know him. He regarded the cackling girls.

"Valentine said a rude word," Tobi snitched.

I pulled a face. "Don't tell your mother."

Though I was reeling over the fact she'd left me a treat. What was that about?

Cameron shooed them inside, lifting his bearded chin to me. "Coming in?"

"With ye and four kids? Naw chance. It'll be carnage in there."

On cue, something smashed in the background, and the two boys howled in amusement.

Cameron winced. "A normal day in parenthood. Believe it or not, it's easier with more. Just need a good set of headphones. You'll find out one day."

A single shake of my head was his answer. "Not me."

"The way the mothers at the school drop-off ogle ye? You're about to be hunted, so if you're not down to be paired off, run, man."

"For fuck's sake. Lucky my school duties are almost over."

Hanging out at the school hadn't been the worst thing ever, though not because of the female attention. I'd volunteered for escort duties a couple of times—walking the kids places as an extra adult helper—and it broke up the day.

"Are ye coming back for Finn?" Cameron asked, his amusement at my plight clear.

"I think his da will. Catch ye later. Stay sane."

He rolled his eyes, and I returned to my car.

Driving back through the lanes to Castle Braithar, I mused over the cookies I'd missed out on and almost contemplated calling Mia. But she was on a fucking date, and she'd made her position clear. I'd already overstepped the mark once. It was enough that I sought her out every day, making sure she hadn't vanished overnight or she didn't appear upset.

Just checking on her was a friendly thing to do.

Perhaps the cookies had been exactly that. A gesture of friendship I'd missed.

At the castle, I left my car in the space I'd claimed and entered through the big front door. Castle Braithar sat on the banks of the river with a thick forest surrounding. Built of thick stone blocks, it was hundreds of years old and had the mythical feel of something out of a movie.

It had also been my home for the week.

The place was owned by Gordain and Ella, and they lived there with their daughter, Viola, and her husband, Leo, plus the two kids. The size of the sprawling building, which housed a dozen bedrooms and the recording studio, meant everyone had their own space, and because they liked having one of the bodyguard crew on site, my brother had lived here until he'd moved in with Daisy.

His rooms had been vacant until Raphael moved in. In turn, Raphael had offered his floor to me.

One thing was for certain, it was a fuckton warmer than the bunkhouse, and quieter, as Raphael usually took to the skies after work for an evening of flying.

The bunkhouse had lost its shine.

Striding through the great hall, I picked up on music and women's laughter over the top of it. Sounded like a party. I slowed my steps, unashamedly rubbernecking to peek into the dining room.

Through the door, I caught a glimpse of several lasses, all who'd arrived in the time I'd been out with Finn. Viola, Ariel, Daisy, and others. All dressed up, most with glasses of wine in hand. Not all that long ago, Jackson and I had interrupted just such a party, and things had got raucous. These ladies knew how to throw down. A grin touched my lips.

Then another woman appeared in the gap. Mia, in a pretty dress with smoky makeup accentuating her already knockout features.

My whole body tightened, and I swallowed at the shock of seeing her. She was here, not out with some fuckhead guy pawing over her.

Her fair hair was down, spilling in golden lengths over her shoulders. She only ever wore it up in a ponytail or braid, and my brain went right to coiling those locks around my fist.

Worse, the dress clung to her tits, not cut low enough for me to have a heart attack, but still breaking my brain. I knew the weight and feel of that gorgeous pair. How Mia threw her head back and arched into my palms when I touched her.

My blood shot south.

"Val," a voice hailed me.

I spun around, instantly guilty at my leering.

My brother approached. I shot a glance back at the door, but no one emerged.

"I wanted to talk about the rest of the renovation works," Ben said.

"What works?"

"To the cottage adjoining Mia's. We've got a week before we leave, so it's worth getting as much done as we can."

I forced my brain to re-engage, though half my attention was on the voices in the room, like I'd become the spy. "The windows are in and the plumbing's done. It's the electrics and kitchen build, like with the one next door. Is there a tenant picked out?"

He'd suggested I take it, but that never felt right. I didn't need a whole house. I was a single guy with no responsibilities. Readying a place for Mia and Tobi made sense. For me? Not so much.

"Aye," he replied, his scrutiny on me challenging as always.

Or maybe that was my imagination.

Then I registered his answer. Well, fuck. The second cottage had a new owner. Why the hell was I disappointed over that?

I shrugged it off. Worse things happened. Like my favourite new friend deciding she couldn't be around me anymore.

"I'll make a start on it tomorrow evening. Just need to order in a couple of things."

"What's on your list? We might have it."

I took out my phone, paging through to my notes, then handed it over to Ben. For Mia's place, we'd had an order in from a DIY store, but I was lacking a couple of fixtures necessary for the other project.

Ben scanned the list. In his hand, my phone buzzed. His eyebrows dove together, then my brother recoiled. Silently, he turned the screen to face me.

Kelly read the caller's name.

Oh, fuck.

The very person I didn't want to talk about with him, and

she was forcing her way into our conversation. Two weeks ago, my ex-girlfriend had texted me, but I'd deleted the message and forgot about it. The woman didn't occupy my mind at all, but when faced with my brother, I got a damning snapshot image of her lips on his.

Taking the phone from him, I stabbed to end the call.

"Kelly's calling? What does she want? Surely—" he started.

"Did ye get that list?" I cut over him. Then, because I just wasn't going to go there, I moved away, storming off to the corridor at the back of the great hall that led to Raphael's rooms. "Never mind. I'll text it to ye. Later."

I locked myself in and blasted out music, almost solely so I didn't have to answer the door if my brother followed.

A while later, I scrubbed shower water from my skin, pulling on a pair of joggers. Raphael was putting in airtime, so I'd had the place to myself, doing a workout to dislodge my bad mood before hopping in the shower.

Seeing Mia dressed up like a wet dream had become a welcome distraction, and I'd beat myself off under the hot water with her on my mind.

Someone tapped at the door.

I crossed to open it, towelling my hair.

Mia stood in the frame, her cheeks pink, and a wine glass clutched in her fingers. Her gaze coasted over my bare chest. "Hi, I found you," she said, a little glassy-eyed and seriously cute.

I leaned on the doorframe, trying not to smile. "Were ye searching for me?"

"Might've been." She peered into the room behind me. "Viola said you were sleeping here tonight, and I wanted to say hello."

She'd been talking about me to her friends. I liked that way too much.

I gestured for her to come inside. Mia grinned and tottered past me.

Aside from the big double bed, there was my single camping bed against the opposite wall, a small sofa, and a long countertop across one whole side of the room that acted as a desk and sideboard. Raphael kept the place neat, and I barely owned anything I couldn't get into two kit bags, so there wasn't much for her to examine.

She perched on the sofa, and I sat cross-legged in front of her.

Mia took a sip of her wine then regarded me. "Stop it."

"Stop what?" I flexed in case she meant my being handsome.

"Avoiding me."

I snorted. "I see ye every day."

"And apart from playing bodyguard at the supermarket, you don't say a word. I miss you. I want my friend back."

Tension crept around me, mixing me up. The way she was looking at me was decidedly sexy. Little Valentine was already getting hard for her.

"Friend," I repeated with a note of derision.

"Yes, my friend."

"Can't be a good friend if I keep thinking about ye the way I am now."

Mia groaned. "Cut that out and put a shirt on before I jump you. We are not going there."

I shrugged, remaining bare-chested. "So we're just talking? How about ye tell me if ye read that paperwork we collected from Molly's."

"I skimmed it."

"And?"

"More of the same legal waffle plus reports on how Tobi's dad's businesses were doing. Badly, which I already knew. My guess is they're just trying to get me to go to them. I won't. They can't make me." She swigged her wine. "There's something I want to ask. A favour."

"Go for it."

"Heck, no. Not face to face. I'll text you later."

She stood, wobbling slightly.

I took hold of her hand, tugging so she dropped back onto the sofa. The remaining wine in her glass sloshed, and Mia giggled.

"Ye came to find me and have something to ask. Ask it," I ordered.

I didn't want her to leave. She was here. Happy. I needed to just stare at her, like some kind of visual drug.

Mia downed the rest of her wine and put the glass on the floor with a *clunk*. Then she reached to take a lock of my long dark hair, fingering the damp lengths. "Do you even own a hairdryer?"

I raised a shoulder. "Tobi mentioned something about cookies when I saw her earlier."

Mia pulled a face. "We made you a batch and brought them to the hangar. You were...occupied."

"What was I doing?"

Her cheeks flushed darker pink. "Don't leave this wet or you'll catch cold."

Neat subject change. There was something strange in her expression now. Not embarrassment, but an awkward kind of vibe. I held her wrist to still her movements, catching her gaze. "What happened? What was I doing?"

Mia tugged her wrist away, her amusement fleeing with it.

"I don't want to say."

"Fine. Then tell me why ye came to find me tonight. One or the other."

"I want you to model a vibrator for me."

The second the words were out of her mouth, she clapped her fingers to her lips, like saying them had been an accident.

My heart thumped. "Ye want me to what?"

I'd heard just fine, but I wanted her to say it again.

"One of the women bought a kit where you can make a vibrator from your partner's... You know what."

"Ye can say dick, little spy."

She laughed and shoved me. "Anyway, I don't have a partner, but I want a vibrator. And your equipment seemed like a good place to start. So I bought a kit and now I need a model for it."

Amusement caught me at her drunken confession, but then was rapidly followed by an image of what she was asking. My mind spread over the idea. Of her on her bed, naked, ready to go with a Valentine-shaped dildo...

But before I could question her, Mia leapt to her feet, sidestepping me with more agility than a drunk lass should have.

"Think about it?" she asked, then she was out of the door and gone.

16

Mia

"I'm so wet," a woman griped across the group of children.

We were huddled under the shelter outside the school, rain pattering down around us. Spring had arrived in a rush of mixed-up weather. The snow had melted everywhere apart from the mountain, and rain alternated with the first glimmers of sun.

Her friend snorted. "Ye dirty B."

The first woman cracked up. "Ye know what I mean. There's been no let-up all day."

"It's all that time ye have bored at home."

Both snickered again.

I hid a smile at their banter. Today, the school was celebrating with a Spring Sing at the local village hall, and we were queued up outside the school, waiting for a gap in the weather to walk the kids across the village.

I'd taken the afternoon off to see Tobi with her friends,

after hearing her practice the songs all week. She'd had Avery over for a playdate, and the two of them had been adorable as they tried to remember the words and actions. Today, after the singing, she was going to Avery's house in exchange, and I planned to get a few things done at our cottage.

At the end of the line of people, the headmistress stepped forward, a hand raised to indicate that we were going. Beyond her, I spotted a familiar figure I was trying to ignore.

Valentine was here again, standing in the rain like it didn't bother him, his black hair loose, and his high-visibility jacket the same as the ones the kids all wore. Except on him, it looked like a uniform, and all of a sudden I had a whole new fantasy going on. Not that I'd tell him.

After my drunken question, I'd been too embarrassed to talk to him. Equally, he hadn't replied to my request. Our friendship had been broken already, and I'd just succeeded in killing it dead.

"Ooh, have a gander." The second woman elbowed her friend. "The bodyguard guy. He's..." She mock-wiped her forehead.

"I asked him out," the horny one answered, her tone pitched low.

"Did ye!"

Her friend gasped, and I inched closer, in sudden desperation to hear what he'd said. Had she been the one in the hangar with him? She was pretty. Taller than me and probably mid-thirties, so experienced. If she was bored at home all day, why not have a little afternoon delight?

Nausea gripped my stomach.

In equal parts, I did and didn't want to know.

"He turned me down," she confessed. "Said something about not mixing work with pleasure, whatever that meant.

Pity. Bet he'd be fun."

I sagged, utterly relieved and with no excuse for how I felt.

The women chattered on, stepping forward as the headteacher moved off. I trudged after, resolutely not looking at Valentine.

Luckily, the bodyguard crew were leaving next week, going on tour with their rock star. Daisy had been talking about it at work this morning, and I felt bad for how much she was going to miss Ben. Ariel was the same with her boyfriend, another one of the team named Jackson.

I had no such justification for how I'd miss Valentine, too.

The crocodile of kids and escorting parents set off from the school. There were no footpaths, so the parents spread out, walking on the outside to protect the kids from any passing cars. It wasn't a long walk, and the country lanes were quiet, but I knew from one of the other moms that they'd had problems with drivers zooming too close in the past.

What moron drove like that around kids? It made my blood boil.

Stepping over puddles, we traipsed down the road, passing the occasional house, the main cluster of streets with the village hall approaching.

Up ahead, an engine roared.

At the front of the queue, the headteacher called out for us to halt. We were at a junction where we needed to cross the road to reach the safety of the pavement which led all the way to the hall. Already in the road, she held up a hand to stop the traffic so the kids could walk safely.

A grey delivery van revved at her, the driver laying on his horn.

The mom who had been ogling Valentine took a shocked breath. "That's so aggressive."

It was. Scarily so.

I tightened my hand around Tobi's, my group of three safely on my left-hand side.

The headteacher said something again, and the van jerked forward, like the driver was trying to force her to let him pass.

Collective shock rippled across all us adults.

If he accelerated, she'd have to jump out of the way, and he'd no doubt speed past us all. Fear trickled into my blood.

Then my gaze latched on to Valentine. He indicated to another parent to watch his group, then strode forward. He barked something to the driver, who laid on the horn again. I strained to hear what was being said, but they were too far in front.

Abruptly, the van lurched another foot forward. Someone shrieked. The headteacher stumbled back. But Valentine didn't budge an inch.

Instead, the huge man slammed both hands down on the front of the bonnet.

"Engine off," he snapped.

The driver yelled something back.

"Engine off or I'm in that cab doing it for ye," Valentine snarled louder. "Trust me, brother. Ye don't want to know what will happen after that. I'll have ye on the ground faster than ye can blink."

The fear in me instantly turned into a kick of heat.

"Good God, that's attractive," the ogling mom whispered to her friend.

This time, I couldn't judge her. It was *incredibly* attractive.

The driver stared Valentine down for a second, then the engine noise ceased with a rattle.

"Now get out," Valentine ordered.

The door popped, and the driver hopped down, his features twisted in a miserable snarl.

Pointedly, Valentine turned his back on the man, arms folded, and stood in front of the vehicle. Then he gestured for us to continue.

With her eyes wide, the headteacher hustled, getting the school column moving again. The kids trotted forward, each of them gazing at the van. As he passed, Finn, Valentine's charge, stared up at him like he'd hung the moon. Valentine gave a nod to the boy, who flushed red and beamed, getting nudges from his friends.

When it was our turn to pass, I was almost ready with the blushes, too.

"Valentine!" Tobi uttered. She stuck her hand out for a high five.

Valentine smirked and reached to tap her palm with his. Then his gaze drew over me in a quick but loaded look. I felt it right through me, a zap of lust that lit me up.

Then he was behind us, my group of kids on the pavement and our destination looming ahead.

What the hell had that been? He hadn't sent me a reply, so why the weighted stare? Did it mean anything, or was I just as horny as the bored school mom?

In the village hall, I forced myself not to glance around for him. Instead, I enjoyed my daughter's first event with her new school and tried not to think about anything else.

Afterwards, with an uneventful trip back to the school, I waved Tobi off for her play date with Avery and returned to the car park. At the back of his black car, Valentine had a small group of parents around him, an equal share of mothers and fathers talking at him, presumably about the driver incident. Over the tops of their heads, his gaze sought me out.

I wanted to talk to him as well. See if he was okay. To see if we were okay.

The friendship I was trying and failing to resurrect.

But he was occupied, so I hopped into my car and drove home alone.

Back in my cottage, I busied myself with tidying up the place. I'd ordered a few bits and pieces with my first paycheque and had picked them up from a parcel box in the village as we didn't have a mail service at the cottage.

My brain stayed resolutely on the big, dark-haired bodyguard.

Fixing up some hanging shelves in Tobi's room? Valentine handing me a hook then tumbling me onto the rug. Sticking a toothbrush holder to the bathroom wall? Valentine in the shower, beckoning me to join him.

Holy shit, that one was hot.

In my bedroom, draping a new throw blanket at the end of my quilt? Valentine on the floor screwing in the electrical plugs. Of course, my brain didn't leave it there. It let me picture him stripping, pushing me back on the bed, and screwing me instead. I sighed, putting the cool back of my hand to my heated cheek.

A thump came at the door.

Good. I needed a distraction before I burned up into cinders.

I rushed to answer. Valentine waited on the other side. He leaned on the wooden post that supported the porch roof above, and gave me an amused grin. "I was going to say hi, but what have ye been up to? You're all flushed."

I pressed my lips together to hide a smile. "Mind your business. What are you doing here?"

Valentine tipped his head at the adjoining home. "Working

next door this evening. I just wanted to give ye and Tobi a heads-up in case of any banging."

I swallowed at the word *banging*. "Tobi's out for a couple of hours."

His amusement switched to careful perusal. "That so?"

"I apologise for the other night," I said quickly, needing to get the words out. "I was out of line."

"Which part?"

I glowered at him. "You know what I'm talking about."

"Not sure I do. Ye didn't say anything to offend me."

"The toy thing. See? You had to make me say it."

Valentine folded his arms, so infuriatingly handsome, I wanted to strangle him.

"Did ye really buy a kit?"

Heaving a sigh, I nodded.

His eyes gleamed. "Show me it."

I gasped in outrage. "No."

"How am I supposed to be the model if I don't see what I've got to do?"

My jaw dropped. "You'll do it? But you didn't say. I was waiting for a reply. I thought I'd humiliated myself."

Valentine merely tutted and jerked his chin. "Wasting time here."

Jumping forward, I grabbed his sleeve and tugged him inside the living room, closing the door after. "Stay," I ordered, then hustled to my bedroom. From a box under my bed, I extracted the kit I'd bought late at night when overconfident and worked up. Now, it felt too real.

I stared at it, the exterior packaging not hiding the contents at all. A large dildo crossed the cover with a guy posing in briefs behind.

My confidence wobbled.

A figure loomed at my back. Valentine reached around me and took the kit from my hands, squinting at the writing and the picture on the front. Then he opened it on my bed, pulling out the instructions and the plastic-encased items that needed to be used.

While he laid it out, I shook, frozen to the spot.

Valentine read through the list, muttering the order in which he needed to mix the solution and the steps that came after. His gaze lifted to mine. "Seems straightforward enough, but I have a question."

"What?" I squeaked.

The whole situation was so unreal.

"The guy needs to get hard and stay hard for a while." His focus slipped down my body. "I want a little help in that department."

A nervous laugh flew from my lips. "There is no way you'd struggle to hold an erection."

"Didnae say I'd have a problem. I want the help. I don't need it."

I just stared. "We can't... I mean, I can't..."

"I'm naw asking ye to blow me. This is a solo gig, for the sake of our friendship. But if you're going to be getting off on a replica of my dick, it's only fair that I get a visual in exchange. Tit for tat."

Without conscious decision, my hand drifted to my chest.

Valentine's hungry gaze followed it.

"A photo," he added quickly. "Both of them."

"In exchange for modelling for me, you want a picture of my boobs," I clarified.

"Exactly. I'll take this next door and get to work. But I'm going to need to keep checking that photo so the model doesn't shrink." He gave a wolfish grin. "I wouldn't want to disappoint ye with the end result."

The heating wasn't on, but it was too hot in here.

He was far too close, and my body was far too interested.

I really wanted that Valentine-shaped dildo. Slowly, I nodded, and he raised his eyebrows.

Then he picked up the kit, tapped his wrist to indicate time passing, and left my cottage with a slam of the front door.

The second he was gone, I dropped onto my mattress and took a deep breath.

Could I do this?

I'd never sexted anyone before or sent a nude. Not of any kind.

My phone dinged. I took it from my pocket to see a picture from Valentine. It was of a tube of gloopy mixture.

God, he'd already started.

Valentine: Fast, little spy. Time's a-wasting. It dries from the bottom up so you don't want a stumpy end result.

Shit. I grabbed my hem and yanked my top over my head. Before I could think too much about it, I activated my camera and snapped a boob pic then sent it.

Valentine: Hot as fuck, honey. But I'm going to need them bare if I'm going to get hard the way you want me.

My breathing shuddered. Naked? God. Jumping up, I drew my curtains closed then unclipped my bra. Quickly, I tried another photo.

On the screen, it came out dark.

I clicked on a lamp and tried again. This time, I took a minute over the angles, finally settling on leaning forward slightly so my breasts filled the shot, heavy and full. My nipples hard.

God, that was sexy.

Wasn't it? I sent it, bold and brave, but also holding my breath.

A minute passed with no reply.

He'd seen the shot, the read receipt told me, but he didn't come back with anything immediately.

Boobs out, I sat there, waiting.

Instead of feeling ridiculous, I could only picture what he was doing next door. If he wasn't texting, his hands were occupied.

I reclined on my new blanket, letting my imagination conjure the scene. He'd be completely naked, of course, and probably kneeling on the floor. His huge dick would be throbbing, as hard as possible with the thick vein running down it. I let my mind linger on his girth and on the precum that leaked out. He jerked his hand up and down his impressive length, his knees wide and his head tipped back in pleasure.

I slid my hand over my breasts, my palm skating over my nipple. I toyed with myself, pinching like he'd done in the times we'd fooled around, and then I let my fingers keep going down to my waistband.

All afternoon, I'd been turned on by him.

He was right next door, hard for me. I couldn't let that slide.

Sneaking my hand into my waistband, and then my underwear, I touched myself between the legs, my fingers wet.

My phone chimed with a text, and I yanked my hand back, panting.

Valentine: This work?

A photo followed. Him, mostly naked so I got a glimpse of rippling abs, and the tube that had come with my kit at his groin.

Oh God. My heart missed several beats. He was hard in that tube from me.

In a rush, I stripped the rest of my clothes and scooted up the bed, staring at the picture. I couldn't see anything, not really, but I knew it was there, and it was obscenely erotic all the same.

Returning my hand to my clit, I got my fingers wet then rubbed.

Another message landed.

Valentine: Answer needed.

I tapped out a reply with my left hand.

Mia: So good.

Valentine: What are you doing next door?

Mia: Never you mind.

Valentine: I'm going to need another shot.

He didn't say why, but there was implied urgency in his words, and the threat of him going soft and ruining the model shot panic through me.

Valentine: Nipples. You touching them.

I took my camera, moving my hand from the juncture of my legs to my breast, and I held myself, my finger and thumb pinching my nipple.

This time, it was easier to take the shot and send it. I was in the zone, and I already knew he'd like it.

Valentine: Fuck, little spy. Your fingers are wet.

Mia: You got me hot and bothered.

Valentine: Shite. No more messages for the next ten minutes or I'm going to mess this up.

I returned to working myself, imagining him holding his

erection in that tube and trying not to come. In reverse action, I was speeding up, aiming to reach climax before he was done.

I stroked myself, imagining him bearing down on me, notching himself to my core then thrusting home. There was nothing like his dick. It was the perfect shape, slightly too thick, the edge of pain giving so much pleasure. And when he'd been inside me, he'd lit me up like a goddamned Christmas tree.

I shuddered, desperately lost and chasing that pleasure hard. It was exactly why I needed a vibrator based on him. Nothing else would do.

I worked my hand, moving fast. Him, moving in and out of me.

Despite everything, I wanted him. That was a problem for another day, because right now, it was really working for me.

Another chime from my phone had me grabbing it up.

Valentine: Just so you know, I fill this tube.

God. My orgasm hit me in a crashing wave, and I cried out, throbbing around nothing and wishing he was with me. Sparks flowed through my veins, and I sank back onto my soft bed, lightheaded and grinning at the ceiling.

It took a solid minute for me to cool, then I hopped to the bathroom to clean up.

When I returned to my bedroom, another message landed.

Valentine: Time's up. Tell me exactly how hot and bothered you got.

He must've finished with the tube. Obviously he wasn't letting the erection go to waste.

I tapped a reply, smiling.

Mia: On my back, fingers moving fast, imagining using that toy.

My phone rang, and I jumped. But it wasn't Valentine. Elise was calling, Avery's mother. I snapped to answer.

"Mia? Sorry to bother you, but I need to let you know that Tobi's just been sick."

"Oh no, is she okay?" My heart panged.

"I think she might have a tummy bug. There's one going around the school."

"I'm on my way," I said.

Hanging up, I dressed in a rush. Then I jogged outside and banged on the door of the cottage next to mine. Valentine swung it open, thankfully clothed.

His smirk faded at my expression. "What's wrong?"

"I've got to go pick up Tobi, she's sick," I said fast. "But that means I can't complete the model."

The rubber mixture needed to be poured into the mould he'd made, the vibrating part added in, too. I could hardly do it in front of her. This was not mother-and-daughter arts-and-craft time.

His dark eyebrows dove together. "Leave it with me. I'll finish it up."

"Are you sure?"

"I want to see how it turns out."

His gaze held mine for a beat longer, but I had a sick child to go fetch.

When I returned, Tobi clinging to me, we went straight inside and heard nothing more from Valentine all evening. I could only hope he had time to complete our project before he had to leave.

17

Valentine

The crowd roared, the wave of sound deafening, though muted by my in-ear headphones. In front of me, Finn stared eagle-eyed at the stage where his father sauntered out, bare-chested and sweating, his guitar slung low to his hips.

"Guten Abend, Berlin! How ya doing?" Leo hollered into his mic.

The audience screamed their response.

Day three of the tour, and energy levels were sky-high. We'd barely stopped, flying out to Germany for the first set of gigs, and tomorrow, the tour buses would take us to France then down into Spain. It was a buzz. Every stadium had been packed full, and so far, no risky shite had been sent to test us. Leo wasn't heading out on the town every night or hitting up the clubs. He had interviews to give and industry shite to manage in the afternoons but mostly wanted to chill with his family. Viola and baby Torran were doing fine, both adapting well to being on the road.

He wasn't allowed to stay up for the whole gig but insisted on being there with his da as long as possible. For the past two evenings, he hadn't slept until Leo was back in the hotel room and cuddled around the boy in his bed. After midnight each time. It had meant a lot of late nights and a cranky kid the next day.

None of the family had expected this, so we were adjusting on the spot.

We watched until Leo's second song came to an end, and I tapped Finn's shoulder. He pushed my hand away, so I crouched until I was face-on with him. In the pit just below the stage, we had space to breathe.

Under my grip, he turned to face me, his chin stuck in a stubborn slant.

I pointed to the wings.

Finn gave a resolute headshake.

For fuck's sake. I wasn't above putting him over my shoulder and carrying him out, but I needed the lad to trust me. Gesturing to Gordain, his grandpa, who waited in the wings on the far side, I held up my phone. Then in front of Finn, I typed out a message so the boy could read it.

Valentine: Can you send us gig pics every ten minutes? We're going to chill on the bus.

The older man read it and peered over. I pointed to Finn, and Gordain sent a reply.

Gordain: I'll keep you posted. Leo's safe with Jackson, Ben, and me here.

I showed Finn, and he darted his gaze to the side. Then the wee lad yawned big. Tiredness was clearly affecting him, but he needed to keep his da safe.

My heart, an organ that I thought had been broken completely, ached.

Reaching out an arm, I brought the boy against me and lifted, waiting for any kicking. Instead, he slumped on my shoulder, tucking his head to mine. I didn't miss the front row of fans taking us in, cameras raised. Leo and Viola never shared pics of their kids, but they were out there. It was unavoidable.

The security team at the back of the stage let us pass, and I carried Finn deeper into the corridors in the bowels of the stadium, announcing our movements to Ben via my earpiece. The sound changed to a muffled roar, and Finn slid off his headphones, his hand drooping over my back. At the rear exit, a guard gave us access to the lorry park, and I trekked over to the family's tour bus, the door opening with a hiss once the reader scanned my fingerprint.

Inside was dark, neon-blue strip-lights along the floor that led through the kitchen to a lounge area. On the couch, Raphael put his finger to his lips then pointed to the depths of the bus. Viola and the bairn were sleeping, then.

I carried Finn through and eased him off my shoulder to the sofa.

He blinked drowsily then sat up. "Your phone?"

I took it out, explaining to Raphael. "Gordain's going to message with POL pics."

POL was proof of life. Not that I was going to explain that to Finn. On cue, one came in. A picture of Leo back to back with his guitarist. Finn soaked it in then slumped.

I snagged a blanket and tucked it around him. "I'll wake ye if one doesnae come in."

The lad nodded. His eyes closed, and his head dropped back. For a minute, the two of us bodyguards just watched him until we were sure he slept.

"He's not enjoying this," Raphael said quietly.

"Not at all. He's scared shitless."

Then I tested Finn, just to make sure he was out cold. "I'm going to grab a carton of chocolate ice cream. Want in?"

Raphael smiled, catching what I was doing.

Finn didn't move, his lips parted in sleep.

For a little while of watching him, I pondered a niggling doubt that had grown in my mind over the past few days. "Do ye believe in intuition?"

"Sure."

"Do ye think that's what Finn's feeling?"

"Like he's anticipating shite going down?"

I shrugged, keeping my voice low. "After the incident on stage where Jackson had to throw himself at a guy, I guess it showed me what people are capable of. It sounds weird, but I'm getting the sense that this panic is something more. And I just realised how daft that sounds."

Raphael's amusement quickly faded. "Intuition is the brain pulling facts and feelings together to produce intelligence, aye? Like when ye get a wary feeling ahead of doing something new. I'm naw sure whether a six-year-old has that capacity, but I know the feeling of thinking bad shite is going to happen to your family. Except in my case, I wanted it for my da. Someone offing him was my dream."

I chuffed a sympathetic laugh, dislodging my worry. Raphael's father was a crime lord who'd wanted his son to work for him. He'd given up on Raphael, everyone hoped, but that didn't change the fact my colleague and friend had experienced a fucked-up childhood where murder, guns, and literal backstabbing were daily occurrences.

"What about now?" I asked. "Still want him dead?"

Raphael shrugged. "If he leaves us alone then I want nothing. I don't give a flying fuck what happens to him. I just can't see it lasting. It makes me not want..."

He trailed off. I waited him out, the cool calm of the dark bus settling around us.

"Gabe and Effie will have a bairn in a few months," he continued at last, referencing his older brother's impending new arrival. "How the fuck can they ever relax knowing our father is out there, ready and waiting to cause damage? I know he agreed to back off after my sister threatened him with a tell-all, but she's happily shacked up, too. I want to talk to Jax about it, but is that my place? Why am I interfering?"

He and Jackson had been close friends for years, and now Jackson was dating his sister, thus putting him in the line of fire of their da. I tilted my head, giving him a gentle question. "What's the real issue here? Jackson's big enough and ugly enough to go into a relationship with his eyes open. Ye don't expect your brother and sister to stay single?"

He exhaled through his nose. "Of course not. I just can't see how they can give away their heart knowing someone might shred it when they get scared off and walk away."

Well, fuck. "That's a risk ye take with any relationship. Ask me how I know."

Raphael's serious gaze returned to mine. His dark hair was messy, falling in his eyes, and he pushed it back. In the dim light, he appeared younger. Vulnerable.

"I was engaged," I said. "Did ye know that?"

Slowly, he nodded. "I dislike gossip and don't seek it out, but I heard someone mention it a few nights before we left. Ye don't have to tell me anything."

I didn't, and I had the distinct feeling I was talking to the wrong person, but there was still a lesson for Raphael in there. "I'll spare ye the details, but the woman wanted someone else. She looked me in the eye and told me she loved me when she never had. If you're worried about outsiders destroying relationships, I'd say it's more likely to come from inside.

Relationships are never risk-free."

Raphael swore softly. "New fear unlocked. There was me panicking about falling in love with someone and my history causing them to leave, now I'm not so sure I want to even start anything at all."

"Is there a lass in mind?"

"Nah. No one. It's theoretical, just on my mind from watching Jackson and Ariel fall into each other's orbit. That happened so fast."

I snorted, keeping an eye on Finn. "Not that fast. Dude was far gone for her way ahead of when they started dating. He nearly bit my head off when I said I was going to ask her out."

Raphael shuddered. "That's my sister."

"It was a joke to test him. I wasnae going there."

A tiny wail came from deeper in the bus. Both of us stilled, listening. Viola's voice followed as she soothed her bairn, presumably feeding him, and after a minute, all was quiet again.

Raphael asked an abrupt question. "Are ye seeing Mia?"

I blinked. Swallowed. "No. Why do ye ask?"

"Any issue with me taking her on a date?"

At my lack of a response, he sat forward, forearms on his knees. "You're making me think I should be less wary of relationships, and she's a sweetheart."

"Didn't know ye knew her," I grouched, suddenly panicked.

"I don't. What's she like?"

Beautiful, kind, sexy as fuck. Four days ago, I'd left a sex toy based on my dick outside her cottage, packaged up, of course, and heard not a word since.

That was fine. She wanted a relationship, I didn't.

She didn't owe me a report on how well fake-dick-me

fucked her.

But if Raphael wanted a girlfriend, I was doing them both a disservice. He was younger than her but still a responsible man. He'd take care of her.

I ground my teeth together, trying to form the words of how fucking amazing Mia was.

Raphael cracked up. "Are ye kidding me? Ye walked straight into that setup and now can't even speak through caveman outrage."

My brain clued me in. I groaned. "That was a test. For fuck's sake."

"Course it was. I'm sworn off women forever."

From under the blanket, Finn struggled up, grasping for me. I gave him my arm so he could sit. At the same second, my phone lit. A photo from Gordain.

"Here ye go," I said softly to the lad.

He clocked his father, sighed, then slumped back down.

It was going to be a long night.

Finally, the bus was moving, and we were setting off into the night, Leo and his family plus Gordain and Ben on one coach, Jax, Raphael, and I on another, travelling in convoy with a shit-ton of other staff and equipment to the next country.

In my narrow bunk, the curtain's drawn, I finally lost my

cool and messaged Mia.

Valentine: Product review request. Please give a rating out of five stars.

It was late. Gone one AM. I wasn't hopeful of a reply.

Mia: Five thousand stars. Would recommend, except I don't want to share.

My fucking heart thundered.

Valentine: What I wouldn't give to see it in use.

Mia: Dammit, Valentine. You and that mouth of yours.

I smothered a laugh, rolling to my back.

Valentine: It would be better if I used my mouth on you at the same time as fucking ye with it.

Mia: I'm sorry, the Mia you're trying to reach expired. Some red-hot guy blew her mind.

Valentine: Woman, you crack me up.

Mia: I aim to please.

Valentine: If I say pretty please, can I get a photo? It's a lonely life on tour.

Mia: Really! I figured you'd be waylaid by groupies left, right, and centre.

Valentine: Outrageous. I've been celibate since the last time you graced my dick with attention.

Mia: Oh, come on.

I narrowed my gaze at my phone, my newly horny state simmering.

Valentine: I don't lie.

Mia: Remember the cookie incident? When Tobi and I came by the bunkhouse to give them to you, we heard noises from inside. Sex noises.

Valentine: I haven't been back to the bunkhouse since you left.

A long pause followed. Did she fall asleep mid-conversation? It rankled that she'd believed something wrong about me. For weeks, too.

I sent another quick reply to be sure she got the message.

Valentine: To be completely transparent, I haven't even checked out another woman. Even the bare tits that get exposed to Leo every night. Well, maybe I peek, but I'm only picturing yours.

Still no reply came in. Fuck. I'd messed up our friendship again and had no idea how to fix it.

18

Mia

*O*nly picturing yours. He was only picturing mine.

"Hey, Mia."

What did that mean? How could he face off with sexy half-naked rock fans and still think about me? All night and most of this morning, all I'd thought about was Valentine's claim.

"Mia?" a voice repeated.

I tuned in to it. *Daisy.* My boss had pulled up outside the building I was cleaning without me even being aware.

"God. I was miles away. Hey!"

"I've got a surprise for you." Daisy approached, a garment bag held out.

"Ooh, what is it? Come inside."

Since confiding my story in Daisy, we'd gotten closer. She was missing her boyfriend badly and throwing herself into work. I led her into the office's kitchen. There were no staff here today, so it was nicely quiet.

"A uniform. Just a tunic to wear over our normal clothes.

but see! It's branded. What do you think?"

I squeaked in excitement and took the bag, drawing down the zipper to reveal a cleaning tunic. Uniforms had been my suggestion when Daisy had asked how I was finding work and whether I had any ideas for the business. She'd been reluctant, though I had no idea why, because this warm blue tabard with a monogrammed company logo was sweet as hell.

Highland Housekeeping, the name read. So classy.

"I love it," I breathed. "We're going to look so official. What made you change your mind?"

"Ariel told me off for letting my mother dictate things when she isn't in my life."

"Your mom? Sounds like a story there."

Daisy perched on a stool. "If I give you the background to this, it means some bad-mouthing of my mother. Do you mind? I don't want to be insensitive since you lost yours."

I brought to mind the framed picture I had of Mom at home, her happy smile so comforting though it always made my heart ache. "Please. She loved a good story. I'm all ears."

"Mom runs a naked cleaning company in the States called Daisy's Delights."

My jaw dropped. "Come again? Naked? Wait, she uses your name?"

My boss cackled. "Right? It's a lot. She cleans houses topless, and yeah, chose my name to use. We don't talk much, but I go find her naked social media posts from time to time to check in on her."

"God." I eyed her phone. "Going to need to see those pictures."

She rolled her eyes but paged through until she located a gallery of photos. An older, nude woman posed provocatively with various cleaning items, stickers and emojis hiding the really racy stuff, along with a small, frilly apron.

"Damn," I breathed. "We'd make so much more money if we did this."

Daisy choked. "You're not wrong, but can you imagine our clients? We'd give them heart attacks."

"True. Eh, that's a bad business model. We want the return custom."

She grinned. "Then it's decided—we'll keep our clothes on." Daisy hopped off the seat. "I came to bring the tabard but also an offer. You remember Cait who you met at drinks? Her mom is Scarlet, and she's a hugely successful businesswoman. A total boss babe but the kindest lady, too. Cait mentioned you to her, and Scarlet offered to help decipher the contracts you've been sent."

I blinked. "God, is it bad I barely remember talking about that?"

"It was a wild night, that's for sure." She tapped the counter, turning to leave. "I need to get to my next job, but the offer is there if you're interested."

"Thank you, and I'll message Cait to thank her, too," I called.

Several hours later, I settled Tobi into bed, her eyes shuttering almost instantly. The full-time hours and the new school were taking it out of her, so early nights were now the new way.

Which left me time to myself.

From under my bed, I retrieved a box with all the things I didn't have homes for yet. One was an envelope I'd snagged to hold the paperwork from the Winchesters. I reached for it, fighting the urge to ignore it for longer. I didn't care about the failing company. I even had the vague fear that Tobi might inherit debt as one third heir to his estate. Not understanding the paperwork felt like the safest solution.

My fingers grazed over the other item in the box. A long, metal container, clipped firmly closed in case of exploring children.

It was the homemade project Valentine had created for me.

He'd asked for a product review, and I'd faked my answer. Truth was, I hadn't been brave enough to use it.

Maybe the paperwork could wait a bit longer.

I tossed the container on my bed and tucked the box away, creeping back out to check the room next door. My daughter was out cold, and if she woke in the night, it was normally during the early hours, not right after going to sleep.

Just in case, back in my cosy, lamp-lit room, I locked the door.

Then I returned to my gift. Valentine had packaged it up securely, leaving it outside my door before he left. I'd peeked, and even touched the rubber, but that was as far as I'd got.

One short conversation with him yesterday had me feeling all kinds of things that only he seemed to generate. I was overheated, over-sensitised. My blood running hot and my breasts heavy, my skin begging to be touched.

I needed an orgasm.

My Valentine stand-in was the obvious choice to give it to me.

The box had two clips on the end, and I undid them and opened it, the rude phallus inside ready and waiting for me like a cheerful stress reliever. I tipped it onto my lap, my breath hitching at the weight. It was a sizeable device, a perfect, smooth replica, even of Valentine's thick vein, and with buttons on the end to control the vibrations.

I flicked the switch, and it buzzed against my thighs.

God, yes.

The thought of pushing it inside me spiked a fever.

I was dressed for sleep in pyjama bottoms and a strappy top, so I brought the vibrator to my chest, nudging the blunt end over one nipple, then repeating at the other side, tipping my head back at how good it felt. My heartbeat sped up, and I wriggled on the bed, my nipples hardening to bullets and my pussy getting wetter by the second. Valentine had no idea what he was missing.

Then I had an idea.

Almost shaking with nerves, I stripped my top and flicked the button to turn off the vibrations, then put the toy between my breasts. Grabbing my phone, I arranged myself and took a shot. Then I sent a quick message first.

Mia: Are you alone? I have a picture for you.

His reply took seconds.

Valentine: Just checked into a hotel and I have the room to myself. Send it. Now.

I loved that bossy tone. I clicked to *send*, my heart racing, then I shifted up my bed to nestle against my pillows, my gaze never leaving the message thread.

Dots appeared as if he was writing a reply, then vanished.

A few seconds later, the phone rang in my hands. A video call from Valentine.

I jumped and dropped my phone to the quilt.

Grabbing it up, I swiped to answer, keeping the screen resolutely on my face.

The screen fuzzed then cleared, giving me the gorgeous man I'd missed so much, his black hair loose and a white pillow behind him. He was tanned, presumably the spring sun in other countries stronger than here, but it was the way he stared back at me that caught me in the feels, his gaze moving over the screen as if he was fascinated.

"Please tell me that picture was just taken," he said.

"Maybe. What's it to you?"

"If my rubber dick gets to tit-fuck ye, it's only fair I get to watch."

I squirmed, thrilled that he'd called. Even more needy now he was part of the evening. "We can't."

"Aye, we can. I have thirty minutes until I have to escort Leo over to tonight's venue," Valentine told me.

"Over video?" I queried, a small worry breaking into the warmth he generated even with just a virtual presence.

"Let me give you a room tour before we start."

"So confident," I grumbled, but I was already halfway to being persuaded.

Valentine jumped up from his bed and panned the camera around the room, even opening the wardrobe, showing me he was alone. He moved to the door and flicked the latch to lock it, then panned to the ceiling and the corners. "No cameras, no one listening in, no danger of anyone seeing this but me."

I chewed my lip.

His smirk increased. "Ye trust me, aye? My bank account number is forty-six, thirty-three, thirty-nine, sixty-eight. My dick is nine inches long. I keep my car keys on top of the front right wheel when I'm away. And just to show ye how interested I am..."

The camera sank down his bare chest, pausing at the V-cut muscles that led beneath his clothes, then lower to his very tented shorts.

I swore, and the camera returned to his face.

"Like what ye see?" The cocky Scot grinned.

He returned to sprawl on the bed.

I took a steadying breath. "How can you be that turned on from one photo?"

"I told ye, it's a gift. Now listen up, I've been tortured with wondering how you're using that toy. So here's the deal. I'm going to talk ye through every little thing I want to do to ye, and you're going to fuck yourself silly with that rubber dick while I watch. When ye come on it, I'm going to fuck my fist and imagine that pretty pussy is squeezing tight on me. Sound good?"

I gave a breathy whimper.

Valentine's smirk broadened. "Use your words, Mia."

"Y-yes."

"Atta girl. First, did ye find the lube in the box?" At my negative, he continued, "Get it, spread it all over that bad boy."

I obeyed him, leaning to retrieve the lube from the metal tin. I uncapped it and drizzled the oil, spreading it over the end of the toy. Nine inches, he'd said. The man wasn't exaggerating.

"Mia," Valentine said. "Lift the phone. I need a permanent visual."

I'd left my phone on the sheet so scrambled for it, still feeling awkward about my body being on display.

Valentine swore. "Holy shit, baby girl. Ye half-naked there? Give me the tour."

"What if someone else can see this?" I said.

"Then they're about to get a show, because I'm not going to hold back anything from ye."

"God, okay." I pulled the camera back and tilted it to showcase my chest, my other arm around my waist.

"Fucking hell, woman. I've got my dick in my hand now and I'm wishing hard that I was there with ye. Touch yourself. Play with them."

I inhaled, a wave of sexiness taking control of me and burning away any lingering concern. Shifting the camera lower, I used the other hand to hold my breast, drawing my fingers over my nipple.

"You're a goddess. Do that with the vibrator," he urged, his tone darkening.

I obeyed, taking the toy to my breast, flicking it on to drive vibrations into my skin. It felt incredible having an audience. Even better than it had solo.

"Fuck 'em both with it like in the picture," Valentine asked.

"How...?" I bent to set the phone on my bedstead, resting against the wall and freeing up my hands for what he asked. "You do the same," I asked. "I want to see you."

"Will it turn ye on to watch me playing with myself over ye?"

At my nod, he sat up and looked around him, arranging a pillow at the end of his bed to support his phone. But every time he moved, it fell over.

Valentine frowned at the screen then gazed around his room. "Using a chair," he grumbled, his cocky expression only returning when he'd solved the problem.

"Can you take your shorts off?" I asked, my voice barely a whisper.

The item in question left his body in an instant, giving me the real-life visual of the gift lying on my quilt. Valentine palmed his dick. I picked up the replica and encased it in my breasts.

He groaned and pumped his shaft. "If only ye knew how hot that is."

My eyes were glued to the screen where an even hotter show was playing out. I moaned at the surge of pleasure from the vibrator and from seeing him.

On my knees on the bed, I palmed my breasts and pushed them together, loving the noises of pleasure and encouragement Valentine gave up. So easily, he made me feel like the sexiest woman alive.

He jerked his chin at the phone, his lips parted. "Lose the rest of your clothes. I need to see that disappearing inside ye."

I moaned, fumbling at my waistband to strip the pyjama bottoms. Despite our previous encounters, I'd never been naked in front of him. Maybe it was easier this way because my restraint was long gone.

"You're so fucking gorgeous." Valentine moved closer to the camera. "If I was there, I'd have ye on your back with my face between your legs. I'm a big lad so you'd need warming up. We're going to do that using the toy, understand?"

I shivered and nodded, awaiting his instruction. It only seemed right for him to tell me how to use his replacement. It made everything hotter.

"I need to see everything, so toss your pillows to the end of the bed and rest back that way. Good girl. Now widen your knees. Rub the end of the rubber dick over your clit."

Everything he asked, I did, my eyes closing at the first pass of the vibrator over my soaking wet and desperately sensitive core.

"Fucking hell, Mia. You're so wet for this. Just like I'm so hard for ye. If I was there, I'd work ye soft at first then getting firmer with each pass. It would be hard not to fuck straight into ye, because your pussy would take me like a fucking glove, but I'd resist, and take my time building ye up. Do ye wish I was there? Can ye feel me?"

"I wish I could," I confessed.

"My dick is leaking for ye. How do ye want to come first?

With the toy outside or inside?"

I was already building up to something powerful, his words, the vibrations, and the ultra-sexy feel of the evening breaking my brain. "I want it inside me."

"Lift your hips. Get it into position."

I drove the toy lower, switched off the vibrations, then notched it at my entrance. My whole world shrank to that point of touch. The imminent intrusion that I so badly needed.

"Now, little spy."

I thrust it inside, my arousal and the lube easing the path. A gasp flew from my lips as it filled me.

Valentine gave a guttural snarl. "You're so fucking sexy. Does it feel like my dick?"

"Yes. I still wish it was you."

"So do I. Ye have no fucking idea how much. Flick the vibrations back on and fuck yourself in my name."

I did, driving the thick vibrator in and out, my hips rising and falling to meet the thrusts. My body was so primed that the building orgasm neared fast. "I'm close."

"I am, too. See what you've done to me," he ordered.

I raised my head to see him on all fours, facing the camera like he was over me, his dick inside me, his muscles doing the work.

"My fucking dick filling your tight pussy."

It was all I needed to tip me over the edge.

I cried out again, my internal walls clamping down on the toy. My orgasm pulsed through me, a glorious spread of wave after wave of pleasure.

On the camera, Valentine gave a desperate growl, and I opened my eyes in time to see him come, too. He dropped onto the sheet, keeping on one elbow so I didn't miss the show.

His expression…

I kept the dildo in me, prolonging my orgasm, in total rapture with the moment. With my other hand, I stroked my clit, neglected as I'd let the vibrator do all the work. Now, I turned off the vibrations and just held the toy in place, strumming myself faster and faster. Around the toy, my stretched pussy throbbed.

Valentine groaned, muttering how hot I was, how sexy he found me, but I couldn't watch now. I just needed to keep going, lit up by his attention on me.

A second climax wrecked me, this time starting from my clit and echoing at every other point. I moaned and curled in on myself, pulsing hard.

"Don't ye dare hide. I need that flush on your skin. Need to see ye," Valentine snarled.

Breathless, I spread out once more, making a show of sliding the dildo out.

But the moment was over. Instant awkwardness descended, my mind offering words that I wasn't ever able to say. Not to this man, the one who was all about the fun and nothing more.

Without waiting for my sweat to cool on my skin, I snapped up and ended the call.

19

Valentine

Grey motorway rushed by the tour bus, visible through a narrow slice of window beside my bunk. I thumbed a message to Mia. Two nights ago, she and I shared a mind-blowing experience, but since, the lass wouldn't reply to me.

Valentine: Earlier, we drove over the border into Spain. Leo has the night off, then he's got gigs in Barcelona and Madrid. The bodyguard team gets to chill. What are you up to?

I didn't expect an answer.

None came.

A couple of hours later, I exited the hotel's lift to the opulent lobby, tall stands of red flowers against black-and-white décor, everything shiny and cold. Outside the Excelsior Hotel's huge tinted windows, night had fallen, but it didn't hide the throng of people in the street. In the exterior lighting, they shifted, not passing each other like in a busy shopping street, but oddly staying in place.

My pulse picked up.

I squinted, hunting for tour merch or items clutched in hands that fans might want signed, any indication that this was for Leo. We didn't publicise where he stayed, but there were a number of methods for that to leak. If they were here for him, it could make leaving the hotel riskier.

The woman at the reception desk looked up at my approach. "How may I help you?"

"They been out there long?"

She peered over thin glasses. "I noticed a few people half an hour ago."

Which meant the crowd had grown quickly.

"How many people are on security tonight?"

"One, our doorman."

"You've got to be kidding me."

She blanched. "Usually the general manager's here in the evening, but the city's quiet. He's left already. There won't be any trouble. It's never happened here, and we frequently host politicians."

Fucking politicians. I turned away. I was off duty, if that was ever a thing, but tapped an alert out to the team. Leo was meant to be heading out for dinner, but that plan wouldn't fly if he couldn't leave the place safely.

My phone dinged, two messages arriving at once.

Ben: On my way down.

Mia: I signed up to a dating site. I'm filling out the profile.

Well, fuck. I scowled at the second text, leaning back on a cold stone wall to reply.

Valentine: Is that safe?

Mia: I'm using a fake name and not showing my whole face in the pictures I just took. The Winchester men would never stoop to using a dating site, so I think so.

I still didn't like it.

Another reply came in.

Mia: Have you ever tried this?

Valentine: Why would I?

Mia: Right. Because you don't want a girlfriend. I'll call Daisy to come help me.

Valentine: I can still help. Show me the pictures you're using.

Two appeared. The first of her smiling in profile, the second more focused on her body. Neither were clearly her, but still I gritted my teeth.

Then I checked myself.

Mia wanted a boyfriend. Who the hell was I to stand in her way?

Valentine: Open two more buttons on your shirt.

Mia: Like so?

She sent a third pic, her delightful tits now the star of the show. A rush of heat eased through my body, chasing the adrenaline from seeing the pack outside. Even while chatting, I didn't take my attention off the danger for long. The high-end hotel's doorman was keeping them at bay, but the lack of any other personnel wasn't my favourite news in the world.

Valentine: Fucking hell, woman. Guys will be lining up to take you out.

Mia: That's the idea.

"Val." My brother crossed the hotel lobby from the stairs, his gaze troubled and his fists bunched.

I gestured at the windows. "It's been building for at least half an hour and is getting thicker. The hotel only has a single doorman on duty."

Ben took in the scene. In a different city, a few days ago, we'd had fans chase the tour bus. In another, they'd hung out around the back of the venue in a crowd so thick we'd needed the police to move them on before we could drive out.

"How many?" he asked.

"Not sure. I'll go check it out. The doorman, too."

A jerk of his head released me from my unofficial lobby guarding. Through the rotating door, I emerged into the night air.

"Banks!" Someone screamed.

Leo's surname. No doubt this was a fan mob.

I sought the person out—a teenager braced by his parents. The lad's expression dropped when he realised I wasn't his idol.

People around him muttered, jockeying for position, only held back by a line of potted trees that marked the hotel's entrance. Most of them were adults.

"What's going to happen for all the fans who couldn't get tickets?" someone else bellowed.

Excited voices took up the call, energy high on the mild night.

The sense of threat built in me.

I'd heard Leo talking on the phone to his record company about issues with this gig. There had been a problem with the online sales platform where it had crashed and dumped out all the people queueing for tickets. A large number had been bought by ticket touts instead and resold at an extortionate figure. There was nothing Leo could do about it, but I knew he'd felt bad.

Apparently the crowd did, too.

Using a block-counting technique, I estimated the size. Fifty, sixty, shite, close to eighty people were cramming into the medieval cobbled alley. We were in Barcelona's Gothic

Quarter, with narrow pedestrian-only streets lined with high-walled buildings. Access was tricky. We couldn't bring a car outside, but there was a private square on the other side of the building.

Down the alley, a covered bridge spanned the street, leading from one building to another. Old stone, like the rest of the buildings, and with open sides.

I'd noted it earlier but now took a good look then turned to the door guard I'd already introduced myself to at check-in. "How's it going, brother?"

The man's eyes focused over my shoulder. His fingers fluttered over his smart uniform. "They keep asking if your rock star is staying here. I've told them no, but more are arriving by the second. Someone must've put it online."

I squinted around to make sure he hadn't just outed me to anyone listening. Luckily, no one seemed to have heard. "Where's your team?"

"It's just me on the door until ten when my shift ends."

In other words, only here to make the place appear smart. No chance of him being able to disperse them. "You're doing great. Keep them out, aye?"

His gaze clung to me. "I'm new to this job. What do I do if they rush me?"

For fuck's sake. I clapped his elbow. "Call the cops and don't get trampled. Now let me back in so we can work out what to do."

He activated the turning door so I could re-enter. Behind the reception desk, Ben clicked a mouse, a low monitor displaying the other exit to the hotel—a gated archway that led to the square they used for deliveries. A few people had gathered there, too.

My stomach tightened.

I relayed what I'd discovered.

"There's a risk of mob action," I concluded. "We need the cops to handle that crowd. Getting out tomorrow for the gig is going to be a ballache, too. Who the fuck picked out this hotel? Security's a joke."

I didn't temper my complaint for the sake of the receptionist perched at the far end of the counter. She watched us with unabashed curiosity.

My brother drew me away a few steps so our conversation wasn't earwigged. "The record company changed the plan last minute so Luke was closer to the place they're meeting him this evening."

Luke meant Leo. We didn't use his or his family's names publicly, everyone getting a code name using their initial. Finn's was Fletcher and even baby Torran had one. We called him Tank.

"Interesting that we were able to walk in untroubled but a crowd appears right before Luke's meant to leave," I said.

We swapped a glance.

"The record company's courting this," Ben decided. "They attempted multiple times to get him to agree to a meet and greet, but of course, he said no."

"Then they leaked his location instead to appease the angry fans. Fuck. Are the family secure?" If Finn knew what was going on, he'd be terrified.

"They're remaining upstairs. Gordain's in the suite. Raph and Jax are taking positions outside the door. Right now, our best bet is to sit tight. Maybe move hotels later."

A prickle of uncertainty rolled over my skin. I slid my gaze to the crowd outside the glass. They'd closed in even more, a couple stumbling over the potted trees to haunt the entrance approach.

"We need a better plan." I turned to the receptionist. "Is there any other way out than this exit and the delivery square?"

She snapped up her attention from her phone. "Sorry, what?"

I narrowed my gaze. "Are ye messaging someone?"

"Only my boyfriend. This is wild."

Ben breathed through his nose. "Do your job and call the police. That crowd isn't going anywhere, and it could get dangerous."

He was right. In the space of the few minutes we'd been monitoring it, the noise level outside had elevated, the crowd getting raucous. Their yells demanded Leo appear.

If they raided the place, the family could only hide in bedrooms with doors that were thick but not designed to hold back a siege. My team would do anything to keep them safe, but facing down what had to now be over a hundred people would be risky as fuck. Horrifyingly scary for the family concealed the other side of the door.

My brother pointed at me. "I'm calling it—"

A crack ricocheted through the reception, echoing across the polished surfaces.

One of the windows splintered, the glass holding but a silver jagged line bisecting one of the huge panels.

My heart thundered.

The receptionist shot to her feet, her mouth gaping open.

"Get the police here," Ben snarled. "And answer the question. Is there another way out?"

Despite the distance between us, I knew my brother. Like me, he could pivot a plan on the spot, balancing out the tipping point to move from one path to another.

The receptionist picked up the phone, her hand shaking.

"No."

"What about that bridge across the street?" I demanded.

She blinked. "Oh, yes. But it's locked. We aren't using it."

"What is the building it connects to?" I urged.

"It's our overflow rooms, used when we're sold out, but we only open it May through September."

The perfect place to hide.

"Who can unlock it?" I asked.

"The general manager has the key. Hola?" She spoke into the phone, her tone fearful in her rapid explanation to the police.

Ben and I took off running.

"The general manager's off site," I told him.

My brother snagged his earpiece from his pocket. I did the same with mine, fitting it into place to allow hands-free communication with our crew.

"Jax, join Val on floor two," Ben said over the comms system, then gripped my arm. "Get access to that bridge by any means. I'll ready the family."

"We're out of here?"

"Aye, brother."

Relief surged. We split up. I jogged down the corridor and past the stairs, seeking out the staff area. The passes we had gave us access to behind-the-scenes areas, thank fuck that had worked out, and I scanned the nameplate on each door, searching for the Spanish equivalent of general manager.

Even luckier, it was there in English.

I knocked once, tried my pass. A red light and a grating off sound refused me access. Stepping back, I centred myself then booted the door. It gave with one kick, smacking off the wall.

A small, windowless room was revealed. I ignored the desk for the key hutch on the wall.

"In location," Jackson reported. "Where are ye, Val?"

"Trying to find a key. We're going to attempt the bridge that crosses the alley to the next building. Have a hunt around and see if ye can see the door."

"Easy. I'm standing right next to it. It's in the stairwell."

I wrenched open the hutch. "Sweet. What kind of key does it take?"

"Going by the keyhole, it's going to be big and girthy. Long, probably, too."

A dick joke came begging, but I held it at bay, tracing my finger over the rows of jumbled keys. The hotel was an old one, so these had to be from before card readers were in use.

I tracked to the lower rows, scanning the labels. Restaurant A, Restaurant B...the last three were blank but held the kind of chunky key Jackson had described.

I snatched all three and took off.

Back in the lobby, a quick glance showed me the doorman had abandoned his post and the mob was at the turning door, the window still standing but the shouting at a fever pitch. I bolted up the stairs, taking two at a time until I reached the second floor.

Jackson waited for me beside an elegantly gated doorway, the bridge visible through the window. I tried the first key in the lock.

"There's a roof, but the sides are just stone latticework," Jackson said, concern in his voice.

I tried the second key, my brain clueing me in to what he meant. "If we walk straight over, we'll be seen."

"Exactly." He took another look, gauging it. "We'll need to

crawl."

My fear for the lad I'd soon be marking grew. I couldn't hide the mass of people after his da, but I'd do anything to protect him.

The third and final key turned cleanly in the lock, and the gate to the bridge opened, the night air coming with it.

I dropped down and skulked across the short length. The door on the other side opened with the same key, the hallway beyond silent.

"Hello, anyone here?" I called.

The stairs only went down, a few rooms with their doors propped open occupying each floor. I entered each, checked, and moved on. In the lobby, a single door was marked exit only. No fancy reception like across the way, no lights aside from low-level emergency floor strips.

Better still, a corridor led through the dark to exit into an alley far away from the Excelsior's entrance. As the receptionist had said, the place was empty.

We had a route out.

"Clear. This is a go. Ready whenever ye are," I said into the comms, jogging back to the bridge.

"Copy. Incoming in two," Ben replied.

I finished my crawl as Jackson strode to the stairwell, blocking the downwards set, though I'd barely seen another hotel resident this evening. Footsteps thudded, the crew and our protected family descending.

Ben appeared first followed by Gordain, then a huddle of the Bankses, and Raphael at the back. Viola clutched her bairn to her chest, Leo with an arm around her waist and the other keeping his older son near.

Finn broke away from his da and ran to me. Seized my hand. "Ye have to protect him. Ye promised."

He meant his father. My heart ached.

"We will. Nothing bad is going to happen. We're just moving away from the noise and fuss until it's under control. This is what we do, and we're good at our jobs. Do ye trust me?"

His rounded eyes held desperation, his hold on my hand not letting up. But finally, Finn nodded.

"Then let's get out of here."

At the bridge, Ben and I exchanged a few words then he crawled across first, beckoning the small group to follow. Viola next, Gordain taking Torran from her arms so she could move more easily, quickly following after her.

Thank fuck, the bairn didn't cry out.

Down below us, the crowd shifted, easily doubled now and so packed together that people fell. Screamed.

I held back, watching from the corner of the window. A cop car was parked at the end of the alley, lights flashing, but the occupants made no attempt yet to move on the mob. Probably waiting for further cars to arrive, not that it did us any good.

If any fan raised their gaze and spotted the figures creeping over the dark bridge, our refuge could quickly become a trap.

Steady as a rock, I guided Finn to the doorway. We had Ben, Viola, Gordain, and Torran on one side, Leo, Finn, Jackson, Raphael, and me on the other.

"You're next. Ready?" I said to Finn.

"If Da comes."

"Right behind you," Leo promised.

Finn switched his serious gaze to me, and I put my hand on his father's shoulder. With a shuddering breath, the lad dropped down and scuttled over, hugging onto his ma the second he was clear.

Leo swallowed then stooped to all fours. Started to crawl.

"Banks, Banks!" a cry went up.

The rock star froze.

I snapped my focus to the mob, but their energy was concentrated on the reception still, two men wrenching at the door, trying to force their way inside. They hadn't seen him. Instead, they were smacking the shite out of the hotel.

"Keep going, Luke," I whispered.

But he'd stalled out, something like shock in his profile. I could only guess his thoughts. In our prep sessions, we'd talked him through the security arrangements and he'd listened in detail, contributing to every single arrangement and plan. He openly discussed his ongoing battle of needing his family safe while still living for performing.

This was the result of his fame.

Threats, vile messages, and now a baying mob, out for any piece of him they could get. His family trampled on their way. Fuck.

"Da!" Finn called out, panicked.

He struggled away from Viola to the edge of the bridge. If he stepped out, he'd be seen.

"Stop, Fletch," I ordered, using his code name. Then I ducked down and belly-crawled until I was alongside Leo. "Let's go," I urged him. "Your family's waiting. Come on, man."

He blinked, tearing his gaze from the writhing mass below. "This is all my fault."

"Get to safety then we'll talk about that."

"Fuck. Yes."

With my urging, he finished the journey, Finn diving into his arms the second he rolled up. The rest of our crew made the trip, Jackson locking the gate behind us followed by the one on our side.

We had no bags, no possessions, but we were safe.

For now.

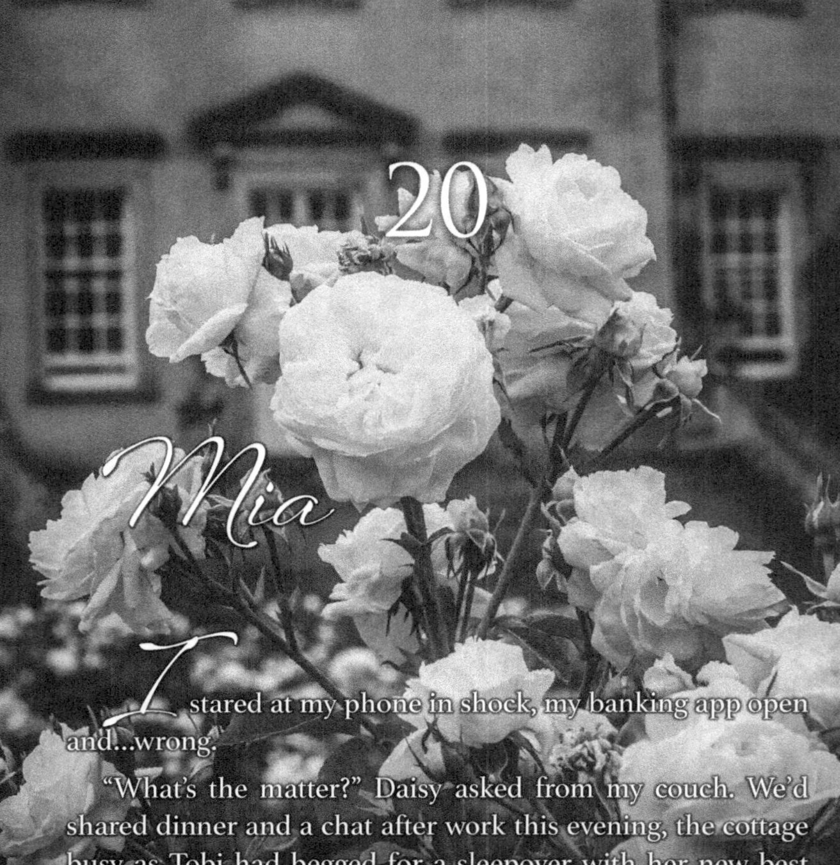

20

Mia

I stared at my phone in shock, my banking app open and...wrong.

"What's the matter?" Daisy asked from my couch. We'd shared dinner and a chat after work this evening, the cottage busy as Tobi had begged for a sleepover with her new best friend. They were in her bedroom now, giggling and high on sugar despite it being past eight PM.

"I've been paid child support."

Daisy cocked her head. "Isn't that a good thing?"

I refreshed the app. The figure was still there. I'd assumed the last lot of money I got from the Winchesters had been my final payment. After Greg Senior died, Vanissa, his wife, paid it from the ongoing business profits, griping about how it wiped out any income they had. I'd felt bad but equally didn't turn it down. By that point, I was caring for my mother and Tobi full time and couldn't work.

"It's not a bad thing. Just unexpected. Vanissa always made it clear they'd only support me if I was under their roof."

"Do they get to decide that? Surely you're owed that legally."

"Maybe if Tobi's dad was alive, but dead people can't owe money. It's up to his executors."

I kept my voice low, not that Tobi could hear.

"Did you think any more about talking to Scarlet? My opinion is you need to lawyer up and get Tobi's rights worked out. Yours, too."

"I got her number but… I've just had such a mental block over this." For more reasons than I wanted to confess.

Both Greg Senior, the father, and Greg Junior, the son, had screwed me over. No one knew how except for me, and exposing that would also expose me to some pretty unpleasant memories. Facing off against that in a meeting of some kind would be horrible.

But Mama didn't raise no coward.

Daisy gave me a sympathetic look. "Call Scarlet. Let her help. At least in telling you what those papers mean."

"You're right. I'm doing it." I took a deep breath and dialled Scarlet's number, introducing myself when she answered.

Her tone was bright, her reply no-nonsense. "My daughter already filled me in. I have a houseful of grandchildren this evening but I can have Ally swing by on his way home from work. He'll pick up the papers, and I'll call once I've read them through. Sound good?"

I agreed and thanked her, even more impressed ten minutes later when her husband—a seriously gorgeous older man with a blond beard—knocked on the door and collected the papers Greg had left me.

I handed them over with more profuse thanks, putting my hand to my heart when I closed the door.

"See?" Daisy said. "Doesn't that feel better already?"

"Actually, yes. As well as scary."

Daisy's phone chimed with a text. She read the screen, her smile dropping in a rush. "God."

"What's wrong?"

"It's Ben. They've had an incident this evening."

My heart thumped. All week, I'd had a lingering fear of Valentine and the others being on the road. There were so many dangers. "What kind of incident? Is anyone hurt?"

Daisy continued, her shoulders hunching up. "I don't think so. They had to flee their hotel because a mob turned up to see Leo. They're hiding out now."

"A mob?" More fear trickled into my blood.

How dangerous must it have been for them to run from it?

Another message landed. Daisy read it then stood. "Ben wants me to go wait with Ella, Gordain's wife. She was due to join them in a day or two as she's been working, but can you imagine your family being hunted like that and not being with them? The poor woman will be in pieces."

"She must be terrified." I helped Daisy collect her coat and check she hadn't left anything. "You must be, too."

Pale, she nodded once and quickly. "Ben can handle anything, I know that. I've seen him in action, and he's amazing. That isn't helping me sleep at night." She hugged me once and went to the door. "Valentine's the same. He's just as capable."

Except I didn't have the right to worry. Not like Daisy, and especially not like Ella. I watched my boss hop into her car and zoom off into the dark.

My stomach had been replaced by a rock.

Concern for Valentine built steadily until my fingers shook.

Turning my phone over in my hands, I peeked into Tobi's room. In her bed, the two mop tops of blonde and brunette hair ducked down, more giggling following.

"Lights out and sleep now," I told the two cute girls.

"Aye, Mom," Tobi replied, mixing up her heritage nicely.

Back in the lounge, I perched on the sofa. To hell with it. I messaged Valentine.

Mia: Are you okay? I was with Daisy so I heard.

To my utter relief, the message was read and a reply started almost immediately.

Valentine: Aw, check you out, worrying about me.

Mia: Daisy said there was a mob. Even writing that is scaring the hell out of me.

Valentine: Can I call you?

My heart skipped a beat. Replying with a fast *yes,* I took a shaky inhale, tapping to accept the call the second it appeared.

"Hey, sweetheart," Valentine said.

His voice loosened my panic a small degree. "Hey yourself. Please tell me you're safe now?"

"Not exactly. We're holed up in a safe-ish place, waiting on permission from the cops to move on. A mistake, if ye ask me." He gave me a quick run-through of the threat that had faced them and how they'd got into a neighbouring hotel building where the family could rest in a bedroom.

Narrow streets. A warm spring evening. The danger the mass of people was creating. It curdled my blood.

"We were ready to leave again and had cars waiting, but I scouted it out and it means walking up an alley and across a public square to the road. In that time, Ben managed to get a line to the cops who are working to control the crowd. They've asked us to sit tight. We're supposed to heed them, though I'm strongly in favour of getting the fuck out of here." He grumbled in what sounded like frustration. "We've even had Raphael up on the roof working out how to land a heli here, but the flight plan got refused."

A horrible sense curled through me. They were trapped.

"So you just have to sit there until the police clear the crowd?" I asked.

"Aye, and they want us to return to the hotel where it all started, but we already vetoed that. Want to know what Leo's record company said? They asked him to go out and address the crowd from a balcony. It's fucking wild that they think that's okay."

I crept an arm around myself, hugging my middle. "Everyone must be so scared."

"They are. Particularly Leo and Finn. Both are beside themselves." His tone changed. "Hang on. I can hear something. Putting ye on loudspeaker so I can leave the phone on the floor. That way I can go to the windows without the screen activating and giving me away."

The sound of the call changed, footsteps mixed with an echoing background.

"A group is being escorted down the alley by cops," Valentine reported.

"That's a good thing, right?" I said.

"Think so. It's the first movement we've seen. Just checking the other window."

He went quiet for a moment. I pictured him in the dark of whatever space they were in, watchful of the hostile people outside.

"Val," another voice said, closer to the phone.

Ben, I was relatively certain.

"What's up?" Valentine replied, more distant.

"While we're stuck inside, I wanted to talk. I was going to do it over dinner, but we didnae get the chance."

"Hold up," Valentine said, presumably intending to cut off my call.

"Kelly messaged me," his brother replied.

Valentine ceased talking. Dead air played out.

"She asked me to get ye to call her, that's all. I didn't reply to her and I won't. Just wanted to say because I know she's been hassling ye."

Valentine's voice returned. "How did she get your number?"

"Not from me." Another pause followed, then Ben huffed. "I'm telling the truth. I'm not in contact with her. She probably got it from someone in the family. I have no fucking clue."

"Whatever. Message received," was his response.

Ben audibly exhaled. "This isn't the time or place, but I'm getting a sense of urgency considering everything she's trying. Judging by your expression, you're not interested, aye? It's the last I'll say on it."

A door clicked closed, then Valentine came back on the line. "Sorry about that."

"Who's Kelly?" I asked.

"No one I want to talk about. Or to."

"If she's hassling you—"

"I said I didn't want to talk about it," he snapped back. "Fuck. Sorry. This is just not a good time, or topic."

My chest ached, the hurt adding to my already overflowing emotions. It was obvious who that woman was, and why he wouldn't discuss her with his brother. He'd been engaged, and it was to Kelly. He'd loved her, and she'd betrayed him.

He was hurting from it still.

Maybe he still loved her.

"It's okay. We all have no-go areas. But if you ever want to talk—"

"I won't."

The finality in his tone cut me off. I opened my mouth, but no more words came out.

Didn't we all have secrets? If he and I couldn't confide ours beyond the gossipy tea sharing of our first non-date in the pub, then what hope did we have of ever getting closer?

"I'll leave you to handle things there," I managed weakly instead.

Valentine started to answer but abruptly stopped. "Shite. Mia, I need to go. Fuck."

"Is everything okay?" I clutched the phone.

But he'd disconnected as fast as he'd called.

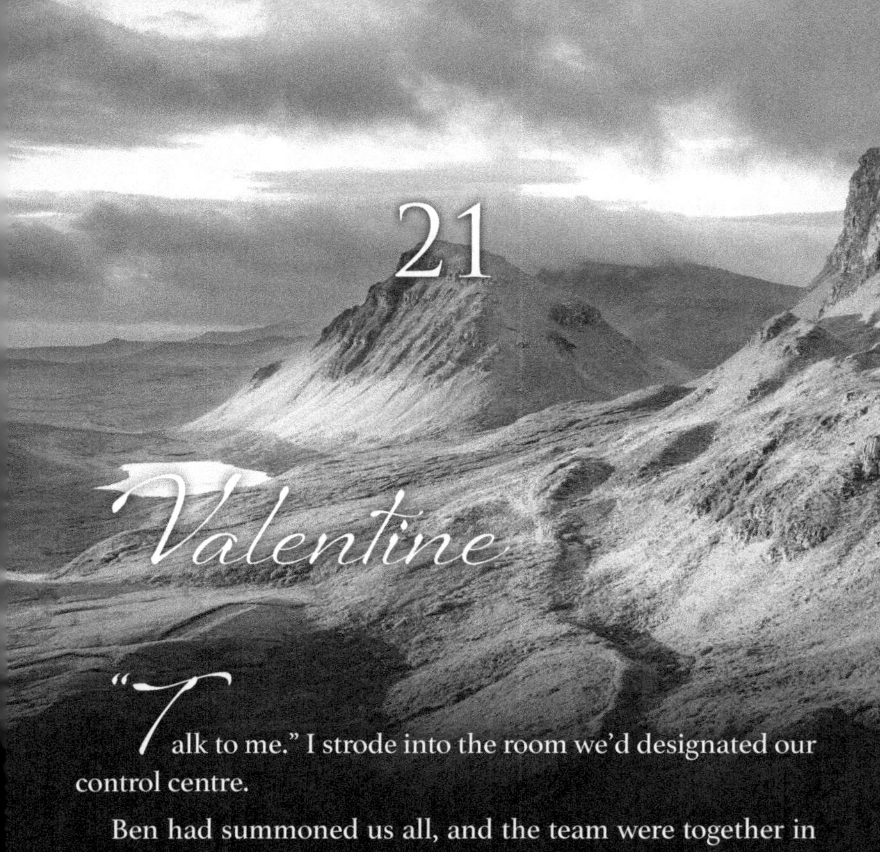

21

Valentine

"Talk to me." I strode into the room we'd designated our control centre.

Ben had summoned us all, and the team were together in the dark, pulled from our locations at various windows around the hotel while Leo and his family were huddled in a bed in another room, trying to keep the kids calm.

My brother lifted his chin to Raphael. "Tell everyone what ye just told me."

Our new recruit held up his phone. "I've been monitoring social media. An hour and a half ago, a post appeared that gave Leo's hotel address in the city."

"The original source," I snarled. "Odds on it was the record company."

He jerked his head in agreement. "It's a throwaway account, but the tagging of the tour, the city, and key people made sure the post was picked up fast. I reported it, but the damage is done, and it gets worse. In the past twenty minutes, the amount of people sharing pictures and live footage from the crowd has spiked. It's going viral."

"Turning into a riot," Jackson said in a deadly low tone.

I took a breath, my adrenaline rising with the new threat. "Ye think? I just saw three uniformed police officers escorting a group away."

Jackson folded his arms. "From my position at the other end of the building, I just watched a flood of people arrive and someone try to kick in the door of the place next to the Excelsior. They're already in the hotel itself."

"What kind of people are the new arrivals?" I asked. The teenager with his parents I'd seen when I was down in the alley talking to the guard probably wasn't the type of fan turning up now.

"Men in their twenties or older."

I understood his riot comment now. Fuck.

Any kind of public disturbance, be it a protest or another kind of gathering, attracted dodgy types, there for the kind of opportunities that could be had under the hubbub. Such as breaking and entering. Or brawling for fun.

Ben listened to us in turn, his gaze touching on each. "That police action is too little, too late. The situation is escalating more rapidly than predicted, and those incomers don't sound like fans of Leo's. More likely they're here for mischief. Let's revisit our options."

Jackson's scowl darkened. "This is no longer a safe house. The surrounding buildings are vulnerable, and we're sitting ducks. We can run, but we might be chased."

Raphael nodded, no fear in the younger man's countenance, only bristling determination and a touch of anger.

I felt it, too. It rippled across all of us.

"We need to leave while it's still possible," Raphael said. "We can ignore police advice because that's been bullshit, but the safest route is going to be by air."

Ben huffed. "The local chief of police is still maintaining that we stay put. They've got a major football match on that kicks out soon, and their forces are concentrated there."

My sense of concern deepened. A flood of sports fans wasn't going to help matters any.

"Walk through the helicopter option," my brother asked Raphael.

"We can do it, just not from here. The problem is that restricted air space. No local pilot will risk losing their licence. The rules are a lot stricter here than in the UK."

"Where's the nearest ye can legally get someone to touch down?" I asked.

His reply was instant, the man having done his homework. "There's a helipad about a thirty-minute drive away across the city."

"Which means getting to the cars which are still on standby," Ben concluded. "Jackson, check our exit. If we can get out safely and make it to the square, we'll have the cars waiting. Raphael, how long until we can have a helicopter in position?"

Our pilot was already calling up something on his phone. "Thirty minutes is plenty. I've had a contact lined up. We'll need a touchdown location and to have something waiting at the other end."

"What about the tour buses?" I asked. "How safe are they going to be if we're pursued?"

Ben twisted his lips, his gaze holding on me for a second while he reached a conclusion. "From experience, mob mentality dies the minute the horde is disbanded. People get their heads back. This isn't paparazzi, so if we can get our family to a new location by air, I'd consider that a solid plan.

We don't need to be on the road for any longer than it takes to get to the helicopter, and the bird can take us to a safe house. Our family with one or two of us, however many we can get in the cabin. The rest will need to continue in the cars. Val, go through our list of secure hotels and find one with a helipad up to an hour outside the city. Make sure they have a private suite ready, then rooms for the rest of us when we arrive."

I didn't even need to ask whether Leo would still play the Barcelona gig tomorrow. Even if he could prove his record company had shafted him, cancelling would be out of the question.

The most important thing was getting his family out of here.

Jackson left the room, Raphael got on the phone, and I began my search.

In ten minutes, our plan clicked into place with cars waiting to whisk us across town, the helicopter on its way, and the hotel secured. As a team, we'd worked seamlessly.

That didn't diminish the immediate danger. Leaving the rooms we were in meant entering an alley then crossing a busy square. We couldn't avoid going on foot.

Ben and Gordain briefed the family. Leo and Viola listened carefully, their expressions muted and the answers quiet. Rapid-fire, we consolidated the single backpacks everyone had brought from the tour buses this evening, and that Raphael had retrieved from the Excelsior while we were hiding out, and the family donned oversized hoodies, hoods up but with no other form of disguise.

Finn sought me out. His hand curled into mine. "I'm scared."

"All ye need to do is stick by my side until we reach the cars. I've got ye."

"And my da?"

"Nothing will happen to him. I swear it."

"Okay," he whispered.

At least he was convinced. Now I just had to deliver on that promise.

Down the darkened stairs, we travelled in single file, exiting swiftly through the portico with its door to the street opposite the Excelsior and into the corridor that led in the other direction—the back route I'd already checked out. The sounds of the crowd outside chased us, though with few windows, we were invisible to prying eyes. At the far exit, a single, windowless door gave way to a small courtyard with a line of high smelling bins, presumably used by one of the surrounding restaurants.

For a beat, Ben waited, then waved us on.

I emerged into the night air, Finn tucked in at my side, the rest of the crew marking their protected family member, Viola concealing her bairn beneath her hoodie.

There were no people out here, thank fuck, but at the end of the high-sided and narrow backstreet ahead, people milled about under streetlights. Beyond that, cars moved along the busy city road.

The square where our transport was waiting.

It seemed impossible that the danger was behind us, and we proceeded with caution, moving swiftly along the medieval street. At best, we had two or three doorways to step into if trouble materialised, but with two hundred yards to go, the sense of urgency to get to our refuge built.

Sweat trickled down my spine. Every sense was heightened, my body primed to fight. This was a risk we took as bodyguards. Another good reason for me not to have anyone at home worried about me.

Momentarily, my mind fixed on Mia.

She'd worried. She'd wanted to know everything. Asked questions like I mattered to her. It was a bad idea to allow that, even if we were friends. I hated the thought of her losing sleep over me.

At the junction of our dark backstreet and the bright, paved square ahead, a large group of people emerged. Ben held up a hand. We all froze. Shrank against the wall.

The all-male group jostled each other, laughing. One carried a long item in his hand. A stick or maybe a crowbar. In the shadows, it was hard to make out.

I prayed the same applied in reverse.

The men didn't stop, set on a path that led them further down the square, not in our direction. But at the last second, one of the guys swung his gaze our way. The pointy-faced, short dude squinted, lingering for a moment, his gaze travelling down the length of our column. But just as I was ready to do something, somehow try to scare him off, he gave it up and continued after his friends.

I released a breath. Ben got us moving again. I didn't like it, though. The little rat-faced arsehole had taken a good look.

Close to the end of the street, Gordain and Ben walked ahead and stepped out, standing casually together while the rest of us waited. The open square was our last hurdle. Our two cars were parked illegally across the way, and all we had to do now was reach them.

After a couple more people crossed our path, Ben finally gave the signal, and we shifted formation to take defensive positions around Leo and Viola, Finn glued to me. As a unit, we left the safety of the backstreet, joining Gordain and Ben who made up the front of our party, Jackson and Raphael forming the left and right flanks, and me at the rear.

There was nothing left to do but swiftly march across the expanse, not slowing or stopping for anyone.

We were a third of the way over before the illusion of safety was shattered.

"Hey," a man shouted.

I performed a defensive glance around us. Oh fuck.

Rat-faced guy hadn't left. Instead, he'd waited. At his shout, his friends paused. Turned back.

"Leo Banks," he yelled, a smirk forming on his fuck-ugly face.

Our aim of not attracting attention was up. The tension hanging over our party peaked, and Viola uttered a small sound of fear.

"Banks!" another voice followed.

Then my brother gave a single order I was waiting for. "Run."

I picked up Finn, sprinting with the boy clutched to me and keeping right behind his parents. With Viola carrying the baby, our party concentrated on matching her pace, the gap between us and the cars narrowing.

Ahead, the drivers climbed out and opened the back doors.

The gang of men pursued us, footsteps on stone telling me how close.

Shouts went up. More people swivelled to watch, gasps telling us they'd realised what was happening. It would be hard to be out in the city tonight without knowing the drama that was going on at the hotel.

Phones lifted, documenting our flight.

It was a thrill, I guessed, spotting a famous person. Maybe the gang behind us fancied their chances in stealing something they could sell. Or getting kudos for taking a swing at a rock star.

Fat fucking chance.

All I could focus on was getting the family to safety.

The last ten metres brought a chorus of yells behind us. But we were there. The cars right in front of us, engines on, ready to go. Leo guided Viola inside the first then reached for Finn, bringing his boy in close. Raphael scooted in beside them, and Gordain loaded into the front.

I went to close his door, the rest of my team readying to take the second car.

Then Finn's voice screamed out. "Val!"

His anxious face appeared in the gap between the front seats. His gaze wide, frightened, and focused behind me.

"He's got a knife. Turn around!"

Steeling myself, I slammed Gordain's door and twisted to face the danger. A slam of a hand on metal told me Ben had released the driver to leave, their engine roaring. But the danger for us was far from over.

My remaining team members came face to face with the pursuing gang. Eight strong. All staring us down.

"Back up to the car," Ben muttered.

"Ye first." I gestured for him and Jackson to go behind me and dropped into a fighter's stance, inching backwards while providing space for them to clear.

Rat-face was focused on me. At his shoulder, his equally ugly friend carried the weapon I'd noted earlier. A metal pole about a foot and a half long.

But it was the knife in Rat-face's hand that snagged my focus.

Thank fuck the family had gone. Their car had pulled out into the traffic and zipped away, the engine sound cluing me in to their movements. In no time, they'd be across the city and to the safety of the helipad where Raphael would ensure they got to the new hotel.

All we needed to do now was follow them.

"Back the fuck off," Ben yelled at the gang. Then he dropped his voice to speak to us. "Jackson, inside. Ye next, Val."

He rounded me to put his hand to my chest, driving me back.

Two things happened in quick succession.

The rat-faced man lurched forward, blade flashing and aimed at my brother.

I shoved Ben out of the line of fire, right as the blade slashed down. Rat-face stumbled as he missed.

His knife embedded in my thigh. He yanked it free and fell back.

Instantly, I knew something was badly wrong. I'd been injured before, and usually there was no pain until the adrenaline wore off. This was different. A dull ache was followed by a rush of blood blooming from the slice through my jeans and flesh.

Far too quickly, the stain spread.

My heart pounded.

Rage swallowed me whole.

He'd aimed at my brother, the bastard.

A couple of months ago, Jackson had neutralised a man wielding a blade, but that was a solo attacker. This fucker had brought his gang. I was going to take every one of them down.

But my attacker chucked his knife and ran, his friends sprinting away with him.

Ben swore a blue streak and tugged me into the back seat of the car, Jackson manhandling me between them.

"Put pressure on the wound. We need a tourniquet," Jackson ordered.

"Hospital, now," Ben ordered the driver.

It took me several seconds to catch up, my brain dangerously slow. I'd been stabbed. Somewhere vital. And my life force was ebbing away.

22

Mia

I paced my room, a check on the girls showing me they slept. I couldn't do the same. After Valentine hung up, my heart rate hadn't slowed. All manner of dangerous situations plagued my thoughts. Anything could've happened.

But Valentine wasn't mine to worry about.

I knew that. He'd told me so.

He still had feelings for his ex, and I had to respect that he wasn't going to magically lose those and change his mind about me. I had to get over my minor obsession with the man and continue with my own life.

Miserable, I lay in my bed and opened the romance app I'd made my profile in. I'd used yet another fake name than the one I was running with at work and the open-blouse photo Valentine suggested.

1,182 potential matches, the app told me.

God. That had moved quickly.

I couldn't bring myself to look at any of the profiles whose owners had liked mine. Nor could I rest for fear of hearing about Valentine. A battle raged inside me. At last, I put my phone onto Do Not Disturb and forced my eyes closed.

It was a long time until I dropped off.

The next morning, I took off my phone's restrictions as Cameron collected the girls to take them to school.

I waved them off, reading the first of the messages.

Daisy: Sorry if this wakes you. I heard from Ben that Valentine got hurt last night. He's in hospital.

My heart stopped. I gaped, jumping to the next text.

Daisy: He's in surgery now. I'll text back when I hear more.

No further message had arrived. With shaking fingers, I dialled her.

"I had my notifications off. I didn't feel like I had the right to worry as much as I was," I babbled.

"He's in recovery," Daisy answered.

I sank to the couch. Took a shuddering breath, fear swallowing me. "God. Was he badly hurt?"

"I think so." Her voice was thick with concern.

"Tell me everything that happened."

Daisy recounted how the bodyguard team had led Leo and his family to safety but encountered a gang on the way. One of the members then stabbed Valentine in the thigh, slicing into an artery.

"He lost a lot of blood, but they saved him," she finished. "Ben's going to call me when Valentine's awake. Ben had to leave the hospital because he needs to be with Leo when he goes to tackle his record company, then there's a gig this evening. Ben will see his brother once they're clear of that. Apparently Raphael got permission to land a helicopter at the hospital so they can come and go easily."

My fingers shook. "Can you please keep me posted if you hear anything more?"

She agreed.

For the rest of the day, I startled at every message.

Finally, by mid-evening, Daisy heard from Ben and called to fill me in.

"Valentine rang Ben himself. He's furious at being stuck in a hospital bed and hating the painkillers he's on. He argued with the Spanish police when they came to interview him, passing out mid-sentence. He only cheered up when Finn demanded Gordain take him to see him instead of going to the gig. He's still there now getting fussed over by the nurses."

I gave a choked laugh. "Valentine or Finn?"

"Both, I imagine. Ella flew out earlier to join them all. She was so scared all night. Leo wanted to cancel the dates, but he's been persuaded otherwise, and they're revising all the plans so they have their own hotel booked by Gordain and with only Leo flying in and out of the venue, the family staying behind. It has to go on, just without Valentine."

No wonder he was grouchy. "Will he come home?"

"I think so." She hesitated. "He might need a friend if he does. I don't know how he's going to handle leaving the crew."

I didn't know either. Valentine struck me as a loyal team player through and through.

The following afternoon, Daisy sent the update I was waiting for.

Daisy: Raphael's flying him home. I'm not sure when.

Mia: Tell me when you find out?

An hour passed. Then another.

Daisy: Apparently he's here! I had no idea. Raphael took him to Braithar. I tried calling him, but no answer. I'm going to go check on him, unless...

Mia: I'll go. On my way now.

In a minute, I was finishing up work and flying out the door. Speeding, I drove to the castle through the dark afternoon. There was no answer at the huge front door, so I walked to the back. There was also no reply at the exit door, but it opened under my hand. My pulse skipped along.

"Hello?" I called. At the tiny apartment he'd been sleeping in, I tried the handle. "It's just Mia. Sorry if you're naked."

It gave, and I stepped inside. The curtains were open and the light off, but that didn't stop me seeing the large figure on the double bed.

Valentine. Breathing, alive, and rolling over to greet me. A wave of emotion had me pressing my fingers to my lips, stifling a sob.

He blinked owlishly and struggled to sit up, his features contorting in pain. "Christ, woman. What time is it? It just seems like five minutes ago Raphael brought me in. I meant to call ye, but fuck knows where my phone is."

Composing myself, I crossed the room. "After two. I only just heard you were back."

"I've no idea how long for. The meds are messing with my head. I slept most of the flight."

"Is no one else here?"

"The housekeeper was earlier, I think. Or I may have imagined her."

"Are you in pain?"

"Naw. Can't feel a thing. Come here."

Taking care not to jostle him, I sat on the bed. Valentine twisted to face me, the quilt sliding down his bare torso. A heart monitor sticker was still on his chest, and small bruises marked his inner arms, but those were the only indications of his hospital stay. Aside from his loopy state.

He eased an arm around me and gave me a heavy hug, a blissed-out sigh leaving his lips. I gently returned his friendly embrace, and another sob shook me. It took a moment to subside.

"I heard what happened from Daisy. That must've been so terrifying."

Valentine closed his eyes, holding on. "It pissed me off. I'm out of action. All because some fucking arsewipe decided to take me on."

"He stabbed you." My voice trembled.

"Aye. Nicked something so I nearly bled out. My brother and Jackson saved my life before the docs had a second go at it."

I went quiet. He did, too. The whole thing could've been so much worse. Valentine could've died.

And in that second, I gave up.

Gave up pretending Valentine wasn't more to me than a friend. That I hadn't been developing something deeper for him than I'd ever felt for anyone before. It was a hopeless endeavour because he was never going to reciprocate my feelings, a painful reality I'd have to swallow, but denying myself wasn't possible anymore.

I cared about him. A lot. It caught up with me in a dizzying rush.

"I'm so, so happy to see you," I whispered.

"Holding on to ye is the first time I've felt grounded in days, sweetheart."

"Hello? Valentine Graham? It's Heather from Nurses at Home," a woman's voice called. A knock at the back door chased her words.

I eased off the bed. "In here."

A nurse bustled into the room. She squinted at Valentine and then smiled at me. "Ah, grand. My instructions stated that this fellow would probably be on his own because he refused to stay in hospital or have an attendant. Not ideal for the first week or two of his recovery. Who are ye?"

"Mia," I said.

"Excellent. Mia, will ye be taking care of Valentine?"

"Of course I will," I promised, my heart swelling all the more.

But a glance back showed me he'd once again fallen asleep.

An hour later, after gently waking Valentine to do observations, meds, and wound care, giving me the horrifying sight of the slash injury in his thigh, the nurse had gone and I needed to collect my daughter.

"We'll come back with food for you," I promised.

Valentine had submitted to the treatment but without his trademark grin. He faked one now for me, but exhaustion sank him down.

At the school gates, an excited Tobi hugged me.

"We have a special mission this evening," I told her. "Valentine got hurt at work so he's in need of a little looking after. We're going to make him soup then go see him. Is that okay?"

Her little rosebud mouth formed an 'O'. "Can I make him a card?"

"I think he'd like that very much."

We drove out to the supermarket then home to make a chicken and vegetable soup that would be easy on his stomach but also rich in protein and nutrients. Then Tobi and I bundled back into the car and drove to Braithar.

In his room, Valentine had pulled on a shirt but was otherwise in the same position. A more ready smile appeared. "My two favourite lasses."

Tobi skipped over, her piece of paper outthrust. "I made this for you."

"What is it, Tobster?" He took the card. "Aw, is that me? What am I doing?"

"Fighting."

He lifted his gaze at me, one dark eyebrow quirked. "Is that so?"

"Mama said you were hurt protecting Finn's family. Were there guns? Did you hit people?"

He choked on a laugh. "Something like that."

Her eyes brightened. "Whoa."

I flapped a hand at her, searching for something to put Valentine's soup bowl on. "Don't go asking for details, it isn't polite. Valentine, I'm just going to pop to the kitchen to find a tray and a spoon. I'll be right back."

I trotted down the hall to Braithar's kitchen, easily finding what I was searching for. It was a little eerie with the echoing place being empty, and I quick-stepped my way back to the tiny apartment.

Tobi was now perched at the end of the bed, grinning from ear to ear. "... then I trod on her foot and yelled at her to stop."

Valentine nodded in earnest. "Smart girl. My brother once told me a good way to handle bullies is to yell the crime at them along with their name and the fact they're obsessed with ye. It embarrasses them. Try that out."

Tobi considered him then inflated her lungs. "Chelle, you're obsessed. Stop standing on my shoes," she screeched.

Valentine applauded. "Perfect."

But his skin was paler now. I set down the tray and took up his hand. It was clammy.

"You're due to take more painkillers," I told him.

"Eh. Later. I willnae be able to eat whatever ye brought me if I neck those now. Food first."

His fingers squeezed mine. I made the mistake of looking into his eyes.

My pulse skipped a beat, and my stomach flipped. Goddammit.

I had to drag my attention away to let him eat.

With Tobi now activated in full bully-repelling mode, something I hadn't known was a problem until now, I kept our visit short. There was a lot more to say. I didn't want to leave him. Instead, I focused on the practical.

"Did you find your phone?" I asked.

He pulled it from under his pillow and waggled it. "I have someone coming to check on me later this evening."

"Can I come back in the morning?"

"You'd better. And Mia? Thank ye."

I didn't need to tell him I'd do that and so much more.

23

Valentine

Pain meds fucked with my sense of time. The shite I'd been prescribed by the hospital knocked me out almost from the minute Mia and Tobi left until Mia's return the next morning. I had six missed calls and dozens of group chat messages from my boys, but I ignored them all in favour of my favourite lass.

She breezed into the room, opened a window, then leaned over my bed to take my temperature.

"You'd be hot as fuck in a nurse's outfit."

Mia pursed her lips in amusement, bending to collect another covered Tupperware bowl from a bag. She found my tray from where I'd set it down by the bed and placed it beside me, uncovering a creamy-looking porridge from the tub, complete with a spoon and a flask of something.

Forcing myself, I took a mouthful of the food.

"I'll see if I can get myself one. How did you sleep?"

"No idea. I was unconscious."

She gave a laugh. "And now? Any pain?"

So long as I didn't move. "Nope. I could use a wash, though, once I've eaten."

She narrowed her eyes. "For real or because you want a bed bath?"

"Both?" I relented with a sigh. Breakfast smelled good, but my stomach roiled at the thought of food. "They rinsed the blood off me in hospital, but I haven't had a proper shower in days. I probably stink."

A quick glance at my groin area told me Mia was picturing my injury, much as I wished it was for other reasons.

"You don't smell. I'm not sure you should get your wound wet. Maybe we'll ask Heather the nurse when she comes by later."

"She's coming back?"

Mia's scrutiny of me intensified. "Daily. Don't you remember her saying?"

I shrugged.

"Okay, then how are you feeling? You didn't answer the question about pain."

"Not complaining," I muttered.

Having Mia here was awesome. Having her worry about me didn't feel so great. She had a day of work ahead of her and a bairn to care for. I really wanted her to see me as the fit and healthy version of myself. Not a man who hadn't moved from his pit in a day, apart from to hobble to the bathroom.

I was no one's burden. I didn't want her to see me that way.

She sighed. "I'll try to finish early so I can be here when Heather comes, but I need to go to work now. Will you be okay until then?"

"Seriously, don't stress about me," I replied.

"I can't help that and I'm not even going to try." She gave me one last glance and backed out of the door.

"I appreciate ye," I called after her.

Then I stared down my food. The bite I'd taken in front of Mia had been driven by sheer hunger, but the moment I tried to swallow, my stomach rebelled. For fuck's sake.

Like last night, I couldn't eat a thing.

My phone dinged with an alarm Raphael had set for me before he left—a reminder of the meds I needed to take which were in packets on my bedside table. I dismissed the notification and flipped off the pills that were curdling my gut. If I couldn't eat, I'd never recover. I wasn't sick, only injured. Meds were working against me, and I could do without them.

A couple of hours later, I woke from another doze.

And a shitty dream. In it, I'd still been with Kelly. I'd arrived at the house we'd shared with a bag on my back, presumably coming home from deployment, but the curtains had been drawn. Shadows moved behind them, noises filtering through the open windows. Two voices I knew well. My happiness at coming home had been replaced with deep sickness.

Dream-me hadn't wanted to see, even though I knew I had to bring an end to what she was doing. It meant witnessing it. Giving visuals I'd never lose.

Thank fuck the alarm had pulled me out of the nightmare.

I flexed my limbs and stretched my spine. My leg ached with a dull throb, but I could handle that if it gave me my appetite back. I took up my phone and scanned my messages. Each of the crew had asked how I was doing, and Ben had sent an update from Daisy, which presumably came from her talking to Mia. I wrote back.

Valentine: None of you arseholes better be buddying up to Finn while I'm out of action. That's my boy.

Almost instantly, two people were typing.

Jackson: How about that, you're not dead.

After the shit I gave him when he'd disarmed the knife-wielding maniac, I expected much more.

Raphael: Did you take your antibiotics this morning?

Valentine: No, Ma.

Ben: Is that a joke? Daisy will make you.

Valentine: She can try.

Ben: Or I can ask her to ask Mia.

Him saying her name gave me a strange feeling. Of the degrees of separation between us. Where she was only connected to me by my brother's girlfriend. I didn't like it.

I squinted at the time, double-taking.

It hadn't just been an hour or two I'd slept but all the morning and half the afternoon, too. Mia would be back soon. Damn. I'd wanted to be a little better presented.

Tossing my phone, I shoved the tray aside and threw back the covers, grimacing at the warm stink that rose around me. God, I really did reek. A shower was even more in desperate need than ever. I sucked in a breath and swung my legs across the bed.

The knife wound pulsed with an evil, dull pain that sank to my bone. I shuddered, pressing my fingers around the hurt until it eased, then I forced myself to stand. My head swam, but no wonder, considering the length of time I'd been horizontal. Still fucking doing this. Staggering, I limped to the wall, using it to keep me upright on my way into the bathroom.

Light on. Shower on. Fucking pain.

I tugged off my t-shirt and boxers without passing out, and opened the shower door. At best, I had thirty minutes to handle this shite.

Steam rose. I stepped inside.

The water beat down on me and soaked my bandage. My skin stung, the heat doing something strange to my brain. I squeezed liquid soap onto a flannel and scrubbed myself down.

My head rushed. It overwhelmed me until all of a sudden, I couldn't breathe. I sank to the shower tray, dropped my face to my hands, and blackness swallowed me whole.

24

Mia

Heather's car was already parked outside Castle Braithar, the nurse at the open door. It was a little after three, but I didn't have the school run today. Tobi was going home with Avery and her family so I could spend longer taking care of Valentine.

"Hey, Heather," I called.

She lifted her head, her expression fraught. It pulled me up short.

"What's wrong?" I climbed out of my car.

"Mr Graham collapsed in the shower. I'm calling an ambulance."

Collapsed. Ambulance.

My heart stopped.

At a run, I took off into the castle and to his room. The blankets were tossed aside, and I continued into the bathroom, fear driving me on.

Valentine sat on the bottom of the shower stall, naked,

aside from a towel draped over his waist, and his long hair wet and straggly though the water was off, presumably Heather's doing. But his eyes were open. His gaze clung to me.

"I know I'm an idiot," he muttered.

I dropped down beside him, kneeling on the bath mat. "Are you hurt?"

"Naw. Can ye tell the nurse I dinnae need an ambulance?"

"I'm not telling her any such thing. You collapsed."

"Aye, because I didn't pace myself."

"Or take his medication," Heather said from behind me. "An ambulance is on its way."

"I'm not going to hospital again," he grouched.

"Let the medical professionals be the judge of that," she ordered.

"If ye ladies step back, I'll get myself up."

He put his palms down to brace himself, but Heather protested.

"Wait for the ambulance, will ye? I can't support your weight if ye go down again."

Valentine eyed her. "I was in the army. I can get myself back to bed. Would've already if my brain hadn't crapped out."

Slowly, he pushed to his feet, so much bigger than Heather and me. I hustled to move in on him, earning a grateful half-smile.

Heather stepped back, then angled to get on his other side. His towel fell, but for once, Valentine didn't make a quip. From his twisted lips and a rapid inhale, it was obvious he was in pain and suffering from his injury.

In the bedroom, he limped to the bed and dropped heavily at the end. He'd paled all the more.

"There. Managed that without expiring," he grumbled.

The nurse popped her hands onto her hips. "Lucky for you. That army comment explains everything. Military men make the worst patients. Your girlfriend here will agree with me."

"We're just friends," I said automatically.

Valentine said nothing.

Turning around to keep busy, I fetched clean towels and brought them back to him. Valentine gave quiet thanks, his fingers taking a quick squeeze of mine.

"I'm going to do some observations, but I'm also going to need to change that dressing ye soaked." Heather took up her medical bag.

"Cancel the ambulance?" Valentine suggested.

"We might need it yet. Ye could have a concussion," she replied.

"I didnae hit my head. Just slid to the floor."

While the nurse took out various pieces of equipment then moved to check Valentine's bag full of medications, I sat beside him, keeping his hand in mine. He shivered, and I tugged the duvet around him then took a towel to his long hair, lightly scrubbing the worst of the water from the lengths.

"Did you really not take your meds?" I said softly.

Valentine drifted his thumb over mine, his skin hot. "I couldnae eat on it. Ye went to such trouble to bring me food."

"Antibiotics start working in a matter of hours, but if ye stop them, infection can take over again just as fast," Heather stated, her back to us. "That's why it's important to take the full course. If ye ask me—"

Interrupted by my squeak of shock, she didn't get a chance to finish her sentence. Valentine's eyes rolled, and he dropped back on the mattress.

"Val?" I leaned over him and cupped his face. "Valentine,

wake up."

He didn't move.

I tore my gaze to Heather. "What's wrong with him?"

She hurried to his other side. Took his pulse.

"We're going to need that ambulance to get here fast."

25

Valentine

My blood rushed cold. Some fucker kept bumping my bed, rattling me. Then a needle stuck my hand.

For fuck's sake. I was in hospital.

My brain kept spinning, so my eyes stayed closed, but machine beeps and the chatter of medics told me I was right.

Some time passed. The place was an ice cavern, the windows open and a draught freezing me to the bones.

Kelly was by my bedside, her fair hair longer than I remembered, but dull, nothing like Mia's shiny gold. Why the fuck was my ex here? Last person I wanted to see. Then I was outside her house and opening the door. Sex noises played out, coming from the bedroom down the corridor ahead of me. No, they were coming from the lounge. Everywhere. If I took another step, I'd see her. And him. My brother. I'd see them together.

"Did his fever break yet?" a worried voice asked.

Mia was here. Warmth spread through my frozen body.

Someone answered her, but I checked out, surrendering to another wave of chills and whatever was messing with me.

Dream-me closed the door to Kelly's house and took a step back.

The next time I surfaced, it was to pain. Someone prodding at my knife wound.

"Getthefuckoff," I slurred.

The weight removed, though the person kept up their work. Cleaning, I guessed.

I faded out once more.

It felt like a single blink to me, but it was dark outside my hospital room when I managed to open my eyes. In a wide blue chair, Mia tapped at her phone, a hospital pillow propping up her head.

"Little spy," I said. My voice came out weak. I tried again. "Yo, Mia."

She jerked her head up. Then the lass flew from the chair to my side. "You're awake."

"How long was I out?"

"You fell unconscious yesterday."

I stared. "I lost a whole day?"

"And then some." She checked the clock on the wall. "It's eight PM. I was just messaging Daisy with an update."

Well, fuck. I shut my mouth.

Mia continued. "Your stab wound got infected, and you picked up a fever. They gave you some heavy-duty antibiotics and you responded well to them. Your body needed rest, according to the doc I spoke to this morning."

"Ye drove all the way here to see me?"

"Twice."

A strange feeling tightened in my chest. I'd felt it before with her. It was either a big dose of gratitude or I was having a heart attack.

"Thank ye," I managed. "Where's Tobi?"

"With Elise and Cameron. Visiting hours are almost over, so I'll have to leave, then I'll go pick her up and get her home."

I exhaled, struggling upright. "Take me with ye."

"No chance. You're staying until they release you." Mia reached for my hand.

"Don't leave me here," I mumbled.

"I have to. You didn't take care of yourself which is why you're back in a hospital bed." Her serious gaze held mine hostage. "But, I have an idea for when they let you go."

"Which is?"

Someone tapped on the door. Mia glanced over and nodded.

"I have to go. I'll come back tomorrow and tell you then."

The last thing I wanted was for her to walk out that door and leave me alone, but there was no choice. Plus I felt fucking awful, so there was no way I could go with her.

I let her leave with a hug and a promise that she'd come back.

The same nightmare haunted me all fucking night. The door. The sounds. The awareness.

True to her word, Mia returned the following afternoon.

She talked to my doc, a stern older woman who gave me the facts of how I'd risked my life for no good reason, then sat with me while I choked down dinner.

"If you're feeling better tomorrow, they'll probably let you go."

"What? The doc told me another couple of days in prison

at least."

She chewed her lip. "I know how much you hate it in here. I had an idea and I asked her and she agreed." Mia's pretty eyes focused on me. "What if you come home with me?"

I set down my fork. She continued quickly.

"I spoke to Tobi, and she's happy to have you stay at ours. You can have my bed, and I'll sleep on Tobi's floor or on the sofa. Whatever. That way, you'll have someone watching over you properly so you don't relapse again. The hospital will release you earlier that way."

"I could kiss ye."

Mia flushed a gorgeous pink. "Better not. I just want to be a good friend. It'll also stop your brother from spiralling and Leo from cancelling the tour so they can come back and see you. This way solves all the problems."

I just stared at her, too many thoughts clamouring for attention. Elation, relief, something heavier, too.

Mia stood with a glance at the clock. "I need to go now, but I'll be back in the morning. It's Sunday, so I'm not working. Let me know then."

As if I could say no.

The following morning, Mia texted before setting out. I'd got the go-ahead from the doc so was ready when she arrived, a very excited Tobi beside her.

With help from a hospital porter, I got to Mia's car, and then we were speeding south into the Cairngorms once more.

Freedom, I wanted to yell Braveheart-style.

Tobi kept up her chatter, twisting around in the front passenger seat to address me in my sprawl across the back. She wanted to know all about my time in the army, the training, the places I'd been, mostly the fights. Mia smiled at her daughter's enthusiasm, sliding me the occasional look.

I couldn't stop my fucking grin.

At the cottage, a couple of people milled about outside the empty place next door.

"What's going on there?" I asked.

"Ben can tell you next time you call him," Mia replied mysteriously.

One of the people peeled away and came to the car. Ally, one of Gordain's brothers who lived on the estate in a house down by the loch, opened my door. "Let me give ye a hand."

I accepted the offer and drew myself up with all my weight on my good leg. I wanted to question him on the next-door cottage, but my head rushed, and I had to focus on limping inside. Ally guided me directly to Mia's bedroom, and I dropped onto her mattress, the solid bed welcome after days in a hospital one.

Mia bustled me under the covers and, as had become my habit, I slept.

The next two days passed in a pattern of sleep, meds, and tender loving care from Mia. The nightmares didn't stop, but my waking time made up for them. Tobi brought me pictures which decorated the bedside table, and by Tuesday, when she was at school, I was feeling a hundred times stronger.

With Mia out for the day at work, I talked to my brother briefly on the phone, finding out that he'd asked for help in fixing up the cottage next door for my sake. I had no intention of moving in but thanked him for taking the work off my hands, then the jackass tried to thank *me* for getting between him and the blade, so I hung up on his arse.

Chatting with my boys on text made me grin.

Jackson: What do you get if you cross Valentine and a gangster he doesn't like the look of? A bodyscarred.

Raphael: Valentine's got a promotion. He's gone undercover.

(Under the bedcovers, geddit?)

Jackson: Dude, you didn't need the explanation.

Raphael: I've spent too long hanging out with you and your pilot jokes. By the way, Valentine, this will make you laugh. The operations manager at the venue we're in today is named Duke Clithero.

I burst out in a chuckle.

Valentine: He's a Clit Hero?

Raphael: EXACTLY. The duke of clit heroes.

Jackson: On funny names, Raph and I had a professor at uni named Richard Tate.

It took me a second to get what he meant.

Valentine: Was he a dick-tat-or?

Raphael: He was the worst, and I couldn't keep a straight face whenever one of his colleagues called him Dick.

Valentine: I used to know a Holden Hiscock.

Jackson: And did he hold his cock often?

Valentine: Not as much as his wife, Anita Dick.

I rolled back, cracking up while a series of laughing emojis came from my boys. It was nice to see Raphael happy after his confession in the darkened tour bus, and Jackson, too, after he endured all manner of drama recently. Then a censoring message landed, cooling our fun.

Ben: Sorry to break this up, but we need to mobilise. Val, take it steady. We need you healed for when we get back. Rest up, aye?

I chucked my phone and slumped on the cushions. Rest up? I was bored out of my mind.

At lunchtime, Mia returned.

This time, I waited on the sofa.

Setting down her bag and hanging up her coat, she took me

in with wide eyes. "Someone's feeling better."

"Much."

"Been up to anything this morning?"

"Called my folks. Ma is desperate to know who ye are, but I put her off."

"I don't mind talking to your mother." Mia crossed the room and put the back of her hand to my forehead. "Nice and cool. Hungry?"

I was, but for more than food. The lass had on a blue tabard with the logo of Daisy's business on it. It stretched over her bouncy chest and fastened at the sides.

All of a sudden, I was picturing her naked and wearing just that.

My dick stirred. Any thoughts of that nature had been suspended while I'd been out of it, but things had taken a turn for the better.

"Why are you looking at me that way?" Mia asked, amused.

"Just thinking how business must be booming if you're walking around like that."

"Like what?"

"Sexy cleaner. Must be a market for it."

She gave a peal of laughter. "Actually, I do know of a topless cleaning firm."

My dick thickened, and my mouth hung open, tongue out like a cartoon dog. "I would pay any money to see that."

"I am not showing you their pictures."

I choked on a laugh. "No, sweetheart. To have ye clean topless for me. Seriously. Take my credit card." I banged an imaginary card on my hand.

Mia's amusement simmered, and her gaze turned speculative. "You're definitely getting back to health if that's on your mind."

"Pretty sure until I see it, it's the only thing that's going to be in my head. Ye don't even have to do any cleaning. Just sit topless in the middle of the room and I'll do the work around ye."

"Oh yeah? I'm not sure much cleaning would get done."

"Neither am I. That would just be the start of it." Heat played out in my voice, my body warming.

Mia's pupils dilated. Fuck, yeah. She was into it, too.

But then she took a breath and rose, dusting her hands together. "Let's keep your blood pressure from exploding, yes? Now, food."

Mia busied herself in the kitchen, and I dropped my head back on the couch, loving the mental image she'd given me and plotting ways to make it a reality.

In the early evening, she brought Tobi home from her school club. I'd taken a shower—carefully—and dressed in clean clothes. I was finger-combing out my hair when they walked in the door, bags in hand, smiles for me, Tobi bursting out with a story about her day.

A new and strange sense filled me. Something poignant. This must be what it was like to have a family.

It was all I'd wanted, once. A wife and bairns. More than one for sure. My work dedicated to giving them a comfortable life. Coming home to a warm house with the sounds of kids playing.

If I'd once wanted it, that had long gone. My nightmare kept reminding me.

It was a crying fucking shame that I'd picked the wrong person to break my heart over. That still didn't help me understand what the hell she wanted with me now.

26

Mia

Laughter came from the living room, and I grinned over the dinner plates I was washing up. Valentine had offered, but I'd told him to park his butt and rest, so he and Tobi were watching cartoons.

When I finished, I peeked out of the kitchen. On the rug in the cosy space, Valentine read something on his phone while reclining against the sofa with his long legs outstretched. Tobi sat behind him, a length of his black hair in her hands.

She tugged on it. "Stay still or it won't go right."

"Sorry," he replied. "Listen to what Jackson said Finn did today. They're in Italy, and Ben, Jackson, and Finn helicoptered into an amusement park and spent a couple of hours going on the rides there." He muttered something to himself about fun thieves, shaking his head.

"I said still," my daughter chastised. With her tongue poking out, she twisted strands into a slim if slightly wonky braid.

I'd just shown her how to do that a couple of weeks back.

She completed one and held it up.

"Put your hand up to feel it," she instructed Valentine.

"Aye, very even. Do another the other side so it's like a Viking."

She snagged another length and began again. "What's a Viking?"

"Like me but hundreds of years ago and on a boat."

"You're too cute," I told them.

Valentine raised his gaze to me. "Hey, Mama."

Of all the names he used for me, that one hit me straight in the feels.

I joined them, picking up Tobi's brush to tease out more of Valentine's hair. He'd let it air dry after his shower, but the black lengths were glossy and thick.

"So unfair," I mused. "If I didn't blow-dry my hair it would turn into a rat's nest. Yours is beautiful."

Valentine gave a low sigh then slightly angled his head to give me a look. He loved his hair being played with, but that was a very different thing from Tobi messing with him to my actions.

She finished her second braid, and I reached to take the leather tie from Valentine's wrist. Then I rolled his hair into a high man bun, taking the plaits in with it.

He turned to face us. "Verdict?"

"So Viking." Tobi grinned.

A little stunned, I blinked to regain my powers of speech. Effortlessly gorgeous Valentine was here in my home, on my rug, and asking if I liked the way he looked.

It would take no effort at all to lean in and kiss him.

"Not bad," I managed.

He pursed his lips in amusement then let me off the hook. He eased back, a wince of pain telling me his movements weren't being kind to his injury. "If I haven't said, your home is lovely. I like the changes you've made." He gestured to the room and to the little touches we'd added. Artwork Tobi had brought home from school. Cushions that gave a burst of colour to the gold couch.

"I want to do more," I said.

"Like what? It's perfect."

"For one thing, get another couch so visitors have somewhere to sit."

He gave me a wolfish grin, like I'd busted him in his plan not to take up too much space. "Is the picture in the kitchen your ma? I said hello to her just in case."

My breath hitched. "Stop being so sweet, or…"

"Or what?"

Something low built in my belly, a coiling heat that warmed my blood. I switched my gaze to my daughter, but she was drooping, staring at the TV and the cartoon playing low in the background.

When I returned my attention to Valentine, he was still watching me, but his focus had slipped down my body. His eyes flared.

Then his phone dinged.

"Your meds alarm," I said with a thick voice. Then I hopped up. "I'll get them. You wait here."

I collected his antibiotics and painkillers plus a glass of water. Valentine accepted the antibiotics and swallowed them down. "Not the others. They fu— I mean I want to get off them. They're bad for my system."

"So's a night spent in pain."

"Tell ye what. If I can't sleep for hurting, I'll take them then. Besides, I want to be back on my feet tomorrow. There's all that hammering and drilling next door, and I want to check out what they're doing. Plus I have plans to use my body for other things."

That last line almost did me in.

The tone change of the evening, and of the whole few days of taking care of him shifted. The old, sexy-as-hell Valentine was coming back. I was powerless against him.

I took a shuddering inhale. "You're nowhere near healed before you go offering to help next door. You're supposed to be resting your leg." If he did too much and tore a stitch, if he did half the things going around my head, he'd be straight back to square one.

"Don't fret, sweetheart. I wised up. I know exactly how much I can and can't do."

Didn't that just give me a slew of images?

Ones that were probably a danger to him if we acted them out.

My daughter yawned, and I took the cue.

"Come on, Tobi. Let's go to bed. Valentine, you probably should, too."

He regarded me. It was barely eight PM, but if I didn't get out of his orbit, I was going to break the man in two.

"Another good night of sleep," I added.

"Fine." He heaved himself up and walked to my bedroom, his limp still there but less now.

And I spent the next couple of hours imagining just how healed he might be.

In the morning, I got a call from Daisy while finishing up my second client.

"We had a cancellation," she told me. "Your ten-thirty has moved to tomorrow, I shifted the rota to make it work."

"No problem. I'll go home for an early lunch and check on Valentine."

"How's he doing?"

"Good. He's healing. Missing work, I think."

"Ben said they'll be back on Sunday right after the last gig rather than waiting until Monday which was the original plan. Raphael will make a couple of flights. Everyone is dying to come home."

A small pang hit my heart. With his crew back, Valentine would have other things to occupy him rather than just hanging out with me and Tobi. He'd probably move back to the castle.

"I'll tell Valentine. He'll be gunning to see everyone."

"I bet. Ariel and I are beside ourselves," she continued. "I love having her stay over with me, but we both want our boys back, so we're going out of our minds."

"Want to come to mine for dinner? We can chat and catch up."

"Love to. I can answer for Ariel as well. It would also be nice to give Ben a report on his brother."

"Are they not talking still?"

"Not much. I wish they'd had the chance to be alone together on the tour and get over their differences. I'll have to work out another plan for that."

We made our goodbyes, and I finished up and drove home.

The closer I got, the greater a kind of urgency gathered inside me. So much was up in the air. My life and Tobi's, Valentine and his brother, whatever he and I were together. I'd wanted a boyfriend but had barely checked the dating app

I'd set up.

None of those things had answers, so I focused on what I knew. The need inside me. The attraction that bloomed whenever I was near the huge black-haired bodyguard. The energy that required an outlet or I was going to go crazy.

At my cottage, I parked up and went inside.

"Hello?" I tossed my things down and went to the bedroom.

Lounging on the bed, and in just his boxer shorts and a black t-shirt, Valentine put down a book he was reading. He tilted his head in enquiry, that teasing, lingering magnetism right there in his eyes. If he was surprised to see me, he didn't say. Instead, he looked...delighted.

An idea struck me. "I'm the cleaning service you ordered."

"Oh yeah?"

"I'm early. I hope that's okay."

Nerves struck me. I stripped my tabard over my head then moved to the curtains, drawing them closed. Valentine sat taller, the light in his eyes darkening and his focus locked on what I was doing.

"We're a specialised service," I continued, drifting my fingers down my body. "There are rules."

"Name them."

"No touching."

He inhaled through his nose, his lips pressed together.

"Also, no exertion from the client. You're to stay put." I peeled off my long-sleeved top. Underneath was just my bra.

My heart sped, my body alive under his avid attention.

Valentine gave a groan. "If I don't move from here, can I touch myself?"

God, I needed to see that. "That's allowed."

"Thank fuck." He palmed the bulge in his shorts.

Not stopping for nerves, I unclipped my bra and freed my breasts. Now, I was topless, only tight cropped leggings on my lower half. I didn't look at him but soaked up his grunt of pleasure at my reveal.

"Holy fuck, woman. Just...damn."

I crossed the room, pretending to examine the place for cleaning work. "You'll need to give me some direction. What's dirty around here?"

"Besides all the things I want to do to ye?"

I hid a smile. "What do you need to see me clean?"

He considered that, giving himself a slow squeeze. "Maybe straighten the duvet."

I rounded the bed and bent to fold back the duvet he'd half kicked to the bottom bedstead. I made a show of it, leaning, working the angle he had of my chest. Once I was done that side, I slowly walked to the other, letting him lift his feet so I could finish the job.

"Anything else need attention?" My voice came out breathy.

Valentine lifted his chin to gesture to the ceiling. "That light might be loose. Why don't ye stand on the bed and check it out."

More heat swirled in me, spreading through my limbs.

I stepped to the top of the bed, right next to him, then set a hand on the wooden frame behind his head. Without touching him, I leaned over, making sure my boobs were right in his face until I felt his breath on my skin. Then I rose and stood over him, and pretended to examine the ceiling light.

From the bed, Valentine would be looking straight up at my chest. He made a sound of pleasure, and I peered down to find his hand now inside his boxers. The patch of white bandage just a little lower was fresh, telling me he'd changed it this morning. He was taking care of himself. It only made me need to do more.

"If I've never said," he said, "the underside of your tits is fucking delectable. Something about that is hot as fuck. Like I know no one else will see it, no matter what ye wear."

"Depends on who I'm working for," I retorted with a grin. I reached to tap the light fitting. "This seems fine to me."

"There's a box under the bed. Fetch it out," he ordered.

Oh, I liked that bossy tone. The greater urgency in him.

I stepped down and bent to find the box. My cheeks flushed hotter when I realised what he meant. My sex toy. The one based on his dick.

I extracted the tin it was inside.

Valentine took a breath. "That's an important tool in there. I'd like ye to demonstrate it for me so I know it works. I'd do it myself but I've been told no touching."

His mind worked at a different speed to mine. He'd taken my dirty maid scene and turned it into something so much better.

"Where would you like the demonstration?" I asked.

"On the bed. Other end to me."

Yes, sir.

I rounded the bed and sat on the mattress, the folded duvet making a pillow as I reclined. Not breaking eye contact with him, I took out the weighty dildo. Ran my fingers over the length.

"Looks good to me," I breathed.

"Ye have no idea. I've been fucking desperate to see it in action. But it only works if the user is naked. Strip."

I hesitated. This was going further than I'd planned. I didn't want to hurt him.

He must've read me right as Valentine stalled. "If you're thinking my blood flow is in danger, that ship sailed the minute I saw ye. See for yourself."

He stripped his shirt then lifted his ass to do the same with his shorts. It left him gloriously naked, his hard dick bobbing from where it lay against his belly. Then he reached for his thigh and tore the white bandage away, leaving just the sutured skin on display.

I gazed at it. At the place that evil bastard had stabbed him and nearly ended his life. It was healing. Pink and healthy, but God.

"Eyes up here," he said softly. "All I need is for ye to keep going. I've been out of my mind with need for ye, the sense getting stronger until it's all I'm thinking about. Clothes off, woman. Let me watch ye fuck yourself in real life with my replica dick. I promise I'm not about to die on ye."

"But you almost did."

I couldn't help my plaintive words. He held out a hand.

"Come here a second."

"Didn't we say no touching?"

"Need to kiss ye."

But if I kissed him, or got on top of him, I'd want to do so much more. My breasts in his hands. His mouth going places. I'd be naked in his arms and endangering his life in a heartbeat and I wouldn't even notice. He had the power to make me mindless.

Instead, I shook my head. "I can't do that."

Frustration crossed his brow. He took a long breath and centred himself.

"But I'll do this," I added.

As he'd asked, I removed the remainder of my clothes and

forced myself to get back into character so I didn't freak out over the nudity. Instead, I tested the weight of the dildo. "The tool appears to be decent quality. Is there anywhere particular you'd like me to try it out?"

"Your lips," he said.

I parted them in surprise then brought the toy to my mouth. I took my tongue to the end, and Valentine licked his palm and ran it over the head of his dick. I enclosed the end like I would if I was sucking on him, and he gripped himself, slowly sliding down his shaft.

Easing it in and out, I kept my gaze on what he was doing.

"Now open those legs and put it against your wet pussy," Valentine urged. "While ye do that, use your other hand to check the size of those tits. I need an estimate."

My smile tried to return, but I kept it at bay, growing more turned on by the second. Parting my knees, I travelled the dildo down my body to lightly touch it to my clit. Then I glided it to my wet centre, hissing at the sensation.

If he was doing this, it would be so much better, but I needed him lying back and watching. His attention made this all the hotter.

"Ye should see how fucking gorgeous ye are." Valentine gripped his dick. "Now push it inside and talk tits to me."

Notching the toy to my entrance, I sank it inside me, a gasp flying from my lips at the intrusion. I'd used it only once, when he'd witnessed the act over our video call, but my memory did me dirty. It felt so good, stretching me and touching places inside that pulsed with pleasure.

At his groan, I remembered the second action and cupped one of my breasts. "Really heavy. More than usual because I'm..."

"You're what?"

"Aroused."

"In the workplace? Is that appropriate?"

A laugh bubbled up. I'd closed my eyes and kept them that way, needing to keep focus so I didn't rush. "Maybe not. I apologise. Tell me how to use the tool, please."

"It needs a good test. Start off slow."

"Right up to the hilt?"

"All the way, sweetheart. Pinch your nipple as ye do it and report on that, too."

I pushed the toy deeper into me, setting off spasms, and squeezed a nipple. "It's rigid."

"Wet your finger and thumb and stroke over it and pinch it. Keep the toy in motion. All the way out then all the way in."

I obeyed, doing exactly as he asked, heat streaking through me.

Valentine gave up a rough gasp. I couldn't resist looking this time. Considering how on display I was for him, I needed to see him in action. The effects of what I was doing to him. His gaze was locked on my pussy where the toy disappeared inside me. His fist worked his dick in long strokes, matching my speed.

I spread my legs wider and moved faster.

He copied me, his hard dick leaking.

Everything seemed to crowd in around me. The dim room, the heat from being so close to him and yet so far. The worry I'd had that could now turn into something better.

A new pang of desire struck me inside, and I moaned, my orgasm sneaking up on me fast.

Valentine tipped back his head, fucked his fist, then came. He groaned, cum landing on his chest. Up to his neck. I stared on, wishing he'd been inside me. But then my climax drove me under. I pulsed around the toy, my body arching then dropping down to the bed while my mind blipped out in spiralling delight. For several seconds, I could do nothing but swim in the waves of pleasure.

When I managed to open my eyes, it was to a grinning man.

"Fucking hell. Sold. I'm booking this service every day."

I laughed again and heaved a breath.

He was okay. I hadn't given him a heart attack or any other injury. And as I scooted off the bed, embarrassed but also elated, I could only think of how I badly wanted to do this again.

27

Mia

Across my kitchen table, Ariel slid Daisy a glance then raised her voice. "How's the dating going?"

I grinned at her. "Fine."

"Fine that you're ready to go out with someone from the app?"

The two women had been part of my original dating conversation, but I'd also made the point earlier in the evening that Valentine and I weren't a couple.

I was easier to read than the first reader book Tobi was working her way through in the living room, Valentine's low tones gently correcting her now and again.

"I have no idea how anyone chooses from a list of strangers and agrees to meet one in person," I replied.

"Show me your list of matches," Ariel asked.

I handed over my phone, open on the app with its enthusiastic red hearts spreading over the screen at each new match.

"God, how many?" she exclaimed.

"The boob pic was Valentine's idea. That's the only reason so many guys want to match with me."

"There's four thousand men dying to meet you. Holy crap."

A figure loomed in the kitchen doorway. Valentine, wearing a strange expression. "Did I hear my name?"

Daisy grinned. "Talking about you, not to you. We're trying to help Mia pick a date."

Ariel squinted at the list. "You can rule out many of these on just their basic data alone."

"How?" I asked.

"Let's sift through the first ten and narrow things down. Guy one is divorced with two kids. Forty-three. Doesn't want more children." She raised her gaze to me. "Is that a dealbreaker?"

A rush of something powerful heated me. I stared at the phone. "Yes."

"Okay, that just made this much easier. There's a filter option for that. We can remove all the men who don't want a family." She tapped the screen. "That took out five hundred. Sweet. On to the next."

I sensed Valentine's gaze on me. I lifted mine to find him staring, his arms folded and his jaw tight.

"Okay, guy two is six-four. Do you have a preference for shorter guys?"

Valentine made an off sound.

I held in a laugh. Ariel knew exactly what she was doing.

"No, height isn't an issue."

"Great. Otherwise he sounds good and his picture is hot."

"Show me?" Daisy asked. She peered at the screen. "Oh, totally. He's bearded. That's sexy."

Valentine craned to see. "Probably hiding a weak jaw under that patchy mess."

Ariel pulled a face. "You could be right. Let's read his opening question. Oh no. That's not good."

"What isn't?" I asked.

"Instead of asking about you, which is the whole point of this section, he says this: 'Flipping this around to let you get to know me. I'm a high earner in a fortune five hundred company. With my bonus this year, I'm investing in my crypto portfolio.' I'm not even reading the rest of this waffle."

Valentine tutted.

Daisy made a yuck sound. "You just know he's the type to slobber when he kisses then expects you to swoon over him."

I wrinkled my nose. "Rule him out, thanks."

Ariel sighed and swiped her finger. "Guy three I'm ruling out for an offensive chat-up line."

Valentine mooched closer. "There's a section for that?"

She showed him. "There is. Say, Val, what would yours say if you were chatting up Mia?"

"Easy." He braced himself on the back of an empty seat opposite me and linked his gaze to mine. "Do ye like my eyes, Mia?"

I blinked, a little dazed from his direct stare. "Yes?"

"Our kids could have them."

There was a pause, then a choked sound. It possibly came from me.

Ariel fanned her face. "Holy hell. You're good."

Valentine smiled, but it was all for me. He was acting. It was just a line. But damn, did that give my heart big ideas. From his devilish smirk, he knew exactly what he'd done.

"Vallll," a holler came from the living room.

He broke that delicious focus and raised his eyebrows. "Back to reading duties. Maybe give this up for another day, aye? Pretty sure I just set the bar at an unreachable height."

He left us, and I slumped on the table.

"Good God. What am I supposed to do with that?" I whispered.

One of the women patted my hair. "Seems to me that you're doing just fine," Daisy replied.

Louder, Ariel said, "We need to bird-test all these men."

"What's the bird test?" I sat up, my cheeks hot.

"It's simple. You tell the love interest something minor, like 'Oh, I just saw a bird'. If they're interested in your smallest musings, and engage with you on it, they're a keeper. The study shows those relationships have much more staying power. If they dismiss you and change the subject, or worse, completely ignore you, they're not all that into you. It's something to do with genuine interest and them picking up what you're laying down. I forget the details, but the principle seems easy to try out."

My phone buzzed on the table in front of Ariel.

She handed it back to me, and I read the name on the screen.

"Oh shoot. It's Scarlet. I've been meaning to call her back. I'm just going to take this." I stood and answered, leaving the kitchen to cross the living room, smiling at the sight of Valentine patiently flipping the page of Tobi's book.

My daughter, on the other hand, was forming her fingers into a small yawning creature. Valentine scowled at her while fighting the inevitable. Both of them cracked up when he fell.

"Hey, Mia," Scarlet said down the phone. "Are you okay to talk?"

"Yes. I'm so sorry. I've been busy with Valentine being here."

"No need to apologise. I just wanted to catch up on this paperwork matter. Did you get my message about the date for Winchester Holdings' board meeting? The two brothers appear to be pushing it."

I sat on my bed, the only light coming from the open door. "I did, but honestly, I blanked on it. I don't want to meet up with them."

Scarlet sighed. "I understand. It's in a couple of weeks, which is why there's a sense of urgency. Can I ask, do you have any other paperwork from before?"

"None, why?"

"No copy of Tobi's father's will?"

A strange sense of cold slithered in me. "I never even saw that. I'm not sure it exists."

"It does. A reference to it is buried in this pack of nonsense they sent you and the basis for them taking control. You're entitled to read it, and I really think you should. I'd like to contact their solicitors on your behalf. It will invite questions from them and probably some form of challenge, but I'll use my office's Inverness address as a reference. They won't be any the wiser on where you are."

"Thank you, and yes please." I held my breath then released it, trying to dispel my fear. "Can I ask why you think those papers are nonsense?"

"It's an investment proposal and a change to the business assets Tobi's father left."

"But they told me the business wasn't worth anything."

"While hiding the will from you and your daughter and setting a conclusion date for managing that money with you not around."

I pieced over that, my mind shifting to rewrite what I'd been told. "Vanissa, his wife, implied there was no money, only debt. She said Tobi wasn't due anything and that she was paying child support out of the business's tiny profits, leaving almost nothing."

"For want of a better word, I think she's full of it," Scarlet said. "Even if her husband didn't leave a will, which I think incredibly unlikely, or if he didn't name Tobi in it, under Scottish law, your daughter is entitled to something called Legal Rights. I'm not saying for sure that there's a big claim here, but there's absolutely something and a share she's due. To determine exactly what, we need more information."

I agreed to everything Scarlet suggested and thanked her again for all she'd done for us, because she really had gone to town for someone who was at best a new friend to her daughter and at worst just a neighbour.

She accepted my gratitude, and we hung up.

I held my fingers to my mouth, not trusting myself not to sob.

So Vanissa wasn't paying the child maintenance in error. It was legally still due. And she'd lied to me. How horrible. But also, I hadn't pushed, so I was to blame for this, too. Acting the coward, I'd run away, not wanting to face anything and letting fear guide my actions.

But I was changing.

For the sake of my daughter, I wanted to pursue this to the ground but I still feared what they could do to us as a family. The Winchesters still had power and threats they could make. With Scarlet making enquiries on my behalf, that only invited retaliation.

Yet, backing down wasn't an option anymore.

"All good in here?"

I raised my head to find Valentine ducking to enter the room. He approached, stopping short of touching me.

"I swear I wasnae listening, but I heard ye finish the call then ye didn't come out. Are ye okay?"

I dropped my hands to my lap. "Maybe. No. I don't know."

Then I don't know what drove me to form the words, but I said something else. "I think I just saw a little bird outside the window."

Valentine's eyebrows drew in. "Ye did? In the dark? Maybe it was some kind of night bird. Or a wee messenger come by to cheer ye up."

My heart squeezed. I couldn't manage a response.

Ariel's bird test had been passed with flying colours by the one man who didn't want the same as I did. What if he was wrong? What if he didn't know?

His gaze burned into mine. "Want to talk?"

I did. Badly. But it wasn't to be that evening. When Ariel and Daisy left so I could get Tobi to bed, my daughter clung to me, not letting me go. Her legs ached, and when she was hurting, my resilient, buoyant, sweet girl needed me. So I did exactly that. I stayed at her side. Slept by her bed.

Any other conversation could wait.

28

Valentine

Brandished like a weapon, Tobi jabbed her breakfast spoon my way. "When you were in the army, did you fight wars?"

"I was deployed, aye. Usually to defend places and people, though."

"Where did you go?"

"All over the place. Canada with the UN, North Africa to help train people. Wherever the Royal Regiment of Scotland sent me."

"What was it like?"

"A lot of walking places or waiting around. No junk food."

Her arms circled the bowl of sugary cereal in front of her. "Did you have a gun?"

"Aye, a big one." I winked at her ma.

"Tobi, eat your cereal and stop bothering Valentine," Mia chided, her cheeks pink.

In that damn blue tabard I now associated with a strip

show, Mia crossed the kitchen behind her lass, reaching to a high cupboard to put a box away. I climbed up and rounded the table to take it from her, sliding it into place and invading her space. I didn't hide my regard for her, and she flashed me a sexy look. Fucking hell did I want her.

Tobi angled her head at me when I took my seat again. "Am I bothering you?"

I grinned. "Nope. Let's turn this around. Is Tobi short for anything or is that a whole name?"

"It's short for October. My granny's birth year."

"Month," Mia corrected. "Also the month we lost her, coincidentally. A week before she would've turned fifty-five."

I twisted to the picture of her ma on the wall. "Ye did a great job with these two, Mrs Walsh. The Tobster is out here rocking your memory, and Mia's killing it at life and at work. I'm sure ye know already."

When I turned back, Mia was still watching me. "I didn't think you knew our surname."

"Not from your lips. It's on the stack of letters there. Not snooping, just observant." I pointed at the countertop then took another bite of toast. "Do ye know mine?"

She tutted at me. "Of course I do, Mr Valentine Bhaltair Graham. I spent enough time with you in hospital rooms."

It was my turn for surprise. Mia's expression became smug. But the moment passed with her alarm going off. She and Tobi hustled, collecting bags and jackets, then headed out into the bright morning for work and school, leaving me alone.

I had two days left until Nurse Heather said I could move normally around my injury, but my brain and body both ached to be useful. If Mia didn't have to work, I had endless ideas of how to pass the time, but I was out of luck there.

Noises came from next door, a familiar sound with the

renovations underway. I headed outside to where bright sunshine warmed the covered porch, the spring day promising to be beautiful. Ally carried a toolbox in the door.

I hailed him. "Need any help in there?"

He stopped. "I appreciate the offer, but naw. After this, I'm done. Want to come check it out? Gordain said you're the likely new occupant."

He gestured with his head, and I followed him inside, limping to keep the weight off my leg.

He squinted at me. "Shouldn't ye be on crutches?"

I huffed a laugh. "Ye sound like Mia and my nurse. I'm fine. Taking it steady. I learned my lesson."

Ally shrugged then gave me the tour. The place mirrored Mia's in shape, the finish as good as how I'd worked up hers. One thing was undeniable—it really was pretty much complete.

"Last thing will be a good clean down, then ye can move in," Ally said. He knelt to tighten something under the kitchen counter then swung the door out, testing it.

I poked around, checking out what could be my home.

From the start, when Ben made the suggestion, it hadn't felt right. It still didn't now. I didn't need a place like this, with two bedrooms and a spacious living room. Yet I couldn't impose on Mia for longer, which meant going back to sleeping on Raphael's floor or to the bunkhouse.

My brain buzzed with too many thoughts and no solutions. Nothing felt clear or right.

"I'm all done." Ally came to stand next to me. "The bathroom's finished, kitchen checked off, electrics and wiring sorted. Job's a good one. Ye okay?"

"Is there any chance ye could do a favour for me?" I asked. "I'm at a loose end this morning, and Tobi was talking about getting her room painted. I don't have my car here and am not supposed to drive yet, but if I had the equipment, I could make myself useful that way."

It was early, and there was plenty of time to do the work. If I picked up a low-odour paint, it wouldn't trouble Mia or Tobi all that much. I even knew the exact shade because the lass had selected it from a colour chart a couple of nights ago.

Ally tilted his head at me. If he found it interesting that instead of making plans for the cottage which could be mine, I was thinking of next door, he didn't say. Instead the man shrugged and offered the ride I needed.

Before we left, I messaged Mia for permission.

Mia: She'll be over the moon. In fact, it's great timing. She wants to sleep over at her friend's tonight. Because it's Friday, I agreed.

So it would be just us this evening. Ally got us on the road, and I made another stop-off request. As houseguests went, I'd prove I was a good one.

Six hours later, the room was painted and Mia returned with a very excited Tobi. The little girl whirled around in her bedroom in delight then hugged me around the legs. My throat clogged, but I chided her to keep off my new lilac walls just to make her laugh. Then, with an overnight bag packed, her ma whisked her away to her playdate.

Meaning I could get on with phase two of my plan.

When Mia returned, I was just sliding a tray into the oven.

She entered the kitchen, eyes wide. "You're cooking? What is it?"

"A slow roast beef. I'm not exactly a great chef, but this is seasoned to within an inch of its life and will taste pretty decent. I'll serve it with roast potatoes and honey carrots then either I can make a gravy or I picked up a sour cream dip that would go well. It'll be ready around seven, if that works for ye?"

"It works." She appeared dazed.

"Go take a shower," I ordered.

"Yes, chef." Mia ran her gaze over me, the haziness turning to something more heated.

Badly, I needed to examine that expression in more detail, but I let her go, taking the time to clean up the kitchen.

This was fucking nice. If I moved in next door, I could cook for her and Tobi from time to time. Maybe they'd even like hanging out with me some evenings. In the back of my mind, that happy scene changed to something darker. The time when I'd see Mia return from a date, or when some arsehole asked if he could move in and play happy families with her and the Tobster. That, I couldn't bear.

So maybe we only had this, now.

29

Mia

Fresh from the shower, I slid the blue tabard back over my naked body—shaved, buffed, and moisturised, of course—then stepped into the living room.

"Valentine?" I called.

"Still in the kitchen, being the host with the most."

"Could you come here?"

I posed in the doorway to my bedroom, my long blonde hair still damp and loose, and the tabard keeping me from feeling ridiculous in my seduction technique. Because damn did I want that man. Right now. On the bed, the floor, wherever.

Across the room, he appeared in the kitchen entrance, wiping his hands with a tea towel. It fell to the floor when he raised his focus to me. "Tell me my eyes aren't lying, Mama. Are ye naked under that?"

I inched back. "Only one way to find out."

"Don't move a muscle." He prowled over, moving more easily than I'd seen since his injury. He reached me. Set a big palm to my cheek. "Aren't ye just a gift all wrapped up?"

Valentine stooped to press his lips to mine. My breath hitched, and I stretched to meet him, the kiss familiar and thrilling in equal measures. This was what I'd dreamed about all day. Having him home and waiting for me, knowing what we could do with an empty house and endless attraction. I loved his height and how he made me feel tiny and petite. I loved even more how his hands ghosted down my body to take two big handfuls of my breasts.

But he didn't stop at his favourite place. With a grunt of pleasure, he slowly descended to kneel in front of me. "I've been dreaming about your sweet body all day. Let's see if your pussy remembers me. Since that rubber version has been in play, I've been getting worried you'd prefer that over the real thing."

Valentine slid his warm hand down my leg, encircling my ankle, then lifted, drawing my foot over his shoulder. Putting him face-on with my core. He delivered a kiss right to the centre of me, and I tipped my head back on the wall, gasping with a rush of desire and too urgent for more to feel self-conscious.

"Well, hello." He took a long lick and groaned. "So wet for me already. Ye do remember who I am. Now buckle in, because I'm ready to prove the real man is better than the model. Oh, and I apologise in advance."

"You're apologising to my pussy?"

"Aye, for the pounding I'm about to give her."

He licked me again, spearing his tongue inside before settling back to suck my clit. I shamelessly arched into his touch. I'd never needed anything so much as this moment with him. I wanted him touching me, holding me, driving into me, over and over. Like he could read my mind, Valentine upped the pressure, lashing me with his tongue while two fingers teased my entrance. He sank them home, a third adding to the mix on the next pass, stretching me, delighting my pleasure zones.

I knew what he was doing, besides wanting to make me come—priming me for his big dick. I was so ready I didn't want to wait, but even tugging on his hair didn't slow him. He kept up his movements, set on a pathway I wasn't about to argue with.

Breathless, I grinded against his mouth, mindlessly matching his steady rhythm though my brain was melting. Heat wound tight inside me. I spasmed around his hand, and a moan escaped my lips. Valentine gave up an almost desperate groan of need, and that simple sound did me in.

Somehow, I'd become hard-wired to needing his pleasure. He was getting off on touching me and driving me crazy. That knowledge broke me. I braced my shoulders to the cold wall and came without any more warning.

Valentine groaned into my flesh, his fingers somehow thicker as they went inside me for a final time. Delicious feelings broke through my senses, and I finally drooped, unable to support myself properly for how boneless he'd made me.

"Fucking hell, woman," he swore. Then he kissed my thigh. "Look."

I gazed down. Valentine indicated to the hand he still had embedded inside me. "Four fingers. Next time, I'm going to get my whole hand in there and fist-fuck ye, okay?"

I whimpered, too turned on to give any more sensible words. Anything with him. If he thought it would bring either of us pleasure, I was sold.

He eased his fingers out of me, setting my foot on the floor. "But right now, I need to fuck ye more than I need air, water, or brain cells. Can I strip ye?"

I nodded, and he stood in a rush, taking the hem of the tabard in his fingers. He lifted it, standing back like the reveal was a gift.

"Ye have the perfect, gorgeous body," he breathed.

A month ago, I wouldn't have believed him. I'd never liked my belly rolls or the stretch marks that came with pregnancy and stayed, but Valentine had taught me to love myself. With a final tug, the single item of clothing was over my head, then he stepped back.

Holding my gaze, he stripped his shirt. His jeans went next, followed by his boxers. Though stunned by the sight of his dick, hard and bobbing for my attention, I touched my gaze on the plastic covering his sutures, and the image restarted my intelligence.

"Lie on the bed," I ordered.

"I'd rather lie on ye."

"We'll try that later if this doesn't hurt you."

He worked his jaw but snatched my hand and pulled me after him into my bedroom. Or his bedroom. I'd confused the fact after almost a week of him in my bed.

On the big bed, he sprawled against the pillows, long and lean and ready for me.

I prowled up the bed, stopping to kiss beside his wound. Another to the base of his dick. Valentine made a sound of pleasure. Flattening my tongue, I slid up his dick then enclosed the end, taking him into my mouth.

"Fuck, no need to prime me. I'm so hard for ye I can barely think. Climb on top of me. Ride me."

I smiled around his dick and sucked him. He'd taken me to the edge and over barely breaking a sweat. I wanted to tease him and get him so fired up for me he lost his mind.

Valentine speared his fingers into my hair, giving up the

complaint to guide my blow job. After a minute, he groaned again, and his dick thickened. Precum coated my tongue. "Warning that this is going to end way before I'm ready for it to."

I came off him. "Are you sure you want me to stop?"

Without pause, I took him deep into my throat this time. No further order came. Instead, he gripped the quilt, his knuckles pronounced and his head tipped back, the gaze he'd kept on me hidden, but the curve on his lips showing me his feelings.

He was fighting finishing while loving the battle.

I reached between his legs and curved my fingers around his heavy balls. Tugged them lightly. Drew my thumb down the centre line.

"God, fuck. Enough. Stop now," he finally snapped.

Beaming, I crawled up him until I was astride his lap, right over his hard dick. I went to get him into position, but Valentine gripped my hip to secure me in place.

"I need a second to play with these."

His hands grazed around my breasts, and his eyes flared. I sat taller, presenting them to him to do whatever he liked with. Valentine moulded and massaged me, cupping them together then lifting each like he'd done before. Holding my gaze, he brought one to his mouth and tongued me.

"Fucking in love with your tits."

I flushed hotter, liking the *love* word way too much. Valentine watched every reaction while he toyed with my nipple. Then he sucked. I gasped, and his dick pulsed under me.

Both of us shuddered with need.

Valentine licked his finger then took it to my neglected nipple, sucking one with deep pulls while working the other side.

He breathed through his nose, that intent gaze still trained on me like he needed to know every reaction. I could only revel in the pleasure, my body on fire for him and all he was doing to me.

Another spiral of desire broke over me, and I reached between my legs and held his dick, notching it to my entrance. I sank down with an undisguised moan of deep happiness.

Valentine stilled and pressed his forehead to my shoulder, his eyes closed. With my knees on the mattress, I rose and fell, taking him in deeper. Another try, and I was fully seated, nothing between us but...

With a growl, Valentine rose and flipped our positions so he was rearing over me, his dick so rigid inside me I knew nothing else but that connection.

Except he didn't move. Valentine swore, appearing to force himself to focus. "I'm bare," he gritted out.

"What?"

"You're fucking me bare. No condom."

I opened and closed my mouth, stunned at myself. It hadn't even occurred to me. Nor could I manage a word, almost every part of me wanting to continue exactly as we were. I needed it. I needed him in every way.

At my lack of a response, Valentine took a heavy breath, his arm muscles trembling and desperation plain. "All I want to do now is pound ye until we both come. I don't want to stop. I would give every-fucking-thing I own to come inside ye just like this. But, sweetheart—"

"Do it," I breathed.

His gaze flew to mine. "Seriously?"

I could only manage a tiny nod. It was enough. He jacked his hips. We both moaned. Then Valentine dropped his face so his mouth met mine. He kissed me, matching his strokes to the presses and care of his lips. His tongue dominated mine just as his body took ownership of every other part of me. All I could do was receive the immense pleasure he was drilling into me.

Soon, I was careening towards that cliff again, the approach hotter, faster, and even more compelling than when he'd delivered an orgasm on his tongue. Having him inside me without protection took any level of sense and smashed it up. Nothing had ever felt like this.

"Need to come," he abruptly said.

It triggered me. My pussy clamped down on his dick, and I was lost to another stunning and powerful climax, something fresh in the mix that drove me to new heights. Earth-shatteringly good.

Valentine gave up a growl of urgent need. He worked his hips once, twice more, then he stilled, and his dick pulsed inside me.

"Fuck, sweetheart. Fuck," he cursed and dropped down on me, his weight delicious.

I clamped my arms and legs around him, rocked to my core, and fighting a wave of emotion. Because God, that had been good. I needed to do it again.

Somewhere in the distance, beeping filtered through my haze. "Hush, whatever that is. We're not available," I breathed.

On me, Valentine gave a rumble of amusement and dropped a kiss to my temple. "I think that's the oven timer. I need to turn the meat."

"Think you already did that," I quipped.

It was barely innuendo and definitely not funny, but he laughed like I was hilarious, kissed me again, then climbed up and left the room. Him pulling out of me brought a sticky sensation that was new and definitely interesting, but quickly enough he returned with a warm washcloth to take care of the mess.

Then he pulled the blanket over my naked, totally sated form. "Be back after I've handled my beef."

I sighed, watching his tight backside and long legs as he walked away. A minute later and he was back, hopping into bed with me and wrangling the covers over us both

Valentine spooned me, his hand delving into my cleavage and palming my breast.

"Quick conversation, though it's stating the obvious." He settled in close.

"Shoot."

"What we just did—I'm clean. I had a health check as part of the job. Thought it was worth mentioning."

"I am, too. Also, on the pill, so we're covered there."

He breathed out. "Aye, I figured. Not that you'd want a surprise mini-Valentine popping up."

"Even if they had your eyes?" I asked dryly, referring to his chat-up line from when Daisy and Ariel had been here.

Valentine chuckled again, his fingers idly indenting my skin, my breast apparently now his stress toy.

I sank into thought for a minute, first over the sexual health check I'd had after my encounter with Tobi's father, and secondly over a happier idea. One where Tobi had a little brother or sister. It had surprised me how easily my answer had come to Ariel's question about whether I wanted more kids. I did. At least one, despite money being tight. I loved being a mother, and Tobi was so independent now, it freed me up to have a babe in my arms.

Which meant a boyfriend who wanted the same. Or a sperm donor who didn't mind not raising his kids, which was probably a lot of men. I snorted a soft laugh.

"What's so funny?" Valentine turned me over to face him. Instantly, his gaze was on my boobs, but he did a valiant job in dragging it back to my face for my answer.

"I was thinking about how some men behave. The shirking-responsibility type."

He blinked. "Am I included in that group?"

"Nope."

"Then get those men out of your head when you're in bed with me, woman."

I grinned at him. "Sorry. I'll save all my thoughts for you."

"Good. Or I'll give ye something else to think about."

My pulse skipped at the threat. Against my leg, Valentine's dick thickened again. It hadn't truly gone soft, pointing to him being still as turned on as I was. It was barely five in the afternoon and broad daylight. We had the place to ourselves until probably lunchtime tomorrow, and I intended to make the most of it. I wriggled my hand between us and stroked him.

His gaze became loaded and heavy. I went to move, but he caught my wrist and drew it above my head.

"There was me thinking we could just cuddle and chat until dinner."

"Your dick says otherwise."

"Valid argument. Hold the bedpost. Both hands."

Stretching myself like that put me on display and gave easy access to my chest for my man's avid attention. Valentine tossed back the blanket and knelt over me.

"How about this, we chat while I play with ye."

"Deal. Just take it easy on that leg. Don't hurt yourself," I warned.

"I haven't and I won't. Now let me get started on my favourite activity."

Without pause, he spread both hands over my boobs, letting my nipples harden against his palms. Then he ducked to blow on them to stiffen them further. Pinching them between his fingers and thumbs, he toyed with me, watching my expression, and with his dick hard but neglected.

"Thought you wanted to talk?" I tried to hide how turned on he was making me. My body responded to him like he'd taken ownership of my central nervous system. I'd come twice already, and another felt greedy.

"I do. What about?"

I laughed, arching into him, my shoulders deep in the pillows. "It was your idea. Tell me something about your last job."

"Ahead of accepting Ben's contract, I worked for a logging company. Spread your legs."

I did, and he knelt between them, his fingers trailing over my belly to glide between my thighs.

"I meant the army," I said on a breath.

But he'd gone quiet, his gaze travelling down me. "You're so fucking beautiful. Do ye hear? I've never wanted anyone the way I want ye."

My heart ached, and I closed my eyes, burying my face.

"No, watch me."

Valentine waited for my focus to return to him. He planted a hand next to my head, some deep intention in his expression that made me shiver to witness it. He kissed me, then pushed my breasts together and buried his face in my soft skin, sucking love bites where he chose.

Then he drew back, his voice coming out gruff. "Feet further apart, knees up."

"What are you going to do?"

"Did ye like my fingers inside ye?"

Slowly, I nodded. He'd mentioned fisting me, and

though it sounded intimidating, what he'd tried had felt so good.

"I'll tell ye about the army and let's see if we can get ye fucking my whole hand by the time I'm through."

I whimpered, earning a devilish grin.

Reaching under the bed, Valentine claimed the box with my toy, pulling out the tube of lubricant. He slicked up his fingers and drizzled the cool liquid at the juncture of my thighs. I shivered, hopelessly aroused by him.

"My school had a link to the regiment, so there was always a presence in the halls and in various ceremonies. I knew the uniform as well as my school colours."

He spread the liquid out, circling my clit then gliding a finger right inside me. I bucked, and a restraining hand landed on my hip.

"Because I was living so far from my family, I boarded at the school, and that meant evenings and weekends were free for all kinds of activities. I signed up for cadets and loved every minute of hiking and camping."

A second finger joined the first. Valentine used his knuckles at my entrance, the sensation driving me crazy, then scissored his digits to create space.

"Atta girl. Relax. Loosen up for me." He released my hip then continued with the story. "At sixteen, I was as tall as the recruiting officer who came to talk to us about options. At eighteen, when I graduated, I signed my soul over to Black Watch, third battalion."

"God," I groaned under his constant motion. "I need to see a picture of you in uniform."

"Gonna get my phone greased up, but okay." He snagged his jeans from the floor with his impressively long reach then paged through screens until he found what he was looking for.

He passed it to me and continued with his work, a third finger added. Heat coiled inside me. I gazed at the ridiculously gorgeous shot of a younger Valentine, maybe mid-twenties and with his hair short, in military uniform. Hot as anything I'd ever seen.

In a couple of short clicks, I forwarded the shot, the whoosh of the message giving me away.

Valentine quirked a dark eyebrow. "Did ye just send that to yourself?"

"For later use."

He eyed the phone I'd discarded on the bed. "Can I take pictures of ye for that purpose, too?"

I squirmed. "You already have shots of my boobs."

"A gateway drug. Ye got me hooked, and now I need more. Like seeing half my hand slicked up and buried in your pussy whenever I want."

To make his point, he tapped a place inside me that had me seeing stars. Denying him anything now was impossible.

"Okay, but just that."

He swore and grabbed the phone, angling it, then showing me the result. I moaned, the sight of myself like *that,* with his fingers buried, deeply erotic. Being with Valentine was a journey into exploring my sexuality, and I was grabbing on to all chances.

He tossed the phone then collected my vibrator, pausing to drown it in lube before flicking it on. "I'm going to use this on low to open ye further. My hand is big, but luckily ye chose a good model for this design so it'll do the job."

To start with, he brushed the toy over my nipples,

smiling as I cursed him, then took a suck of both in turn. He drove the vibrator down the centre of me and passed it over my clit then straight inside me, his hand removed. I keened, the rush of desire overwhelming. Valentine didn't wait around, drawing it in and out and taking first one then two fingers back in with it. Soon, he had all three alongside the dildo.

"Fucking hell, woman. Ye are so clever. So good. Your pussy is taking this so well."

Despite the fact all I was doing was lying there, I got a burst of pride at his praise.

Valentine slowed again, just teasing me, the vibrations not enough to tip me over the edge yet and his fingers a steady presence.

"I loved military life," he said, though his voice was gruff and his gaze never strayed from where he penetrated me. "Even if it was tough, I was never bored, and I enjoyed the camaraderie with my unit."

"Did. You keep. In contact?" I stammered, fighting my eyes closing against the onslaught of good feeling. Higher and higher, he was driving me, the orgasm kept at bay but the pressure building.

"Aye, with a couple of guys. We text from time to time, but both are still serving. Becoming a recluse didnae help my friendships."

The vibrations kicked up a notch, Valentine obviously having pressed the button. Still moving slow, he pulled the toy almost all the way out, his hand thick at my entrance.

"Four fingers," he uttered like a curse.

Spreading me with his fingers wide, he sank my vibrator back in and circled it in wide arcs, aided by the lube and how slick I'd become. It hit so many pleasure sensors that tears filled my eyes. Not in upset but the sheer intensity of it. I drove my heels into the bed, letting the tears fall.

Abruptly, we were there.

In a push, the toy went away and Valentine's whole hand replaced it, lodging deep. I gasped, mouth open at the intrusion. He groaned, holding completely still.

"You're doing it, little spy. You're taking my hand. Going to form a fist now."

I breathed permission, every part of me focused on that full feeling, on the reverie in Valentine's voice. Inside me, the shape changed to a thicker presence. It touched all the places the vibrator had done when he'd driven it in a circle, but at the same time. I'd never felt anything like it.

"Your pussy is closed around my wrist. Christ, woman. How does that feel?" he demanded.

"Incredible."

"Can I show ye with a picture?"

I nodded, and he took it, showing me the sight on his screen. I moaned again, needing him to move. To deliver on the promise from every flex of his fingers and bring a crest to my building need.

"So fucking perfect. Your body is beautiful. You're amazing," he said almost in a chant.

"Make me come," I managed.

"Yes, ma'am."

Valentine began a slow thrust with his fist. There was so little space for him that even the slightest move charged me up. His words of praise did the same to my brain, the irresistible force of him owning and dominating me in all ways.

I could only surrender, letting him play me, work me, fist me into submission.

So quickly, the heat caught alight. I spasmed around his hand. A warning my mouth couldn't give.

"That's it. Come for me," he commanded.

His other hand went to my clit. One pass. Two. All I needed.

With a broken cry, I splintered, squeezing and throbbing around his hand. The full occupation of my insides blitzed my nerves. My legs shook, my body jerked. My entire being was eclipsed by the stunning force of the orgasm he delivered with his fist.

In the recesses of my mind, I picked up on Valentine shifting, urgency still in him. He flexed his hand, and I sprang open my eyes to see him fuck his fist.

"Can I come in ye?"

"Anything," I whispered.

He knelt up and brought his dick to my entrance, at the same moment, easing out his hand until there was space to thrust inside me alongside some of his fingers, though I couldn't tell how many now. Like before, I could only feel and take.

I focused on his clenched jaw and the honest desperation in his expression. Neck muscles taut, body gleaming with sweat, his muscles working hard.

"You're so beautiful," I said, surprising myself with my words.

Valentine's gaze flew to mine. He pulled out his hand so just his dick filled me then braced over me on the bed, bringing his mouth to mine. He closed his eyes, kissed me deeply, and came.

I held him close, loving every shudder. Valentine was in my body and under my skin. I held in words that crammed forward in my mind.

Ones where I confessed how I felt about him.

I'd given him my heart. I hadn't meant to, but there it was, beating for him. I'd fallen in deep with the big, stubborn Scot who didn't believe in love anymore, and against his orders.

It was my own fault if the answer was a sorrowful smile and a no-thanks rejection.

31

Valentine

Wrapped around Mia, I sank into the pillows, blissed out. Satisfied, at least temporarily. I could never get enough of this woman.

"We didn't finish the military conversation," she said after a long while of us both drifting on endorphins, or whatever great sex delivered.

"That's what you're thinking about right now?"

"It's the uniform. I'm hooked on that photo."

I chuckled, hugging her closer. "While you're picturing me like that, what else do ye want to know?"

"Why did you leave?"

"My term was up. Not that this is a great conversation while I'm holding ye, but my heart had been broken right as I'd signed up for four more years, and the next time it rolled around, I didn't have the commitment my unit needed. In a better way, I had choices, either to take up a lifetime of service or build a career outside of it. Something for myself."

"Do you think your relationship would've survived if you hadn't been away so much?"

I raised a shoulder. "Never really considered that."

"Was Kelly a reason for leaving, too?"

"Cart after horse, Mama. She'd already cut and run."

"I meant did you want to get her back."

"Hell no."

From the kitchen, beeping sounded, the oven announcing the food was ready. Time had flown while we were hidden away in here.

Climbing up, I swatted Mia's ass. "That's dinner. Let's go eat. We'll need refuelling for the evening I have planned."

Adorably flustered, she sat up, pink on her cheeks and down her throat to her bare tits. While I dragged on my boxers, she shook out her hair then ran her fingers through it, twisting it into a fast braid.

"Could you grab my dressing gown? It's on the back of the door."

Hunger swept over me that had nothing to do with the meal I'd made. With a low growl, I crowded her, stealing another kiss. "How about ye sit at the table naked?"

"You'll spill more food than you plate up."

She grinned, and my mouth curved to match, her happiness infectious. Also, she had a point.

The dressing gown wasn't where she said, so I picked up my t-shirt. "Wear this?"

"If you like." She let me tug it over her head.

"I do. It doesn't hide ye from me but is enough to keep my dick under control. I can't promise for how long, though."

Mia laughed, leading me out of the room. My shirt drowned her in length but clung to her curves, her ass a thing of beauty where it moved under the thin material. I groaned, reaching for her hand.

"Nope. I made a mistake. Ye look too hot in that. The food can burn."

She darted away, making a break into the kitchen. Huffing pretend annoyance, I paced after her.

Under the bright spotlights, she waited on me. "What can I do?"

"Suck me off."

"I meant with the meal."

"Fuck the meal. Sit on my lap."

"Valentine! I'm hungry."

"So am I, little spy." But her need for food beat down every other priority.

After washing up, I took the beef from the oven, the top nicely charred but a cut inside showing me it was perfectly done. "I didn't have time to make sides, so how about rolls with pickles and sour cream?"

"I'm drooling already."

At my side, Mia made up the rolls while I carved the beef. Then we sat at the table and devoured the food. This was all so easy, being around her. If I had a wish, it would be to keep everything exactly as it was now.

The notion broke down a wall I'd constructed. My little spy, peeking through at my dark interior.

After dinner, we returned to bed, cuddling up like it was the most natural thing in the world. My happy state simmered, words needing to go out into the world. But my long-held practice of not talking about that kind of shite kept my mouth closed.

"Talk to me about something," I asked instead. "Anything. I

just want to listen to ye for a while."

Mia lifted her head from my chest. Her gaze was troubled, an indent in her furrowed brow. "Weird. I was just about to speak."

"What about?"

She arranged herself with her arm under her chin, watching me. "You know how Scarlet is looking into my issue with the Winchesters? I've been on edge about it for a number of reasons."

"What scares ye the most?"

I'd burn the whole fucking family down if they tried anything.

"I'm worried that they are planning to use my mental health as a lever in some way. Logically, there's no case for them, I'm almost certain, except that one really bad night I had after mom died is on record."

I nodded. "No judge is going to do shite with that."

"Right? But if I have to go face to face with them in a room with lawyers and they use that against me, I'm scared I'll burst out crying and prove their point." She said the words fast like they had been haunting her.

I interlaced our fingers. "I'll go with ye, if it helps. I'll hold your hand, and if they attack ye, I'll be there to remind ye there's nothing they can do. The lawyers will do the talking, I'll glare them down, and they won't be able to touch ye."

Mia's gaze intensified. "You'll really come?"

I flashed a grin. "Anytime. Now what else is there? Ye said a number of reasons."

A heavy sigh followed. "Only that I fully expect them to be vicious. Greg particularly."

"Orange car guy. The oldest, aye? Therefore probably has

the most to lose. I'll handle the bitter little fuck. We have a score to settle after he pursued my car anyway."

Mia took a breath like she had something else to say, but then her gaze shuttered. "I have a score to settle with him, too, but I don't want to talk about them anymore. Your turn for a conversation starter."

Getting fired up to defend her had somehow loosened my tongue. The words that didn't come earlier were right there and ready. I took a breath.

"How about the time I stood by, my whole family around me, and watched my brother kiss my fiancée?"

Her jaw dropped. I reached to tap it closed.

"It's that or I fuck ye seven ways from Sunday again. Your choice."

Mia gave up a sound of frustration. "I pick both but talk first. Ben really did that? I'm horrified. I thought he was a good brother."

I tracked back through my words, realising where I'd gone wrong. Then I sighed, because wasn't that the core of the problem between us? "I misspoke. Kelly kissed him. Sit up a minute. I need some space so I can get this off my chest without it spoiling how I touch ye."

She obliged, arranging herself cross-legged facing me. I'd already teased her hair out of the braid, loving how the yellow lengths framed her face. She rarely wore it down, and I loved that it was something private only I was seeing.

"I told ye already that Kelly had no issue with our long-distance relationship? For one thing, she loved my family and was content being a part of it. For the second, she was actually in love with Ben and had been the whole time we knew each other."

Mia squinted. "But she dated you. And agreed to marry

you. Why would she lie like that and for so long?"

"I can't answer that. I never asked. All I know was the duration. She wanted him, couldn't have him, so she turned to the next best thing—his younger brother. I was a safe option because I wasn't there, plus she liked the vibe of being a military spouse. I paid her rent, too, so she only needed to work part time. It was a sweet arrangement."

Red flushed Mia's cheeks. "Sweet? She was using you for everything she could get. How long did this go on for?"

"Years. I was the idiot who couldn't see what was happening under my nose. Right up until the moment when it all came crashing down."

Her gaze gentled. "What happened?"

"There's four of us siblings, another brother and a younger sister alongside me and Ben. Our brother was getting married, so I'd applied for leave, but it hadn't been guaranteed, and I only knew I would make it at the last minute. Instead of being happy, Kelly acted weird with me, blaming me for not giving her notice. Like I had any control. Military leave can be shaky at the best of times, and I had been fucking elated to see my brother and his bride walk down the aisle. Anyway, barely talking, Kelly and I went to the wedding together. At the reception, my mom gave a speech about the happy couple, then Ben stood up for his. He cracked everyone up with making jokes, one of which was about him being an even sadder single man now his brother had fallen."

I swallowed, and Mia's gaze became stricken like she could predict the coming train wreck.

"Kelly left our table and marched up to Ben, right as he was finishing speaking so all eyes were on him. She grabbed his lapels and told him he didn't need to be sad. She loved him. It had always been him. True love only came once in a lifetime yada, yada."

Never once had I talked this out with anyone. My voice grated.

"Then she kissed him. One by one, people turned to stare at me, as if expecting some big argument or a fight. But I'd frozen. Kelly spared me one glance and said, 'Sorry, Valentine, it was never you', so I did the only thing I could and walked away."

Mia, with her fingers pressed to her lips, gave a deep sigh. "That was such a shitty thing for her to do."

An unfunny laugh came from me. "Wasn't it? According to Ben, who tried to call me after but had to leave a message, the kiss was unexpected and unwelcome. He had no feelings for her and zero intention of speaking to her again. He'd been in shock but had followed me outside but lost me. I didn't want to see him, her, or anyone else. I packed up, got on a plane, and cut all ties with her. Stopped paying her rent and the other bills I'd taken on."

"Good for you. She didn't deserve a minute more of your time." Mia tilted her head. "Why's she trying to get in contact with you now?"

"Fuck knows. I don't care enough to find out. If it was anything real, Ma would tell me."

"How so? Does your mother still see her around?"

"Kelly works for her."

Her jaw dropped. "How could your mother even talk to her after that? I'd want to slap her silly."

"I know, but bear in mind the wedding and breakup was five years ago, and this was a more recent occurrence. My mother put up a job advert for a receptionist at their inn, and Kelly applied. Ma called me in outrage over it, but I said to employ her if she fit the job requirements. It didn't bother me. They needed someone, and pickings were slim in their small town. Everyone's happy."

A dubious expression met mine.

"Is anyone actually happy with that arrangement, though? It must hurt your mother to see her, considering what she did."

"My family is pretty forgiving. Or maybe Ma prefers to keep her enemies close."

"And what about you? Visiting must be awkward."

"I can count how many times I've been back to the inn since she took the job on one hand."

Mia toyed with the edge of the duvet. "Where does that leave you with Ben? Not in a great place, I take it."

I slumped, weight descending where I'd hoped it would be taken off. Apparently sharing problems didn't halve them, instead they just multiplied. "Strained at best. At worst..."

Her eyes rounded. "You think he lied to you about her?"

"No, not at all. I believe him. I just wish my brain would get the message."

Mia waited for me to explain. I was doing a shite job of it.

"I've had nightmares," I finally managed.

"Of him and her?"

"Exactly. The dreams were regular right after it happened, then recently, they came back." I dried up, suddenly sick of this.

Why the hell was I ruining a fucking amazing evening with Mia over nonsense from the past? What a waste of time. Her stories, on the other hand, I wanted to hear. They were active and still ongoing, needing resolving. Mine was a body dead and buried. Digging up the grave wasn't going to help anyone.

I inflated my chest and pushed down all the hurt and misery into the little box where I kept it. Then I installed my smirk once again and hauled Mia onto my lap. "Enough of all that. We're wasting time when we could be doing way more fun things."

I kissed her, and to my utter relief, she allowed it. Then I spent the rest of the time putting my mouth to much better use than talking.

32

Mia

Darkness and warm strength surrounded me. Beautifully broken Valentine stirred in his sleep, a possessive hand taking a squeeze of my breast. We were naked again, having sunk into sleep after multiple rounds of mind-breaking sex.

Need for him had taken me over almost entirely. I was insatiable.

His fingers flexed again, feeling me up, then his lips pressed to my neck from where he spooned me from behind. I gave up a small sound of pleasure, and his arms tightened around me.

Without further warning, I was lifted and rolled so I was on him, my back to his chest. One of Valentine's arms braced me and the other snaked down my body, straight between my legs. His fingers speared into my wet centre, and he groaned.

Drowsiness made every move all the more delicious. I followed the path of his arm and slid my hand over his, finding his hard dick nestled between my thighs. I stroked him as he played with me.

"Put me inside ye," he said in my ear, his voice thick with sleep.

I guided his dick to my slick entrance, and Valentine thrust home. He filled me so perfectly. We gave twin sounds of relief, but his hips remained still, and a kiss landed on the side of my face, the press somehow intense.

He took my fingers to my clit. "Play here but go slow."

Boosting us higher on the bed, Valentine arranged me so my head rested against his shoulder and I was comfortably reclined on him, my legs over his so my body was exposed. His hands travelled up to my breasts.

He cupped both, taking the weight. Inside me, his dick pulsed. "How do ye walk around all day without constantly wanting to stop and play with these?"

I smiled into the midnight-black room. "It's a challenge."

"I bet. The size alone would distract me."

"How about having a big, swinging dick? Doesn't that do the same?"

"Eh. It does half my thinking for me. I go where it leads."

"Which was right to my tits."

Valentine choked out a surprised laugh. He nudged the side of my face with his, asking for a kiss. I twisted to meet his lips, leaving my body alone to hold his head, allowing a better fit. A deeper connection and a fusing of our mouths.

If only we could get a picture of this. The covers had been kicked away, leaving us both bared to the silent dark. His big body framed mine. His dick lodged inside me, my legs spread over his, leaving nothing concealed. Everything wet and swollen from use. His hands on my breasts and his mouth on mine.

This was lovemaking. Nothing fast or furious about it—we'd already done that multiple times, just a perfect fit and unstoppable need to make the other feel good. To claim and connect and own.

His touch started up again, those big hands massaging and teasing my breasts until my skin burned with pleasure. At a murmured order from him, I returned to play with my clit, lightly drawing a finger over it, every pass giving me a burst of fresh desire.

Our kiss didn't stop. It continued with our rhythm, slow, winding, and perfectly timed.

Valentine tugged on my nipples, elongating them. I echoed the action with my clit. Still deep inside me, his dick pulsed. I throbbed in time, the reminder that he was in me but not moving spurring me on.

Rolling my hips, I started to fuck him. But he broke the kiss.

"No. I want to come from just feeling ye. Is that okay?"

God, why did every little thing he said make me emotional? I'd already been in pieces from hearing his heartbreak at that wedding. Though he'd been light on details, I felt every piece of his shock. Of how his safe world had been dismantled by dishonesty and misuse. No wonder he didn't want to risk another relationship. He'd been burned so badly. Yet here he was with me in every way but a label.

I stopped and returned to the kiss and my light playing with my clit. Valentine kept up his steady action, working my breasts until my breathing came hard and heat flashed over me.

Every breath he took mapped to mine. Every tiny shift in our bodies was both of us in perfect unity. Need grew and grew in intensity. A dark wave of pressure and delight.

A precipice fast approached. I tore my mouth from his, dropping my head back to gasp. Around him, I pulsed, then another beat and I was coming. I moaned, throbbing hard around his dick, the sensation washing all over my form and all the heavier for the barely there movements.

Silently, Valentine hugged both arms tight around me, his head down and pressed to mine. He took a shuddering breath, his dick thickened, and the sensation pulled a choked cry from me. Then he groaned, coming inside me, my climax triggering his.

It took a long moment before my brain engaged again and I drifted back to earth. Tuned in to the man at my back, I reached to stroke his face, not risking any words of deep emotion he wouldn't want to hear. Valentine kissed my hair, then took his hand back down me to the place we were still joined. He stroked my thighs, my clit. Felt over where he impaled me still. Then holding his dick in me, he finally slumped down. Like he needed to remain in place all night long.

I drifted to sleep happier than I'd ever been in my life.

The following morning, I woke to an empty bed. Momentary panic struck me that he'd got overwhelmed. I'd understand. I'd panicked over it, too. But a minute later, his clattering around in the kitchen let me breathe easier.

I snuck to the bathroom and cleaned myself up, hardly recognising the woman in the mirror with her hair tousled and cheeks pink. Naked, I stood for a second and just let myself stare—something I never did, usually remembering harsh words about my size. Now, I didn't care. It didn't hurt me. I liked me just fine.

When Valentine returned to the bedroom, I was back in bed, his black t-shirt covering me for the sake of us being able to eat and not instantly screwing again. My eyes rounded for the tray he carried.

"Coffee and toast. Just a quick refuel so we don't have to get up yet." He offered it out then climbed in beside me. "Woman, ye look well fucked."

"Understatement of the century."

He grinned, so perfectly handsome, and gestured for me to drink my coffee. "It's weird not having the Tobster home. I'm used to her noise in the morning. When do we go get her?"

My heart panged in a way that was getting worse and more familiar. He'd always been so respectful of my little girl, keeping clear boundaries as a house guest, but he missed her, too.

"Elise said to come by at noon." I leaned to grab my phone, finding a photo waiting. "Look, they're having breakfast in a den."

The kids had a tent up in the living room with cushions on the floor and snack trays laid out in front of them. Elise's son sat behind them, and the three beamed at the camera.

Valentine grinned. "Cute. I bet Finn would be in there if he were home."

"They come back tomorrow, is that right?"

"Aye, right after the gig, so it'll be the early hours by the time everyone's flown in."

"Daisy and Ariel will be so happy. You will be, too. I bet you've missed your crew."

He raised a shoulder, chewing on toast. "I've been pleasantly distracted, if ye hadn't noticed."

Breakfast gave way to another turn in the sheets, then a shower ahead of getting dressed to fetch Tobi.

Shortly before we had to leave, Valentine surprised me again. At the front door, standing in a beam of sunlight, he gestured to the perfect spring day. "How about we drive out somewhere for lunch? There's a café on the beach at Loch Morlich that Tobi will love. The sun's out, and it's naw that cold. We can take a ball. Maybe even paddle in the water if ye fancy it?"

Two thoughts struck me at once, arrows to my aching heart.

I'd fallen for him so hard, I'd been ignorant of anything else. But that couldn't hide the truth right there in my face. Valentine loved me, too. He'd deny it, I was sure, but he did. He didn't take the option of space, which I could've given him by going out. He didn't mention leaving though he was back on his feet again. Instead, he wanted to bring the family unit closer together, to join in with us. Be part of us.

For the first time since letting myself get tangled up in his orbit, I felt hope.

"Love that idea," I managed.

"I do, too." He leaned to peck my lips.

My stomach flipped, my whole being rotating to become his. So simple and easy, and something I had to work out how to keep.

In my car, we trundled out to pick up my daughter. She flew into my arms, but her glee was all for Valentine being there and his plan to go to the beach.

Throughout the afternoon, I had to remember to catch my breath. To pinch myself to remind me this was real. Loch Morlich was the prettiest spot, with snowcapped mountains rising all around and thick fir trees coming right down onto the sand. Other families had the same idea of enjoying a Saturday on the beach, and kids played in the surf, some brave souls out on canoes or windsurfing.

But it was Valentine at my side who stole my thoughts. Or him running with Tobi in and out of the waves. When she splashed him, he laughed, taking care to only lightly splash her back and not drench her.

If ever I'd pictured the perfect father for my little girl, he was there on the sands, carving out a place in our lives.

My phone ringing in my bag broke my reverie. I pulled it

out—Scarlet calling.

"Hey," she said. "Sorry to call unexpectedly, but there's been an odd occurrence with regard to my lawyer talking to the Winchester family."

A chill descended over me. Of course they'd crop up now. "Go on."

"After ignoring many of our questions and requests, they've this afternoon sent through a list of demands. Primarily centred around getting visitation with Tobi."

Down the beach, my daughter claimed her ball and tossed it at Valentine's head. He snatched it from the air, his pretend outrage making her stuff her hands to her face in glee.

"No," I breathed, horror threatening my perfect afternoon. "They're trying to get her alone? No way. I don't want that."

"I doubt they really do either. It's a chess move. There's more, and some of this is going to sound scary, but hear me out before you panic, okay?"

I swallowed and asked her to proceed.

"The mother has threatened to take you to court for custody of your daughter."

"She what?" I whispered.

"She has no case. We've pushed back, and she instantly returned with a counteroffer. She's claiming she just wants to know her stepdaughter is safe, and the method she proposes is by seeing her in person. If she's satisfied, she won't push for custody, but she also wants a promise that you'll attend her sons' company stakeholder meeting a few days later."

My mind raced, tripping up over itself. "Why would she threaten a custody case without any chance of winning?"

Scarlet's tone turned serious. "To present this as a bargain. She won't get custody, but she knows a challenge in court could be messy and time-consuming to handle."

"All to get me to come to their meeting? What would that give them?"

"The chance to persuade you to vote on their side. The paperwork they left at your friend's house outlines a proposal that ties up Tobi's inheritance and gives her no control or access for years."

"Then there is money." I shrank in on myself.

"Undoubtedly. Mrs Winchester also begged forgiveness for not handing over the will yet. She gave the excuse that her lawyer's office had suffered a flood and they lost access to all systems. She's happy to supply a hard copy in the access meeting."

"Where she wants to see Tobi in the flesh." My tone came out dull. "When does she want to do that?"

"Monday, in Dundee."

I shivered, suddenly freezing. "What do you suggest? All I know is I don't want to go near them."

"Hard question—are you worried that they'll try to snatch Tobi?"

I gave it a moment of thought. "No. Honestly, they seemed to like her when we lived with them, but taking her from me would destroy any case they had, wouldn't it?"

"Entirely. My lawyer suggests you show willingness and go ahead with the initial meeting. They see Tobi, we have it on paper that you attended and that your daughter is fine, then we get that will and have time to read it before the shareholder's meeting. I'll go with you, and my lawyers will be there, too. They can do all the talking. Is there someone else you can ask for moral support?"

From the water's edge, Valentine sighted me. He cocked his head in enquiry, his arm swinging to toss Tobi the ball even as his attention was all mine.

"Yes, I think so," I replied.

"Good. Should I agree?"

I took a breath. The only danger, when coming face to face with the Winchesters, was to me when seeing Greg, for he'd attend, I was certain. I hadn't told Valentine the full story, stopping short of my most embarrassing act. Of how Greg had turned on the charm and idiot-me had accepted his flattery and been led in. That humiliation was mine alone. I could bear it for the sake of seeing this through.

I'd run, I'd hidden, and I'd ducked issues. Now I needed to wise up and claim my daughter's rights.

"Please do."

33

Valentine

Fury had me stabbing buttons on my phone.

My brother answered right away. "Good timing that ye called. I just heard from the Spanish police. They made an arrest. The guy who stabbed ye is a known criminal and he's facing—"

"Grand. Hold that thought. I have a favour to ask. It's urgent."

"Name it." He waited on my word.

I never asked anything of him, ever, but I was going in all guns blazing now.

From the moment Mia had taken her phone call on the banks of Loch Morlich, I knew something was wrong, but it was only once Tobi fell asleep this evening that she'd given me the details along with a request for me to be there with her.

Of course I fucking would.

I'd told her so in her bed and I'd meant every word.

"I need to form a guard for Tobi at a meeting on Monday

morning. I'm going regardless, but if I have the rest of ye there, I'll feel a whole lot easier."

Ben made a gruff sound. "Switching to a group call. We're all available. Ask us all at once."

My heart damn well ached. Jackson then Raphael linked up. In ten minutes, I had a strategy in place. We'd fly Mia and Tobi in and out of the meeting so there was no chance of being followed and provide a show of force like those fuckers never saw coming.

Then we were done, and I had to let them go as Leo was due to leave his dressing room and take to the stage.

"Ben?" I said after our colleagues had disconnected.

"Aye?"

"Thank ye." Then I hung up on him and took Mia to bed.

She asked me to help her forget. I worshipped her body until she did. All night, I held her. The lass had a nightmare, and I hushed her, hugging her until it let her be. Then in the morning, I rose before Tobi could know where I'd slept.

Sunday passed with tense quiet. We took Tobi for a walk around the loch with Cameron's lass, me testing my strength as much as anything. I needed to bring my A game tomorrow and I'd slacked off with all things fitness related. I spoke with the crew again who were preparing to come home, while Mia went to see Daisy and Ariel for coffee.

Then we were there.

Monday morning dawned bright and cold.

Ben had texted when Raphael had flown him home. They were the last to come back, so the crew were suited, booted, and ready to go.

Mia sat Tobi down on the couch. "We're going on a little trip this morning to see some old friends."

Tobi bounced on the seat. "Who?"

"Vanissa, Greg, and Simon. They want to say hi. Plus there might be a few others around, but it's just the family we're going to talk to."

The little girl's eyes brightened. "Greg promised me riding lessons at Christmas. Do you think I'll get them?"

Pale, her ma touched her cheek. "I don't know, baby. But we don't expect gifts every time we meet people."

My phone chimed. "The heli's ready," I told the lasses.

"We're going by helicopter?" Tobi squeaked. She hopped up and ran to me.

Without thinking, I lifted her into my arms. "Aye. But if I get scared of heights, I might have to close my eyes so I don't cry."

She snickered and flung her arms around my neck. I caught Mia's expression, half expecting her to tell me off for overstepping. When I'd taken care of Finn, I'd thought nothing of carrying the lad when he needed it. I'd seen my brother put him on his shoulders, and it felt normal to do. But Tobi was different. I didn't have a role with her, aside from her mother's friend. Yet Mia's lips curved into a faint but perfect smile, and the band that had been around my chest for weeks tightened like a clamp.

I took a breath to dispel the odd feeling. I couldn't lose focus on my priorities. "Ready?" I asked her.

"As I'll ever be. Let's go."

At the airfield, Raphael loaded us into a helicopter with him and my brother in the front and me, Mia, and Tobi in the back. Jackson had already left, driving down country in convoy with Scarlet who was meeting her lawyers en route. Jackson would pick us up at the helipad and drive us the short distance to the hired hotel conference suite that was our neutral destination. Raphael would stay with the aircraft, giving us a fast getaway should we need it. The rest of us would guard Mia and Tobi come hell or high water. As plans went, it was pretty slick.

Heaven help the fucker who tried anything today.

We lifted off. Tobi squeaked and clutched her ma then was all eyes for the view and jabbering questions and a rolling commentary over her headset. The trip seemed to pass in the blink of an eye. Soon, we were touching down at Dundee's tiny airstrip and loading into the big car Jackson had waiting. Conversation was sparse, even Tobi stopping her cute but endless chatter for a muted peering out of the windows.

"Are we going home?" she asked.

"No, we don't live there anymore," Mia answered.

"Good. I like our new cottage," her daughter announced.

We turned left into the city centre, and Mia indicated up the coast, speaking to me. "They own several properties here—the head office of the place I used to work, and a big Victorian home in West End which is that way. Vanissa's house is beautiful, but we lived in an annexe in their garden. It was always cold as it had night storage heaters. I wish we'd moved a long time ago."

I took her hand, not missing Ben noticing from the front passenger seat.

At a big, modern hotel, we pulled over. Mia took a shaky breath, and all of us climbed out of the car.

A man lurked in the hotel's entryway. Tall, though not as tall as me, and with sandy hair, he took us in, focusing on Mia who had her back to him while she helped Tobi down. Then he tossed a cigarette and stormed away around the rear of the building.

Greg. Mr Shiny Orange Truck. Had to be. His nasty expression gave him away. If he'd expected them to come alone, he was as stupid as he was ugly. I linked gazes with my brother and indicated the direction Greg had gone. He inclined his head, clearly having noticed, too, then spoke in Jackson's ear. Jax peeled away from the group as Mia faced forward.

"Ten minutes. In and out. We can do this," she said under her breath. To her daughter, she said, "Ready to go say hi?"

Tobi produced a smile, but it was a small one. Together, we entered the hotel. The receptionist led us into a lift and to the second floor.

Through the glass doors of a conference room, I spied Scarlet plus a man and a woman one side of a wide polished table, and a group of people on the other. We reached the door, and I scoped out the strangers. A polished woman in her late forties had to be the mother, Vanissa Winchester. A twenty-something lookalike lad was her son, Simon, then, which confirmed it was Greg who'd haunted the place outside. I wondered if he'd show his face or if my and the team's presence had scuppered his plans. Jax would report in when he found him.

I moved on, summing up the group. A team of four in suits were lawyers. I sneered at the clear intimidation attempt and placed a hand subtly on Mia's back. "You've got this. We're all here, and in a few minutes, we'll be gone."

She gazed straight forward, nodded, and entered the lion's den.

At the door swinging open, all eyes trained on us filtering in.

Mrs Winchester stood, her focus shifting to the girl she'd called her stepdaughter. "At last. We've been waiting so long. October. I've missed you. Come here for a hug."

Tobi hid behind her ma.

The Winchester woman's forehead lined. "Don't you remember me? It's Vani. How about you give Simon a hug?

Didn't you miss your brother?"

Mia took a seat, and Tobi curled on her lap, ignoring the woman's demands. I concealed a smile and leaned on the wall, watching the mother, who started talking about the shock of finding Mia and Tobi gone one day, then switching to eyeball the younger son. Dumb fucker had his attention squarely on Mia. He didn't sneer like his older sibling but he needed to stop fucking staring.

I cleared my throat quietly. Simon stared at me. With a pinning glower, I raised a reproving eyebrow. I knew how I appeared. My size, how I probably weighed twice what he did.

Dude dropped his gaze to his lap. Yeah, like I thought.

Vanissa huffed at Mia. "Well, are you going to offer any explanation for your behaviour or just sit there?"

Scarlet's male lawyer raised a hand. "This meeting will be short and with the solitary purpose of enabling the attending parties to see October in good health. As you can see, the child is hale and hearty."

"The sole purpose? Am I not owed answers?" the mother snipped.

"I'm afraid that isn't necessary to the proceedings," the lawyer answered.

"I put her up. Fed and clothed her. She hasn't said a word." Vanissa twisted to her team, all leaning in to listen to her whisper.

In my earpiece, Jackson spoke. "Found our lurker. He's waiting at his car, engine on."

I scowled. Ben's eyebrows drew in, too. He went to gesture to Raphael, but I held up a hand, pausing him.

"Excuse us for a moment." Vanissa exited the room into a chamber to the side, her son and her lawyers going with her.

If for some reason she was stalling, I'd take the opportunity for an investigation.

Kneeling beside Mia, I whispered in her ear, "The other brother's outside. Jax is monitoring him, but I want to check him out. All right if I step away for a minute? You're both safe here."

Her throat bobbed, but she inclined her head.

Badly, I wanted to hold her to me for a moment, to still her trembling, but I was here to do a job. I trusted Ben and Raphael to watch over her, plus with Scarlet and all the legal folk, I knew she'd be okay.

The bigger threat was outside.

Beyond the room, I followed the corridor to the rear of the hotel. From the windows, I scanned the car park below. The orange truck stood out like a sore thumb, Greg standing in the open door with one foot on the tread.

If he was here to take Tobi, I'd bury him with that fucking truck on top of him.

A set of stairs led down to an exit, Jackson waiting the other side, keeping a watch while not engaging yet.

He lifted his chin as I slipped out the door. "Need a hand?"

I snorted. "If I can't take out this miserable arsehole with one hit, I shouldn't be in this job."

"Use your words first, Val." He chuffed a laugh and held his position.

I strode on, making a beeline for Greg.

Adrenaline tightened my muscles, and anger threatened my composure. Fuck this guy. If he ended up with my fist in his face, it could only improve his looks.

He clocked me immediately and straightened from his lean.

I let my hostility show. "Why the fuck does it seem like you're planning an abduction?"

He reared back, his expression of disgust still installed. "Who are you?"

"Valentine Graham, here with Mia and Tobi. Answer the question."

"I don't need to tell you shit."

I let a cold smile curve my lips. "Aye, but ye might prefer that to my alternative way of getting information from ye. Try to enter the building, and my man is there to persuade ye against it. If ye even get that far."

He shut his mouth, his gaze jumping to Jackson before returning to me. "Mia can't afford security." Then his eyes narrowed. "One of you is fucking her fat ass, then."

As a bodyguard, there were lines I shouldn't cross. Despite my comment to Jax, I knew I wasn't above the law, and there was clear delineation between protective and aggressive behaviour. That was all that kept me from grabbing him by the throat.

Greg centred on me, sniffing out my rising rage. "It's you, then."

I tilted my head in cold assessment, not acknowledging a thing, but the moron only got more excited.

"Damn, she's got better at leading men on, then. Used to be the other way around. Did you know she used to follow me about like a sad and desperate bitch? One click of my fingers and she'd sit up and beg. She's always been mine."

"Bullshit," I gritted out. He was talking crap. Trying to rattle me. If they'd been in a relationship, Mia would have told me.

Greg shifted forward in an attempt to reclaim his space. I didn't budge, as much frozen to the spot as not giving an inch, and he rocked back on the balls of his feet.

"You care about her, don't you? Didn't she tell you why she left? My brother opened his big mouth and gave up the game so she didn't believe I was serious about her. But just as easily, I can get her back. If you think she cares about you, guess again, because that bitch is taking you for all she can get. Mia wants me and she always has."

A slew of images of the two of them together suddenly hit me. Her in his arms. In his bed. Her wanting him, not me, all this time.

History repeating.

Greg gave me a final smirk of victory and climbed into his car, reaching for the door handle. I stepped aside. It was better for him to go than be here, even if I wanted to throttle answers out of him.

Through the open window, with his blond hair slicked back, Greg gave a final parting comment. "When I'm ready, I'll take her from you, and it'll be as easy as breathing because she's loved me all along."

He revved the engine then drove out of the car park, leaving me to stare. And fucking reel in horror. My worst nightmare, bigger than any Kelly had ever given me and unknown until this second, had just come true.

34

Mia

Valentine entered the room behind me right as Vanissa took her seat once again.

She formed a pretend shaky smile to address the room. "I feel like we should start over. It wasn't my intention to get so emotional, but that's an undeniable effect of having my family torn apart. I've always tried to be reasonable. From the first moment I found out about Mia and our sweet Tobi, I've tried to do my best by them. We gave them a home. Help when her mother was dying. All the attention she deserved."

She was building up to something, and it couldn't be good. I shot a look at Scarlet who nudged the lawyer to her right.

The man cleared his throat. "Noted. We see no need to draw this out further. Are you satisfied that October is content and well cared for?"

Tobi cuddled into me, her face buried in my neck.

As if I'd do anything other than the best for my baby. She'd been the first priority from the moment I'd taken a pregnancy test.

Vanissa smiled in sympathy at us. "Yes, I'm satisfied. But you see how much she missed her family? Mia, be reasonable. Such rash actions as you've leapt to can't be good for the girl's mental health. What if a child psychologist reported that your abduction caused October trauma?"

My lips flew open. Trauma?

Scarlet's lawyer spluttered. "Let's be clear, no such report exists, nor is there any justification in ordering an assessment."

At last, the true colours of Vanissa Winchester shone through. She brushed strands of glossy blonde hair back from her face and took an easy breath. "That remains to be seen. It might be very appropriate with regard to access or even custody arrangements."

My heart cracked. I hugged Tobi closer. "You wouldn't dare."

I wouldn't put my daughter through anything like that. She was already scared enough in this meeting.

From the end of the table, Scarlet glowered and took control. "This is over. The only thing remaining is for you to provide a copy of the will, Mrs Winchester."

Vanissa indicated to one of her lawyers who extracted an envelope from a briefcase and placed it in the centre of the table.

"Here. I doubt you'll find anything interesting in it." Vanissa stood. Her gaze returned to me, cold and calculating. "The details of the board meeting to decide the fate of my late husband's business are also in the envelope. Your attendance is required, Mia. With Greg and Simon, the three of you form the basis for the board and hold all the votes. To make things perfectly clear, decide in my sons' favour and we need never speak again. Vote against them, and my lawyers will throw the works at you that no team of apes you've somehow amassed will protect you against."

Without another word, she left the room, Simon and her people going with her.

I slumped. Scarlet and her two lawyers collected the envelope and pulled out the contents, a fast conversation commencing about changing goalposts and underhand tactics. I could only focus on breathing. On comforting Tobi who I hoped hadn't understood any of what Vanissa had threatened.

I expected Valentine to set his big hand on my shoulder, providing warmth where I only felt cold, but when I peeked around, he was holding his position, something troubled in his gaze.

"Can we go home?" I asked him.

He blinked, then nodded, moving around me with his team.

For the entirety of the trip back to the McRae estate, he barely said a word.

At the hangar, Finn and Leo were waiting on the helicopter, both of them there to see Valentine. He'd been a hero on the tour, and they crowded him, full of happiness to see him back on his feet. Gordain joined them, slapping Valentine on the back.

I needed to get home. Scarlet was driving while in conversation with her lawyers and required input from me. I placed a hand on Valentine's arm. "I'll see you back at the house."

He spared me a look, but it was that same pensive, cooler one. "Aye. I'll pick up my car now I'm allowed behind the wheel. We'll talk later."

Why did that feel ominous?

At home, I made us food and called Scarlet. She was nearby so made the arrangement to come straight to us. Tobi was overjoyed to be home. She asked if she could see Avery, having missed her at school today, and a quick message to Elise had them picking her up for an hour or two's playdate. They swung by right as Scarlet appeared.

Of Valentine, I'd seen and heard nothing.

Brandishing the paperwork, Scarlet laid it out on the kitchen table. "My lawyers took copies at the hotel and have done some fast work taking it apart."

I scanned the official-looking will, the paper thick and embossed, and a logo for a solicitor's firm in the corner. "What did they find?"

"Greg Winchester Senior wrote this when he formed the business as a man of thirty-five. It wasn't amended to include Tobi by name, or either of his other children for that matter, but fortunately the language used still accounts for your daughter. In summary, it awards his entire estate including property and any business concerns to be split equally between any biological children."

"So three ways: Tobi, Greg Junior, and Simon," I said. "Not his wife?"

"No, and she isn't on the board either. You said she owned her own home, so perhaps he felt she was already provided for."

"Do we know what the business is worth? With all the evasion, I'm almost certain they're lying about that, too."

Scarlet lifted her gaze. "They didn't include the asset report, which is frustrating, but at least we now know which solicitor firm is handling the will. My lawyers have already got in touch, and they'll call you when they get it. My guess is it's of significant value. Why else make all this fuss?"

I shivered, everything flipping around from what I'd believed in the past.

"There's something else," Scarlet continued. "If that's

correct with the three children splitting everything, the Winchesters have the majority. The two sons hold a shade over sixty-six percent of the business so don't need your vote, which you have on Tobi's behalf, for the restructuring plan to go ahead."

"The restructure that puts the sons as Chief Exec and Chief Operating Officer and locks in profits for silent partners, like Tobi," I concluded. While waiting, I'd tried to read the information Greg had delivered to Molly's for me.

Something bugged me.

I couldn't put my finger on it, but it had my heart racing.

"This isn't adding up." Scarlet stood and paced the room, seemingly affected by the same energy as me.

"Exactly what I was just thinking. What happens if I don't go to the meeting?" I asked.

"Presumably the vote would carry."

"Except they're doing everything they can to ensure I'm there."

"True. The mother made you jump through hoops, changed dates without notice, then resorted to the basest tactic she could in threatening your daughter."

"They changed the date again?" I asked.

"Shoot. That was on one of my messages. It's tomorrow. No doubt to give you even less time to think this through."

We gazed at each other.

My blood heated, anger mixing in.

"They're scared," I uttered. "Of what, I have no clue, but it's real."

The older woman nodded. "I'm inclined to agree. Interesting that the older brother didn't show today."

"He did, at least I think so. Valentine went to accost him

outside. I'll see if I can find out what happened."

Scarlet waited while I texted Valentine. A short reply came, saying he'd found out nothing useful but would come by later to talk. I relayed that worrying note.

"Without further information," Scarlet said, "it looks to me that you have a decision to make. The harder option is to call them on their bluff and ignore their demands, leaving the ball in their court."

I sighed. "I don't want to take the easy route of just going along with them because I know they're acting in their favour, not ours. But if she sues me for access or custody via her sons, I can't afford to challenge it. You've been so helpful and generous in giving up your time and your lawyers, but I can't ask for more."

Her expression morphed to one of sympathy. "I've really loved helping. Your story of injustice is inspiring, and I know from my own personal history how a tricky family background can cause all kinds of problems."

I angled my head, wondering what she meant.

"My father, the man who raised me, wasn't actually my biological father. I didn't know until I was a teenager, and my parents never acknowledged it until that point of discovery. We had all the angst and drama you can imagine, but it resolved okay in the end. So believe me, helping you has been cathartic in all things right and true."

I reached and took her fingers in mine, pressing them once. "Thank you. I had no idea about your family. I'm more than grateful you've helped mine."

Scarlet smiled. "But on that note, my limit of usefulness has probably been reached. My people aren't specialists in family courts. They can untangle legal wording on a standard contract, but you'd need to hire a lawyer with the right credentials if the Winchesters carry out their threat. We can offer general help but we're also snowed under from tomorrow on a big new contract."

Her phone buzzed, and she held it up. "My husband. Be back in a sec."

Scarlet stepped outside to take her call.

I mused on what I had to do next. Or maybe I didn't need to consider a thing. Today, I'd been scared out of my wits but I hadn't let that fear own me. I'd shown up.

Tomorrow, I'd do the same, except this time on my own two feet.

Scarlet returned. "Ally's finished work and was wondering if we were done."

"We are. I know what I'm going to do. Wish me good luck in telling the Winchesters to go fuck themselves tomorrow."

"You're going in person?"

"With bells on."

Scarlet beamed and rounded the table to hug me. "I want a blow-by-blow account of all that goes down."

"You'll have it."

She drove away, and I sat alone in my kitchen and let all the facts and different pieces of information filter through my brain. Stress had been eating at me for days, giving me the worst brain fog. If only I could work out the missing piece of the puzzle.

A hidden will, votes and tied-up cash, pretend acceptance, lies, and threats. It all whirled around in my head. Maybe I could talk it through with Molly. She knew the family and had lived two streets over from the Winchesters before her marriage broke up and she'd moved to Stirling. I vaguely remembered her aunt, the lady who drove the school bus, had been friendly with them, too, being of the same generation. Maybe she'd have some insight. Then I pulled a face. She'd gotten Greg Junior's name wrong when we last spoke. Still, it was worth a try.

I tapped out a quick message to Molly.

Mia: Remember that paperwork I picked up? Tobi will split her dad's assets with his sons, but they're making it hard on us. Do you have a minute to talk it out?

Another engine roared outside. I peered from the window.

Valentine was home, his expression dark as he exited his big black car and approached my door. It couldn't be a coincidence that he'd gone down to talk to Greg and had come back miserable.

I heaved another sigh and straightened my shoulders, ready to face whatever else today had to throw at me.

35

Valentine

The door swung open without me even touching it, and Mia appeared in the frame.

She peered at my raised fist. "You were going to knock?"

I shrugged. "Not like I live here."

"Even though you have actually lived here for a week." She blew an exasperated breath. "Go sit down."

I ducked under the frame and trod inside. "I'll stand."

"Suit yourself. I'm exhausted, so don't mind if I collapse. Today has been a battering ram that just keeps swinging. Not even just today." She shook her head, like she had to dislodge a sense of being stunned. "So, during the meeting you went out and spoke to Greg. Tell me about it."

I hated his name on her lips. Despised it.

All afternoon, I'd wallowed in misery at what I'd discovered. Coming here was the very last fucking thing I'd wanted to do, but it was better to have this out then walk away. I'd been in the situation before and didn't want history repeating more than it already had.

"He told me everything," I forced out, waiting for the flash of guilt on her face.

Mia had the cheek to raise her eyebrows. "And that included what exactly?"

"About the two of ye."

"Elaborate, please."

Frustration rushed in me, hurt and pain too close to the surface, an afternoon spent imagining her with him driving me crazy. "Do ye really need me to spell it out?"

"If you don't mind."

"Tell me the truth. Is it real? Do ye care about him?"

Mia's face flushed red. "That isn't spelling out anything."

"Answer me," I yelled.

Instant horror struck me at losing my rag. At shouting at the woman I... I...

She goggled for a second, then fury and disbelief descended over her features. Mia stood and planted her hands on her hips. "Oh, you idiot."

She took a step. I matched it, moving back.

"I see what happened. Greg told you I was in love with him and you believed him?"

At my lack of a reaction, she continued, moving closer still.

"That's it, isn't it? Good God, men are the worst. Once upon a time, Greg made a pass at me. Mom was gone, and I was in this weird place of starting a life without her. It made me decide on one last attempt to be nicer to the Winchesters. Family-wise, they were all we had and the only home left for me and Tobi. I'd tried to be friends with Greg and Simon, but both had shown obvious dislike from the moment I appeared at the funeral. They cared for Tobi, but even that was fake, I think, considering Simon didn't look her way once today. His own sister."

"Lucky she takes after ye and not that side of the family," I couldn't resist the jibe at the brothers.

She paused as if a thought had occurred to her, but then her ire returned, and she got back to educating me.

"The result of my efforts was Greg asking me to go to the local pub with him. I thought it a nice gesture, but when I went to the main house, I overheard him and Simon through the open window. Simon, who always had a loose tongue, was revolted at his brother taking me on a date, and while I stood there expecting Greg to correct him, in my pretty dress and with my hair done for the first time since Mom's funeral, he replied to him that yes, he was taking the stupid cow on a date and she was dumb enough to believe he was really interested. He was taking one for the team. I disgusted him."

Mia's flush paled to white. "Both laughed at me. They joked about having to have sex with me. I was humiliated, Valentine. Not because I cared about him, or that he'd led me on and broke my heart. But because after everything I'd been through, I couldn't take another hit. From the minute their father had plied me with drink and taken me to his bed while I was too drunk to even remember—"

My jaw dropped, but she held up a finger so I didn't dare interrupt.

"To their mother pushing papers at me and issuing her quasi threats. Their coldness and hostility just tipped the balance. I was alone and lost. I missed my mother so much, and every little thing hurt. I cried the whole evening then went to see Molly the next day and sparked my plot to leave. So how does that map to what he told you? Is it helping your scowl any? Do you believe me in the slightest?"

Ah fuck. Fuck all of it. I passed a hand over my face, lost for words. "Just wish you'd told me."

"Told you what? There was nothing to tell. Greg isn't an ex. I never kissed him. Never even hugged him. Besides, when did we have even the smallest conversation about our relationship since you came back injured from the tour? We aren't going there because the moment we do, you'll get scared and run."

"What the hell are ye talking about?" I demanded.

Mia dug her fingers into her tied-up hair, the other hand going to her throat. She looked exhausted. Fed up. So over my shit I was scared what was going to come out of her lips.

"You're in love with me," she finally said.

I tried to speak. No words came out.

"You love me and you panicked the moment something threatened that. I get it. You went through hell with your engagement. But you stood there and listened to Greg and believed every word he said. Did you even challenge him, or yourself in believing it, or did you just mope until gathering the courage to come yell at me?"

She waited for my reply, but I was still reeling. Denying it. Rocked to my very bones. In my employment, I could pivot on the spot, evading danger and coming up with a better plan fast, but faced with the same in my personal life, I was fucked.

"I just need to know if it's all an excuse to leave?" she uttered quieter.

"No," flew from my lips without me even forming the word.

Surprise and relief added to her visibly warring emotions. "That's something at least. But I think I just found my limit with you, too. I'm done with being the doormat people walk over. I'm done with any and all levels of BS. Tell me I'm wrong about the rest of it," she commanded.

I forced out my words, panic driving cold through my veins. "You're wrong. This isn't love. I know what that feels like. I've been there, and it is nothing like this.”

“Describe the love you shared with Kelly.”

I stopped. Thought about what I’d felt when I’d been in love. It had been nothing like what I’d seen of my parents’ relationship. Of Ben and Daisy. Of all the happy couples on the estate. “Paranoid. Painful. Strained for me. For her, it didn’t exist.”

She put her hand to my chest. Her fingers shook. “Love is like how we are together. Happy. Caring. Devoted. Wanting the other in all ways including outside of the bedroom. Giving your time, making sure they’re fed. Housed. You go out of your way to protect them. You drive through the night for a favour. You pass the damn bird test, for heaven’s sake.”

What the fuck was a bird test? “I can’t give ye what you’re asking for.”

“You’re right. Not like this.”

I was utterly stumped.

Her shoulders rose and fell. “Let’s find an easier way into your self-discovery. What do you want, Valentine?”

“For things to stay like this. Nothing changing.”

“With you sleeping over but not living here? For me to not be your girlfriend? For us never to be a real couple? I deserve better than that. Tobi does, too. She deserves a father who’ll love her and is proud to take on the title. I deserve someone who wants everything with me.”

Emotion hit me thick and fast. “You’re breaking up with me?”

“No, you idiot, I’m telling you to sort your shit out and be that man if we’re what you want. You’re torn up over your past and never healed. Talk to your brother. Call your ex and find out what she wants then tell her she hurt you. Forgive her or don’t, just do whatever you need to move on from it. If you’re lucky, I'll still be waiting. If not, I understand. I can bear the pain of losing you because I know loss. I've survived it once and can survive it again."

Her voice broke, and tears lined her eyes. Jagged pain slashed through me so vicious it nearly brought me to my knees. I wanted to grab hold of her. Apologise. Tear up all the words she'd said and get back to where we'd been.

But Mia rounded me and opened the door. She pointed outside to the darkening late afternoon.

"Why would it hurt you?" I muttered, needing more from her than I had the right to ask.

"Because I'm in love with you, too. Now get out of my house."

36

Mia

Alone, again, I fled the lounge for my bedroom and slid to the floor, bringing my knees to my chest. Then I let the tears fall that I'd kept in while he'd just stood there.

It wasn't love for him. He'd said so. A knife to my belly.

Or did I trust my instinct that told me he'd got so twisted up he didn't know the truth about himself? It smacked of pathetic to even think it.

For a minute, I let myself wallow. Then I cooled, dried my cheeks, and climbed up, hunting down my phone.

I hadn't been kidding when I said I'd survive Valentine. Loss felt like the end of all things, but that was never true. It merely concluded one direction of life and set you in another minus a person, an idea, or the way your heart beat.

I wanted everything with him. I'd laid my cards out. If I even thought about him coming back, it would break me, and I had a problem to fix. A niggling idea in my mind that needed all my brainpower.

A text waited for me.

Molly: That's so weird. My aunt asked after you this morning. She drove through Dundee a few days ago and happened to spot one of the Winchesters.

I perched on the sofa and tapped a reply.

Mia: Don't suppose they were doing anything suspicious that could help me work out this inheritance issue?

Molly: I'd love to say yes, but nope. Let me forward her note.

Another message arrived.

Aunt B: George Winchester was at the crossroads, yelling at some old dear in her car for not moving off quick enough. He was always a wrong 'un.

Mia: She called him George to me when I saw her last, too. Must have the wrong name stuck in her head.

Molly: Oh, I corrected her once. It isn't wrong. He used to be George when he was little.

That same warning played out in my mind. A deep spike of intuition that I needed to follow this trail.

I hit the button to call Molly, excitement soothing a tiny edge of my sorrow for Valentine. "Can you get your aunt on the phone? I think the two of you might've just uncovered something vital."

In an hour, I had the answer I'd been looking for. All I needed now was the ovaries to deliver the killing blow when the time came.

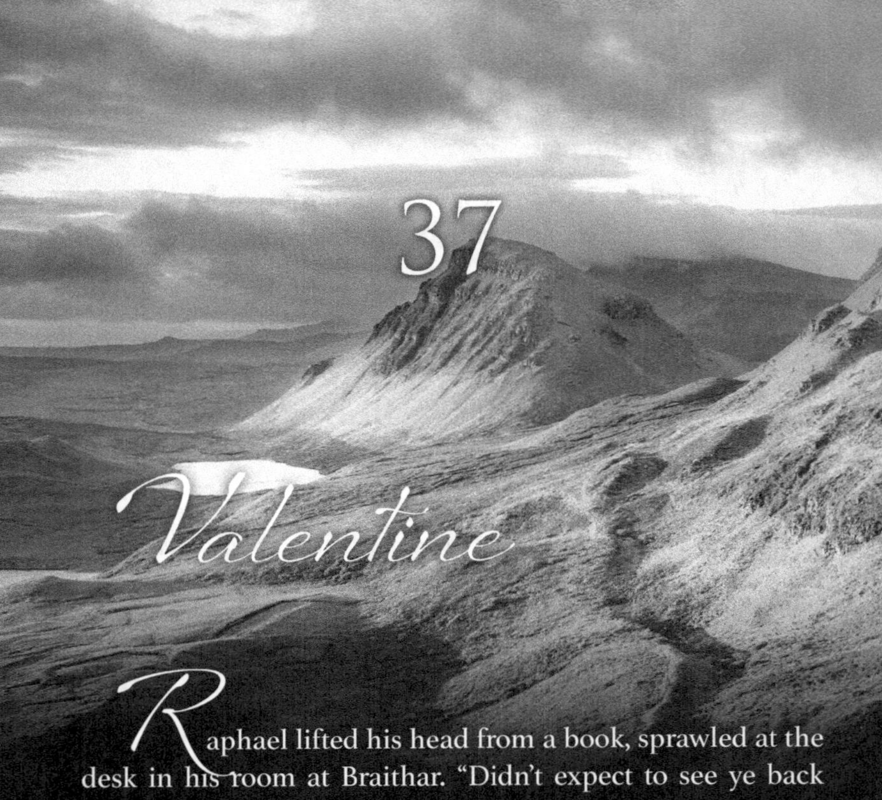

Raphael lifted his head from a book, sprawled at the desk in his room at Braithar. "Didn't expect to see ye back here."

The lad jumped up and came to me, arms open. I took the embrace. Needed it. I'd clued in early that Raphael was a hugger. He made a point of throwing an arm around Jackson whenever he went quiet for too long, and was now doing the same with me.

Made me wonder if Raphael himself needed comfort more than he said.

He slapped my back and pulled away, his ready smile morphing into a frown. "Ye okay?"

"Not really. I'm about to call my ex. For some reason, she keeps messaging, and I haven't spoken to her since she kissed my brother at my other brother's wedding. Want to listen in?"

He widened his eyes then plopped back into his seat. "For some morbid reason, yes. Won't it be weird?"

"Eh." I took out my phone and went to my blocked numbers. There were two for Kelly. I picked the one she'd texted from recently. "I want ye to see the contrast between a failed relationship and one that's going to work."

"I take it the latter's with Mia?"

"If she'll take me back."

He winced. "Did ye do something daft? Atmosphere was tense in the heli, but I figured that was from the meeting."

"Yeah, that was mostly me. I'll give her tonight while I fix shite then I'm going to make up for it."

I hit the number to call Kelly then sat at the end of Raph's bed, thankfully stripped and remade by someone since I'd collapsed here. My camp bed was still against the other wall. Looked like I'd be sleeping there tonight.

I deserved nothing better than the floor.

The line rang loud in the room.

"H-hello?" Kelly's hesitant voice followed.

"Kelly, it's Valentine. I'm with a friend. You've been trying to get hold of me." Nothing but cool indifference filled me. Until now, I'd thought talking to her the worst thing ever. To my surprise, I was entirely calm.

"Yes. Wait a minute. I'm getting out of my car." Sounds came of a door closing and footsteps on a path. "I'm in the house now. Did you say you're with someone?"

"One of my team. Listen, I've got a lot to do this evening, so if ye could get to the point quickly about why you're blowing up my phone, I'd be grateful."

A pause followed. "It's been years, Valentine."

I shrugged, not that she could see. "And?"

"You're still angry at me."

"That isn't true." Even if I still needed to hold her to account,

I didn't care enough for any strong emotion.

Kelly sighed. "I just assumed things would be different now, since, you know, everything got resolved. It is, right?"

"I'm drawing a blank here. What's been resolved?"

"You know what I mean. *He's* engaged to be married."

It took a long second for the answer to dawn on me. "Do ye mean Ben?" A startled laugh flew from my lips. "Are ye saying you've been waiting all this time for him?"

Raphael mouthed, *Ben's engaged?*

Unofficially, I mouthed back.

"Don't act shocked," she said, her voice trembling. "We used to be friends, didn't we? You knew me better than anyone. If things had gone as they should've, you'd have become my brother-in-law. We would've been family."

The years I'd spent with her hit me in flashes of memory. All those long-distance phone calls when we'd chatted about our future, all the shite she'd purchased for the place that would be our home, and the whole time, she'd been living a lie. I'd expected to feel annoyance, but only pity followed.

"Ben's very happily settled down with a woman who's perfect for him," I told her. "Daisy's the best. She's kind and sweet, and Ben adores her. I can't imagine a better partner for him."

"Don't," Kelly uttered.

Mia's words came back to me, how I'd never tackled this. Never faced Kelly and told her off for what she'd done. It was true. What was the motto of my regiment? Nemo Me Impune Lacessit. *No one provokes me with impunity.*

I'd let her get away with it for far too long.

Taking a breath, I said what needed to be said. "Kelly, once, I had endless time to listen to ye, but that tolerance dissolved when I realised how you'd lied and cheated every second we were together. I'm not saying this to be cruel, it's just a fact. I also discovered something about myself. I gave ye up without any kind of a fight. Now, I know that's because what I felt never went to any real depth. It couldn't, because ye weren't there to meet it. I know that now because I'm with someone who actually has depths worth exploring. So let me wind this up by stating for the records that ye hurt me in the most underhand, shitty way. I carried that burden of regret for a long time and never told ye off for it. Consider this me telling ye."

She sniffed. "You never loved me. If you had, you would've left the army and wanted to be with me. You liked the idea of me more than the reality."

"That's probably true. Doesnae excuse what ye did. I never lied. I never cheated on ye."

"Oh, come on. All that time away and you never screwed someone outside a bar or snuck them into barracks?"

"Not once." Though the way she so easily assumed that told me she most likely had.

Kelly gave a noise of derision. "If I was a shitty girlfriend then you're a shitty liar."

Raphael sat forward, his dark hair tumbling in his eyes. "After all he just said, you're still missing the point. For fuck's sake. Apologise to Valentine. He deserves it."

"Who's that?" Kelly asked.

"None of your business," Raph snapped back, my ally in this weird-as-fuck coming of age for my emotional development.

"Fine. I'm sorry," she bit out. "I'm more sorry for all the years I wasted on Graham men. I'm twenty-nine now and I have to compete with women a decade younger when I go out—"

Aaand I was done. "I couldnae give a damn. I'm assuming there wasn't anything real ye needed to talk to me about?"

"No, I just wanted to be sure about Ben."

Click. I disconnected and in a couple of swipes, blocked her once again. Then I heaved a deep breath.

"Brutal," Raphael breathed. "How did it feel?"

"Unreal. Freeing. I avoided that for so long because I thought if I spoke to her, I'd have to handle emotions I really didn't want to feel again." I eyed him. "I figured she'd broken my heart so badly, but I know I was a fucking fool."

He pointed at me, grinning from ear to ear. "Because you're in love with Mia."

On that, I bit my tongue. No way was I telling him before her. Even though Mia had been the one to inform me.

"Next stop, I need to talk to my brother," I said instead.

"Ben and Daisy are out for the evening. By the end of the tour, he was cranky as fuck over missing her. Can it wait until morning? You'll get a better reception if he's... Ye know."

"If he got laid all night? Fuck. Fine."

Raphael chuffed a laugh.

Alongside his competence at the controls of the helicopter, his hand on the cyclical, or whatever the fuck it was called, and his easy confidence in all things mechanical, I could imagine the youngest bodyguard laying on the charm with a lass. He usually talked to women in the same way he did men, with careful words and respect. But all the lad had to do was smile at them and he'd have someone willing to risk the things he feared.

I raised an eyebrow. "Have ye considered finding a girlfriend?"

"After what I just listened to? Fuck, no. Not happening. It isn't worth it."

I wasn't going to push, but I'd be ready with advice when he needed it. I tipped my head at the door instead. "Fine. Want to go hang with Leo and the family for a couple of hours?"

Earlier, when I'd seen them, my mood had been foul. I wanted to spend some time with Finn again. Nowhere near as much as I needed to bang down Mia's door and beg to see her, but she'd told me what I needed to do, and I was only fifty percent of the way there.

I wasn't returning until I could prove I'd listened and done the work.

Tomorrow would change everything.

*E*arly the next morning, I rolled up outside Ben and Daisy's cottage and climbed out of my car. It was so early, the crisp air iced my face and the sky was barely light.

My brother opened an upstairs window and gazed down. "Valentine? What's wrong?"

"Nothing bad. Need to talk to ye. Got a minute?"

"Aye, funnily enough, seeing as I was in my fucking bed." He gave me a reproving smirk that was as much tolerance as censure. In that second, it was just like looking at the boy I'd spent years with at boarding school. The big brother who'd got me out of trouble and colluded with me in stupid pranks.

I'd missed him so much.

Moments later, he was letting me in, a long-sleeved top hastily dragged on along with worn jeans.

Daisy skipped down the stairs in a thick dressing gown. "Got to say I'm surprised to see you here."

I squinted at her. "Sorry to disturb."

"That isn't what I meant." She threw a glance at my brother. "Anyone for coffee?"

We both shook our heads, and Daisy disappeared into the kitchen. Gesturing for me to take the couch opposite his, Ben watched me, his forehead furrowed and his dark-blond hair in whorls and scruffy from sleep.

I'd resisted doing this, summoning memories and drawing in the conflict it brought. But I was the problem and I was over myself.

"I called Kelly last night."

He jerked. Passed his hand over his face. "Fuck. Not what I was expecting ye to say."

"It was about time I told her off for what she did."

His lips parted, but he let me have the floor.

"Ever since that night, I've had this block over handling it. I shut down. It gave me nightmares."

"Was that the first time ye spoke to her since?"

"Aye."

Ben winced. "I'll probably regret asking this, but what were the nightmares about?"

"The two of ye together."

He swore. "I was never alone with her. Not once. Nothing ever happened, and I never suspected her...preference. At the wedding, I was standing there in shock, not enjoying the moment. I've always wanted to explain that."

"I believe ye. I'm sorry, for that and for freezing ye out."

An apology long overdue but necessary.

Ben ducked his head, like he'd needed this as badly as me and it was hitting emotional shite neither of us got to easily. In the background, the coffee machine rumbled and splashed, the sound giving us privacy.

"I understand," he said. "I've thought about it a lot and I never blamed ye. If Daisy suddenly decided she loved my brother instead, I'd want to end ye. Getting over that would be hard."

"Fuck." I cracked a shocked laugh. "It isn't even that. More humiliation. I've come to realise that in the past few weeks—the relationship was never all that. It made the phone call a thousand times easier."

"How did it go?"

"She wanted to suss out if your relationship was endgame. I told her it was. Whatever fake reason she had for needing to talk to me was given up."

He blinked. "Holy shite. All this time."

"And she still loved ye? I don't think she knows the meaning of the word. But aye, now she has to finally move on. I wish I could feel sorry for her, but truly, I couldnae give a fuck what she does."

My brother tilted his head. "Because..."

"Because what?"

"Ye found something real."

My grin matched his. After this, I was going straight to Mia's. I'd make her breakfast if she let me then ask her out this evening. "Hope so."

Ben reached out and punched my shoulder, lowering his voice. "Maybe the two of us will get engaged at the same time."

"Is there a reason ye aren't already?" I asked.

"Daisy needed proof of my staying power." He choked at

my delighted expression. "Not in bed, for fuck's sake. In the relationship. She gave me a six-month time limit, then I can ask."

June, then. An interesting deadline that gave me ideas.

Ben continued, his eyebrows merging. "I wondered why ye were here and not with Mia at that board meeting, but I'm guessing she wanted to go it alone?"

"That meeting isn't today."

Ben leaned to see into the kitchen. "Daisy?" he called. "When Mia asked to rearrange work today, it was for a meeting, aye?"

Daisy came to the door, a flowery coffee mug in hand and her eyes rounded. "The board meeting. Please tell me you knew this, Valentine? The family she's battling changed the date on her. She left earlier to drive down to Dundee and take them on."

"Today?"

"Yes! It's in an hour."

The shock didn't hold me still for long. I was on my feet and out the door, dialling Raphael and barking a request for a lift in his heli.

Somehow, I'd fucked up again. I needed to catch up fast.

38

Mia

I'd only been to Tobi's dad's head office once in the past, when I had to drop off my ID and signed contract when I'd started my cleaning job. Then, the woman from Human Resources who'd come down to talk to me had barely given me a second glance. She'd done the same when calling me to discuss my maternity rights. I'd obviously been beneath her notice.

To this day, I'd never told any of them who Tobi's dad was. It was none of their concern, and I knew how gossipy office chatter would've branded me—the woman who slept with their married boss and got knocked up.

The same HR woman stood at the reception desk now. She narrowed her gaze at me as if trying to work out where she knew me from.

I ignored her and smiled at the man behind the counter. "Mia Walsh. Could you please show me to the boardroom?"

He bobbed his head and stood. "Of course. Follow me."

"Wait, please," HR lady said. Jennifer, her name came

back to me. She frowned at the receptionist. "It won't be the boardroom. Check your meeting list again."

He blinked. "I did. That's correct."

Her snooty gaze shot my way. "You're just the cleaner, aren't you?"

"It's Mia, and yes."

She tutted annoyance and turned back to the receptionist. "As I thought. You're taking her to the wrong place. You're lucky I'm here. The board members wouldn't look kindly on her being shown in, not on such an important day."

I took over answering on his behalf, donning the biggest pair of lady balls I'd ever owned. "No, Jennifer. You're wrong and speaking out of place. I've been invited to that meeting, and you're holding me up."

Stepping away, I peeked back for the man who needed to lead me through the intimidating building. Luckily, he caught up, throwing an apologetic glance at Jennifer who appeared like her head was about to explode.

I could've laughed. The lowly cleaner was here to clean them out. But nerves had me in a tight grip.

Outside a room with tall and polished dark-wood doors, we stopped. The receptionist opened the nearest for me, revealing an even more daunting scene. A long table made of wood the same colour as the panelled walls was surrounded by around twenty people in a variety of grey suits. Ninety percent older white guys with just a couple of other women.

I knew Vanissa wouldn't be here, not being a board member, but Greg and Simon held court at the top of the table.

A few people gave me cursory glances, monitoring my movement down the side of the room to the opposite end to the Winchesters. In contrast to the sea of grey, I'd worn a bold red dress. It wasn't expensive or fancy, but I needed to stand out. If not right now then at a key point in the meeting for sure.

However, in this second, I couldn't imagine saying a single word.

The receptionist pointed out a refreshment table then left me, closing me in with the wolves. I couldn't hold a cup. I'd spill the drink and embarrass myself. It was all I could do to sink into a chair and remember why I was here.

God, why was I doing this alone?

Daisy had offered to come, and Ariel said the same, but I was determined to do it by myself and prove how I'd wised up. Now, I regretted that choice hard.

Down the table, someone clapped once.

A grey-haired man in his sixties with a grey suit, mid-grey tie, and glasses perched on his nose, peered at the attendees. "Gentlemen, if everyone can take their seats, we can commence. And ladies," he added as an afterthought.

People settled down. Chatter ceased with squeaks of seats and clearing of throats.

The man waited for a beat then picked up a pile of paperwork, tapping it to straighten the edges. "The first order of the day is to confirm attendance. We'll go around the table and introduce ourselves and our roles. I'll go first. I am Peter English and I am the chairman of the board for Winchester Holdings, and I have been in this position for almost ten years. Beside me is Frank who is taking the minutes."

Peter's gaze landed directly on me. "We'll move on to the new face in the room."

I started and swallowed. "Mia Walsh." My words came out in a whisper.

"Ah, Miss Walsh. We were expecting you. Please state for the record your role here today."

I nearly went in with the I-don't-knows but caught myself.

"Voting rights," I said instead. "I represent my daughter, October Walsh. Daughter of Greg Winchester Senior."

Murmurs followed. Other attendees swapped glances. Clearly this was news to most.

The chairman dipped his head. "Interesting. Next."

He gestured to each attendee in turn, but I barely heard a word over the blood rushing in my ears until it reached the Winchester men.

"Greg Winchester. Here to represent the family business and aggressively pursue the future success of the company my father built."

Beside him, Simon smirked then leaned to speak in his ear. They simultaneously looked my way. Then both of the bastards *laughed*.

Oh, fuck them. Anger stripped away my fear. I sat taller and straightened my shoulders.

"Simon Winchester. Here to vote for my brother who knows what he's talking about," Simon said, amusement unhidden in his voice.

The chairman nodded. "Excellent. Now that's out of the way—"

From the hallway, a commotion sounded.

A man's voice made it through the heavy doors. "Aye, I will. If she wants me there then what's it to ye?"

Valentine? My heart squeezed. I'd recognise his tone anywhere. Hastily, I stood and made my way to the door.

"Miss Walsh, you cannot leave while the meeting is in progress," the chairman said.

"Actually, I think I can." I raised my eyebrows at him so he'd try to challenge me again.

He glared at me over his glasses but didn't say another word.

I stepped out into the hall. Jennifer from HR and the receptionist blocked the way, creating a human shield for their precious boardroom. Beyond them, Valentine glowered, a bull ready to plough through them. With his hair tied up and in jeans and his close-fitting black jacket, he was out of place, big and rough in the polished environment, and everything I needed to see right now.

"Let him pass," I ordered.

Jennifer twisted to goggle at me. "Excuse me?"

"I said let him pass, Jennifer. He's with me."

At least I hoped he was. It almost didn't matter. He was here. I'd needed him so badly, and he'd shown up out of the blue.

Valentine took the opportunity and shouldered between them, sparing a scowl for the HR lady. "Aye, Jennifer. Now go away."

He took my hand in his and positioned himself at my side.

I sucked in a breath. "I'm entitled to have someone here with me. Don't worry. I'll make sure the notetaker gets his name," I said with a saccharine smile.

Jennifer huffed but spun on her heel and clipped away, the receptionist scampering after her.

I didn't waste any more time on them, turning to face Valentine. "You're here."

"I am. I didn't know they'd moved the date or I'd have been outside your door this morning before ye left, begging to go with ye. As it was, I had to catch a ride with Raphael."

I pressed my fingertips to my lips. "You flew here in a rush just to be with me?"

"Of course I did. At a minimum to say that ye were right. In everything. I'm so fucking sorry for how I acted."

I could only stare up at him. In his eyes, all manner of

emotion played out, his breathing hard like he'd run to get here. He continued speaking.

"After ye kicked me out, I did everything I should've done a long time ago. I talked to Ben. And Kelly."

"You called her?"

"I told her off. It needed to be done, but it also showed me how the hurt I'd carried wasn't real. How could it be when I'd had no idea what love was until I met ye?"

"Me?" My bottom lip trembled.

"Aye. I'm so fucking in love with ye. I want all the things ye said. To be your man. To be to Tobi whatever she needs."

Relief, hope, and utter happiness danced through me, strengthening me and warming me from the cold place I'd been all night. It made me want to abandon my plans with the board and continue this conversation where random people weren't in danger of overhearing, but I had a job to do first.

I put a finger to Valentine's lips. "Stop. Please. Not another word or I'm in danger of losing my mind. Wait until this is over, then say all those things while we're in bed together."

He kissed the finger. "All I need to know is I'm naw too late."

I pushed up on my tiptoes to kiss his lips. Just once, but pressing my answer into his skin. "Not for me, or for the fun that's about to go down. You're right on time."

"God, woman. I can't wait to see ye throw down. From everything ye told me yesterday—"

"Yelled at you, you mean."

He grinned. "With absolute justification. It wasn't just my shite I took away. Their da hurt ye." He tilted his head at the room holding the Winchesters, his voice low in a whisper.

I cast my mind back to what I'd said. "You mean how he got me into bed?"

"Aye. It was an assault. Getting a lass so drunk she can't consent is rape."

He mouthed the word.

I sighed. "You're right. I made my peace with that a long time ago for two reasons—I would've said yes if I'd been sober—he was the boss and I crumbled under his presence—but mainly because what he did brought me Tobi. I can't regret her in any way. I was also too meek to even recognise it, let alone challenge him."

Valentine's eyes flashed with venom. "But now you're a warrior, ready to claim what you're owed."

I was. Stronger than I'd ever been and here to do battle for my girl.

Holding his hand, I marched back into the room.

Every single gaze flew to us.

Peter the chairman goggled. "You can't bring a stranger in."

"Please stop telling me I can't do things when it's patently untrue." I pointed at the man beside him taking notes. "Frank. Please add to the meeting list Mr Valentine Graham. See? Not a stranger anymore."

Frank dutifully made the note.

"This is most irregular," Peter sniffed.

Fearless, I cocked my head at him. "Is it? Then buckle up, because things are about to get super irregular from now on."

Valentine dragged a heavy chair from the edge of the room, the legs screeching on the polished floorboards, and forced the people to my right to budge over for him. He winked at me, and I returned my attention to the chairman.

"I have a question. Is everyone here legitimately allowed?"

I spoke to them all but watched Greg and Simon.

Greg schooled his features, suppressing an interesting

glare at Valentine that looked like a challenge. "Mia, please. I wouldn't expect you to understand how this meeting works, but we follow an agenda, then you'll get to contribute to the vote. I think my mother made herself clear in her guidance to you?"

"Oh, she did."

He held his gaze on me, an arrogant tilt to his chin. "I'm glad to hear it. You and I always were on the same wavelength. After this, I'll take you for lunch so we can catch up properly. How does that sound?"

Simon snorted.

I wrinkled my nose. "Sorry, George, I'm not interested."

He made an off sound and gestured to Valentine, his expression slipping into ugly derision. "Surely you're not interested in this—" Then he stopped. "What did you call me?"

"George. It's your name, isn't it?"

Greg, because I couldn't change his name in my head now, though someone else had done so long ago in real life, switched his astonished gaze to his brother.

"I was never interested," I continued. "Even when you begged for a date. I agreed to go out with you as a friend but I'd never settle for someone as average as you."

"Average?" Greg sputtered.

"Unexceptional," I offered an alternative.

"Mediocre fits nicely," Valentine supplied, stretching his legs out under the table like he owned the place.

"Yes." I pointed from him to the notetaker. "Write that down. Greg Winchester, really George Winchester, is a mediocre man, and I refused him."

Greg gripped the edge of the table. "Don't write that. We need to get on with this meeting."

"So I stop talking?" I produced a happy smile. "But I have so much to say."

The chairman peered over his glasses at me. "It appears to me you have a point to make, Miss Walsh. Please proceed so we can get on."

"The agenda," Greg snarled. "That's what your job is here, Peter. Don't waste our time. Get to the vote."

I centred myself and readied my stunning blow. "By all means, but it seems a little futile to vote when there's just one eligible party."

A commotion broke out.

Peter held up a hand. "Do you mean your daughter is that only eligible voter? Therefore you as her proxy?"

"Exactly. And I have proof." I took the envelope from my bag and slid it down the table to Peter.

He opened it and pulled out the will, a copy of Tobi's birth certificate with Greg Senior's name on it, and the other record I'd found. The one where Vanissa, George, and Simon *Johnson* were named.

"George Johnson," the chairman read the words I'd highlighted.

Greg jumped to his feet. "You can't do this. Ignore that. It's irrelevant."

Next to him, Simon lifted his phone to his ear. "Mum, she knows."

Under the table, Valentine's hand slid to my thigh. Squeezed.

Victory suffused me, so close I could almost taste it. From the moment the mis-naming by Molly's aunt had clued me in, through the evening of phone calls and research, and a chat with Scarlet to make sure I'd made no missteps, I'd finally discovered the truth they'd been hiding. The reason they were trying to rob my daughter of all she was due.

"Miss Walsh," Peter said over the fuss. "Could you please explain to me precisely what I'm looking at?"

"Happy to." I indicated to Simon. "Is that your mom? Put her on loudspeaker, please."

He froze then tapped the screen.

"Mia, what the hell do you think you're doing?" Vanissa snapped.

"Me? I've done nothing. You, on the other hand, lied through your teeth for years. You already had two kids when you married Greg Senior, neither in any way a blood relative to him. I found several references to you as a family unit long before Tobi's father came on the scene. You were the Johnsons. You ran the parent-teacher association which gave me a nice repository of information on your previous life. Then Greg Senior came along, married you so you all changed your surnames, and you relied on the fact he called your boys his sons to actually make them so after his death. Nobody here knew, am I right? Nobody once questioned how the Winchester boys were suddenly taking over."

I drew a breath, my heart racing, then continued. "You know, if you'd have been honest, there would be no issue here. Greg Senior raised your children as his own. Even though he didn't adopt them, he presumably let you change George's name to Greg in honour of him. I would've expected him to want them to share in his estate, and yet his will wrote them off. They got nothing. Not any part of the business. Not one penny, despite how long he knew them. Why is that? Remember, it's fraud to misrepresent yourself in a proceeding such as this. I believe it comes with hefty jail time."

"You... I mean..." Loud on the phone line, Vanissa tried and failed to continue a sentence.

Simon took a short breath then said in a rush, "Mum

cheated on our dad with our stepdad. The two men hated each other and never agreed on anything. The divorce, definitely not George's name change. I mean Greg's. He just used it then changed it himself at eighteen."

"Simon!" his brother chided.

"Wait, they couldn't agree on a divorce? Vanissa and Greg Senior weren't even married?" I said in shock.

It painted a new picture again. One where Greg Senior's kind care for our newborn daughter spoke of him having an heir at last. Where his homelife wasn't as settled as at first glance. Had he got me pregnant on purpose? If he'd lived, I wondered if he would've confessed it.

"No, they were, but there was a prenup so our dad couldn't get his hands on—"

"Greg, stop your brother's blathering mouth," Vanissa started.

I took a calming inhale, letting years of her superiority over me wash away. "It all makes so much sense now, Vanissa. If I'd known the truth, I wouldn't have objected to you contesting the will. But you tried to con Tobi out of her rightful inheritance. You tried everything under the sun to control us, and in doing so made my life miserable. You bet your ass I'll fight you now. You don't have a leg to stand on."

Silence fell.

Simon choked. "She'll take the house, too, Mummy. Where are we going to live?"

His brother grabbed at him. Someone shrieked. A tussle broke out between the brothers.

Valentine's careful touch on my arm brought my focus to him. "Is that right? None of it is theirs?"

"I got the asset list in an email this morning. Vanissa's lovely house, the one we weren't allowed in much, belonged to Tobi's dad, along with the business. Which, by the way, isn't losing money like she claimed, but thriving."

"And that all belongs to October." He stood up. "I cannae think of a more worthy lass than her. Come on. Let me take ye somewhere to celebrate."

All I wanted was to be in his arms.

Against the clamour of voices, I took his hand in mine.

At the door, I threw a parting comment over my shoulder. "In case it isn't clear, my daughter is now the sole owner of Winchester Holdings. Peter, please have Jennifer fire Greg and Simon from whatever jobs they have here. They are no longer welcome on the premises. Oh, and this meeting is over and the agenda denied. My lawyers will be in touch."

Then I left the boardroom and walked away with the man I loved.

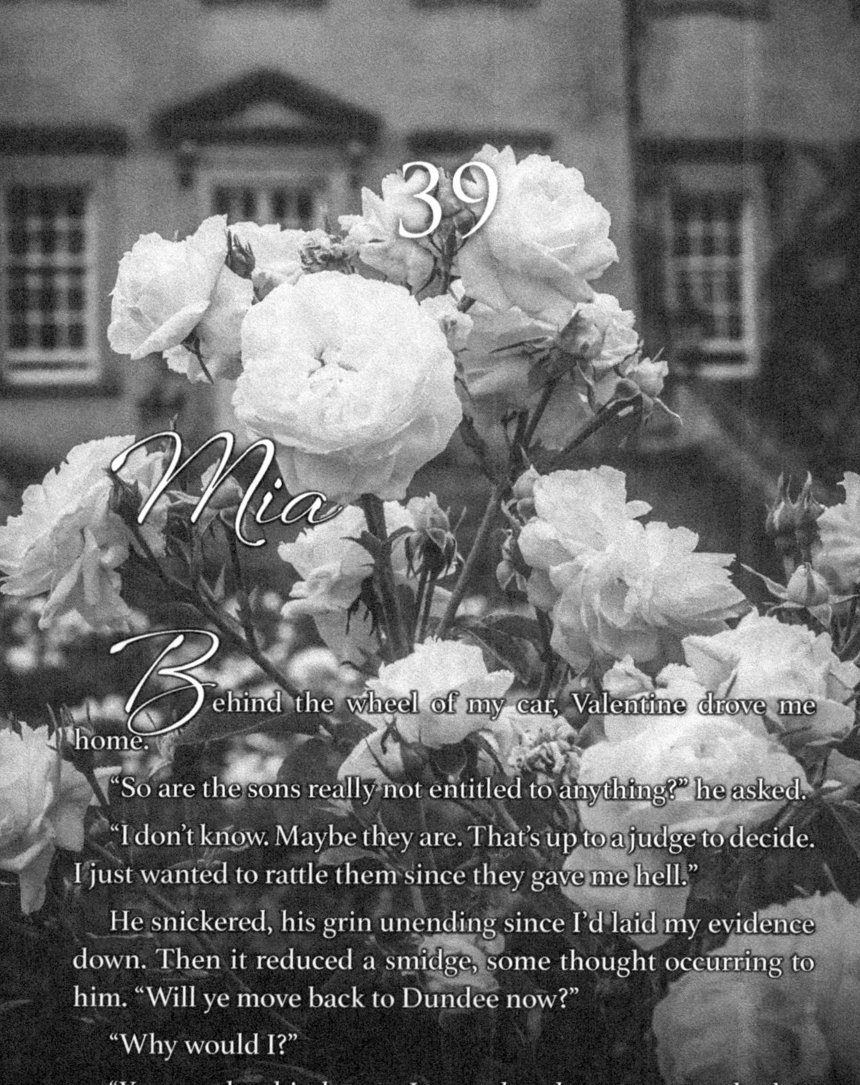

39

Mia

Behind the wheel of my car, Valentine drove me home.

"So are the sons really not entitled to anything?" he asked.

"I don't know. Maybe they are. That's up to a judge to decide. I just wanted to rattle them since they gave me hell."

He snickered, his grin unending since I'd laid my evidence down. Then it reduced a smidge, some thought occurring to him. "Will ye move back to Dundee now?"

"Why would I?"

"Ye own that big house. It was the place ye spent the last days with your ma. It would make sense to take ownership."

I opened my mouth and stared him down. "Pull over."

Valentine checked his mirrors then halted at the side of the road. "What—"

I leaned across the car and kissed him. He gave up a hungry sound and mapped his lips to mine.

"Didn't you just fly all this way to be by my side? Why do you think I'd be in such a hurry to leave yours? I have a home. It's a beautiful cottage made perfect for me by the kindest man."

He rubbed his nose against mine and kissed me again. "Thank fuck for that. Now tell me everything that happened after I left last night."

So I did. My research, the things I'd been told, and even the tears. We drove with him holding my hand and taking my heart.

After stopping off for lunch, which Valentine called an official date, we returned just in time to collect Tobi from school. Together, we crossed the playground to wait for the doors to open.

Purposefully, Valentine interlaced our fingers.

The pretty mom who'd asked him out was off to the side. "Look, he's off the market. Lucky bitch," she whispered to her friend.

I shot her a grin. I was lucky. At least I hoped so. There was still a conversation to be had, but I was almost certain how that was going to go after the events of the day.

Tobi sped from the door and bypassed me to hug Valentine's waist. "Where were ye last night?" she complained.

He knelt to her level, his expression full of regret. Her Hello Kitty hairclip was in danger of falling out, her blonde bangs in her eyes, so Valentine unclipped it and set it back into place. "I had some important work to do, but if it's okay, I'll come home with ye now?"

"You're not going to leave again?" she demanded.

He looked at me. Smiled. "I don't plan to, but that isnae up to me."

We went home together, and I turned the thought over in my mind. There was no doubt what I wanted—for him to be with us always. But yet again, he'd put our needs first by never assuming.

A couple of hours later, Valentine drove out to fetch dinner from the village pub where we'd shared our first kiss what felt like forever ago, and I sat Tobi down on the couch.

"There's something we need to talk about. Some things I discovered about your father's family and his business."

Swinging her legs, she waited patiently for me to go on.

"You know your dad was Greg Winchester?"

"Aye, Mom. He was old and now he's dead."

"He is. I went to see your stepbrothers again today." I introduced the new word. Vanissa had always insisted on *brothers*, and now I knew why.

Tobi twisted her hands in her lap. "I don't want to go back to see them again."

"You won't have to. I promise. But as the only child of Greg, you inherit his house and his business."

"Not Greg or Simon?"

"They might get a share, but I think it'll be just you. What that means right now is that I'll take care of it all. When you turn eighteen, you can decide what to do with it."

My daughter would have the world as her oyster. She'd never worry about money like Mom and I had done. Or move in with people she didn't like just to have a roof over her head.

Tobi bounced up. "Okay. Avery asked if Valentine's going to be my da. Is he?"

I blinked, sideswiped by the question. "Um, well…"

"If you married him, he would."

God, if only. My lip trembled, but I clamped my jaw. "Normally people are together longer than a few weeks before they have conversations like that. What would you think about it if I did?"

"I'd love it! I want him to live here."

"Why don't we decide that when we're ready to ask?"

Luckily, she accepted my answer, and not long after, Valentine arrived back. We ate together at the kitchen table like the decision had already been made, Tobi stealing Valentine's food and him pretending to sneak bites of hers.

This was happiness. I was sure already, even if I'd take my time to ask.

After we'd demolished the food, Tobi grabbed her reading book from her bag, and I poked around in the cupboards for dessert options.

"Want something sweet?" I asked Valentine.

"This right here, forever. Isn't that right, Ma?" With his hands behind his head, he addressed my mother's picture.

My heart panged. "I meant food."

"Aye, that, too. Feed me and breed me."

I gawked and shot a look to make sure Tobi hadn't heard, but she was still out of the room. "Don't say things like that."

"Why not? Ye want it?"

I managed a nod. I'd begun to pine for another baby.

"Trust me, little spy. I do, too." He shrugged. "All the things ye told me went through my mind on repeat last night. Viola gave me baby Torran to hold, and all I could picture was a bairn made of ye and me. Ye, Miss Walsh, I plan to wed, bed, and all the rest. So be ready for it."

Tobi skipped back in and slapped the book on Valentine's chest. While I stood there stunned to my core, he hoisted her to his knee and they read together.

The perfect happiness morphed into a vision for the future. One where Valentine asked Tobi if he could be her dad and she had another person to love her unconditionally. Where we gave her a baby sister or brother. Where a man told me he loved me and I was everything he wanted.

Abruptly, I choked on a sob and ran from the room.

A while later, once Tobi was asleep, I clambered up from her floor, exhausted and half in a daze from a near constant state of stress and worry over the past several days. Or weeks, or months. In the doorway of her room, Valentine leaned, watching me. Silently, he crossed the floor and lifted me into his arms.

"Bed," he whispered.

I could only nod yes.

In our room, he peeled my clothes from my body then nestled me into the pillows, kissing down my body to take me to the brink of an orgasm in easy, confident slides of his tongue.

Just as I was getting there, he stopped, came up me, and notched his dick to my entrance. I wound my legs around him and bucked to drive him into me.

Valentine groaned and sank home, banding an arm around me, the other hand going to my belly. "I'm so in love with ye. I want ye. Need ye. One day, you'll carry my bairn. Be mine, Mia."

"I love you, too," I managed, then all other words were lost.

He made me come then built me up for another. Made love to me then slept, holding me so close.

I'd made the best decision of my life when I'd leapt on the job advert that brought me to the McRae estate. Forevermore, with Valentine, I was home.

"Can I ask Valentine to move in with us today, Mama?" Tobi skipped out the front door and along the concrete ground, asking the same question she did every morning.

"When we're ready," Mia replied with the prettiest smile for me.

The two of us sat on chairs on the porch outside the cottage, the early summer sun warming us. It was June now, and a gorgeous Saturday morning. The changing season was marked on the landscape around us, with purple and pink heather blooming and birds flying in and out of trees, nesting.

It was giving a man big ideas.

For weeks, since the showdown between Mia and me, I'd fought to prove I'd changed. I'd let her down with how I'd treated her, and it broke my heart to remember the words I'd thrown her way.

In the same way that other aspects of life had settled for her, with Vanissa and her sons taking a payoff suggested by the lawyers instead of challenging the will, time was healing old wounds.

I only hoped what I had planned this evening would make up for it for good.

"It's a shame we're going out for the day," Mia said with a sigh. "As much as I love spending time with Daisy and the other women and kids, I could just sit here in the warm sun and watch the world go by for hours."

"Tomorrow, we'll do exactly that."

I leaned in and kissed her. Tobi grinned, staring between us. Where other kids might yell at their grown-ups showing affection, she seemed to crave our closeness. If we hugged, she'd wiggle between us and demand her share and to be squished with us both holding her. Slowly, Tobi had crept into my heart just as much as her ma.

"What are you doing today?" the girl asked me.

I raised my eyebrows. "I have plans with my brother."

A truth, but hiding a thousand thoughts and sneaky conversations.

"Hope you both have fun. It's so lovely that you're getting close again. We'd better go." Mia stood, ready to head out for a day of subterfuge planned by me.

As she passed, I tugged her hand, landing her back in my lap for a last squeeze. "Can't wait."

Then they were gone, and I needed to get on with my plans.

Several hours later, and midway through my stringing up lights, my phone buzzed with a video call. I swiped to answer to my mother.

"Ma, please tell me you're on the move."

"We are! Gordain just picked us up. It's so lovely being back in Scotland, and even better for what you boys have planned." She beamed, my father leaning across the car to peer at the phone.

"Ben," I called into the depths of the house. "The old folks are on the phone."

Ma muttered outrage, and Gordain complained from elsewhere in the car. Ma and Gordain were old friends from when Ben was a bairn, but that was a story from a lifetime ago.

While Ma filled me on how Kelly had recently quit their inn and left town to elope with some previous boyfriend, my brother jogged down Castle Braithar's broad staircase.

He joined me, throwing an easy arm over my shoulders. Sweaty fucker that he was from the work he'd been doing. "Hey, Ma. Da, did ye bring what I asked?"

Our father beetled his thick eyebrows, his frown deep. "Of course I did. We'll be an hour then I'll help out."

I sucked air through my teeth. "I don't know. Wouldn't want ye popping out a hip through anything too strenuous."

Ben twisted away, hiding a laugh. As kids, we'd plagued our father with teasing like this. He always took the bait.

On cue, Da glared. "I've been working my arse off daily since before ye were born. Harder than ye could imagine. I built a house from the ground up—"

"Bull, hush now. You know they love to antagonise you." Ma stopped him with a kiss.

We both made faces of disgust.

"Leave your father alone," our mother chided. "We'll be there soon, and I can't wait to see Daisy again, Benji, and meet Mia and Tobi, Valentino."

We let them go and got back to work.

"Benji," I said with a snort at the nickname no one used but Ma.

"Shut up, Valentino," Ben countered.

We shared a moment. We were really doing this. It had been such a perfect plan, but fuck, it was getting real.

By six, the work was done. Braithar's hall was thick with people, almost all families, our kin, and I'd driven out to lead Molly, Mia's friend, back with me. She'd brought her three kids and her aunt, and had got hopelessly lost in the remote mountain roads.

Only a few key people were missing. Mia and Daisy, plus Ariel who was our wingwoman and an essential part of our evening.

Elise and her family entered the big space, Tobi with them. The little lass I wanted to call mine spotted me and ran, leaping into my arms.

"Why are you dressed like that?" She tugged at the lapels of my suit.

"If I tell ye, it means you'll know a big secret."

Tobi nodded, entirely serious. I carried her to the side of the room. Not that anyone else in the room was ignorant of the events, but I needed a moment with my girl.

"I'm going to ask your ma to marry me. Think she'll say yes?"

Tobi's mouth fell open. "Ohmigod." She hugged me, ducking her face.

To my horror, she sobbed.

"Hey, hey. It's okay. Dinna cry," I hushed, rubbing a hand up and down her back.

Tears slid down her pink cheeks, soaking the sleeve I wiped them with. My heart ached and expanded all the more.

"I'm just...so...happy," she uttered between sobs.

"It means I can be your da, if ye want." A mini proposal to lead into my main one.

She sobbed harder, her nod and the tight hold bringing tears to my eyes. I boosted her higher and dropped my head down by hers. Around us, people took awed breaths then cooed.

This Scotsman was getting things right at last.

Tobi calmed, letting me blow her nose and dry her eyes. Her last question let me know all was going to be fine.

"Can I be bridesmaid?" she chirped.

Her best friend, Avery, trotted over, Cameron in tow. "Can I be one too? We can match our dresses!"

"Av," her da warned.

But his grin was all-knowing. Cameron had called this months ago. I was glad to prove him right.

The girls chattered about what happened at a wedding, then I sensed someone's gaze on me. Finn sidled closer, Zander with him.

I gestured for him to come to my side. "Just who I wanted to see next."

Finn blinked. "Me?"

"The lad who saved my life by calling out a warning about that bad guy. That was excellent work, and it meant I only had a small cut and not something much worse."

He flushed red, throwing a proud glance at his friend. Zander's jaw dropped.

"So," I continued, "a question for ye, Finn. I wondered if you'd be my ring bearer, if I'm lucky enough to get engaged this evening?"

The wee lad wrinkled his nose. "Aye, but... Do I have to wear a costume? I'm too old for that."

"A suit will be fine."

"So I don't have to be dressed as a bear?"

A bear? I squinted, totally lost but picturing an animal at my wedding.

Cameron came to my rescue. "Ring bearer, Finn. Not a ring bear. It means ye carry the wedding bands. No costumes needed."

He gave a relieved sigh and accepted while Cameron and I tried not to crack up.

Across the room, my mother watched with her hand at her lips, emotion in her eyes. Another element of my plan fell into place. Something Mia had agreed to without even knowing.

"Tobster, I've got someone for ye to meet first. Granny Graham. Your Gigi now."

"I have a granny?" She led me and danced all the way.

Another twenty minutes, and the text I'd been waiting for landed on my phone.

Ariel: Public.

Ariel: Oh, and five minutes.

"Five minutes," Ben yelled out from across the hall, clearly having got the same message.

Or had he? Maybe not both.

"Public or private?" I stomped over to him. "What did Daisy vote?"

"Public," he breathed.

"Mia, too."

Both of us shared a scared, excited, fucking thrilled moment. Ariel had been under instruction to take our lasses home with plenty of time to dress up fancy. Then, assuming both sniffed out the plot, she gave them the options of how we were going to do this thing. One on one, or in the middle of the space we'd spent all day decorating.

Looked like our beds were made.

A horn sounded outside, and a ripple of excitement crossed the group of family and friends. I slapped the back of my hand to Ben's chest, and he grabbed me, both of us staring at the door. Voices sounded.

It opened.

Show time.

First, Daisy entered, her mouth open and her bottom lip already trembling. She stared up at the white fairy lights and then at the crowd. When her gaze finally landed on Ben, she burst into tears.

He broke from his position and went to her, drawing her into his arms and uttering quiet words in her ear while slowly leading her back to the centre of the floor.

But my attention left them and went to the next person slipping inside the room. Mia sought me out, her eyes just as wet as Daisy's. She wasted no time in coming to me, holding on to me, but the tears fell just as hard.

Like with Tobi, I found it a challenge to control my own.

"I havenae even asked yet," I whispered.

Mia sobbed.

Over her head, I caught Ben's eye. Both of us sank to our knees. We'd tossed a coin, and he'd won and opted to go first. A good thing, because my throat was so thick I could barely breathe.

"Daisy Devereux, ever since I saw ye escaping out a window, my heart has been yours. Will ye do me the greatest honour and consent to be my bride?"

Daisy wiped her eyes, her smile so big joy shone from her. "Oh, Ben. Yes. Of course I will."

He rose and kissed her, sliding on a ring Da had brought all the way from the States. Ben had found it online, and nothing else would do for the woman he'd chosen for life. Applause rang out. I clapped, too, then held up my hand. Perfect quiet resumed.

"Mia Walsh."

Mia's eyes widened. If Ben had first seen Daisy at a window, our first sight was far more entertaining. But I'd save that one for later.

"I knew from the moment I first laid eyes on ye that there was no other woman for me. It might've taken me a while to find the words, but now I have, they'll never stop. Marry me. Make me the happiest man alive."

She laughed in pure happiness. "Yes!"

I stood and kissed her, then broke away and beckoned for Tobi. The girl skipped over and held up the ring box I'd asked her to keep hold of.

"Thanks, sweetheart," I said.

"That's okay, Da," she quipped back.

Then she scampered back to my da, her grandfather-to-be, who she'd been tormenting with making him yawn, beaming all the way. Shocked, I spun back to Mia.

"She's been wanting to say that for a long time," my fiancée—the only one who ever mattered—filled me in.

"I love it. I love her. I love ye endlessly."

I placed the ring I'd picked out just for her on her finger. A perfect fit.

Then I kissed the woman who owned me, and listened to the applause. When I was ready, I'd introduce her to my folks. Find Molly so her friend could see I'd taken care of her as I'd promised.

Mia and Tobi were my world now. All it took was a little give and take.

EPILOGUE

Raphael

A message from Ben took me from my jog back to the hangar and his office. Not that I strayed from the building for long. For weeks, I'd been busy with the compromise Leo had put in place for his gig schedule. He hadn't wanted to let his fans down, but at the same point, had been so shit-scared by the attack on Valentine that repeating that risk had been out of the question.

A relief for all of us to change up the process. Even more for his lad, Finn, who needed some distance from the event to feel safe again.

Now, Leo never stayed in the city he was playing. I flew him in and out, sometimes for long hours with refuelling stops to get him home. It was safer for everyone and had worked while he was in gig season, but as of today, the rock star was back in his recording studio.

The off season we all needed. Except... I couldn't settle. I loved my home, but something burned in me to be out there. For what purpose, I had no clue.

I reached Ben's door and thumped. He hollered for me to enter.

At his desk, which he always looked too big for, he peered up. "Raphael, come in and sit down. I have something to talk to ye about."

I dropped into the chair, a sweaty mess, but that was normal in this job. "Happy to help, whatever it is."

My boss pursed his lips. "This is a slightly unusual request. Remember Barry who I contacted to lend us personnel to cover Valentine?"

I picked out the contact in my mind. "Owns another bodyguard firm?"

"That's him. He's made a request of me. He's snowed under with a big event in London and needs someone trustworthy for a VIP assignment."

He meant me, obviously. I tilted my head. "Aren't they always VIPs?"

"This one's different. Another level with its own challenges and risks you'll need to take into consideration."

"Who is it? Who will I be guarding?"

He turned his laptop to show me a client file complete with photo on the screen. A lass more beautiful than could be real was in three-quarters profile. Expensive jewellery at her throat, a sparkling gown, her expression tormented in a capture that appeared like it had been taken at some fancy event she didn't want to attend.

My heart thumped out of time, and my stomach did a weird flip.

"Your mission, Raphael, is to guard a princess. I can't think of anyone better to do the job. What do you say?"

"Aye, I'll go." The rest of the words, ones that I needed to state, didn't come.

I'd met this woman before, a long time ago, at least it felt that way. Her Royal Highness was not going to enjoy seeing me again.

The End.

To read and spicy and sweet bonus scene for Valentine and Mia click here: https://dl.bookfunnel.com/qeso93uu9o

Please note that downloading any free material from me adds you to my reader list (or gives you the option). You can unsubscribe at will.

Want to find out exactly how Raphael upset a princess? Order his book here.

https://www.amazon.com/dp/B0CW1DNGV5

ACKNOWLEDGEMENTS

Dear reader,

We're done with another deliciously spicy adventure from our world of hot Scots! Valentine and Mia gave us a dose of friends-to-everything romance. Valentine fell without realising. He had no idea what was happening, and it took him a minute after Mia called him on his BS. Lucky for him, she had the patience of a saint to let him come to understanding in his own time. Our brave heroine had a journey of her own with facing up to the controlling relatives who'd lied to and manipulated her.

SECRET CODES (there's one in each McRae Bodyguards book, and the answer is given in my reader group, newsletter, or in the back of the next book).

Valentine's openness was super attractive to Mia. Did you note him rattling off his bank account number during a particularly spicy scene while he was away on tour?

That bank account number is this book's hidden code.

Go find it and have a guess. You'll need to use your phone's alphanumeric keypad (i.e. 2 = ABC, 3 = DEF etc) to turn the numbers into letters.

In order, they give a message from Valentine to Mia.

Take her from You's code will be revealed in my Jolie Vines's Fall Hard Reader Group https://www.facebook.com/groups/JoliesFallHardFans a week or so after launch and also at the end of the next book (Raphael's story).

I'll share it in my newsletter, too. You can add yourself here - https://www.jolievines.com/newsletter

Previous book's code

Did you spot the code in book two – Save Her from Me? Guess it here then find the answer below!

On the picture of Ariel's spicy list at the end of the story, there's a hidden code on the bottom right of the page.

GMHTFM,LF.

Can you guess what Jackson wants Ariel to do? (This is not one for kids to guess, just to be clear.)

I've included it at the end of this letter so you can confirm your guess.

Big thanks go to my readers who give me the love that fuels my writing. To Elle, Zoe, Emmy, Sara, Shellie, and Liz – you're the best and I couldn't get anything done without you. To Cleo, you make such pretty graphics and beautiful formatting. To Aaron and Addison, Troy, Kathleen, and team at Dark Star, the audio is fabulous. To my ARC and Street Team, I can't wait to hear what you make of Valentine and Mia.

Lastly, as always, I thank N&M, my whole world.

Jolie x

--

Jackson's code spells out Get Me Hard Then Fuck Me, Little Fox.

Did you guess right?

ALSO BY JOLIE VINES

Marry the Scot series
1) Storm the Castle
2) Love Most, Say Least
3) Hero
4) Picture This
5) Oh Baby

Wild Scots series
1) Hard Nox
2) Perfect Storm
3) Lion Heart
4) Fallen Snow
5) Stubborn Spark

Wild Mountain Scots series
1) Obsessed
2) Hunted
3) Stolen
4) Betrayed
5) Tormented

Dark Island Scots series
1) Ruin
2) Sin
3) Scar
4) Burn

McRae Bodyguards
1) Touch Her and Die
2) Save Her from Me
3) Take Her from You
4) Protect Her from Them

Body Count
1) Arran's Obsession

Standalones
Cocky Kilt:
a Cocky Hero Club Novel
Race You:
An Office-Based Enemies-to-Lovers Romance
Fight For Us:
a Second-Chance Military Romantic Suspense

ABOUT THE AUTHOR

JOLIE VINES is a romance author who lives in the UK with her husband and son.

Jolie loves her heroes to be one-woman guys.

Whether they are a brooding pilot (Gordain in Hero), a wrongfully imprisoned rich boy (Sebastian in Lion Heart), or a tormented twin (Max in Betrayed), they will adore their heroine until the end of time.

Her favourite pastime is wrecking emotions, then making up for it by giving her imaginary friends deep and meaningful happily ever afters.

Have you found all of Jolie's Scots?

Visit her page on Amazon and join her ever active Fall Hard Facebook group.

www.ingramcontent.com/pod-product-compliance
Lightning Source LLC
Chambersburg PA
CBHW072043190726
48294CB00005B/1379